THE ECHO BELOW

by

HEATHER CAVILL

Edited by Kyle Robertson

This is a work of fiction. Names, characters, businesses, organizations, places, events, and incidents are either the product of the author's imagination or used fictitiously. Any resemblance to actual persons, living or dead, or actual events is purely coincidental. Except for Troy Richardson.

This story contains themes of water-related trauma, including drowning and near-drowning, as well as abandonment and complex parental relationships. Reader discretion is advised.

First Edition

ISBN: 978-1-0698954-0-0

For Charlie, who believed I could.

PROLOGUE

The sky was the color of bruised coral; one of those beautiful, painted evenings that cast a soft glow over a restless sea. Wind lifted the sand in faint curls, twisting through the seagrass and dancing across the half-erased footprints behind them.

Coraline March walked ahead, her shoes in one hand and a smaller pair belonging to her grandson in the other. Cold sand pressed between her toes, grounding her with every step. She had stopped feeling the bite of the wind years ago and lived for the feel of the breeze sweeping through her silvering hair. It was the rhythm she loved: the sound of tide and time folding together as she walked the shoreline.

Behind her, seven-year-old Silas hummed. It wasn't an actual song; not one she'd taught him, not one he should've known, but his voice carried it all the same: a sweet, lilting melody with no words. Just open vowels that seemed to stretch and rise with the gusts of sea air. It was familiar to her in a way she didn't want to name. Coraline didn't ask him where he'd learned it, some part of her already knew.

Silas was trailing about ten feet behind, staring down at his feet and the impressions they made in the wet sand. His small hand clutched a conch; a medium-sized spiral shell that had washed up on the shore below the bluff, as they did on rare occasions.

"Stay on the dry sand, Silas," Coraline called, glancing back. "The waves are turning now."

"I know," he said, not looking up.

Like any seven-year-old, he was easily distracted and drawn to the edge of things. The second born by only minutes, Silas was the more cautious one. Isla would've raced him into the tide.

Coraline turned her eyes back to the sea and continued walking, listening to the churn of the waves in that steadying rhythm she loved; but when she looked again, he was gone. Her body moved quickly, scanning the shoreline, heart knocking against her ribs.

"Silas?" Her voice rose as panic bloomed in her chest. "Silas?"

Further back, at the edge of the water, she saw a flicker of movement where he had stopped. He was crouched and reaching toward the shell that had slipped from his hand and rolled forward, caught in the retreating foam. Without thinking he followed, every step wading further into the surf. Hands outstretched toward his small treasure, he tried frantically to retrieve it as it tumbled into the waves.

"Silas!" Coraline dropped their shoes and ran toward him, her voice cracking as she called out.

The wave that hit him wasn't very large, but it was fast, sudden, and angled like it knew what it wanted. It broke at his knees, knocking him forward, flat onto his stomach. With one sharp, panicked cry, his arms flailed, and he was under the water, the rogue wave engulfing his small body.

"No! Silas!"

Coraline's feet splashed through the curling whitecaps, pushing forward as fast as she could go. Resistance fought her every step, costing her precious seconds she couldn't afford. By the time she reached where he had been, Silas had already disappeared beneath the steady churn of water.

Rushing further in, her skirt ballooned and tangled around her legs as the tide surged to her waist. The cold bit into her bones as his name ripped from her throat in panicked cries, her arms flailing, searching beneath the surface.

He's just under. I'll see him any second now. He can't be far below!

Hair lashed across her face as she spun around in circles, eyes searching the surrounding water. Coraline dove, and dove, clawing at the waves. Salt seared her nose, her mouth, and her eyes, blinding and burning; every sense drowning all at once, yet still the sea kept him from her.

"Silas! No! Where are you? Not him, not yet!"

There was no splash, no bobbing head, no sign of a struggle as she continued to search the shallows. Eyes raking the waterline, she prayed for any trace of him. Throat raw from shouting, her knees split open, but she was blind to the pain of rocks tearing at her skin. All she saw was water. All she wanted was him.

"Silas, please!"

Nothing. Her body shook, half from fear, half from rage.

"No. No. No."

Coraline staggered forward once more, stumbling deeper and diving lower, calling his name with everything she had left, but there was only silence; a stillness too sudden. Everything in her gave out at once. The strength that had carried her through the water drained from her limbs, leaving them leaden and trembling as the terrible reality settled in. No hope left to hold on to, her knees buckled, and she sank into the wet sand.

Grief swelled in her throat, thick and painful as a guttural sob welled up from inside. *This isn't happening. This can't be happening.* Her eyes searched the shore without focus, unwilling to accept what they saw.

Nothing and no one. Just the thundering silence in her ears and the weight of the reality setting in. Everything was distant and muffled, like a nightmare unfolding behind glass.

As tears fell from her eyes, a soft sound emerged from the silence and jolted her back to the present. It was the faintest hum: not above the water, but within it, winding through the tide. A sound so much like Silas's song that her breath caught, and she held it, listening. Coraline trembled as the hair on her arms lifted and for one impossible moment, she believed he was there, just beyond her reach.

The sound lingered for only a second before the waves swallowed it up, leaving nothing but the dark roll of the sea and Coraline alone in its aftermath.

He was gone.

ONE

The kettle gave a damp cough, pulling Isla from sleep. She didn't remember turning it on before drifting off to the TV. The futon creaked in protest as she sat up. Her spine was tight, her mouth dry, like cotton had been stuffed behind her teeth. The air in the apartment felt stale. She looked over at the humidifier only to realize it had turned off during the night, or maybe she had forgotten to fill it. Either way, the damage was done. Her sinuses ached, and her joints pulled in protest when she moved.

There was no need to check the clock. Light filtered through the blinds in hazy bars that said it was late afternoon. *Another wasted morning*, she thought. And another shitty, restless sleep.

Thin padding sagged over the thin metal frame of the futon as Isla swung her legs over the edge. Falling asleep here rather than her bed was a regular mistake she never seemed to learn from, and her back paid the price. Damp hair greeted her fingers as she combed through the tangled strands falling around her shoulders. Sweat soaked through her shirt until it clung uncomfortably to her skin. Peeling it off, it fell to the floor, and she padded barefoot into the kitchen.

It really wasn't so much a kitchen as a suggestion of one. A narrow stretch of countertop at the far end of the living room housed a compact fridge, a two-burner stove, and a sink. In the corner, a washer-dryer unit stood taking up what little space was left. It wasn't much, but it worked. And for Isla, it was enough.

Steam sputtered from the kettle as she poured hot water into a stained mug before adding a tea bag. Elderberry and nettle, leftover from a naturopath's expensive cleanse she'd abandoned after the second week. Isla's throat relaxed as she sipped, and then came the deep, familiar cough. A pressure caught behind it; wet, metallic, and she leaned over the sink to spit. The faintest pink laced the fluid, but she didn't bother to examine it. This was nothing new. With a practiced motion, she turned on the faucet and washed it away.

Canvases and paint supplies cluttered her space, and the air carried the faint scent of linseed oil and old paper. Most of her blank canvases were stacked sideways against the wall, while a few others still dried on their easels.

One caught her eye: the unfinished painting nearest the window. It made her uneasy when she looked at it. A jagged coastline under a slate-colored sky, waves crashing violently against sharp, uneven rocks. In the foreground, something dark and blurred twisted up from the surf. It could have been seaweed, or maybe hair. Either way, it was abstract and terrifying. She'd noticed it one morning last week after waking from another strange, half-remembered dream. There was no clear memory of painting it, but the brushstrokes were undeniably hers. And lately, waking up to unfamiliar art was happening with unsettling frequency.

Her phone let out a quick vibration on the counter. Three missed calls, all from the same number. No name attached, no voicemail left behind. Just the same string of digits flashing across the screen repeatedly. Irritated by the persistence, she set the phone down, dimming the screen.

As Isla sipped her tea, she looked to the far corner of the apartment where her sketchbook lay half-open beneath a curling paperback that fluttered next to the open window. She crossed the room and lifted it to see the black pencil that had filled the last page. Kelp strands tangled around a woman's throat, mouth stretched in a silent scream and water blurred a pair of wide, unblinking eyes.

"Lovely." She sighed, tossing it back down next to the window with a roll of her eyes. No caption, no date, and no recollection of drawing it. Just the drowning stare fixed on hers as if those eyes knew something she didn't.

~

The midweek lull of the late shift meant the bar wasn't busy. A couple of regulars hunched over whiskey sours like much-needed medicine, and an unfamiliar face tried to flirt with her. Isla barely registered it. Flirting was par for the course in this line of work, background noise in a job that paid the bills when her art didn't.

At five feet six inches with long espresso-colored hair and crystal green eyes that shifted with her mood, Isla drew more than her share of unsolicited pickup lines. Most couldn't remember her name by the time they left the bar, and she preferred it that way.

Working well under dim lights, her hands moved faster than her brain as she slipped into her easy routine, the chaos of other people's lives drowning out the static of her own. Pour, nod, wipe, repeat. She moved on autopilot and kept her smile a subtle curve. Just enough to look friendly, not enough to invite conversation.

"You look like shit. You okay?" Ivy leaned against the bar and flashed a teasing smile. "Seriously, you don't look like yourself tonight."

Heavily tattooed and unflappable, Ivy was a thirty-something blonde charmer who ran the bar with sharp efficiency. Quick to shut down drunk nonsense, she was skilled at handling customers with tact and authority but gave a steady warmth to her staff.

Isla gave a tired shrug. “I didn’t get much sleep.”

The neckline of Ivy’s low-cut leopard-print top dipped low enough to draw attention, though it never seemed like she was trying. Everything about her screamed bombshell: glossy blond waves, red lipstick, curve-hugging jeans.

“Have you been to that hippy clinic I told you about yet?”

“I have,” she said, scooping ice into a tumbler. “They can’t find anything wrong with me. A virus, or ‘chronic fatigue syndrome.’”

“So, you’re just tired, and they don’t know why?” Ivy slid a lime wedge into a glass filled with vodka and soda. “Did they at least give you a magical vitamin shot or something?”

“They took some more blood to test for autoimmune disorders and said they’d get back to me.”

“Maybe it’s that old kissing disease everyone got in high school.”

“Mono?” Isla laughed. “Definitely not what I have. That would require the kissing part.”

“Damn. I was hoping that meant you’d finally gotten some.”

“I appreciate the support.”

“If you ask me, which I know you didn’t, you’ve been burning the candle at both ends.” Ivy leaned closer, lowering her husky voice so the regulars couldn’t hear. “You’ve taken every shift you can get your hands on, and you aren’t sleeping much. You can do better than this. You’re young and I’ve seen your art. You’ve got so much talent, Isla. Stop pouring drinks seven days a week for men who leave you mediocre tips and go have a life. Push your paintings.” She cut herself off and flashed a smile at a passing customer.

“Having a life doesn’t pay the bills, and sadly, neither does my art.”

"Well, then for now, try not to fall face-first into someone's drink." With a wink, Ivy sauntered off to check on the kitchen. She was straight up, no bullshit, but the last thing Isla wanted to talk about was her squandered talent or her body's slow collapse.

Grateful for her break when it came, she slipped out the back door and into the narrow alleyway behind the bar. Rain had been falling lightly for hours, and the air smelled of damp concrete and metal. The drain below the building trickled with runoff from a gutter, and sirens passed in the distance.

Perched on an old crate, Isla lit a cigarette, as was her break time ritual. The routine steadied her hands and calmed her nerves, and the buzz that spread from her head to her feet made her forget the throbbing shoulders and mild headache that was coming on.

As she took another deep inhale, she noticed the faintest sound: not quite music, but a distant voice in a woman's tone, stretched long and soft, echoing quietly. There wasn't another bar for blocks that she knew of. A private party somewhere nearby maybe.

The cigarette warmed between her fingers, its smoke curling lazily around her knuckles, acrid and oddly sweet. She quieted her breath to listen, but before she could pinpoint the sound's location, it was gone. All that remained was the hiss of the drain and the soft patter of rain on metal siding.

"You're tired," she said aloud, "and possibly insane." Then she took one last long drag, smoke coiling past her lips, and flicked the cigarette onto the ground to stomp it out before stepping back inside.

Isla stumbled up to her third-story walk-up apartment, out of breath from the steep flights of stairs and a little tipsy from some post-shift drinks with Ivy. The deadbolt stuck as she tried to open the front door, and she had to pull the handle back to unlatch it. Sweat, smoke, and the pungent odor of dried alcohol emanated from her. She needed a shower.

Even though she wasn't hungry, she opened the fridge to browse its contents. A Diet Coke, expired milk, and a jar of pickles she couldn't remember buying sat on the top shelf and half a loaf of moldy bread lay forgotten on the bottom. Grocery shopping moved to the top of her to-do list.

Goals of eating healthier had long been her plan, but fresh groceries were expensive, cooking was a pain, and the pad thai practically delivered itself. Between tending bar and selling the occasional painting, there wasn't much extra cash for organic wholefoods. Big-city living was already a grind. Rent swallowed most of her paycheck, and art supplies and bills took much of the rest. Now, with doctors' visits and medical tests all paid for out of pocket, she had barely anything left. Vegetables didn't seem to make much of a difference, anyway. Feeling like shit was something she had gotten used to, so she was learning to live with it.

Isla's health issues had started just before her last birthday and gotten gradually worse. Two different doctors told her they believed her problems were mental.

"All in your head," they'd said.

After an assortment of expensive tests, they'd recommended some talk therapy, exercise and Vitamin D. A naturopath at the clinic Ivy recommended suggested supplements, more sleep, and laying off the smoking, then took another few hundred dollars to test for autoimmune diseases and allergies.

Maybe it *was* mental. At twenty-six, her joints felt like they belonged to someone twice her age, and no amount of kale smoothies or stretching seemed to make a difference. Web MD said depression could cause physical symptoms, but she didn't feel sad.

She plopped herself onto the couch and picked up her cellphone. Three more missed calls while she was at work, all from the same number as before. This time they'd left a message. Fingers moved to the screen, curiosity nudging her to listen.

"Miss March, this is Sheriff Alan Wright calling from the Greyhook Police Department. I'm trying to reach you regarding your grandmother, Ms. Coraline March." Frustration echoed in his tone. "I hate to notify you by voicemail, but I seem to be having a hard time reaching you. I need to tell you that Coraline seems to be missing. We'd like to locate her or at least get in touch to make sure she's all right. You are listed as her emergency contact, so I'm hoping you can shed some light on this matter or may have been in touch with her. Please call me as soon as you can. Thank you."

The message was calm but clipped and his words didn't feel real at first. Isla stared at the phone long after the voicemail ended, thumb hovering over the callback number.

Coraline was missing. Slowly, she lowered the phone and set it face-down on the counter. A slow, sour, and thick with guilt punch to the gut rose inside her. Isla didn't remember the last time she'd spoken to Coraline. Still, her grandmother had always made her presence felt in Isla's world: a signed holiday card when she didn't go home for Christmas, birthday wishes with a few bills folded inside an envelope, tinctures or homemade presents sent just because. Every note arrived in the same elegant handwriting on plain stationery, a quiet indicator that Coraline was still there, still present, even with the distance.

Now, that presence would go silent. There would be no more letters, no more packages, no trace of her on the other end. All that remained was an empty suitcase in the corner of her apartment, a quiet accusation of all that had been left unsaid.

~

The shower ran hot enough to scald, filling the room with steam. Isla stood motionless under the spray, her arms hanging loose at her sides, forehead resting against the wall with her eyes half-lidded.

Pressure lingered just under her skin: a constant, dull ache that never fully let up. There was tension in her chest, a light ringing in her ears, and a weight in her spine when she bent over the bar for too long.

The water poured over her shoulders, down the line of the old scar that lived on one of them. It was slightly raised, thin and pale pink. Not overly noticeable, but she remembered every inch of how she got it.

At sixteen, she'd snuck out to meet her friends at the edge of the cove, trying to prove to herself that she wasn't worthy of her grandmother's constant concern for her. The air had been thick with moisture that day, and she'd climbed too far out on a set of slippery black rocks. Sliding down the algae-covered ledge, she'd fallen and split her shoulder wide open. With severely wounded pride, Isla returned home bloodied and shivering to meet her judgement.

Fury in every step, Coraline had marched her into the clinic, then paced the room while Isla's shoulder was cleaned and stitched. The doctor had remarked she was lucky not to have been knocked out and drowned, a verdict that only stoked Coraline's anger. Meanwhile, Isla had just laughed, kept alive by bad decisions and the sheer, stupid will to keep going and doing the things her grandmother advised against.

The warmth of the shower dulled the sounds and smells of the night, loosening her aching muscles and bones. The hot water soothed, but nothing cured. Steam clung thick to the mirror when she twisted the faucet off and stepped into the fog-heavy bathroom, towel wrapped tight across her chest. The clouded mirror gave way with a creak as she swung it open to reveal the clutter behind it. A pill case sat wedged between bottles, pulled free with practiced ease before the tablets went down one by one. Iron, magnesium, B-complex, something expensive for adrenal support. And two Advil. Always Advil.

Pulling on an oversized T-shirt that clung to her damp skin, she poured herself a glass of water and slipped on fluffy slippers to warm her feet. Hair still dripping, she sipped as she stood in the middle of the apartment and stared at a canvas sitting on the floor next to her closet.

An ethereal seascape of blues and greens, that had started as a dream and consumed her for hours until it was finished. A shadowed figure floated just beneath the waves at its center, face blurred. The water around bloomed with sea-glass green, washed-out turquoise, and faint coral pink along the edges, while kelp forests rippled overhead like an inverted skyline, tendrils drifting down in strands of silk. It was one of her rare paintings that hinted at something gentle, maybe even beautiful, though the figure at its center remained mysterious and unreachable. This painting spoke to her, though she wasn't quite sure why. And whether she liked it or not, the sea always seemed to find its way onto her canvas.

Isla moved through the apartment, clinging to the mundane. Tea, a cigarette, a quick tidy. The kettle clicked on, and she reached for a mug, focusing on the motion, the promised warmth, anything but the unease beneath. Her mind felt as frayed as her body, but still, tea sounded good.

Something small, something normal. Then her gaze landed on the phone, still on the counter where she'd left it.

It had been over two years since she'd seen Coraline, and nearly that long since she'd heard anyone say her name. She picked up the phone and held it to her chest a moment before playing the voicemail again. This time, as she listened, she noticed a faint whooshing behind the Sheriff's voice, right after he said Coraline's name. A rush of sound, static maybe, or wind. It could have been nothing, but to Isla, it sounded like the sea.

~

Perched on the edge of her stool, Isla sat in a loose white tank top that slipped from one shoulder, navy overalls streaked with old color, and nothing on her feet but the chill of the hardwood. Black paint coated the brush in her hand as she stared intently at the canvas in front of her.

She always drew the curtains before painting, more out of habit than secrecy. It was unlikely anyone would peer inside on the third floor, but the idea of unseen eyes watching her work creeped her out. This space was sacred: one of the few things that cleared the static from her mind.

There was a time, fresh out of art school, when Isla painted with intent and the work felt malleable, something that could be shaped into beauty and scenery someone might want to display. That joy had slipped from her hands somewhere along the way. What came now were fragments of her mind, haunted and half-formed. Always shadows, always waves.

The sheriff should have been on the other end of a returned call by now, a bag packed with her things. Instead, she sat at her easel, paintbrush in hand, paralyzed by a choice she wasn't ready to face; to go home, or to stay.

Coraline was missing, but it was Isla who had been disappearing these past years. Drifting further with each unanswered call, each text left sitting in silence. Visits became phone calls, phone calls became messages, and eventually, even those were left unread.

There had been love, of course there had, but there had also been rules. So many rules. Coraline had raised her with the mandates of a soldier, not the freedoms of a child. Isla often felt like an outsider; a girl told to keep her distance from the very thing that defined their town. No swimming past the jetty. No wandering the cove alone. Absolutely no beach parties, especially at night. Not that she obeyed, but disobedience never came without lectures, punishments, and inevitably, more rules.

Isla knew what they were born from. Though she hadn't understood as a child, she saw it now for what it was; fear shaped into structure. Silas, her twin brother, was only seven when he'd vanished into the tide. After that, Coraline rarely spoke of him. She traded laughter for vigilance, and joy for control. The softness that had once existed between them was slowly replaced with only caution.

When Isla was thirteen, she had asked Coraline why.

"You know why." Coraline hadn't looked up when she'd answered. "The ocean listens, and it's dangerous."

It listens. Insanity was what it sounded like. The kind of cryptic nonsense whispered after spending too many years alone in a small town. Yet beneath her strangeness was the buried truth – Coraline was scared. Losing Silas had changed her. After that, even the most ordinary dangers took on monstrous shapes. So, she clung, wrapping her rules around Isla like armor: tight, rigid, and suffocating. Curfews that didn't make sense, boundaries that felt arbitrary, answers that never came. Not because she didn't love Isla, but because she did. And fear, real fear, doesn't always look like pleading or softness. Sometimes it looks like control, like silence.

Despite understanding this now, admitting she missed Coraline wasn't something Isla was ready to do. The thought of Greyhook filled her with something she couldn't name. There was an unhealed wound there. A past life with a tyrant ruler, where conflict and love had lived side by side.

What if this wasn't as urgent as it seemed? Perhaps Coraline took a trip, or maybe she just needed some space from a town where everyone was always in your business. Coraline had disappeared during a meteor shower one summer just before Isla's graduation and hadn't told anyone she was leaving. She'd come home after twenty-four hours with eyes a little too bright as if she'd been on a secret adventure. Isla wanted to believe that's what this was, but she could already feel that belief coming undone.

It was time for a cigarette. After searching her purse for a solid two minutes, she finally located her lighter at the bottom. The kitchen window creaked as she pushed it open, and the extractor fan above the stove beside it rattled to life as she switched it on. To spare herself the hassle of climbing six flights of stairs several times a day, she had perfected this sly strategy. Leaning out, she lit up. The first drag curled through her, steadying her hands and quieting her churning mind. It fixed nothing, she knew, but the floaty calm was enough to make the temporary lie worth it. The last cherished puff had her feeling much more at ease, and she returned to her canvas.

Dipping the brush in green, then black, the cave slowly emerged. Thin streams of light filtered down from above into a small tidepool below. Smooth, dark walls dripped with moisture, and seaweed hung like curtains over a small opening shaped like a mouth. Isla painted until her shoulders ached and her eyes hurt. When she finally called it a night, her hand was cramping, and the clock read 4:47 a.m. Exhaustion consumed her, but she felt calmer after expelling some of her tension onto the canvas.

Bypassing the TV and futon, she climbed straight into bed and curled beneath the blanket. Sleep didn't come easily, it rarely did, but she closed her eyes and let her thoughts drift, the rhythm of her breathing slow and steady. Eventually, the world slipped away. The sound of the waves began to fill her subconscious. That piece was consistent now.

In her dream, she was barefoot, standing in the water near sand and rocks, surrounded by a deep, endless blue ocean. Millions of stars lit up the sky, and the moon was full above her. The waves lapped in a peaceful, hypnotic rhythm that soothed her, until a terrifying scream fractured the silence. Then the dream collapsed, like a wave folding inward.

Isla jolted awake, heart hammering against her ribs. Her pillow was damp with sweat, the air around her thick and still. The fact of Coraline's disappearance surged back, followed by the familiar sting of guilt. She lay back slowly, eyes wide in the dark, listening to the silence that surrounded her. Minutes dragged by, until exhaustion began to dull the edges of her thoughts. Just as sleep crept back in, a single, darker thought rose to the surface.

Maybe dreams weren't just dreams after all.

~

It was late morning when she woke again, the sun already dragging long lines of light across the ceiling. Her pillow was dry now, but the faint trace of salt remained on her lips. Isla sat up slowly and rubbed her eyes, then reached for the phone still plugged in beside the bed. One voicemail, the same she'd already played a handful of times. Clicking it open, she played it again.

“Miss March? This is Sheriff Alan Wright calling from the Greyhook Police Department.”

She paused the message there. To the sheriff, Coraline was just a name on a page: another missing person among a roster of phone calls. A family on a list they’d never asked to be on. Sheriff Wright may have spoken to Coraline a handful of times, but he didn’t really know her, so would he know how to find her? Isla might. She knew the edges, the habits, the contradictions. The small intimacies that built her grandmother out of more than her current circumstances. If anyone could bridge the distance between missing and found, it had to be someone who knew her. Didn’t it?

A sharp thump on her third story window pulled her from her thoughts. When she looked up, there was no one there: just a smear of green pressed flat against the glass. Leaning closer, she realized the damp, leafy thing didn’t belong anywhere near her building, or even in this city. It appeared to be seaweed.

Isla stared at it for another minute before turning away from the window and pressing the call-back number. It rang twice before a deep male voice answered.

“Greyhook Police.”

“Hi. This is Isla March. I got your message about my grandmother.”

There was a brief pause as papers shuffled, and a door closed in the background.

“Hello, Miss March. We were hoping you’d call.”

Isla’s gaze drifted back to the window. The strand of seaweed was now gone. No smear, no dampness, nothing to prove it had ever been there at all. For a moment she wondered if she’d imagined it.

Beyond the glass, the sky stretched pink and gray, the kind of sky that always came before a change.

TWO

The bus crawled northward, its windows streaked with rain and roadside grime. Wipers lurched across the windshield in uneven sweeps, never quite keeping pace with the mist. Near the back, Isla sat alone, her coat balled between her shoulder and the rattling window, her duffel shoved beneath the empty chair beside her.

Beyond the glass, the city had fallen away into fields, then trees, then those other trees: tall and dark, older than highways, and dripping with moss in green curtains. A nameless town slid by outside the window: a rusted food market, a parking lot gone to weeds. It was the kind of nowhere that sat between somewheres, the kind of place Coraline would have known the name of.

Isla's spine ached less than usual today, the pain dulled but not gone. The idea of time away from leaning over the bar for hours on end felt like luxury. It was a rare breath, one she hadn't taken in quite some time.

Before leaving town, Isla had called Ivy to ask for someone to cover her shifts.

"Take all the time you need," Ivy had said, very little surprise in her voice. "We'll be fine. Just take care of yourself. Maybe there's a rugged cop or two who can help you 'interrogate' the local population."

Knowing Ivy, she'd likely had an entire fantasy arc mapped out, complete with backstories, before Isla had even started packing.

With Isla's health faltering, time off would not have been unexpected. The beauty of bar work was that it was fluid, gloriously non-committal: a job you could disappear from for a while and no one would bat an eye. Unless you showed up like Naomi did last fall; six months pregnant, sunburned, and back from Arizona with a spiritual awakening and a restraining order courtesy of a man named Bruce.

The bus jolted over a pothole, dragging her back to the present. As it rounded a bend, the road narrowed into tight curves, the trees leaning inward as though they were conspiring over the asphalt. Wet ferns curled like claws across the slopes, and moss carpeted the ground beneath. With each turn, the drive fell quieter, the outside world drawing its veil. The hills rose steeper, their edges sharpened, and somewhere in the back of her mind, Coraline's voice surfaced.

"You can smell the ocean before you see it. You can feel it on your skin."

Isla inhaled reflexively. She could smell it, not the sharp tang of fish and brine, but something subtler like damp stone, salt clinging to bark, and the faint trace of seaweed. To her, it smelled of nostalgia.

Her fingers rested pale and still in her lap, less shaky than they'd been, her chest not as tight. Drawing another breath, she let her head fall back, savoring the scent that loosened something inside her. Ahead, the highway bent west, toward the cliffs and the ocean. Toward Greyhook. Isla didn't want to admit it, not even to herself, but she knew: the closer she got to home and to the ocean, the more she felt whole.

As her senses took her back in time, she thought of Silas. Not the way she usually did in flashes of waves, screams muffled by water, or the thick, awful silence that followed in her dreams. Not just of the loss, but of the boy. Her twin. She was six in this memory, one of only a handful she had left that remained clear and unclouded.

Their room was dark except for the octopus-shaped nightlight Coraline plugged in every evening when it was time to wind down for bed. They'd built a blanket fort using broomsticks and binder clips between their twin beds that once sat side-by-side. Inside that fort, Silas had curled up cross-legged, whispering into one of his seashells. The shell, a broken conch, was split through the middle. He had fallen in love with it for the zigzag pink stripe running down its center. Coraline had warned him not to touch it or the sharp, broken edge it bore, but he'd taken it anyway. Hidden away, it became his confidante, the keeper of his whispered secrets. Pressed to his ear, it spoke to him in the murmurs of the ocean, and he hummed while he played, the melody soft and unfamiliar.

"Where'd you learn that?"

"It tells me," he'd said, tapping the shell against his temple.

"Liar," she'd scolded.

Silas had only shrugged and kept humming. Isla hadn't thought about that night in years. Maybe she'd buried it, or perhaps it got swallowed under all the therapy sessions and quiet apologies. People never knew quite what to say when you were the other twin, the one who was still here.

After all these years, the boy himself was harder to remember than the day he'd vanished, but their bond remained. Not just a memory, but a thread woven through her marrow. A quiet tether that had once pulsed with shared breath, mirrored thoughts, and unspoken knowing. Even in his absence, occasionally Isla still felt that phantom hum of something once a part of her, a connection that had been so vital.

She hadn't been there the day he'd drowned, but she'd carried the story with her just the same, repeated so often she could picture it. Police reports, sympathetic stares, the sound of condolences echoing through her mind. But Silas as a boy; that part of her memory had eroded, the edges worn smooth.

It hurt in a way she hadn't expected – today's grief held a different shape. Isla closed her eyes, but she didn't cry. She just let herself remember what it had felt like to share a world with him, even if it had only been for a little while.

~

Passing trees thinned just enough to reveal the green and gray coastline below. Jagged cliffs slick with black rock; the tide smearing its way up the shore. The ocean was still too far away to hear, but Isla could feel it in the weight of the air, sharp and crisp.

The cold glass on her temple felt soothing as she leaned against the window. She hadn't eaten since yesterday, but her stomach didn't feel empty. It was full of something heavier: anticipation, maybe. Or dread. Her mind drifted to the place she'd grown up, the March house. A cliff-side manor, tall and wind-battered, its shutters stained, and windows fixed on the endless sea. Lavender, chamomile, and salt always lingered there, even in winter.

The strict mandates of that home flooded back to her before the warmth did. Coraline hadn't cared much about curfews or missed assignments, her rules were dictated by tide charts and storm warnings. Isla grew up learning the moods of the sea before she'd ever learned to ride a bike. And while her grandmother had raised her, it hadn't always felt like care. More like containment, and a giant pain in Isla's ass.

Still, there were bright spots, and Isla clung to those now. Warm rice bags wrapped in soft yarn sacks, tucked into their beds during winter storms. Quiet mornings with laughter, stories read from books with worn pages, and Sundays sweetened by baked treats and evening walks along the shore, their pockets filled with sea glass and clam shells. One year when Isla had the flu, Coraline had sat by her bed every night. While steeping herbs for healing teas, she'd press cool saltwater cloths to her forehead and whisper, *"This too shall pass,"* and *"It will only make you stronger."*

Isla hadn't believed her when she'd said it then; a well-meaning mantra spoken over scraped knees or a childhood heartbreak. She'd believed it even less after Silas died. Words like that had shriveled under the weight of the silence that was left in his place.

Coraline had been different before: playful, relaxed, the kind of grandmother who let the twins run barefoot by the shore and come home dripping with seawater and happiness, smiles plastered to their faces. After Silas drowned, something in her calcified. What once was freedom near the tide became a regimen of caution, as if control could bargain against loss. Coraline grew quieter, more introverted, and spent more time reading and writing letters. Chimes were placed on doors, and locks slid over the windows at night, like vigilance itself could stand guard over them. The home that had once opened its arms felt like it had walls too tall and too thick.

When Isla turned eighteen, she'd left without saying goodbye. No screaming match, no slammed doors. Just a one-way bus ticket tucked into her bag and a note left on the kitchen table. For years, she'd told herself there were no regrets, but now, with the road winding closer to the coastline and the one person who'd always been there no longer waiting at the end, she wasn't so sure.

By the time the bus passed the mile marker for Greyhook, the ringing in her ears was gone. The world no longer sounded muffled, as though filtered through gauze. She had been blaming trapped water, or TMJ, but now she could hear the steady rhythm of tires on wet pavement, the soft patter of rain against metal, each sound distinct and clean.

Outside, the clouds sagged low, stitched across the sky. Coastal trees blurred past the window with trunks wrapped in ivy. Behind them, the ocean finally appeared. With hoodie sleeves tugged over her hands and one knee drawn in close, Isla leaned back in her seat. She breathed deeply, the air drawing in clean without that familiar snag at the top of her chest. Something inside her had released, like a cork drawn from her lungs, and she watched, entranced by the familiar shimmer along the water's edge. Then, she closed her eyes, bracing against the feeling it carried in with it.

This too shall pass. You'll be stronger because of it. Maybe Coraline had been mad, but maybe mad people weren't mad all the time.

The bus shuddered to a stop in the gravel lot behind Greyhook's only gas station. It stood alone at the end of the main street with two pumps, one flickering sign, and a sagging bench that hadn't been painted since the Clinton administration.

Isla stepped down onto the slick concrete, her duffel strap slung over one shoulder. The ocean air hit her like a wet hand: salt, cedar, and a faint rot, like seaweed fermenting beneath a boardwalk. The town hadn't changed, not really. Power lines still leaned overhead, rooftops still drooped under moss, and the same names flaked in blue and white across shopfronts: Jo's Diner, The Reef Pub, Julie's Cuts (Walk-Ins Welcome). Every corner of every building was worn down as though slowly chewed by wind.

Her boots hit the wet pavement in a steady rhythm, the sound echoing through the street as she walked. The mint-green hardware store stood out, freshly painted against the gray morning: Murphy's Hardware & Marine Supply. Beside it, a little bookstore sat quaintly next to a coffee shop called The Little Bean. Both were places Isla had spent countless hours.

Two old-timers lingered on a bench beneath a faded awning, paper cups of steaming coffee in their hands. Their conversation broke off as she passed, one just blinking, the other offering a single, slow nod. She recognized him: Duncan Lee, a man she remembered from her teen years bussing tables at The Reef, and Isla guessed his cup held more than just coffee.

At the corner of Marine and Oak, where the sidewalk narrowed, a slight figure stood under a crooked, wind-beaten alder tree.

"Well, look what the tide dragged in."

Isla turned. "Oh! Mira. You surprised me."

Mira Baird looked mostly the same. In her late sixties now, she had silver-streaked hair that was neatly tucked under the waxed hood of a rain jacket that was too big and patched at the elbows. Laugh lines etched like weathered wood covered her cheeks, and her eyes, always just a little too sharp, bored into Isla. In one hand she carried a cloth tote that looked to be full of fruit, and in the other, she held a book.

"I heard about Coraline," Mira said, tone gentle, eyes cool and assessing. "Sorry to hear it."

"Thank you. I don't really know what's going on yet, I just arrived."

"Well. I guess that's why they called you home."

Isla blinked. "Who?"

"Them."

A pause stretched.

"You mean the Sheriff's department??" Isla asked.

Mira's gaze slid toward the west, where the fog sat thick along the horizon. "The house," she said finally, as if that should be enough. "And the sea."

Isla opened her mouth, then closed it again, unsure how to respond.

“Things here have been a bit strange here lately.” Mira went on. “Stranger than usual, anyway. I’m surprised you came back.” She stared, as if waiting for Isla to connect the dots she would not name herself. “The tide’s been higher than it should be, and we’ve had sea lions sleeping in our yards instead of the bays.”

“Well, sea lions can be social, can’t they? Maybe they just needed a change of scenery.”

Isla gave a small, awkward laugh. “Anyway, it was good to see you.” She took a slight step back, lowering her voice. “I think.”

Just as she thought, people here were still odd. She gave a small nod and continued down the sidewalk. She refused to glance back, though she felt Mira’s eyes lingering, following her every step. After crossing the street, Isla turned onto a narrow side road that climbed toward the bluff. Only then did the weight of Mira’s gaze seem to fall away.

As she made her way closer to March Manor, the number of houses thinned, their porches weathered and familiar: fewer mailboxes, less noise, just the wind rising against her ears. Trees grew sparse, their branches leaning permanently toward the ocean, bent by its pull. Isla had walked this route daily as a child, an adolescent, and then a teenager. She’d gone barefoot most days, the gravel rough against her feet, and she’d stumble up the road with laughter on her breath and stolen liquor in her veins, anticipating the punishment for coming home with wet hair and damp clothes.

Night swimming was at the top of Coraline’s long list of forbidden things. Too dangerous, too reckless, too much like tempting the sea to take another. The more rules Coraline set, the more Isla had wanted to break them. Now, with each step uphill, the wind pushed harder against her, carrying a sense of return that was as unsettling as it was familiar.

Then, there it was: March Manor. The front of the house was in fact the back, as it sat with its rear door toward the land and its face toward the endless sea. Half-swallowed by mist, perched at the edge of the bluff, it looked less built than grown: two stories of wind-battered wood rose against the sky, windows glinting like watchful eyes. The roof slouched slightly, its shingles curling up like brittle fingernails, clinging to whatever years it had left.

From the road below, the house seemed both fragile and immovable. This was the place she had run from, desperate to breathe free of its walls, but also the place she had carried inside her every day since.

Now, as the mist thinned, the house waited, unchanged and unyielding, as though it had known she would return all along.

THREE

The front gate was just as she remembered. Its frame bowed with age, hinges loose and rusted to a dull orange. The metal *MARCH* nameplate still clung stubbornly to the bars, the letters half-faded from generations of wear. To the right, the leaning fence posts were held together by a sun-bleached knot of rope, its weight shifting slightly with the movement of the air.

The gate yielded with a low groan as Isla pushed it open. Paving stones shifted under her boots as she stepped onto the moss-covered path. The short garden wall had crumbled in places, missing chunks like broken teeth, and a long crack ran through one of the porch columns, a fine fracture from crown to base.

Above the stairs, Coraline's wind chimes hung in a tangle. Strands of salt-worn glass glinted dully in the light, clinking in a whisper of song.

The house was smaller than she remembered, though it felt like it was watching. The paint had gone gray where it had once been white, and the shutters hung loose on their hinges. Wooden stairs leading to the door moaned as she climbed, a sound more warning than welcome, and the planters that lined the porch were empty, their lack of annual flowers unusual for this time of year.

For a moment, she tried to picture it as it must have been when it was new. She imagined the paint unblistered, the stonework square, the porch standing straight against the wind. It had seen other lifetimes before hers. It must have been beautiful once.

A small iron key waited in its old hiding place, tucked beneath the watering can on the thick windowsill beside the door. No one in Greyhook locked their doors, but Coraline always had. The key was cold in her hand, but before she used it, Isla tried the handle. It turned easily, unlocked, and the door opened with a loud click that echoed into the quiet.

As the door swung inward, she stepped into the house and into the past she thought she'd left behind. The stale air greeted her with stillness as she crossed the threshold. There she stood, listening, as dust floated in the half-light, catching on the edges of her vision.

No creaks. No voices. No Coraline.

The silence in the house felt uneasy. It didn't feel abandoned exactly, but more like the hush left behind when footsteps have only just faded. It felt paused, as though Coraline had only stepped out for the afternoon. Lemon balm and sage still lingered in the cool air, threaded with the papery musk of old books and hidden dust bunnies. Apothecary teas lined a shelf. Reading glasses resting on a closed newspaper on the table nearby. Even the obsessively scrubbed floorboards looked untouched, gleaming in the dim light.

Isla stood there, taking in her surroundings. Coraline's boots waited neatly on a woven mat by the door, her shawl hung from a peg by the stairs, and her carved walking cane with its driftwood handle leaned in its familiar place against the wall. A half-full teacup sat on a little round table in the sitting room, its rim stained with rose-colored lipstick, only a thin trace left inside.

She wandered slowly, running her hand along the back of the worn leather chair near the fireplace, fingers grazing the knit blanket draped over the arm. The same faded sea-foam green throw Coraline used to wrap around her shoulders on stormy nights. Isla lifted it to her face, breathing in the faint traces of wood smoke that still clung to the fibers.

More habit than thought, Isla lit up the kitchen with an easy flick of the switch. On the stove, the kettle waited, clean but not polished, while a neat row of jars lined one side of the counter. Honey, dried citrus, sea salt. No dishes in the sink, no clutter left behind.

Inside the cupboards, Coraline's careful order continued. Jars of lentils stacked side by side with bottled fruit, catching the light in amber containers labeled in her steady script. Next to them were half empty spice jars. In the fridge she found the same story: nothing spoiled, but nothing fresh beyond a bowl of apples and a few lemons. It hadn't been cleaned out, nor had it been restocked.

Coraline had always cleaned before a storm and said it was bad luck to ride one out in a messy house. Chaos outside required order inside. So she'd sweep and scrub like the weather might judge her, going on about how no one should sit through a storm with dirty floors and dishes in the sink. Isla would roll her eyes and call it ridiculous. She'd stomped out of this kitchen more than once, muttering under her breath. Now, standing in the same room years later, she felt regret for choosing distance over patience, silence over answering the phone.

Had a storm come for Coraline? Nothing about the room suggested haste. It felt methodical, organized.

Isla made her way toward the narrow staircase that led to the second floor. As she set her hand on the banister and began to make her way up the steps, a sharp knock fractured the silence. Jolting, her hand flew to her chest. Three more raps followed, harder and more impatient, reverberating through the wood. She hadn't been expecting anyone.

A hand still on her chest to cushion her thudding heart, she stepped down and opened the door. Two men stood on the porch, their jackets damp with mist. Of the two, the older was tall and broad, his gray hair cropped close, his tired eyes set deep beneath the brim of a trooper's hat. Brass buttons trimmed his dark brown uniform, and a gold shoulder patch caught what little light the mist allowed. He looked relaxed and gave a polite smile with his greeting as he tipped his hat.

"Hello, Isla."

Beside him stood a younger man, lean and not yet settled in his uniform. The stiff crease of his trousers was still too sharp, the brass too polished. A manila envelope was clutched in his hands and when his eyes met hers, he managed a nod that landed somewhere between respectful and uncertain. He looked, she thought, like he was still learning.

"Sheriff Alan Wright," the older man said. "This is Officer Troy Richardson."

Isla remembered him now. Sheriff Wright had been a young deputy when Silas drowned. He was quiet back then, still finding his feet. Not long after, he'd left Greyhook to work in a bigger city, and by the time he'd returned, Isla was already packing her bags for art school. Their paths had crossed only in passing, with fragments of recognition. Rumor had it he'd messed up somehow, and coming back to Greyhook wasn't so much a choice as it was a punishment. This was where they sent you when you'd slipped up, where it didn't matter whether you were competent or not because nothing ever happened here.

"Sorry to stop by unannounced, but we didn't want to leave the papers in the post box, considering the circumstances." He paused, reading her mind. "It's a small town. People rarely come and go unnoticed around here."

Mira. Once a town gossip, always a town gossip. Isla gave a single nod of understanding; the irony of his statement not lost on her.

Sheriff Wright looked around the foyer like a man who'd stood there before, not recently but long enough ago to remember it differently.

"May we come in for a moment?" Without waiting for an answer, he wiped his feet on the rug and stepped inside. The younger officer followed.

"Doesn't look much different than I remember," the Sheriff said.

Officer Richardson smiled, then shifted the envelope and held it out to Isla. She took it without speaking. It seemed heavier now that it was in her hands.

"Go ahead," he said, motioning to the envelope. "It's from your grandmother. Not the way things are typically done, but she signed it, so it's legal." His eyes were kind, clear and direct beneath the brim of his hat. He gave a small nod, professional but unforced. It was easier to look at him than at the Sheriff.

Inside were three documents: two typed, one handwritten. The typed pages bore the letterhead of Greyhook Legal Services and included a warranty deed transferring title to the March House and the required property transfer form for recording. The house was described in careful legal language, its boundaries measured, its bluff noted, its view of the ocean reduced to coordinates and parcel numbers.

The handwritten page was unmistakably Coraline's. Looped and elegant in that impatient, old-school way. Isla slipped it from the envelope.

In the event of my prolonged absence, Isla H. March shall inherit the March House and all its contents, provided she remains in Greyhook and resides at the March House through the rising of the full moon during the spring equinox of this year.

- Coraline March

Isla looked up from the document. "What does this mean?"

"We were hoping you'd know. It was delivered by courier with instructions to pass it on to you when you arrived."

Arrived. Had Coraline been expecting her?

"When was it delivered?"

"About two weeks ago."

Isla had no plans to come back to Greyhook until Coraline disappeared, nor had she told anyone she was coming. Yet, the envelope had been waiting for her.

Coraline had known. Not hoped, planned.

"How long has she been missing?" Isla asked softly.

"We don't know, exactly. We received a request for a wellness check a few days ago, but it would seem she'd been gone for some time before then. You weren't aware she'd transferred the house into your name?"

Isla shook her head.

"When was the last time you spoke to her?"

Isla didn't remember the last time. Coraline had tried to call. Memories of her phone buzzing on the counter replayed in her mind, clear and unforgiving. The last attempt had been about a month ago, and she'd let it go to voicemail. Guilt curled her fingers hard around the envelope until the edges bent.

"A long time. We weren't close these last few years."

Sheriff Wright sighed, seemingly out of frustration at the lack of useful information.

"Well, we won't keep you. If you think of anything else, give us a call." Officer Richardson handed her his card.

Both officers turned to leave, their boots thudding against the wet porch.

Silence folded in around her after the door clicked shut. The house seemed to exhale, breathing again with her as the faint clink of wind chimes carried through the entry way. Isla stood motionless with the papers in her hands, Coraline's conditions burning in her mind.

Reside in Greyhook, and in the March House through the rising of the full moon during the spring equinox of this year.

It sounded less like legal language and more like a riddle left for her to solve. The equinox was only a few weeks away. She checked her phone; the full moon would fall on the same night. The tides would be higher then, they always were.

Why had Coraline taken the time to transfer the house with such precise instructions? The condition hadn't been accidental, and that thought settled uneasily. Had she planned to disappear?

Sherrif Wright and his deputy had barely made it to their vehicle when the next knock came, this time from the back door. Two light taps, delivered in a way that suggested familiarity.

"What now?" she said to herself as she stalked through the kitchen.

Isla breezed past the baker's rack where stems of lavender, sage, and rosemary still hung drying. With a tug at the semi-sheer curtain over the window, she peeked out. An older woman stood on the stone steps, bundled in a long blue coat, hair pinned back in a loose silver chignon. Eyes small yet kind shone behind rain-speckled glasses, and the neat fold of her hands tempered Isla's irritation. With an exhale, her shoulders loosened, and she opened the door.

"Isla," the woman said brightly, confirming something she'd already suspected. "You look more like your grandmother than I remembered. You're so grown up."

Isla blinked, struggling momentarily to place the familiar woman, whose name hovered just out of reach.

"I'm Eloise Danner. I live down the road on the other side of that big hedge by the white fence." The woman gestured toward her home and the shrub that separated the March House from the neighboring property. "You probably don't remember me."

"I do." Isla smiled as she placed the face in her memory. Eloise was a kind woman who lived alone but always lifted a hand in greeting from her garden, where she spent most of her days. Her tiny cottage sat halfway down the hill, tucked behind a massive, gnarled apple tree: close enough to wave from a distance and to enjoy the quiet comfort of neighbors, but far enough for her to enjoy her privacy. Now and then she'd bring up baskets of apples, the fruit still warm from the sun. That memory softened Isla, and she stepped aside, holding the door open.

"Would you like to come in?"

"Oh no, thank you, dear. I don't want to bother you. I just came to tell you that I was the one who called the sheriff about your grandmother."

Isla's fingers stiffened slightly on the edge of the door, and she nodded faintly, unsure what to say.

"I'm usually out in the garden in the afternoons, and Coraline would often stop by on her way back from town. It was always nice to enjoy her company. Recently, I'd noticed she was going into town more often as the pull cart she used for the market was getting too heavy to haul when it was full. When I didn't see her for several days, I thought she might be ill, so I came up to look in on her. There was no answer, and I could see her walking cane through the window. That's when I thought it best to call the Sheriff."

"Thank you for looking in on her."

"It's no trouble, dear. I didn't want to leave it too long before someone checked in. When the deputy said the house was empty, I thought she'd probably just gone out of town."

"I appreciate you letting him know." Isla looked down at the floor. "I didn't know she'd been missing."

"Don't feel bad, Isla. Coraline talked about you all the time! Your big move to the city, that you were selling your art. She was so proud of you."

The words came as a surprise. *Proud.* Coraline had been proud of her? The thought shot warmth through the ache in her chest. That wasn't something Coraline had ever said to her.

"I wasn't trying to intrude, it's just that things felt a little off after that. As you know, she was rigid in her routines. Every Saturday she picked her herbs, and I hadn't seen her in the garden for a couple of weeks. That's when I called them again and told them something wasn't right." Eloise slid her hands into her pockets.

Weeks. Isla cleared her throat.

"Did you notice anything else that was unusual? Anything different before she disappeared?"

Eloise blinked, gaze shifting as she took her mind back. "Well, no...but now that you mention it, Coraline had been spending more time down by the water these past few months. Sometimes out in the bay, even when it was cold. That wasn't really like her; not that I had seen, at least."

Isla nodded slowly, Coraline's stern rules running through her mind. She had always treated the ocean as if it were alive and dangerous.

"I figured it to be some kind of exercise or meditation," Eloise said, her tone uncertain. "Now and then I thought I saw someone down there with her in the water, but I couldn't tell you who. I don't really understand that sort of thing. New-age practices or whatever they are don't suit me but I have heard that water therapy and aquacise is good for your joints as you get older." She waved a hand, brushing off the thought with a laugh. "Mostly she just stood on the bluff staring out at the sea."

For a long moment, Isla didn't speak. The idea of Coraline breaking her own rules, the very rules she'd drilled into Isla as a child, didn't make any sense.

"That's all I can tell you dear, but if you need anything, you know where to find me." With that, she smiled, and walked back down the stairs, the sound of her footsteps dissolving into the fog.

~

March Manor was never quiet the way normal houses were. It creaked, settled, and breathed. The wind whistled through the eaves and murmured around the windows. Its wallpaper looked older and more worn than she remembered, a warm, sandy neutral, touched by decades of sun, now peeling in some corners.

Isla brushed her fingers along the wall as she climbed one step at a time. On the second-floor landing, everything was as she remembered: a deep red rug, now threadbare at the edges, and flickering sconces with dust-fogged bulbs casting long shadows that shifted as she did. She moved down the hall, past the bathroom, past the linen closet where Coraline's towels were still stacked with rigid precision. Framed photographs lined the walls, each one working loose another memory, until she reached her grandmother's bedroom door. It was closed, the brass knob tarnished, a lace tassel hanging stiff with age. She lifted her hand, then hesitated. Instead, she leaned closer, pressing her ear to the door. At first, there was nothing, just a steady silence broken only by the living room clock ticking downstairs. Then, gradually, a faint vibration emerged. A thread of sound so quiet she almost mistook it for breath. It was barely there, but it stirred something inside her, collapsing the years between then and now.

Silas used to make sounds like that, little melodies that slipped out of him without his knowing.

With a slow push, she opened the door. The bedroom was empty. It looked the same. The bed was made tight, hospital-style corners still holding. A floral quilt stretched flat across the mattress, sun-faded in patches where the light had settled through the same bright window for years. Curtains stood open just enough to let in the soft wash of the afternoon, and the faint scent of salt and rosewater seemed to linger. Isla wasn't sure whether the smell came from the room or from the memory of the woman who'd once slept there.

On the dresser sat a ceramic tray of hairpins, a half-empty perfume bottle, and a framed photo of Silas and Isla as toddlers. They were sun-kissed and wind-blown, laughter frozen mid-snap. Her arm encircled her twin's shoulders, their grins wide and wild. She stared for a moment, caught in the memory, a smile touching the corner of her lips.

The smile faded as another memory. She turned toward the window and thought of the last real fight she'd had with her grandmother in this room. Coraline had stood by the window, stiff, arms crossed, while Isla hurled anger over not being allowed to attend a party at the pier before graduation.

"You are not going to that party," she'd said, each word clipped and final.

"But everyone's going! There are only a few parties before graduation, and you're making me look like a freak!"

"You don't belong on those piers after dark. Not now, not ever."

"Why not? Everyone else gets to go!" Isla's voice had cracked as it rose.

"You know why, Isla. The sea takes what it wants, and I won't let it take you."

"I'm not a child," Isla spat. *"Silas was just a little boy. I'm almost an adult. I can take care of myself!"*

Coraline's arms only folded tighter as she stood her ground. *"The answer is no."*

Something inside Isla had snapped then. *"Just because you couldn't protect him doesn't mean you get to control me!"*

The words hung between them. Coraline had flinched as if struck, but no reply came. Not one word. She kept her back to Isla, gaze locked on the window, shoulders squared in rigid defiance, jaw tight, blinking hard against the tears she refused to let fall.

That silence had been worse than any fury. Isla had stormed out, and later, after the house fell quiet, she'd slipped down the stairs and gone to the party anyway.

Not long after, she'd left Greyhook, certain she'd never come back. Yet here she was, standing in the quiet of the same room, the weight of Coraline's absence pressing harder than her presence ever had.

FOUR

Cal Thatcher opened one eye to the dim gray ceiling. Paint peeled in curling strips, and a water stain shaped like a horseshoe settled overhead, unchanged but always there: a quiet reminder of how much work the place needed. The lighthouse was mostly all original and almost never quiet. It creaked and moaned, its joints settling like an old body. Ocean winds wound through the seams of the walls, carrying the hiss of the sea that broke against the base of the tower.

He sat up and swung his feet onto the cold floorboards. The mattress groaned beneath him, its tired coils wheezing in protest at his movement. Nothing in this room belonged to him. The furniture was borrowed, the bedding was borrowed. Hell, even the job wasn't really his. He'd only gotten it because his uncle Ray had died.

Ray had been the last official lighthouse keeper in Greyhook, a post he'd held for over thirty years. When the Coast Guard automated the station, the town no longer needed a full-time watch. Still, the residents insisted that someone local remain, someone who knew the tides and shoals, someone they trusted if the machines failed. So, Ray stayed on, unofficial but necessary. The man in the tower when storms rolled in and the sea swallowed the horizon.

"Tradition," they'd said. *"Something to reassure the fishing families."*

When Ray's heart gave out six months ago, the post had been offered to Cal. He hadn't said yes for the money or for the hours; he'd said yes because he needed to come home. This post gave him a quiet place to live, and a safe place to start over.

Greyhook wasn't just where he'd grown up; it was where he'd always imagined his life would take place. Before his marriage fell apart, he'd told Lina they'd raise kids here. Saturday mornings on Main Street with coffee and croissants, the same faces every week. A cottage by the water, with shutters warped by salt, and rosemary spilling from clay pots. It might have seemed like a slow life to others, but to him, it was perfect.

This wasn't just the kind of town where people knew your name; they knew your grandfather's fishing stories and how you got the scar on your left eyebrow. They let you know Miller's Pet Supply was sold out of your brand of dog food as they passed you on the street or paid for your coffee when they ran into you in line at The Little Bean. Cal loved the crooked-floored bookshop that smelled of paper and vanilla, and the diner where you couldn't order a burger without someone trying to set you up with their cousin or brag about their nephew's ball game. Greyhook was small, safe, and close to the ocean. It was everything he'd wanted when it came time to raise a family, and when those plans had unraveled last year, this was the only place he could imagine coming back to. It was home.

At the far end of the cove, the lighthouse clung to the rocky hillside just below the bluff. Its whitewashed tower weathered by salt and wind had been worn down to a soft grey beneath years of storms. Perched above the rocks, it sat low enough for storm tides to lash its base with spray, yet high enough for the beam to command the bay and the waters beyond.

From the upper gallery platform, Cal could see it all: the curve of Greyhook's shoreline beyond the cape, the tide curling into the cove, and across the water on the opposite bluff, the March House.

It stood like a sentinel, its windows casting light when the fog thinned, watching the sea in quiet rivalry with the lighthouse. That house had drawn his attention often since coming home. It was difficult not to, with its history tied to his own.

In the last few months, he'd crossed paths with Coraline March only a handful of times, their conversations polite but brief. Kind enough, though still edged with that not-quite-friendly rigidity he remembered.

He and Coraline's grandchildren, Silas and Isla, had once been inseparable. After Silas drowned, Cal had sat with Isla through the long shadows that followed, quiet company in a silence too heavy for their age. They'd remained close growing up, but the years after high school had scattered them, as years do.

The wind rattled against the glass, pulling him back to himself. He shifted and stood to stretch, his joints popping against the chill. Coastal damp got into everything here. Bones included. The lighthouse offered little protection with its thin walls, drafty windows, and an iron furnace that rattled whenever it bothered to kick on. He pulled on a hoodie, laced his boots, and pushed open the heavy side door to the main stairwell.

A gust of briny air rushed in, sharper than usual for this time of year. The sky was still dark, thinning to a washed-out pink and gray. He stepped out onto the gallery and tilted his head toward the tower. The beacon light was out.

"Automated system my ass." He checked his phone. Nothing. "So much for your no-good alerts."

"Can't trust technology!" Ray had always said.

The beacon was supposed to run on its own: sensors and timers wired to a rotating lens, programmed to flash its sequence through fog and darkness. A backup generator was supposed to keep it running during outages, and the system was supposed to replace the bulb automatically and trigger an alert if anything malfunctioned. The Coast Guard conducted monthly inspections that were supposed to catch mechanical failures, but a town of fishermen and salvage divers didn't bet their lives on "supposed to." That was why the town council had fought to keep Ray on as a part-time keeper, even when the National Park Service was ready to eliminate the position altogether.

Now, it was Cal. Someone local. Someone who would climb the tower if the light went dark.

On the outer stairwell, a low fog drew close, grasping like ghost fingers. Cal mentally reviewed his morning tasks: check the foghorn on his way up first, then the beacon. The old horn could be temperamental, but he'd already heard its wail twice since waking up. Built into the belly of the lighthouse, the horn was a steel-mouthed relic wired decades ago, half-digitized and mostly trustworthy like older things often were.

Stepping through a hatch into the chamber, he flipped on the auxiliary light. Everything looked steady: battery readouts solid, no systems tripped overnight. The test button worked, and the horn bellowed its long, mournful blast. Behind it came something else, more faint, threaded through the fog like the echoing of a delayed harmony. Old locals called it the sailor's echo, a ricochet carried back across the water. Today it was less echo than hum, and it vanished as quickly as it had come.

The skin on the back of his neck prickled. The sea could play tricks, but ghost stories and scraps of town lore only seemed to find him on mornings like this. Dark, eerie, fog hugging in, the world muted like he was the only one left in it.

Cal ran the test again, listening harder for the reverberation. Nothing. Just the long, low exhale of the foghorn, that whale-belly groan that made tourists jump but the locals found comforting.

He closed the horns chamber with a heavy thud and started the climb toward the beacon. Halfway up, a rogue wave smashed against the base of the tower, the impact rattling the iron spine beneath his boots. Spray burst across the stairwell slats, dousing him in a cold slap of salty mist. As his boots slipped, he gripped the railing hard, breath jerking sharply as the entire structure seemed to shiver with the sea's force. For a moment he stood frozen, fingers stinging from his hold. The sea's reminder was blunt and undeniable: she had enough reach to shake iron and stone, and she wanted him to know it.

At the top of the stairs, in the center of the lens room, stood the great Fresnel lens, prismatic panes catching what little light the fog allowed and glinting like a watchful eye. Cal set his toolkit down and swung open the service panel, his hands moving by habit. Bolts were tightened, wiring connections secured, an old rag passed over the condensation beading on the glass. This work suited him. He liked to think the light, this old guardian of the bay, still answered to him and not just to a screen in Seattle.

He closed the panel, reset the breaker, and waited. For a breath, nothing. Then the mechanism caught with a low mechanical hum, and the lens began its slow rotation, prisms taking hold of the thinning dawn. A white beam cut clean through the fog and swept across the sea.

Cal leaned back and wiped his palms against his jeans, a deep satisfaction settling within. He stepped to the railing and looked out over the misty cove. The tide moved gently below, unseen currents stirring beneath the haze.

He didn't know yet that somewhere beyond the fog, Isla was already home.

The main keeper's quarters were in shambles. The living area was stripped to bare boards, the kitchen half-furnished, and the bed's sagging mattress along with his unpacked boxes took up most of the space in Cal's room. He'd thought he'd have made the place his own by now, but everything around him still felt like Ray's.

A mug of coffee steamed beside him on the desk, his work orders for the coming week spread out in front of him. With the lighthouse only a part-time gig, Cal filled the days with whatever jobs kept the bills paid and his hands busy: electrical work, mostly. Today he was rewiring a trawler's busted navigation lights and patching the faulty breaker in a fishermen's cottage where the wiring was older than he was. It wasn't glamorous, but it paid steady, and the people here trusted him.

As he sat reviewing the days' appointments, his eyes strayed to the letter lying on the edge of his desk. There was no need to unfold it again: every clipped word of Lina's writing was already memorized. Neat, clinical, efficient. Perfectly matched to the way she'd organized their lives, right up until the day she'd decided Cal wasn't going to change.

Cal,

The last of the documents from the lawyers are enclosed. You don't need to sign anything else unless you contest the accounts, which I hope you won't. The boat is yours. I don't want it. I'm glad you're back where you belong. You were always more married to Greyhook than you were to me.

Lina

No friendly sign-off. No affection. Just the clean break of someone who'd stopped waiting to be convinced and had moved on with her life.

After folding the letter in half once more, he fed it to the wood-burning stove and watched the flames curl it black.

For months he'd tried to convince Lina she could learn to appreciate a slower life, but she wanted skylines and restaurants and cities that never stood still. Cal wanted the exact opposite. After graduating from college, they'd moved to Seattle together. She had refused to give Greyhook a chance, never even tried to imagine a life with him here. Faced with her unhappiness, he'd given in to the city. But no matter how hard he tried, that life never felt like his. City life held her, not him.

Eventually, his frequent trips home and long days sailing had become their own kind of confession. To her it was simple: she had never been his priority. And maybe she was right.

Doomed from the start, he thought. Though he held no regrets.

Cal leaned back, coffee cooling in his hands. Beyond the window, the lowering tide stretched thin over sand and stone, the southern bluff curving in a crescent around the bay. It was then that he saw her: a figure, pale in the fog, barefoot on the wet sand. One hand trailed in the air beside her, as if brushing against something invisible.

He squinted through the condensation-streaked glass, then reached for the binoculars he always kept within arm's reach. It was a habit born from watching boats drift past and seeing whales breach in the distance. He lifted them to his eyes, adjusting the focus with steady fingers.

Isla. It had been years since he'd last seen her, not since she'd fled Greyhook as if her boots were on fire. She'd vanished without a word like Greyhook had meant nothing. Like *he'd* meant nothing. Now, there she was. It shouldn't have surprised him that she'd come back. Word was Coraline was missing; of course Isla would come home.

Cal leaned closer to the glass, its chill whispering against his skin. Mist curled around Isla's legs, unraveling in pale strands as she walked the same stretch of beach just below the place he'd last seen her all those years ago.

She never looked back. She didn't know he was watching her. Didn't know the balance of the tide itself had shifted the moment she'd returned.

FIVE

The beach slept under a dull sky. Clouds stretched unbroken across the night, heavy and pale over the water. The tang of salt and spilled beer drifted in the breeze, and the drum of the shoreline carried farther than usual.

Their tent, an orange dome of nylon and grit, breathed gently in the coastal wind, the sea sighing against the sand just beyond the driftwood line.

They'd camped here before, though never this early in the season. Josh and Beth had left Alaska a week earlier with a truck full of gear and no real deadline, only a loose plan to explore the Pacific Northwest before starting the West Coast Trail once the weather steadied. Greyhook was meant to be nothing more than a quick night's stop, a place to rest before moving on.

Inside, Josh stirred in his sleeping bag. Something had roused him. Not a sound, exactly, but a sensation. It was vibration more than noise, a low, steady thrumming, just enough to rouse his half-dreaming mind. It arrived gradually, starting in his chest and growing into his mind. Familiar and longing, but soft. It became a song without words, and it moved like blood through the walls of his body.

Groggily, he opened his eyes and slipped from his sleeping bag, then unzipped the tent and stepped out onto the cool sand. Their fire pit was nothing but stones and charcoal now, and the trees loomed behind him like sleeping giants. Before him, the cove lay stretched and silver, the tide moving toward him in slow, deliberate breaths.

Josh walked slowly, his bare feet carrying him past their packs, past the weathered log where they'd sat hours before, toward the lapping waves. His arms hung slack at his sides; his eyes, half-lidded and heavy, barely registered what lay ahead. The sand beneath him grew cooler, wetter, firmer. When the first wave licked his toes, he did not pause. Water rose to his ankles, his calves, his knees. Still he kept moving, drawn by something waiting just beyond his reach.

On the shore, the tent rustled. Beth turned, shivering as she shifted closer to where Josh had been. As she curled in tighter, the breeze tugged at the open tent flap, the cool air kissing her cheek. Still drowsy, her hand brushed the space beside her, and she frowned as she sat up, blinking hard in the darkness. Josh's sleeping bag lay empty, and the tent flap hung open, revealing the dark sea beyond.

From somewhere down the slope came the delicate, unmistakable slosh of water. Every muscle locked as she listened: another splash, and another. Her heartbeat ticked faster as she crawled to the tent opening, the night air rushing in as she pushed it open. Below the shoreline, she could just make out Josh's silhouette as he stood waist deep in the bay. Dulled to pewter beneath the clouds, the water caught what little light remained, glinting where it rippled around him. Without urgency, he moved forward as though he was right where he intended to be.

"Josh?" It came out brittle and small. Goosebumps covered her skin, and she scrambled out of the tent. "Josh!"

No reply. He didn't even flinch.

"Josh! Stop!"

Beth broke into a sprint, stumbling down the sloped beach as the sand dragged at her feet, stealing her momentum. Ahead, he was already chest-deep, still moving forward with unwavering steps. When she reached the waterline, she stopped short and a sharp cry tore from her throat as confusion knotted in her chest. *Why wasn't he turning back?*

Then, it hit her. He wasn't going to stop; he was going to keep going until he went under. With a rush of panic, she lunged forward, crashing into the surf. Cold overwhelmed her, soaking through her sweatpants as she pushed further, and further out until her fingers closed around his wrist. Finally, Josh stopped, blinking as though waking from sleep. He turned toward her blankly.

"Beth?"

"What are you doing? You're in the damn ocean, Josh!" Both hands gripped his wrist harder than she meant to, her panic shifting to rage.

"No, I…I came out to pee." He looked down, confused by the water that rose to his armpits.

"No, Josh. Look around you!"

Slowly, he took in his surroundings: the cold water, the empty beach, the darkness. A flicker of awareness crossed his face, raw and vulnerable.

"I'm sorry." His voice was quiet, uncertain. "I don't remember how I got here."

Beth didn't speak again. She simply reached for his arm, and together they turned toward the shore. Step by step, the sea seemed to release its hold. As they walked out of the water and onto the sand, neither of them noticed the faint humming that still lingered around them, a vibration that would remain long after they were gone.

SIX

Cal and Rory slid into their usual booth, the cracked red leather benches snagging at their jeans. The old laminate table wobbled slightly, just like it always had, its base never quite properly balanced. The diner smelled like sizzling bacon and over-boiled coffee, a scent that had seeped into the walls.

Morning filtered through the fogged-up windows, and the sky outside was pale and soft with a wet light that blurred, making the world look still half-asleep. Neither glanced at a menu; they hadn't needed one in over a decade. Jo's Diner hadn't changed, and neither had their orders.

Cal and Rory had gone to high school together, working crab boats the summer before senior year and again after graduation. When Cal left for college, Rory stayed behind, fixing outboards and running his dad's repair shop at the marina. They never talked about feelings or futures, but they shared an easy friendship. When Rory's mom had passed away, they spent the days fishing in silence. When Cal's marriage cracked, they finished a case of beer on the dock and watched the sun come up. Years of friendship had taught them each other's rhythms, and when one of them showed up, the other made room. No questions, no explanations: just the quiet loyalty of two people who'd weathered enough to know the value of their bond.

"Did you not sleep last night? You've been yawning since you walked in." Coffee steamed in Rory's mug as he raised it to his lips.

"Barely." Cal rubbed his eyes with the heel of his palms. "That mattress predates electricity, and the springs feel like they're made of crab traps."

"Ray never did like to replace anything. You're a grown man; go to Murphy's and buy one that wasn't made during the Great Depression. I think they've got memory foam now, and those fancy ones that come in a box and expand when you cut open the plastic wrap."

"I'll get to it eventually. Work's been crazy. A kinked neck builds character, anyway. Isn't that something we're supposed to brag about as we get older? Back problems?" Cal rolled his shoulders until something cracked loud enough to make Rory wince. "See? That's the sound of character."

"Sounds like your spine is filing a complaint to me."

Cal had been back for months now, but Rory still seemed broader than he remembered. Sun-browned and slightly wind-cut from years on the docks, he had a grin that came easily. Grey had begun to thread through his beard in places, and his brown eyes carried faint lines that stretched to his hairline, but the rest of him carried the same energy he'd had since high school.

"Still good to be back, even if my spine never forgives me," Cal said.

"It's Greyhook's divorcee welcome package. Damp boots, shit coffee, and a very old, very empty bed for the really lucky ones." Rory raised his mug in a mock toast.

"What about the sleepwalking tourists? It's all part of the local charm." Cal lifted his mug and then winced as he turned his neck too quickly. "Oof, maybe I will go by Murphy's and see what they've got."

"I heard about that on my way here," Rory said with a laugh. "Marlene at the general store opened early for them. They're lucky she lives upstairs and heard their truck running outside. Apparently, the girl came in shivering, looking for wool socks and hand warmers. Said she had to drag her boyfriend out of the water. It's Arctic out there right now, you'd think he'd have woken up the second he set a foot in it."

"Probably drunk and thought he was peeing in a pool." Cal set his mug down. "What's your week look like? Think we've got time to get some fishing in?"

"Fog rolls in, idiots roll out, so it's gonna be busy." Rory shook his head. "Every guy with a rental skiff becomes a saltwater cowboy until he hits the rocks. But by Wednesday, I'll need a fishing rod and at least five beers."

"It's a date then."

At a nearby counter, Mira Baird poured coffee into a white mug for Walter Shipp, one of Greyhook's older fishermen. Walter came from a long line of men who made their living on his daily catch.

Next to him sat Duncan Lee, twice widowed, face like driftwood and hands like oars. Tattooed letters spelled out his last name followed by an anchor in bold blue letters spread across his knuckles. Both men were weather-worn, with voices like rotted rope and permanent seats at the diner.

"Walked right into the water, I heard," Walter muttered over his shoulder as he stirred two sugars into his coffee.

Duncan raised a white eyebrow. "Sleepwalkin'?"

"Well, you know me. I just mind my own business…" Mira topped up Duncan's coffee. "But I heard his girlfriend had to go in after him and pull him from the water. Said he didn't hear her calling him, and he only snapped out of it when he was almost under the water. Sounds a bit suspicious if you ask me."

"That's how it happens," Duncan leaned back into the stiff cushion of his stool.

"Same as in '62," Walter grunted. "Out past Gull's Point. Lost a deckhand that way. He heard the song and never came back."

Not bothering to hide it, Duncan slipped a small silver flask from his coat and tipped a stream of honey-colored liquid into his mug, then took a long sip.

"It's the Water Song. Every now and again it rides the tide, and if you're not careful, it'll take you with it."

Walter tapped the table between them. "It's called the Sailors' Song, and don't tempt the sea by sayin' the name out loud. We don't need it haunting our waters."

"She'll take what she wants whether we talk about it or not." Duncan's eyes stayed fixed on his coffee as his voice dipped low. "Something's going on out there though. The water's getting restless, I can feel it."

Cal and Rory had known Duncan, Walter, and Mira for most of their lives. These weren't just locals: they were fixtures. Walter and Duncan had captained the same weather-beaten boats Cal and Rory spent summers crewing after high school.

Gruff by nature, Walter spoke little but listened well. There was a quiet wisdom to him, the kind you only earned from years spent reading the sea as well as people. He valued his privacy and preferred work over words, but when he did speak, it meant something.

Duncan on the other hand, was a solitary fisherman who drifted in and out of the docks like smoke, usually with a story and always with a flask. He wore mismatched socks, believed boats had moods, and talked to seagulls like they were old drinking buddies. But he was kind and always had a dry quip or inappropriate joke ready to lift the mood. For the residents of Greyhook, he was a legend. He gave away outlandish stories few believed and butterscotch candies from his coat pocket, pressed into your palm whether you wanted one or not.

Mira was her own special breed of stubborn. She had worked in the diner for as long as anyone could remember. Sharp-tongued and allergic to any appliance that didn't work the first time, she'd been giving the local kids grief since they were small. Still, she had a soft spot for Rory and an even softer one for Cal, who had spent most of his adolescence fixing things for her.

Behind them, Cal and Rory eavesdropped on the old-timers' conversation, exchanging a glance as their outrageous story took shape. Listening in had become something of a shared pastime, one they never admitted to but always smiled through.

As Mira cleared Walter's plate, her eyes flicked to the window where the morning light was filtered through thick, grey clouds. "You boys be careful out there on the water."

Walter leaned back with a low grunt, "You know, when I was twenty-three, maybe twenty-four, I heard the song. It was in the middle of the night, out past Deception Point. I was anchored up, dozin' in my cabin. Dead calm, stars out, nothin' but the sound of water lappin' at the hull." He ran a weathered hand along his scruffy jaw, like the memory had texture to it. "I woke up to the most beautiful sound, the most beautiful voices. Soft and sweet like nothin' I've heard before or since. I couldn't tell what direction it came from, it was just all around me in the pitch black, and it was calling to *me*."

He paused to take a sip of his coffee.

"I got up and walked right outside to the edge of the deck. I remember the water looked as black as oil that night, and as flat as glass. I leaned over, tryin' to see where the sound was coming from, when my old mutt Bruce bit my sleeve and started growlin'. The old boy wouldn't let go. He pulled me back away from the water and into my cabin. It stopped after that, and it was the last time I heard it." He looked up finally, blinking away the memory. "The next morning, there wasn't a ripple, and I haven't anchored out there since."

There was a beat of silence before Rory leaned toward Cal and smiled. "Is he sure it wasn't the whiskey?"

"Most men who work on the water long enough have some experience or other." Walter finished his coffee and went back to reading his paper.

Rory laughed now, voice a little too loud. "The Water Song, huh? Sounds like a sad indie band that only plays basements and laundromats."

"The Sailors' Song." Walter corrected, without looking up from his paper.

"You young guys joke," Duncan called over his shoulder, "but it never ends with just one. The sea isn't polite when she makes requests, and when she comes calling, it's to collect. She gets greedy when she's angry."

"Come on, Duncan! Are we blaming, sirens now? What's next, vampire whales and magical sea lions? That's all just old coastal lore."

Ducan turned to look back at Rory. "Magic doesn't announce itself. It hums just beneath what we dare to believe." He paused to take another swig of his spiked coffee. "You only need one voice out there: that's enough to turn a man's feet in the wrong direction."

Rory opened his mouth again, but Mira interrupted before he could speak. "It could have been you, Rory Haller. That boy could have drowned out there, and that's not something to make light of."

Rory stilled. Nobody wanted front-row seats to a Mira lecture, so he didn't say another word.

"I hope you boys never have to find out." Walter stood, picked up his hat, and nodded before stepping out into the brisk morning air.

Rory watched the door swing shut. "Well," he muttered, "that was uplifting."

Mira strode over to their booth; her order pad tucked beneath her arm. "You two kids want the usual?"

They both nodded, but Mira's eyes landed on Cal.

"You enjoying being back here with all this breezy morning small talk?" A pen appeared from inside her apron pocket, and she clicked it open.

"You mean the part about the sea haunting tourists?" Cal lifted an eyebrow. "Or the part where people don't seem to find it all that strange?"

Mira's face softened as he smiled an easy smile that could win over just about anyone. "Well, I'm glad that you're happy to be back."

"You know I couldn't stay away. You're stuck with me."

"God help us." Scribbling something on her notepad, she winked, and then lowered her voice, "I saw Isla the other morning. Did you know she's back?"

Rory's head tilted, suddenly interested. "Isla Maaarch?" He dragged her name like bait. "Well, hell's bells. She still got all that attitude, or did city life tame her a bit?"

"She came in on the bus the other morning. I saw her walking up to the house."

"Is she staying?" Rory looked directly at Cal.

Mira answered. "Don't know. It's none of my business, but word is she's inheriting that old house."

"Inheriting it? Did they find Coraline?"

"Nothing yet. According to Penny over at the county clerk's office, Coraline signed the deed over to Isla months ago. But I just mind my own business, so I don't know much. Have you seen her yet, Cal? You two used to be close."

"No. I haven't seen her."

Cal seemed lost in thought as Mira looked at him incredulously. Then she wandered back to the kitchen, muttering to herself as she clipped their orders onto the ticket wheel.

"So, how about that?" Rory leaned in, watching his friend curiously from across the table.

Cal sat motionless, his expression not quite readable as his gaze drifted to the window where the morning fog smeared the world behind it.

"If you ask me, she still looks like trouble." Mira returned with plates and cutlery before leaving again, her voice trailing behind her. "But as I said, it's none of my business."

"Did you ever hear from Isla again after she left town?" Rory unfolded his napkin onto his lap.

"Not since that summer," Cal replied. "Not after the night of the party."

"I wonder what's up with that whole house thing. She must be planning to stay if she's inheriting it."

"There are a lot of ghosts in that house." Cal shifted in his seat.

Mira's ears were sharper than her pour as she returned to top up their mugs, sloshing coffee onto the table. "The whole town's talking about what happened to Coraline and where she could've gone, so I'd imagine she wants some answers as well. But she didn't look so happy to be back, if you ask me. Though, nobody ever does. So, I just mind my own business."

A moment later she returned with a damp cloth, wiped up the spilled coffee and then disappeared into the kitchen again.

Rory snorted. "If I have to hear that woman say she minds her own business one more time…I swear, she hasn't minded her own business a day in her life."

The two men sat in silence for a beat before Cal spoke, more to himself than to Rory. "I haven't seen her since that night."

"Yeah, you mentioned that already, buddy." Rory sat back, eyeing Cal's expression with a low chuckle. "Sounds like maybe you've got some things to sort out there. You wanna talk about it over our Wednesday beers?"

Color rose in Cal's face, and Rory took the hint.

"Right," he said lightly, "So, Coraline goes missing without a trace, last seen heading home, then the ocean sleepwalks a tourist into the cove down below her house." He raised a brow. "Coincidence? Or are we starring in one of Duncan's bedtime stories?" The glint in his eyes made it clear he was only having fun.

Cal pulled his composure back into place, settling into a casual tone. "We should put it on the brochure. 'I Survived Greyhook, Washington.' It's a missed marketing opportunity."

Rory grinned. "I'd wear the T-shirt."

The smile slipped. "Coraline doesn't seem like the type to just up and vanish on purpose, does she? She's got roots here. Her family's been in Greyhook for generations. Hell, Marlene's probably already sold through most of Coraline's salves and tonics at her shop. Tourists eat that stuff up."

"I don't know." Cal stared into his coffee for a moment. "Coraline was complicated." He exhaled slowly. "Her husband bailed. Then Silas…" His jaw tightened at the name. "Her daughter walked off and left her and Isla behind. And when Isla left for school…" He gave a faint shrug. "Maybe she just got tired of being the one who stayed. That pattern has to wear on a person after a while."

Isla's name lingered in the space between them. Cal didn't try to cover it this time. The humor from earlier had drained away, leaving something quieter in its place. He wasn't sure what he wanted from Isla March, if anything at all, but her being back had stirred something in him, something he hadn't felt in a long time.

SEVEN

Isla stood in the Greyhook Market comparing two brands of vinegar. It shouldn't have mattered to her whether Coraline used cider vinegar or regular vinegar to clean the salt-streaked windows, but for some reason, today it did. The entire house was so stuffed with memory that it was leaking into her thinking, and staying busy was the easiest way to cope with the silence.

When she turned down the next aisle, she felt the subtle shift of attention. The butcher glanced up and held her gaze a moment too long. An older woman in a raincoat flicked her eyes away just a little too fast. This was nothing new: people had stared at her all her life — or at least they had since Silas drowned. The surviving twin from the strange family on the bluff, whose brother was swallowed up by the water. The girl who was raised by her grandmother, an odd woman who peddled tinctures and remedies before fading into silence and vanishing without a trace.

Isla held the vinegar bottle closer to her chest. She feigned indifference, but their stares sat with her uncomfortably.

As she made her way toward the checkout, something caught her off guard, wood smoke. Just a trace of it, caught in someone's jacket or drifting in from the parking lot.

Eighteen again, sneaking out to a party by the pier. The air thick with spilled beer and smoke curling from a bonfire at the edge of the sand. It rolled through the crowd, into her hair, into her clothes. Laughter, music thudding from a speaker balanced on driftwood. A plastic cup pressed into her hand. Nathan Hackley, the athletic golden boy who'd believed himself to be God's gift to women and who hadn't forgiven the careless way she'd brushed him off, had seized the moment. He'd raised his voice over the music, all teeth and beer-sour bravado.

"What are you doing here, Isla? Isn't your grandma gonna come drag you home? Or is she too busy mixing up her creepy potions?"

The words had landed loudly, cutting through the noise. Around them, the sounds of the party had faded, and people stared. Feeding off the silence, he grinned wider.

"You're a freak with a dead brother who lives with the town witch." Then he high fived one of his idiotic friends.

The crowd had shifted. Some kids had laughed, eager to belong. Others had stared into their cups, pretending they hadn't heard his cruel comments. Isla's skin had burned hotter than the bonfire as it popped and spat sparks into the dark. She could feel the sticky beer underfoot, the weight of every gaze pinning her in place.

She'd always floated between groups, friendly with everyone, close with no one. The rules at home made it hard. Coraline had kept her on a short leash, but Isla hadn't realized how far it had set her apart until moments like this, when no one quite knew how to step in. At barely eighteen, it was too much to carry, and she'd left, cheeks burning, the wind off the water cold against her stinging eyes.

Cal had found her halfway down the bluff, sitting alone with tears in her eyes. The two of them had always been good friends, but he was a year older, already graduated, and that summer he'd been working overtime to save money for college. Most nights he was off with Rory and the other guys his age, making plans to pack up their lives. But that night, when he'd heard what had happened, he'd left them and gone to find her.

"Don't waste your tears on that clown, Isla," Cal had said. *"He's a prick who peaked in high school. This is as good as it's ever going to get for him. The rest of us, we've still got better days ahead."* He'd paused, a faint smirk tugging at his mouth. *"I don't know what's wrong with that asshole, but whatever it is, I bet it's hard to pronounce."*

Isla had wiped her tears away and smiled.

"Seriously, the guy needs to start tree planting to replace all the oxygen he's wasting."

Laughter had broken free, shaky but real, and Cal had leaned toward her, delighted with the smile he'd put on her face.

"If his mother had had a little more self-esteem, he wouldn't even be here. And have you noticed that he only wears Velcro shoes? It makes so much sense now."

Isla had laughed even harder, and Cal had watched as though the only thing he'd wanted was to keep her laughing. She'd laughed until she cried. A laugh that had unclenched her chest and washed away everything Nathan had said.

Placing his hand on hers, Cal had looked her in the eyes.

"Isla, someone can only insult you if you value their opinion, and no one values his."

Then, he'd kissed her. He'd kissed her like it was the last good thing in the world, and she had kissed him back. It had felt right. It had felt perfect. And for a moment, it had felt like letting herself fall for him would mean she'd never leave Greyhook behind. By the next morning, she was packing to leave.

The memory of that night at the pier was still vivid, but what lingered after all these years wasn't Nathan or his cutting remarks. It was Cal. The way he'd found her on the ridge, coaxed a laugh from her until it washed away her sadness, and kissed her like she was something worth having. For once, she let herself sit in the warmth of that memory instead of pushing it away.

When she reached the checkout counter, she paid in cash and slipped the bag onto her arm, then pushed through the door onto the street.

The clouds outside had thickened from a soft cover into a slate ceiling that hung over the horizon, and the wind had picked up. It weaved sharply through the alleyways and trees, carrying the sound of the ocean.

Despite the weight of the sky, she felt lighter than she had all morning. A quiet, airy melody slipped from her lips as she headed up Greyhook's main street toward the bluff. Barely audible, she hummed the same tune that had haunted her dreams. Instinctively, she glanced toward the water. The tide moved steadily against the shore, and somewhere, maybe only in her mind, she thought she heard it humming back.

Wind pushed through the open kitchen window of the March House, carrying the smell of storm-washed sand and damp driftwood. Isla stood at the sink, watching the tide crawl back beneath the failing daylight. The sea had a way of settling her, of quieting the noise she carried inside. For the first time in a long time, she didn't feel the need to fill every moment with distractions. The stillness here didn't demand anything of her; it simply let her be. This was a kind of emotional rest she hadn't realized she'd needed.

Sleep also seemed to come easier here, though not from weariness. Each night she drifted under as the sound of the waves lulled her. The dreams still came, slow, salt-soaked, and shadowy. Sometimes she swam and sometimes she floated, suspended in a calm she didn't quite understand, but they no longer chased her into waking. They weren't nightmares anymore. They were something else entirely: something that stirred curiosity now more than unease.

A low vibration stirred against the surface beside her. She picked up her phone and glanced at the screen. Dr. Lydell, her naturopath, was calling. Isla realized she hadn't thought much about her health or her bloodwork since returning to Greyhook. For months she'd been chasing answers and getting nowhere. Now she wasn't sure whether bad news or no news would be worse.

"Hello, this is Isla."

"Hi Isla, this is Dr. Lydell. I'm calling because I received the results of your blood work and wanted to give you an update. There's nothing overly concerning, but it did reveal elevated sodium levels. They're not dangerously high, but they are unsual. The rest of your results are fine, which is baffling given your symptoms. There is a condition called hypernatremia, though I wouldn't necessarily say it applies to you. It's normally associated with not drinking enough fluids, excessive sweating, vomiting, diarrhea, or kidney problems. You reported none of those, which makes this, well, odd. Cut back on your sodium intake for now, and we'll talk more at your next appointment. Book something online when you're next available."

"I will. Thank you, Dr. Lydell."

Hypernatremia. Too much salt.

Salt on her tongue. Salt in her dreams.

Isla almost laughed.

~

Light spilled through the thin curtains of her old bedroom as morning arrived, soft and golden against the faded pink wallpaper. Everything was still just as she'd left it. The narrow bed sat near the window, its patchwork quilt the same one Coraline had made for her twelfth birthday. A bookshelf lined the side wall, where a row of sketchbooks leaned against a stack of worn out how-to-draw guides, their spines broken from use, pages torn out and then shoved back in. Near the door, the carpet still bore the faint blush of spilled nail polish, a small accident that had never quite disappeared no matter how many times she'd tried to scrub it out.

It was strange, waking up here alone. No footsteps in the hall, no kettle whistling on the stove, no low hum of her grandmother's radio. The house felt empty, lonely. Was this how Coraline felt?

Isla sat on the edge of the bed and let the silence stretch. This was the room where she'd learned to sneak out past curfew, to defy the rules that held her in these walls. Where she'd once lain awake imagining a life that wasn't fenced in by a woman she'd begun to resent. A life where her brother was still alive and where she didn't have to fill every moment of quiet with work or worry.

It was time to get out of here; to shake the ghosts loose and walk until the air outside replaced the memories inside. The floor creaked as she crossed the room, stretching her arms as she went. She threw on some clothes, grabbed her coat, and stepped into the morning where she let her feet find the old route into town.

The streets sloped down toward the harbor as if the whole town leaned toward the sea. The air was cool, the light still soft. The sidewalk was cracked and uneven, lifted in places by the roots of ancient trees. She had once spent whole afternoons here beneath them; sketchbook balanced on her knees while Coraline ran errands nearby.

The bench in front of The Little Bean stopped her. She could almost feel her grandmother's fingers braiding her hair before school, the scent of cinnamon and coffee spilling into the street as the town woke up.

Murphy's Hardware Store was near the end of Main Street, nestled between a defunct barbershop and a still-thriving bait and tackle. The bell over the mint-green door jingled as she stepped inside, prompting a tall man behind the counter to look up from a box of spray paint he was labelling with price stickers. *Noel* was stitched above the chest pocket of his shirt, and he stood with the easy slouch of someone who didn't expect many customers before noon.

"Good morning!" He straightened and blinked twice, smiling and brushing his chestnut hair from his eyes. "You need help finding anything?"

"Just an indoor lightbulb and some weather seal if you have it."

"Sure, aisle five on the back left wall for the weather seal and the bulbs are in the next aisle over. I can show you if you'd like."

"That's okay. I'll find it. Aisle five, you said?"

He nodded, still smiling.

"Thanks."

"Are you from around here? I don't think I've seen you before." Noel studied her with the focus of someone trying not to stare, but his eyes lingered with an interest he didn't quite hide.

"I used to be."

"That explains it. I'd remember you. I've only lived here a couple of years."

With a polite nod, she slipped into the aisles. Noel's attention didn't carry the same weight as the stares she usually drew in Greyhook. His wasn't laced with memory, it was interest.

Men tended to notice Isla. The lean grace of her petite build, the dark hair that fell in loose waves down her back, the hard-to-read green eyes rimmed darker at the edges. But today felt different. Noel wasn't the only one looking. An older man by the gardening gloves glanced up, then glanced again. Another near the paint thinner did the same. Not long enough to be deliberate, not quick enough to be innocent. Their eyes didn't slide away when she met them, they lingered.

A flicker of unease passed through her. Was there something on her face? She fought the impulse to reach up and touch her cheek and instead stepped toward a dusty mirror at the end of the aisle by the sunglasses.

Same dark hair. A little windblown maybe, but nothing unusual.

Still, the looks followed.

Heat crept up her neck and she felt suddenly aware of the space her body occupied, conscious of how she stood, how she moved.

As she picked up a pack of lightbulbs, she noticed Noel had drifted closer, rearranging a rack of extension cords that didn't need adjusting.

"So," he said, trying for casual, "are you in town long?"

"I'm not sure yet."

"Let me know if I can help with anything while you're here."

Isla arched a brow, smiling only enough to soften her dismissal. "Like lightbulbs?" She lifted the box.

"Or…you know. Heavier stuff. Or like, if you just want to hang out."

"I'll keep that in mind. Thank you."

She slipped past him toward the counter, and the man with the paint thinner fumbled. The can slipped from his grip and struck the floor with a hollow thud. He flushed, startled, but his eyes didn't stray. They stayed fixed on Isla, as if caught in an invisible current between them.

A chill crept over her. The quicker she paid, the quicker she could leave. Isla slid her card across the counter just as Noel reappeared, then gathered her bag and stepped outside.

"I'll be around if you need anything..." he called as the door clicked shut.

The fog had thickened, curling low along the street. She drew a long breath, the strange tension of the moment loosening. Out here, the air felt clearer. Out here, she could breathe again.

Instinct carried her hand to her coat pocket, and her fingers brushed the edge of a cigarette packet where she paused. It had been several days since she'd last smoked; not since she'd first arrived in town. She hadn't craved it, hadn't even thought of it until now. Even with the pack within reach, the urge wasn't there. So, with her jacket collar pulled higher around her neck, she continued on her way.

The trail home was crowded by seagrass. Decades of footsteps had worn a shallow groove into the dirt, but it was quiet this morning: no dog walkers, no tourists. Isla walked slowly, one hand brushing the stalks as the wind tugged at her sleeves.

As a child, this path was full of adventures. Exploring, running, playing. After Silas, Coraline had taught her to treat it with caution. At dusk, when the shadows deepened and Isla lingered too long, her grandmother would call her back with the same words.

"The sea pulls harder at people like us. You need to get home before dark."

At the time Isla had assumed she'd meant people tainted by loss, affected so tragically by the sea. She'd chalked it up to another superstition in Coraline's long litany of warnings.

When she reached the bend where the overlook jutted out like a crooked elbow above the cove, she could see the water below shifting in dark, restless swells. Off to her right, halfway down the bluff, the lighthouse clung to the rocks, weather-worn and silent, its beam nearly invisible in the daylight. That beacon of light had always been a steady comfort to her: proof that someone was always there, watching the coastline. On nights when storms rattled the March house, she and Silas would whisper beneath their quilts. They'd imagine its keeper, Ray, as a kind of guardian over the sea. When morning came, Isla, Silas, and Cal would meet to explore the rocks around its base for washed-up treasures, inventing stories about shipwrecks and pirates.

Even now, the sight of the tower soothed her, layered with memory and the faint ache of an emotional safety she couldn't quite reclaim. But as she stood there, that comfort shifted. Something beneath the surface of her calm began to stir. Her shoulder tightened, and instinctively she reached up, fingers finding the scar she'd carried for years: slightly raised, stubborn, and still pink at the edges. The rest of her body felt steady, but the scar pulsed with a deep ache, like something dormant had woken beneath her skin.

Isla held her shoulder for a moment, waiting for the ache to fade, watching a cargo ship in the open water beyond sway gently. The tide breathed against the rocks below, morning light catching in small, shivering flashes across the water. Everything looked ordinary, just as it should be. Yet with her grandmother gone, even the calmingly familiar seemed borrowed and fragile. And one question lingered that she believed only she could find the answer to.

Where was Coraline?

EIGHT

After slipping out through the back door of the pub, Cal walked the narrow alley behind the bait shop, then moved toward the marina along the road that led to the lighthouse. Heavier fog had rolled in just before midnight, wrapping Greyhook in its folds. He liked nights like this. The air felt softer when the mist settled and the sounds were dulled. There was something eerily calm about it: the way the weight of the world shrank to the reach of a streetlight's glow.

However, when the fog lingered too long, it could drive some of the locals a little mad. By the time he'd finished his third beer with Rory, the talk started turning. A few old-timers gathered around the corner booth in The Reef pub, mumbling about how the fishing was poor and the tides were strange. Before he finally made his exit, Duncan Lee had launched into a slurred monologue, swearing up and down that his compass had spun when he left the marina and passed the cove just after dawn.

"Ripples flanked my boat, but the sea was dead calm! It was like something beneath was keeping pace just out of sight."

Cal had nursed his drink, nodding at all the right moments, finally slipping out with an Irish goodbye for everyone but Rory. The walk home was quiet, but with each step, his lower back complained: a dull, familiar throb that was threatening to become a part of him. *Too many nights on that lumpy mattress,* he thought. This week, he decided, he'd finally replace it.

The path split near the dunes: one trail leading into the marina, the other toward the lighthouse and on to the cove. Ahead of him, the tide had drawn back, revealing a stretch of wet sand where a lone figure moved along the shoreline: barefoot, wrapped in a thick sweater, hair drifting loose in the wind. For a second, he thought the fog was playing tricks on his eyes.

"Hello?"

The shadowed figure turned, illuminated slightly by the hazy path light.

"Isla?" he squinted, trying to get a clearer look at who stood ahead. The fog seemed to be dancing at her feet.

They stared at each other across the dark sand, neither one moving as a quiet cadence shimmered at the edge of his hearing. Not wind, not tide — were his ears ringing? Cal shook his head once, dismissing it.

"Is that you?" Cautiously, he stepped closer, not wanting to startle a woman alone on a dark beach at night.

"Cal?" Recognition spread slowly into a smile, and her face lit up as she stepped toward him. Arms loosely folded against the wind, her posture was relaxed, open. "The fog looked so beautiful sitting on the water, I thought I'd take a walk. What are you doing out here?"

A small flutter pattered in his chest. He hadn't expected to see anyone, let alone her. "I was over at The Reef having a drink with Rory. My God, how long has it been?"

"Don't make me count." She smiled that same soft smile that always made his stomach flip. "The summer I graduated, I think." *She knew*. "Do you live nearby?"

"The lighthouse. I just moved back a few months ago."

"Of course you do." She laughed, a familiar warmth nudging at the memories of all the time they'd spent there as children. "Truthfully, now that I think about it, I suppose I can't really picture you anywhere else."

Cal had forgotten how beautiful she was; how good it felt just to see her face.

"Though I have to admit, I did at one point think maybe you'd end up halfway around the world living on that boat of yours."

That wasn't entirely true. What surprised her most was to hear that he'd left at all. Cal had always loved Greyhook more than anyone she knew, and she'd known he'd end up right back here.

"Well, turns out I have a soft spot for old fishermen and corroded structures. Plus, my boat's busted and the lighthouse is free."

"Are you fixing it up?"

"The lighthouse?" With a nod, he moved to stand beside her. "Along with everything else that breaks down around here."

"I meant the boat." She smiled.

"I'll get to it eventually."

"I was sorry to hear about your uncle. I know how close you and Ray were."

"Thank you. I'm sorry about Coraline."

"I'm not sure what there is to be sorry about yet." Isla's voice was calm, but her eyes drifted out toward the water. "No one seems to be able to tell me much. It's like she just up and left."

"Yeah, I hear they don't have much to go on yet. I'm sure she'll find her way back."

"Still the eternal optimist, I see. Some things never change."

"You have." Cal glanced sideways at her. "Changed, I mean. You look more grown up. Older."

"Wow. A poet. Charming, truly."

Oh Lord, he thought, and winced.

"I meant more mature! Like wiser, in a good way."

Shit, shit, shit.

"Mm-hmm." She narrowed her eyes playfully. "Try digging upward, Cal."

"I'm sorry, I panicked."

Isla laughed and a moment passed between them, comfortable, nostalgic.

"I saw your name posted on the board at Murphy's for repairs. Inspections and consulting, too?" Isla smiled. "You're practically the mayor now."

"Don't even joke," Cal groaned. "Mayor of Greyhook? Could you imagine? Mira would harass me every day while telling me she's just minding her own business. I've got enough squeaky floorboards and haunted plumbing jobs to last me a lifetime as it is."

"Haunted plumbing? Exciting!"

"Is it? Pipes that 'whisper.' Toilets that 'sigh.' Last week I had to exorcise a dishwasher."

"A priest as well! Impressive. Putting your degree to good use, then."

"It would seem I am the last line of defense between Greyhook and total supernatural collapse."

They stood together, smiling for a few quiet beats before Cal broke the silence.

"So, you're really back. For good?"

"No. Not permanently. Just here to tie up loose ends and figure out what happened."

"Do you know how long you'll stay?"

"I haven't decided yet. What about you? Planning to grow old here with Rory? I did hear a rumor that you're newly single." The humor in her voice was gentle, not teasing, and the soft tug at one corner of her mouth carried something quieter. An apology she didn't quite say.

"Word really gets around hey?" He let out a gentle laugh and a sigh. "It's true. Divorced. Though I wouldn't say newly. It just took some time to sort everything out before I could move back. And for the record, Rory is an excellent conversationalist, if your idea of conversation is nodding, grunting, and twenty-minute monologues about fishing bait."

Isla had forgotten how funny he could be; how easy it was to be near him. Their eyes met momentarily and something passed between them. Familiarity, maybe. Or the ache of something left unsaid for too long.

"Divorced," she breathed. "I'm sorry."

"It's okay. It sounds horrible, but honestly, I'm not really that broken up about it anymore. I think once you accept that you aren't meant to be, it makes it easier. It was just never going to work. She wanted adventure and noise."

"I can understand that. And you…you wanted this." Her chin lifted toward the water, as if to underline the last word.

"I did. I do. I wanted quiet, the ocean, something simple. Something real." Cal's eyes followed hers toward the water.

They stood quietly before Isla turned to study him. Cal had always looked like he belonged near the sea. Tall with broad shoulders, he was strong in that way that came from hauling gear and hoisting sails, not hours spent in the gym. Dark hair curled slightly at the ends, the salt air forever tugging it loose around his face. A faint scar arched through his right eyebrow, a souvenir from some childhood dare gone sideways. But it was his eyes that caught her attention now: a hazelish green, ringed with thick, dark lashes. Still deep, still searching, and somehow, still caught on her.

"You haven't changed."

"I haven't?" He glanced over, amusement in the curve of his mouth.

"Nope."

Cal began to speak when she interrupted him.

"I know, I know. I have." She laughed as she brushed a strand of hair behind her ear. "Wiser."

Cal rolled his eyes. "I'm never going to live that down, am I? I promise I've learned my lesson."

The corner of her mouth slowly softened. "Do you ever think about him?"

He didn't have to ask, he knew she was talking about Silas. The lines at the corners of his eyes tightened. "All the time."

"Being here again…I feel like I should see him. In the fog, at the edge of the rocks. Just a glimpse of him, somewhere. It feels like he's still here."

Cal didn't speak, but she didn't need him to.

"I should get back," she said at last.

"It was really good to see you, Isla."

Her smile was small yet genuine before she turned and walked away. The mist gathered around her, blurring her outline until the sea fog swallowed her whole. First a figure, then a shadow, then nothing at all.

Once again, Cal was surrounded by stillness. He had told himself the past was settled, buried beneath the years, but standing here now with the dull roar of his own heartbeat in his ears, he wasn't so sure. Just like that, he was back on the bluff kissing her under a star filled sky. Back in the empty space she'd left behind when she'd disappeared without a word. Without a goodbye.

Isla made her way upstairs, one hand on the banister, the other rubbing at her tired eyes. It was cooler upstairs, the kind of chill that came from drafty windows in an old house.

Coraline's bedroom door stood slightly ajar, just an inch, as though it had been waiting for her to return and to notice. Isla pushed it open, taking in the room again. Everything was still in order, quiet and undisturbed. Bed still made, curtains still drawn halfway. Not a single thing out of place. She wasn't sure what she was looking for. Maybe nothing. Maybe something.

She crossed to the vanity that faced the window. A wooden brush rested on a silver tray beneath the mirror, a few grey hairs remaining in its bristles. The handle was smooth, worn by years of use. Hairline scratches caught the light along the lip of the tarnished tray where the brush lay across a lace doily, its edges curled and fraying.

Isla reached for the top drawer and gave the knob a gentle tug. Locked. Frowning, she looked over the surface of the vanity. Nothing out of the ordinary: just Coraline's hand mirror and the old brush. She lifted the tray slightly to peek underneath when she heard a faint, hollow clink. She paused, then lifted the brush and then the doily.

A small key lay beneath the aged lace fabric, tucked just out of sight. Hidden so neatly it might never have been found if the tray wasn't disturbed.

The key slid into the drawer's lock and turned easily. With a soft click, it slid open. Inside were six small leather-bound journals, some cinched with old elastics, their moisture-warped pages bulging against the strain. Others lay loose, corners curled from wear. Isla stared. She'd never seen them before.

Opening the topmost journal, she stroked her thumb over the first page. Coraline's handwriting was unmistakable, neat and delicate. The first entry dated two weeks after Silas died.

I don't understand what happened. It wasn't supposed to take him. It shouldn't have. He was far too young, and I wasn't ready.

Isla swallowed, but her throat felt dry. Flipping open a second book, she kept her eyes moving. Another entry dated years later.

The salt is stronger in me lately. My throat stays dry no matter what I drink. I can feel it pulling, my body aging. I believe that Salt-Blood Syndrome has begun.

Salt-Blood Syndrome? The weight of the words hovered there, and she closed the journal slowly. The lamp on the vanity flickered once, then held steady, causing her to look up. No draft. Nothing moved. Just stillness.

She lifted another journal from the drawer, this one salt-cracked and palm-sized. It contained dates, sketches, and fragmented thoughts. No full sentences, just patterns and instincts scrawled across pages. A tide table, sketches of the coastline, notes in shorthand. Isla paused on the third page.

I can't protect her from the pull...I can only guide her through it if it comes for her. When it comes for her. Will that be enough?

Again, she read the line. Then a third time and her fingers tightened on the edge of the paper. *The pull? Guide her through it?* The words felt dramatic, but she had no idea what they meant. There was no context, no explanation, but something in the back of her mind couldn't let go of the phrasing. What was Coraline talking about? Who was '*her*'?

Isla slid the notebook into her cardigan pocket and stacked the rest on top of the vanity. Then she moved on to the lowest drawer where a gentle tingling met her fingertips as she knelt beside it and touched the knob.

Unlocked. She pulled it open.

Inside, wrapped in worn velvet, lay a conche shell. Larger than her palm, it was pink-lipped and beautiful. Its outer ridges were worn to a shade as pale as bone, but it had a striking, shimmering blue vein that ran along its curve like captured lightning. Inside, the hollow gleamed a deep violet, dark as a storm.

Lifting it, she instinctively held it to her ear. When it touched her skin, a faint sound began. Not anything with notes or words, but something that bloomed in her chest, thick with a memory she couldn't name. Her grip tightened. The sound of rolling waves in the rhythm of the sea, then a voice. Not hers or Coraline's. A child, maybe. A boy. Faint and far away. Not placeable.

Then, suddenly, there was nothing at all. The sound evaporated, and the shell slipped from her grip, landing with a soft thud on the velvet wrap. When she finally caught her breath, it was quick and shallow.

"What the hell was that?"

Back in her own room, Isla sat cross-legged on her bed with the stack of journals on the table beside her, curtains open so she could see the ocean. The bedside lamp cast a soft amber glow across the room, just enough to hold back the dark and to shield her from the restlessness that was squeezing at her shoulders.

The conch was tucked inside the bottom dresser drawer at the far end of her room, shut tight, with a piece of driftwood from her bookshelf jammed against it. Somehow, that made her feel better, though she wasn't sure why.

The journals sat unopened. Not yet. She wasn't ready for what else they held; what else they wanted her to find.

Out her window and beyond the bluff, she could hear the sea licking the cove in slow, gentle swells, the wind moving in unison with the waves. Isla told herself she'd rest her eyes, but only for a moment. Curled up in a room that wasn't really hers anymore, sleep came quickly. Somewhere, deep beneath the quiet drift of her dreams, her heart began to echo the conch's song.

Warm gray light bled through the curtains as the sun pushed past the fog and clouds outside. Isla's bedroom felt colder than it should. The furnace was on, turned up as high as was reasonable and the morning was calm, yet a chill had crept in through her open window while she slept.

The wedge of driftwood had somehow shifted, slipping away from the dresser drawer in the night. Her dreams had been strange and ungraspable. Blurry and full of lilting melodies that slipped through her fingers the moment she opened her eyes.

Needing air, caffeine, and something warm in her hands, she threw on a jacket and walked into town for the biggest coffee she could find.

The door of the Little Bean swung open, releasing a curl of dark-roasted air as Isla stepped onto the sidewalk, an extra-large coffee warming her hands.

"I didn't expect to see you out and about this morning." Cal stood a few yards off, one hand in his jacket pocket, the other gripping a ceramic mug of coffee. His jeans were streaked with sawdust, his flannel collar half-popped against the spring breeze.

"Good morning."

His eyes landed on the oversized drink in her hand. "Good morning indeed. What's that? Liquid ambition?"

"I needed to bring in the big guns this morning."

"Clearly. That looks like a coping mechanism with a lid."

"What about you? What's with the mug?"

"Fair play." Cal lifted his mug. "I left the house with it. Forgot I had it in my hand, so I just rolled with it."

Together they stepped down off the curb, falling into stride beside one another as they walked.

"What are you up to today?" Isla took a deep sip from her blue and white to-go cup, its warming glow flowing into her chest.

"Working on the lighthouse. Storm season knocked out one of the backup generators. I'm slowly replacing…well, everything."

Cal taking over Ray's station wasn't surprising to Isla. He'd spent a lot of time there as a child climbing the stairs and watching the waves. They all did. All three of them.

"You want to come see it?"

Caught off guard by the invitation, she hesitated. Torn between the mysterious journals waiting at home and the ease of spending an hour with Cal, she didn't hesitate for long.

"Sure. Maybe I can pick up some fix-it tips. Judging by what I've seen so far, I may have to personally stop my grandmother's house from crumbling into the ocean."

“That house has been trying to fall into the ocean for years. I can help, if there’s something you need?”

“I think I can handle it. Mostly little things so far. I’m mostly just trying to stay busy, but I’ll let you know. Thank you.”

They curved behind the back of Main Street and slipped between the town’s familiar buildings. Brick turned to gravel, and the scent of salt and kelp grew stronger in the air. As the marina faded behind them, the trail thinned to a strip of dirt, hemmed in by seagrass and the rocky shoreline.

“Still nothing new about your grandmother?”

“No.” Isla kept her eyes on the trail ahead. “From what I can tell, there isn’t much to go on. In fact, there’s nothing. It’s like she just up and walked away.”

Cal nodded slowly. “That’s the hard part. If someone wants to disappear, they can. No forced entry. No note. Nothing out of the ordinary. Nobody notices anything if nothing looks wrong.”

“I don’t even know where to start.” She rubbed a hand over her forehead.

“Maybe you don’t. You wait. You ask around. You hope somebody remembers something small. You let the police do their jobs.”

“Well, Greyhook doesn’t miss much so if no one knows anything by now…”

“Sorry,” he said gently. “I didn’t mean to overstep. You know how this town is. People talk. Everyone’s worried about Coraline.”

“No, it’s all right. I didn’t mean it like that.” She exhaled. “I just feel so helpless. And guilty.”

“Guilty? Why?”

“Because I didn’t know. I didn’t know she was missing, or that she was unhappy. Or lonely. Or whatever she was.” Her voice thinned. “I didn’t know anything.”

“Isla, this isn’t your fault. You were off living your life. Whatever was going on with Coraline isn’t your responsibility.” He stopped walking for a step, then continued. “She’ll turn up.”

They walked the rest of the way in silence, the gravel crunching beneath their boots. Ahead, the lighthouse stood between the broken edge of the coast and the bluff, whitewashed by years of wind and spray but still rising against the sky.

Cal climbed the stairs first, tugging the heavy metal door open. At the threshold, he stepped aside for Isla to enter. The familiar smells of wood, oil, and metal greeted her, and it was warmer inside than she’d expected.

“It feels smaller than it used to.” She looked around, noting the signs of renovations that Cal had taken on.

“I think we just grew up,” he chuckled, “but it’s true, everything feels smaller. I’ve already cracked my head on two doorframes since I moved in. And with all these tools lying around, it’s pretty much an obstacle course. Whoever designed this place didn’t know or like people over six feet tall.”

“It’s mostly like I remember it.” Isla turned in a circle. Stacks of drywall, coiled rope, and an array of rusted toolboxes surrounded her.

Cal moved past her and picked up a pair of pliers, rolling them in his hand as though the weight might steady the nervousness in his fingers. Having Isla here lit up an electric feeling that he couldn’t shake. It was ridiculous, really. He was a grown man, trusted to ride out storms and keep the beacon steady through the worst of nights. Now, he felt like he was nineteen again, fumbling for words he couldn’t quite find and feeling slightly unmoored.

Isla stepped to the curve of the spiral stairs, where a wooden beam rose through the center, partially hidden at its base. A messy scrawl of names covered the back side of the beam, carved into the wood, just out of sight. Isla ran her hand over them tenderly.

Silas. Isla. Cal.

Transfixed, she stared quietly.

"He carved it the week before..." Cal's voice trailed off.

"I remember. He was so proud, but then so afraid he would get in trouble."

"He kept trying to rub it off with his sleeve afterward, like he could just wipe it away from the wood." Cal's smile filled with memory.

"He never wanted anyone to be disappointed in him."

They stood in silence next to the stairwell, a place that still held space for all three of them. The quiet between Cal and Isla held its own frequency, woven from memory, loss, and the gentle warmth of a small piece of Silas that remained.

~

Together, they climbed the spiral staircase. The metal groaned at their steps, echoing against the walls of the old watchtower. At the top, the entire coastline stretched out in the distance below. Quiet and smaller from up here were Greyhook's weather-beaten rooftops, the straight line of Main Street, the jagged black rocks flanking the mouth of the cove. Out beyond, the sea was shifting silver and blue under a sky that was trying to remain open to the afternoon sun.

Cal watched as Isla stepped forward toward the railing. Her face was still as striking as ever, but time had refined it some. The softness of youth had given way to defined features, sharpened not just by age but by certainty. She carried herself differently now. There was composure in the way she stood, in the ease of her expression. She wasn't a girl anymore. She was a woman, and she knew it.

"It still gets to me." He leaned on the rail beside her.

"What does?"

"This view. The town looks so peaceful."

"That's the lie of elevation." Isla angled her head, looking at him.

Cal's gaze traced the curve of her expression. When they were kids, she would leap across tidepools like she didn't believe in falling. Cal and Silas always followed reluctantly, one step behind. Isla had saltwater in her blood, wind in her hair, and Coraline's rules nipping at her heels. She'd been wild, but not reckless. Alive in a way most people never dared to be. Then Silas drowned, and everything had changed. Coraline clamped down on her like a storm shutter. No more swimming. No more exploring. No more playing by the water after dusk. Isla, bright, stubborn, beautiful Isla, had curled in on herself like a sea fern. Still fierce, still stunning, but quiet. Sharper-edged and less trusting.

"I remember Silas used to hum when we climbed up here."

"He was always humming." Isla smiled at the memory.

"So were you."

"I was?" A strand of hair had blown across her face, and she brushed it away. "I don't remember that."

"You did. It was kind of comforting. Also, mildly annoying. Your voice wasn't as good as his." He chuckled and took a step back, bracing for the gentle swat to the arm she delivered, her smirk locked firmly in place. And he didn't mind, not even a little.

"Remember that summer you got stung by a jellyfish and refused to go home because you didn't want Coraline to know we'd snuck out? What were we, fourteen? Fifteen?"

"I limped around for a full day."

"You did, like a pirate with scurvy! You had a welt the size of a pancake." Cal's face pulled into a pained grimace. "That had to have hurt."

“It was worth it! Night swims in the summer were the best.” She grinned. “Remember when we tried to rappel down from that lower balcony,” she pointed below where they stood, “using your dad’s extension cords?”

Cal groaned. “You insisted we use dish gloves for grip.”

“They had texture.”

“They were cheap rubber.”

“I was optimistic.”

“They shredded halfway down, and you got rope burn.” He dragged a hand down his face. “You screamed like you had been pushed off the ledge.”

“I did not.”

“You absolutely did.”

“I was ten,” Isla reminded him, folding her arms. “I guess I should be grateful your knots held. Would’ve been a disaster if the cord came undone and I plummeted to my doom. What were we thinking?”

“You would have stuck the landing.” Cal said easily.

“Wasn’t that one your idea?”

He smiled without shame. “It was always *your* idea.”

“You always participated.”

“Someone had to supervise, didn’t they?”

She didn’t answer that. Instead, she smiled and glanced toward the drop, fog dispersing beyond the waves. “We really thought if we climbed high enough, we’d see past it.”

“Some days I’m still convinced I can.” His face softened as he looked at her.

“What?” Isla’s expression was wary.

“Do you ever think about that night?”

“What night?” *She knew.*

Without pushing, Cal gave a half-shrug.

Isla looked back at him, giving nothing away. "I think about a lot of things."

There it was. The ache that had never healed right. The kiss that had meant nothing and absolutely everything. A moment balanced delicately between grief and desire. And when it shattered, so had they. Isla had left town, and they'd never spoken again. Not until now.

"I do think about that night." She said finally. "I'm sorry. I shouldn't have ghosted you."

"Don't be." Cal placed a hand on her arm. "We were kids. You went on with your life and went after your dreams. I know it was hard for you to be here, in this town."

They made eye contact, and with his touch, she felt that same gravity again. "Thank you."

"For what?"

"For understanding that."

The gulls wheeled lazily in the distance, and her words lingered.

"Do you want to have dinner?" Trying for casual, Isla adjusted the collar of her sweater and finished the last of her quickly cooling coffee.

"Now?"

"It's noon, Cal," Isla smirked. "Later. An early dinner? After we make this place less of a death trap."

"Early dinner? What are we, seventy?"

"Speak for yourself," she shot back. "I like eating early. It means more time for wine!"

"All right. What I heard was, if I buy you dinner, you'll help me clean this place up a bit so it's not such a disaster." One dark curl fell over his eye. "How about burgers?"

“Perfect,” Isla headed toward the stairs. “But don’t forget the onion rings.”

∽

They spent the afternoon clearing clutter from the keeper’s quarters and shifting old tools and boxes into storage until Cal had a good amount of clean, livable space. Work came easy, and so did the laughter.

As the sun thinned into soft afternoon light, Isla walked the winding bluff path back to the March house, her long hair moving gently with the breeze. The air felt calm, and so did she.

Dinner. She couldn’t remember the last time she’d had dinner with someone without it carrying some weight of expectation. But this felt simple, comfortable, like stumbling across something she hadn’t known she’d lost. For the first time in a long time, she was excited and alive in a way she hadn’t realized she’d needed to be.

Kicking a pebble down the walk, she played with a loose tendril of hair that fell across her shoulder. A playful fog came and went, finally disappearing into the trees like unraveling gauze, revealing the promise of a beautiful evening.

When she reached the house, she kicked her boots off at the door and sauntered up to her bedroom, where the journals still waited on her bedside table just as she’d left them.

Not now; later. The day had been too lovely, too easy, and she wasn’t ready to sink into something dark and tangled when she finally felt light.

As she readied herself, Isla reached for one of her favorites: a loose-knit, sea-foam sweater. It felt heavenly the moment it brushed her skin, and it brought out the color of her eyes. Comfortable but flattering, the weave fell easily over her slim frame. She put on a fresh coat of deodorant, a touch of nude lipstick, and gathered her loose waves into a ponytail. As she headed toward the stairs, she caught her reflection in the hallway mirror. There was color in her cheeks today. She looked more like herself than she had in months.

At the end of the hall, she paused as she passed Coraline's door. The sight of it half-open tugged at her, so she closed it firmly, refusing to let her emotions unravel around the woman who had vanished. *Not now. Not tonight.* Still, the image sat with her: her grandmother sitting on the bed beneath a warm wool blanket, a book in her hand. Tea on the nightstand as she'd turn the pages without a sound.

Isla moved down the stairs and stepped outside. The clean bite of the ocean filled the evening air, but the temperature was mild and the breeze gentle. With her jacket hanging around her shoulders, she stepped off the porch to follow the trail. Across the bay, the lighthouse rose in silhouette, fixed against the slow-burning light of dusk, its beacon just visible in the darkening sky.

There was something in the air tonight. Not quite hope, but something close enough to it.

Cal was setting a grease-stained paper bag with burgers and onion rings from the marina shack onto the small table outside when Isla arrived. In his other hand, he held a bottle of red wine, a 2015 Bordeaux. The label was worn, but she recognized the vineyard. The table was already set with two white fold-out chairs that sat across from each other on the main landing outside the keeper's quarters. A candle flickered inside the hollow of an old lantern, and two mismatched plates waited patiently beside the food.

As she stepped out onto the veranda, she smiled. "Rustic charm. I love it."

"I aim to please. Also…" Cal gestured to the makeshift lantern. "I haven't exactly fixed the outdoor lighting yet, so this might be our only light once the sun's gone."

He hadn't meant for it to feel romantic, but standing here now with the soft breeze off the water and the candle flickering between them, he couldn't deny that some part of him hoped it would. The feelings he thought he'd tucked away were returning quicker than he'd anticipated.

Isla picked up the wine bottle and raised an eyebrow. "I'm no sommelier, but as a seasoned bartender, I've seen bottles like this go for over two hundred bucks."

"Then it's perfect for tonight. Though I can't take credit. It was part of the very small collection Ray left me. I figured he'd want us to drink it before it turned to vinegar."

"A tribute to your uncle's taste and your fear of wasting expensive alcohol."

"It's a special occasion."

"Is it?"

"Of course. I'm drinking wine with *you*."

Isla's eyes softened, the teasing edge giving way to something gentler. "Just like old times."

He eased the cork out with a soft pop, giving it a quick sniff like he knew what he was doing.

"You're not fooling anyone."

"Damn." Cal laughed.

The bottle tilted, and he poured smoothly into her glass, the deep red catching what was left of the sunlight. He handed it over before filling his own.

"To Ray," she said.

They raised their glasses.

"To Ray."

They clinked and took a sip. The warmth settled in, and they smiled at each other over the rims.

"It sure beats the cheap beer we used to steal from your dad." Isla swirled the wine in her glass.

"This is a little bit better."

The food was simple. The wine was lovely. They talked about everything and nothing: old classmates, Greyhook gossip, whether crabbing season had gotten shorter or if people had just gotten lazier. Isla asked about Lina, gently, without prying.

"She would never have been happy here. I should've known that. I tried, but we just…hit an impasse. We couldn't move forward together without one of us being unhappy."

Cal ran his finger along the stem of his glass as he watched the candlelight dance across it. A gust of wind fluttered the paper napkins, the tiny flame between them bowing briefly, then holding steady. Below, the sea moved steadily, endless and hypnotic against the rocks.

"I think we both went into it with the idea that we could bend in opposite directions and still meet in the middle. This place was always home for me, but for her it was never in the cards. It would only have been somewhere she'd want to escape."

Isla watched him from across the table, his face half-lit by the glow. She couldn't help but feel the twist of irony in his words. The echo of her own feelings. *A place she'd want to escape.* A place that felt too small, too soaked in grief. But now, she wasn't sure she felt the same way. Something had changed. Or maybe she had.

"Well, first marriages don't really count do they? Statistically, they're just practice rounds, right?" The corners of her mouth lifted.

Cal raised the back of his hand to his lips to avoid spitting out his wine as an unexpected laugh escaped. "Wow, that's grim."

"It's optimistic. Second ones get all the benefit of hindsight. By the third, you're a marriage Jedi."

"Let's hope the next one doesn't require lightsabers."

"So, you'd do it again?"

"I think I would, yeah."

"Eternal sunshine of the divorced mind."

"What about you?" Cal asked, refilling her glass. "Ever come close? Do you have anyone special?"

Isla tilted her head, considering. "Well, the only relationship I've had that lasted longer than six months was with my dentist."

"Romantic."

"He told me I was his favorite anxious clencher. I thought that was sweet."

"That sounds like it was serious."

"I was committed. I wore a night guard and everything."

"That's more commitment than some marriages get."

Tipping her glass toward him, she smirked. "Well, when I give my jaw to someone, I go all in."

"That's a hell of a line, Isla."

"You can use it."

"So, you're not seeing anyone right now?"

"No." She smiled. "There were a few maybes along the way but no one that felt right. And no one right now."

He studied her. "What do you do for yourself these days? Are you still painting?"

"I stopped for a while," she swirled her wine. "The colors kind of dried up for me, so to speak."

"What brought them back?"

"I don't know if they are fully back. I'm still figuring that out, but I have been painting some." She didn't say that most of what she'd painted this past year was dark and murky and emerged while she was still half-asleep. That some were made from nightmares.

Cal listened closely as she spoke: about painting, about the hopeful return of inspiration. Isla had that same draw she'd always had, softening him at his edges in a way that made him want to lean closer. He hadn't realized how long he'd been watching her until the silence stretched, and he blinked, clearing his throat and shifting in his chair, like the movement might disguise the lapse. She didn't seem to notice. Or if she did, she let it pass.

"Do you remember the time you threw your dress shoes off the dock?" Isla asked.

"Wow. I forgot about that."

"You said you couldn't stand the way the toes felt. '*Too round and smug,*' I think was your exact phrase."

"They were smug. They made a noise when I walked, like tiny judges."

"You didn't even know what that word meant."

"I thought I did."

"Then, ten seconds later, you panicked because you knew your mom was going to kill you."

"I hadn't thought it through. I thought they'd sink and I'd be off the hook somehow. *Lost at sea!*"

"Thankfully they floated. Silas found that oar and fished them out in a loafer-rescue mission."

"He just handed them back to me like it was no big deal."

"He was always like that. Just kind. I miss him. He's been gone longer than I had him, so why does it feel so fresh – like he's just out of reach?"

"I don't think that kind of missing goes anywhere. It just gets quieter."

The last edge of light clung to the horizon, casting a quiet reflection between them. The kind of understanding only shared by those who've weathered the same loss. They stayed like that for hours, trading laughter, memories, and companionable silences until the candle burned low and the night settled around them.

"Had I known lighthouse dinners on my patio came with great wine and even better company, I would've made this a habit a long time ago."

Isla smiled over the rim of her glass. "Had I known what I was missing, I might've come back to claim a seat here a little sooner."

The wine gave her extra courage, and she felt the heat rising in her cheeks. To mask what her face was giving away, she rose from the table and wandered toward the railing, allowing the cool salt air to meet her face. The evening had been perfect, the weather sublime, the company outstanding.

It didn't take long for Cal to get up, his shoulder brushing lightly against hers as he joined her. Behind them, their plates sat empty, a second bottle of wine opened. The waxing moon had begun its climb overhead, breaking through the speckled clouds to illuminate their view of the ocean in a dancing column of soft light.

"Do you see that?" Isla pointed. "There. What was that?"

Just past the break line, something had rippled in the water moving slowly under the surface.

"A harbor porpoise?" Cal squinted. "I don't see it."

"It looked too big to be a harbor porpoise."

"A whale? Was there a spout?"

Isla's gaze stayed fixed on the cove as she shook her head. Whatever it was had vanished as quickly as it had appeared. The surface stilled, the tide rolled steady. Yet the water felt aware, as if it hadn't swallowed what stirred, but concealed it. A chill slid over her. She couldn't shake the sense that she was being watched: not from above the surface, but from below it.

"I guess I should probably head home before the clouds roll in and the fog swallows the path."

"I'll walk you," Cal offered, disappointed that the night was ending.

"I'd like that. Thanks."

Isla felt relief at his offer. The dark had unsettled her more than she cared to admit. The chill under her skin remained, and she wasn't eager to say goodnight, either.

Together, they tidied the remains of the evening, tossing burger wrappers and napkins into a garbage bag and blowing out what was left of the candle stub flickering in the lantern. Cal shook out her jacket and held it open, waiting as she slipped her arms in. Then he offered her the crook of his arm, a quiet, old-fashioned gesture that made her smile despite herself. She slipped her arm through, letting it settle there. Side by side, they set off down the gravel path, the hush of evening wrapping gently around them.

Dew settled into the grass, and the faint chorus of crickets serenaded their steps as they walked. A soft veil began to drift in from the water, curling across the ground, turning the road ahead into something hazy and dreamlike. Before they knew it, the March House rose ahead of them through the fog.

"I used to beat you to this gate nearly every time we raced." The iron creaked as Isla pushed it open.

"That's because you always cheated."

"I just started early." Smiling, she leaned a hip against the fence and turned to face him. "Thank you for walking me home."

"It was my pleasure." Cal reached out and took her hand. "I had a really good time."

There they stood, soft mist curling at their feet, the night air holding its breath. Isla felt the warmth of his palm, the steady weight of his eyes, and something in her chest urging her forward. The space between them sparked with possibility, yet she hesitated just long enough to hear all the reasons not to flash through her mind. She leaned in and brushed a gentle kiss against his cheek, so close to his lips that she almost remained there before finally pulling away.

"Goodnight, Cal."

"Goodnight, Isla." Amusement flickered across his face. He could see the debate in her eyes. That kiss had strayed far nearer to danger than to friendship, but he watched her disappear into the shadows of the porch until the lamp in the front room blinked on.

He started back toward the lighthouse along the dark, empty road with his hands in his pockets and a smile on his face. The night played through his mind. The joy of hearing her laugh, the way she would touch her hand to her mouth when her giggle escaped unexpectedly. How she let her glass linger by her mouth after she took a sip. And the way she smiled at him with those bright green eyes.

Thirty yards was all it took before the need to turn back slammed into him. Already, he wanted to see her again. Needed to see her again. Tonight had been effortless and familiar in that beautiful way that felt safe. Yes, she was beautiful: she always had been, but it was more than that. The evening had felt easy. Real. Like something between them was beginning to blossom again.

The faint scent of sweet jasmine danced across the breeze, and with it, an airy note slipped through the fog. It was so soft he almost missed it. He slowed, glancing back toward the house where something soft and distant seemed to drift out through an open window.

Cal listened. The sound wasn't coming from the house. It didn't seem to come from any one place. It moved through the air, faint and melodic, twisting around him along the path. It was wordless and disarming, and he stood frozen until the mist pulled it back into the silence. Just the waves now, and the faint rustle of the grass swaying in the dark.

With a quick shake of his head, he walked on.

Isla slipped inside just after eleven, carrying the lingering thrill of Cal's touch. Kicking off her boots, she moved through the house and climbed the stairs. For once, she didn't pause at Coraline's door; just kept walking toward her own room, then slipped out of her clothes and under the covers. With her mind content, her eyes drifted closed, and sleep took her swiftly.

In her dream, Isla stood waist-deep in the ocean. The sky above was dark but not starless, and warm water curled around her in tender waves. Overhead, the moon shone full and bright, and when she turned, someone was there beside her. A boy. No, a young man. Familiar, though not quite known to her. His hair was dark, slick and curling with seawater, his eyes as pale as sea glass.

As she stared, a voice rose through the silence. Not from his mouth, but from the water around him: a melody without words, built of wispy, open vowels that swelled with the tide. The sound flowed into her lungs and into her soul. In that instant, the song spoke to her mind, and she knew him.

"Isla," he said, his lips never moving, though the words were clear and bright.

Then he pointed past her, and at first, she saw only the dark sheen of the waves. Then, his hand lifted higher, seawater trailing from his fingertips in thin rivulets as he guided her gaze toward the horizon. There, the March House stood in the distance, half-submerged beneath the tide, its windows glowing faintly under the waterline. Something moved in the upstairs window, and she narrowed her eyes gaze trying to make it out. A woman's silhouette.

Coraline? Who was it? Isla blinked, salt stinging her eyes. When she turned back, the young man beside her was gone. The sea stretched out before her, vast and empty beneath the moon, then came voices. Whispers in a frantic, half-drowned language. Broken fragments she couldn't understand, rising from the depths as though the water were trying to speak to her. She strained to listen, but the sound rushed past too quickly, closing in from every side in a tongue she couldn't understand.

Suddenly, the water churned angrily around her, hissing whispers that scraped against her mind. There was a shift beneath the surface before her: something she felt but couldn't see, like a hidden eye opening underwater, its attention focused only on her. A single bell tolled, distant and hollow in the darkness. Once. Twice. Then, silence.

Gasping, she woke and bolted upright. The sheets twisted around her legs, her skin damp and clammy. The bedroom window flapped open: she was sure she hadn't left it that way. Frigid gusts curled across the sill, carrying the heavy scent of salt and sea.

At the edge of her bed, a sheet of paper lay face-down on the floor. Isla bent to pick it up, and every muscle stiffened. The sketch trembled in her hands. It was hers: she recognized the sharp angles and the heavy lines but had no recollection of drawing it.

On the paper, a young man floated upward through shadowed water, visible only from his midsection up, his mouth parted in a soundless call. His hair drifted, hands hanging slack at his sides, and he smiled. Waiting.

She brushed her thumb on the corner of the page. Scrawled there, quick and uneven, was a single word.

Silas.

Beyond him stood the March House, just as it had appeared in her dream, listing slightly as if it had grown weary of resisting the sea. The lower half was already swallowed by the dark water, the ocean beginning to claim it piece by piece. A woman stood in the upstairs window, motionless under the rising water. Isla raised the paper closer to her face, heart beating in recognition.

The woman in the window was her.

NINE

The air felt all wrong. The fog wasn't the usual low-hanging veil that softened the shoreline and muffled the call of the foghorns. It was thick, like wet wool thrown over the town. It swallowed light whole and clung to the docks, laying so still it looked as though the sea had stopped moving.

Duncan Lee was alone on his boat, the *Lady Marion*, as he usually was. He was a man who trusted sharp knots, loved long silences, and lived by the rules of keeping his boots dry and respecting the ocean. Duncan had lived in Greyhook so long he'd become part of its legends. Twice widowed, salt-worn and weather-cracked, he was as stubborn as they came. Moored in the marina below the local inn, his boat was always rocking gently. With his bushy eyebrows, thick white beard, and the slow, spectral way he drifted across the main deck, more than one tourist had mistaken him for a ghost.

Duncan had grown up on these waters, the son of a fishing boat master who sang as he pulled nets through the swells. His family had been in Greyhook for generations, one of the first to settle here. Folks joked Duncan had saltwater in his veins. Some whispered that was why trouble followed him. Two wives buried, one storm-lost cousin, and now the old man himself was drifting out to sea like a character in a ghost story.

No one saw him go. The *Lady Marion* drifted out of the harbor silently through the heavy fog and into the darkness. Engine off, lights out, boots left neatly side by side on the dock. By morning, the *Lady Marion* had completely disappeared.

Eli Lee, Duncan's younger brother, found his truck abandoned at the far end of the marina parking lot, driver's door open, keys still in the ignition, along with a thermos half-full of bitter coffee and bourbon.

The sky had turned from pewter to ash as Rory, who ran the harbour marina, pulled up to meet Eli.

"The boat's gone. So is Duncan."

"He went out in this?" Rory leaned out the window of his truck, squinting at the slate-colored sky and the barely visible water.

"Not a chance." Eli shook his head, one hand braced on the ledge of Rory's car window as he scanned the horizon. "He knows the ocean better than anyone, but he's no fool. I haven't seen him go out in thick fog for over a decade. His boat is an old girl: no radar, no GPS. I don't understand."

They waited as long as they could, but when Duncan and his boat hadn't appeared by mid-day, Eli called the sheriff and Rory texted Cal. Cal arrived without asking questions, because in Greyhook, that's what you did. You showed up.

"Duncan took his boat out last night." Rory passed him a set of binoculars.

"In this?"

"That's what I said."

"What time did he leave?" Cal raised the binoculars and looked out over the water.

"We don't know. Sometime after midnight. The security cameras went out with the power."

"What happened to the generator I installed?"

"It didn't kick in but it's working fine this morning."

"And no one's seen the boat since?"

"Nope. The fog was so thick last night you couldn't see beyond the marina's fingers. That windstorm rolled in hard early this morning. If he was out in that without any instruments…" Rory didn't finish.

"I know. I couldn't see anything from the gallery deck. Duncan's stubborn, sure, but he's not careless."

"Well," Rory speculated, "maybe with the drinking…" His voice trailed off.

Eli's arms were clamped tight across his chest, his jaw working. He didn't look at them: just kept scanning the horizon like he could will the boat, and his brother, to reappear.

Sheriff Wright pulled up in his older-model SUV, the paint dulled by salty air and time. The light bar on top was sun-faded, and GREYHOOK SHERIFF was stenciled in white letters along the side. He eased the SUV into park, the engine ticking as it cooled. Stepping out, he pulled his collar up against the wind and headed toward the three men.

"Boys." He tipped his hat as he greeted them. "Does anyone know if Duncan had plans to go out and anchor somewhere last night?"

"When's the last time he's done that? He's getting too old for it; he would have told me." Taking the binoculars from Cal, Eli scanned the horizon again.

The sheriff rubbed a hand over his jaw. "All right. Standing here won't help us find him. We'll take my boat out and sweep the south coast first, then loop back north."

Rory shut off his engine. "Great. Cal and I will join you. Eli?"

"Let's go," Eli agreed.

“We’ll need more eyes,” the sheriff said. “Rory, can you round up a few of your dockhands? Anyone experienced enough to man a skiff in this fog. Send them north toward Kettle Point and tell them to stay near the shoreline. I’ll put out a call for Walter and his boys. Their commercial boats have got the instruments and fuel to search further out.”

“What about the Coast Guard?” Cal asked.

“Already notified, but you know how it goes. They’ll be busy after last night’s fog and will take their time unless they’ve got an SOS call for a boat or a body. We’ll move faster on our own.”

Eli lowered the binoculars, his mouth a thin line. “Then let’s stop talking and get out there.”

Two hours later, the *Lady Marion* had been located, gently marooned on a narrow beach inside a small bight about ten miles down the coast. Tilted in the sand, the trawler sat almost untouched except for a scatter of scratches along her hull where she’d scraped over rocks and eddies.

The three men stood in a loose semicircle on the shoreline just beyond the boat, their boots sinking into the wet sand as they examined the exterior.

“Hell of a place to end up.” Rory said.

Cal nodded. “Looks like he got lucky. She doesn’t look wrecked, just displaced.”

“Duncan? Duncan!” Eli moved to climb aboard, but the sheriff held out an arm, stopping him.

“Eli, let me go first,” he said calmly, already stepping toward the edge.

Just then, Cal caught movement in the water. A man, fully dressed, drifted not far from shore, barely visible in the fog-slicked light.

“There!”

Duncan floated on his back, arms splayed open wide. His lips were tinged blue from the cold, eyes fixed and open.

Eli didn't wait. The moment he saw him, he was already moving. "That's him! Get a blanket!" Voice sharp with panic, he waded into the cold, but he didn't slow down. "Hang on, I've got you!"

The water stirred as he reached out and found the weight of a coat and the slack arm inside it. Eli grabbed hold, heart hammering at how limp the body felt: too limp, too cold. But he didn't stop. He slid his arms under Duncan, half lifting, half dragging as the current helped push them both toward shore. The other men's voices called from behind, boots splashing into the sea.

Eli didn't look back. "He's breathing," he said, more a plea than fact as Rory and Cal grabbed hold. "He's breathing."

When they pulled him ashore, he didn't move and didn't speak, but he was alive.

"His pulse is thready. Probably has hypothermia." Rory crouched beside him, checking his vitals and laying a blanket over Duncan's ragdoll body as they waited for the EMTs to arrive.

"You outta your damn mind?" Eli grumbled, not expecting an answer. "What were you thinking, Duncan?"

Sherrif Wright stood a few paces back, manning the radio, calling off the search.

The EMT's arrived, sirens blaring, and carried a stretcher to where Duncan lay on the rocks and sand. They dropped the stretcher and moved quickly, working in practiced silence. One of them checked Duncan's pulse again while the other unzipped the thermal sleeping bag: a heavy-duty, foil-lined cocoon meant to trap what little body heat he still had.

Duncan's skin was pale, almost translucent in the overcast light. His expression, unblinking, was fixed somewhere between confusion and awe, and his tattooed fingers were stiff with cold, locked around something solid in his right hand.

“What’s he got there?” Sheriff Wright tried to ease Duncan’s hand open, but his grip was rigid, fingers clenched with a force that didn’t match his otherwise limp body.

“He’s cold and responding to stimuli, but not alert,” one of the men muttered. “Let’s get him inside.”

They shifted Duncan gently, rolling him onto his side to slide the insulated bag and stretcher underneath, then guided him back down. One EMT leaned in with a penlight, checking his pupils, while the other draped a reflective blanket over his legs and chest before moving to tuck him into the bag.

“Okay, bud. Let’s take a look at what you’ve got in your hand,” one of them said, noticing Duncan’s closed fist. “We have to make sure it’s nothing that can hurt us, okay?”

“Let me,” Eli said quietly, still crouched beside him.

He reached for Duncan’s hand, working his fingers gently apart. They were frozen around the thing and it took effort to separate them. When at last his grip gave way, a small object slipped into Eli’s palm. About the size of a pocket watch, it lay flat and cold in his palm, rusted metal, or perhaps dark granite, worn smooth by sea and time. At its center, barely visible under the tarnish, was a small spiral marking, carved deep and brighter than the rest of the surface. No one said anything at first; then, Cal stepped forward.

“What the hell is that?”

“Doesn’t look like much.” Eli turned it over once more to look at it when Duncan began to moan, his hand reaching out toward Eli’s. “Maybe an old oil cap or fossil? Can I give it back to him? It’s not sharp.”

The EMT nodded and, after inspecting it, placed it back into Duncan’s hand. Plastic buckles snapped into place as they secured the insulated bag around him, zipping it to his collarbone.

"He could've picked that up off the beach when we hauled him in." Rory straightened, motioning toward the sand.

Cal frowned. "There was an imprint in his hand from holding it. Shouldn't that go into an evidence bag or something?"

"Evidence of what? Getting caught in a storm?" Sheriff Wright made notes on his notepad, then turned and walked back toward where he had parked his boat in the sand. "Can you boys push me out? I'll see you back in town. I've got to notify the Coast Guard of the circumstances and file a report. Eli, you ride with Duncan to the hospital. Rory, can you get a tug to haul the *Lady Marion* back to your shop? Deputy Richardson is three minutes away with a truck and some warm towels and blankets for you and Cal."

"Sure thing."

As the paramedics lifted the stretcher into the ambulance, something sounded under Duncan's breath: an unintelligible word, or a gasp, but no one could make it out. Wrapped in his cocoon and thermal blanket, temperature slowly rising, he was being taken back to town. No signs of a struggle. No cuts. No bruises. Just the strange medallion he wouldn't let go of.

~

Greyhook Health Center sat on the far east side of town, tucked behind a row of wind-gnarled pines and a weathered "Emergency" sign that flickered almost as often as it glowed. It had exactly two doctors, six nurses, and a single ambulance that was occasionally shared with the next town over. The vending machine in the lobby was permanently stuck on "*Out of Order*," but the staff knew most everyone by name.

Duncan lay in a large observation room under a warming blanket. The walls were sterile white, and the overhead lights hummed, their too-bright glow sharp against the man lying in the bed below them. Eli, Rory, and Cal waited with him, each of them restless in different ways.

Cal stood in the doorway, eyes focused on Duncan's chest, watching the rise and fall. Too shallow, too fast. It looked as though he were breathing in time with a metronome none of them could hear. He hadn't spoken a word since they'd pulled him from the water, but he'd finally drifted into sleep, and his vitals had remained steady.

"He's had some kind of mental break." Eli kept his voice low, leaning toward Rory.

"Well, he's breathing. That's what matters now."

That's not breathing; that's something else, Cal thought as he shifted in the doorway.

As if in reply, Duncan's hand flexed against the edge of the blanket, fingers twitching. A faint sound rattled in his throat, not quite a moan, not quite a gurgle. All three men turned toward him at once.

"You heard that, right?" Eli stood, pushing his chair back and left the room to fetch a nurse.

Returning promptly, the nurse checked the monitor. The numbers glowed steady. Blood pressure normal, heart rate strong, oxygen sitting at ninety-three. Low, but not critical. She nodded, satisfied.

"He's stable. I'll give him a little time and check back in thirty minutes. If he starts talking or anything changes, come and get me." The nurse marked his chart and hurried out of the room.

An hour passed. Then two. A heavy silence settled over the room, broken only by the hum of the fluorescent lights, the beeping of the pulse monitor, and Duncan's shallow, restless breaths. Nurses came and went, offering the same reassurances: everything steady, everything consistent.

Paper cups stacked on the side table told the rest of the story. Endless waiting and too much coffee. Phones buzzed as updates were sent to family and friends; the same words repeated until they felt thin. *Still no change.*

At last, Duncan stirred, his head turning toward the window and his lips parted to speak for the first time. A dry mutter slipped out.

Snatching up a cup of water, Eli rushed over and brought the straw to Duncan's chapped lips. He blinked slowly, lids heavy.

"What's that, Duncan? What did you say?"

"It was her. She called to me."

"Who?"

"She knew my name, and she knew my pain." Duncan's voice was raspy, like a rope dragged across wet stone.

"He's out of his head." Rory exchanged a look with Cal.

"Who called to you?" Eli persisted

"The woman…in the water." Duncan's voice tripped over itself, half thrilled, half frantic. "She was waiting…waiting for me."

Eli stroked Duncan's head, trying to calm him as his pulse quickened on the monitor.

"It's okay, Duncan. You're safe. You're in the hospital. I'm here, and it's going to be all right."

Duncan's heartbeat eased slightly, the monitor's beeps stretching into a slower rhythm. Then, his face softened, wide with a childlike awe.

"She was…so beautiful. Skin pale as the moon, black hair moving like the sea. Her eyes, they were like glass. Green, blue, silver, all at once. She said she could feel me." His hand flexed weakly against the blanket, twitching as if reaching. "She sang to me, and it filled me whole. I was happy. Where is she? Where is it?"

"Hell," Rory stood, running his hand through his hair and turning toward Cal. "He's delirious."

“What’s he looking for?” Cal asked. “That rock he had?”

Rory glanced at the bedside table, then Duncan’s other hand, and then the floor. Empty.

“Eli, I think he’s looking for that medallion.”

“Where is it?” Duncan moaned. “It’s all I have left of her.”

Eli looked around. “I don’t see it.”

“It was right here.” Cal crouched, scanning the sheets, the floor beneath the bed. “Maybe he dropped it.”

Eli crossed the room and tugged gently at the edge of Duncan’s wet jacket that hung drying on the chair. Something small and heavy thudded to the floor. There it was: sea-glossed and slick with its spiral vein glinting faintly in the light.

“Here,” Eli whispered, picking it up and placing it in Duncan’s open palm. “It’s here.”

At once, Duncan’s breathing slowed as his fingers curled around the medallion with desperation and he brought it to his chest. Breaths rising in longer, steadier pulls, the panic eased from his face, leaving only relief.

“The Tide Song.” Eli whispered the word as if testing it. “Our granddad used to talk about it: a melody only for the chosen to hear. Nobody believed him. We thought he was old and crazy.”

“Come on Eli. We aren’t believing it either. It *is* crazy.” Rory was already heading for the door. “I’ll get the nurse since he’s talking.”

Cal stayed silent, arms still crossed, gaze set on Duncan.

The old fisherman’s eyes had drifted to the ceiling.

“She’s waiting for me. She said I belonged to her, that I already knew the way.” And then he smiled: a soft, unsettling smile that never reached his eyes.

Word spread quickly. By sunset, the town had already twisted the story into something else entirely. At the diner, rumors boiled hotter than the chowder. Duncan hadn't fallen from his boat; he'd jumped straight into the sea, calm as a man stepping through his own front door. Or at least, that's what someone said Eli's cousin's friend's uncle had heard.

"John March, nearly a hundred years gone now," whispered Walter Shipp, "disappeared the same way, or so the story goes."

Others swore it was just like that fisherman out near Kettle Point about thirty years back. Voices overlapped, each insisting on a different version, all of them feeding the same unease. Duncan Lee hadn't gotten lost or fallen in: he'd gone on purpose, willingly. He'd been drawn out.

"It's the Sailors' Song," Walter nodded with conviction. "Same as that rogue squall back in '99. Two men went out just before it hit. No distress call, no mayday: they just vanished. Them and their boat. Many said it was because the weather turned so fast, like it does out at sea. But the sea doesn't usually take without warning, and to be claimed by it is not the same as being lost to it."

"Don't start that again." Suz, a local in her late forties who'd worked at the diner for over ten years, waved him off as she placed a lobster roll and a cup of chowder down in front of him. "You lot said that about the flood two years ago, and it was nothing more than a cracked pipeline. You fishermen and your tall tales. You need to stop trying to scare the tourists."

Walter dug his spoon into the steaming chowder and raised it to his mouth. "The *Lady Marion* was run aground miles from here, and Duncan was just floating beside it like a lily on a pond. You don't find that strange?"

"Men go missing, boats run aground. That's life on the coast."

"It was quiet as death out there last night before that wind kicked up. You ever heard a man half-drowned talking about a woman in the water before? Because I have. Duncan isn't the first and he won't be the last."

"It's odd, sure." Suz cleared a few dishes from a neighboring table. "But I'd be willing to bet that favorite bourbon of his was involved as well. Lost in the fog, brain short on air."

Mira leaned against the counter with her arms crossed. "The timing is strange after what happened with that young man in the cove. There's no such thing as a coincidence."

"I agree. Odd is just another word for a truth you don't like." Walter bit into his lobster roll.

Rory had quietly slipped into a booth by the window like a man trying not to be noticed. With a plate of meatloaf and fries in front of him, head down, he'd nearly made it through half the meal without getting pulled in. Suz appeared beside him, setting a bottle of ketchup on the table with a sharp thud.

"Rory. You were there," she said, arms crossed. "Was he drunk as a skunk, or what?"

Fork paused halfway to his mouth, Rory looked up like a deer in headlights. "I…uhhh…I wouldn't say drunk, exactly."

"He said someone called to him," Mira interrupted as she breezed past with a water jug, lips pursed like she was trying not to say more. "Not that it's my business."

Suz rolled her eyes. "Would've been a real shame if the sea took him before the whiskey did."

Walter let out a low chuckle from the counter.

"I'm just saying," Suz went on, ignoring Mira's sharp look, "if he says a mermaid sang him into the water, I'll believe it. But only because I'm sure the bottle was doing the backup vocals."

“That’s one way to explain it,” Rory muttered, smirking into his plate.

Mira leaned on the counter, eyes narrowed just enough to mean business.

“I’m not saying anything,” she began, which always meant she was about to say something, “but I do find it disturbing. Coraline disappears, the March girl shows up again, a kid nearly drowns, and now Duncan’s out there taking a midnight swim fully clothed? That seem like coincidence to any of you?”

Rory set his fork down, finally looking up. “You think Isla being back is making people drink themselves into hallucinations? Come on, Mira.”

“I think,” Mira said, pouring more coffee without asking, “some families carry things with them. Old things. The kind of things most people don’t have names for, and if the sea wants something…” She gave a pointed shrug. “Well, it’ll have its way. Doesn’t much matter how far they run.”

A silence settled over the group before Suz finally broke it. “Nice try, Mira. More likely Duncan just wanted a midnight cruise and forgot he can’t hold his liquor. Wouldn’t be the first time someone’s nearly drowned that way. And it surely won’t be the last.”

Rory picked up his fork, done with the conversation. “And it doesn’t mean it has anything to do with Isla or her missing grandmother. Let’s not be cruel.”

Mira dried her hands on her apron and continued with her puttering. “Well,” she said lightly, “I’ll just keep minding my own business, then.” She paused just long enough in the kitchen’s doorway to add, “But my guess is, you’ll see.”

TEN

Isla stood barefoot on the porch, wrapped in the borrowed beige housecoat she'd found hanging on the back of the bathroom door. Her hands were cupped around a chipped, green mug of steaming coffee, hair still tousled from a restless sleep.

Morning arrived gently. No fog, no wind: just a soft marine haze and golden sunlight that made the ocean look like glass. The air was crisp, but not cold, and a soft breeze rustled through the trees around the house, their leaves whispering a soothing soundtrack for an unhurried day.

She curled into the wicker chair facing the sea, legs drawn to her chest, a blanket wrapped loosely around her knees. The water beyond was calm, barely moving, stretching out in soft blue ripples. From the garden below the porch, the scent of rosemary drifted up on the breeze, earthy and cheerful.

Coraline's stack of six journals sat on the small bistro table beside her. She reached for the one on top, held closed by a worn black elastic band. When she opened it, a faded pressed flower rested just inside the first page, flattened like a forgotten memory. In deep blue-black ink, Coraline's younger hand curved across the paper: the same script, but with a carefree loopiness.

Isla smiled at the familiar handwriting, a warm nostalgia blooming, and her mind drifted to Cal and the way he'd looked the night before last in the fading light. The way his eyes still curled around her in that familiar way they used to and how that easy, dimpled smile still found its way past her guard with little effort. Whatever was sparking between them was yet to be seen, but it felt good to be near him again. Safe and curious. Less like the girl she'd been when she'd left, more like the woman she could be now.

It was strange to admit to herself that she liked being back here in Greyhook, but she had settled in a way she hadn't expected. Her body felt good, stronger and steadier, like something inside had finally begun to heal. It frightened her a little, how easily life here could make her forget why she'd come back, how settling in felt like a betrayal while her grandmother was still missing.

The old house still creaked around her like it remembered every version of herself she'd tried to outgrow, but being back didn't feel so much like a cage anymore. She wasn't a little girl with rules to follow or a clock to race. No one was timing her walks along the shore. No one was monitoring her comings and goings. For the first time, she was here on her own terms. No curfews, no whispered warnings: just her, the ocean, and whatever came next. And Cal.

The image of last night's dream returned: standing in the shallows, the water welcoming. A man close to her age now, close to the age Silas would have been. The woman in the window and the low toll of the bell. Was it just trauma circling back after all these years? Or was her mind quietly unraveling what it had spent decades trying to forget?

She took a sip of coffee, letting the warmth ground her, then turned to the second page of the journal and began to read.

The water sounds different. It's louder, like it's all I can hear. I've had that twitchy feeling in my hands again. It comes and goes, but it seems to go away if I stay near the sea. The more I go inland, the worse it gets.

Isla read the entry, her finger drifting unconsciously over the ink. Coraline wasn't writing for anyone else; she was unraveling something as well, trying to make sense of it on the page. It felt less like a record and more like a conversation with herself. On the next page, another entry:

Today I woke up with wet hair and damp clothes. Again. I don't understand it. Is it the dreams bleeding through? I keep going over the details, trying to find a piece that makes sense, but nothing fits. Am I sleepwalking into the sea?

Isla exhaled slowly and closed the journal, resting it in her lap as she tried to process what she'd read. It all felt very familiar. Too familiar. Her gaze drifted back to the water; still calm, beautiful, and unmoved by the questions clawing at her.

Coraline had grown up in this house, like Isla. No mother. A father lost to the sea before she ever knew him, not unusual in a village like this. Back then, the ocean was everything: a provider and a thief both feared and worshiped in equal measure. The sea giveth, and the sea taketh away.

Now Isla was here, alone, as Coraline had been before she'd gone missing. No parents. No grandmother. No Silas. Just her…and the sea.

~

The sound of footsteps near the gate pulled Isla from the journals. Cal was approaching the house, hands tucked into the pockets of his perfectly fitted jeans, a soft-knit sweater loose across his frame. His hair was windswept, his pace easy, and that dimpled smile played at the corners of his mouth, warm and entirely disarming.

"Hey, stranger! I brought you a lightbulb." Cal said by way of greeting.

"A lightbulb?"

"For the porch. I noticed that the light by the door was out. I figured you probably hadn't gotten around to replacing it since you can't reach it." He winked.

"So, this passes for flirting now?" Rising, she rested her weight against the weathered post that marked the top of the porch stairs.

"Only for the lucky ones."

"You want coffee?"

"I'd be a fool to say no to caffeine."

She stepped aside, motioning for him to come up the stairs. Hanging from inside the porch lantern was an old light bulb. Cal walked over to examine it.

"Looks like the sea air's been eating at the socket a bit, too. I'll bring some tools and take a look at that bit for you next time I'm here."

"That would be great, thank you."

Isla slipped inside and returned a moment later with a steaming cup. The sight of Cal with his arms lifted and a strip of lean muscle visible just above his waistband sent an unexpected thrill down her spine. She lingered in the doorway and watched as he moved with quiet economy, then found herself reaching for something to say to tame the sudden flutter of butterflies in her stomach.

"I found some old journals that belonged to Coraline. I've been reading them, trying to figure out what might have happened."

"You think there's something in those pages?" Cal asked, nodding toward the pile of journals stacked haphazardly beside her.

Isla scanned the half-finished page of jumbled thoughts that sat in the chair she had risen from. "I don't know yet," she admitted, "but I figure it's better than just waiting."

Cal finished installing the lightbulb and swung the glass panel of the lantern shut. Reaching just inside the door, he flipped the switch. The lamp buzzed to life, casting a soft, golden glow.

"My hero," she said dryly, batting her lashes.

He smirked. "Have you been reading all morning?"

"Pretty much."

"Come on," Cal stepped down into the garden. "Let's take a walk before you go cross-eyed."

"Tempting offer. Where to?"

Cal looked back at her, the ocean breeze dishevelling his hair. "I'll pretend I have a plan, and you can pretend to be impressed."

She rolled her eyes, but her smile gave her away as she turned toward the house. "Let me grab my jacket."

It was quiet along the bluff, with only the sound of distant gulls beneath a blue and white-streaked sky. They walked side by side, not saying much at first, the rhythm of the path and the wide-open view enough for a while.

"Duncan went home this morning. Did you hear about what happened to him?"

"I did. Mrs. Danner down the road told me when I passed by her garden yesterday." Isla tucked her hands into her jacket. "How is he?"

"It sounds like he's okay. Eli says he's eager to get back to his rig, but she's still in the shop. Apparently, he's been mumbling about counting the boats as they come in."

"Counting them?"

Cal shrugged. "He told me Duncan just sits on the dock watching the water and counting the boats as they come home. Says, and I'm quoting here, '*The sea remembers him*" and he's '*Listening for the pull.*'" He glanced at her sideways, brows raised. "He also found this strange old rock looking thing. It's cool, actually — it's got a carved spiral in the middle that looks like a whirlpool. Eli made it into a necklace for Duncan because he's barely put it down."

"A necklace? Nothing says emotional recovery like a handcrafted talisman from your near-drowning experience. How very healing."

Cal stifled a laugh. "I guess he's trying to make sense of it in his own way."

"Thread a chain through it and call it closure." Isla smiled. "Honestly, that sounds exactly like something Coraline would do. She used to say, '*The ocean leaves you gifts, but they don't belong to you; they're just on loan.*'" Glancing toward the edge of the bluff, she watched the sea glitter faintly under the light. "She also used to say that the sea remembers. That it pulls harder on some of us. Maybe it's a Greyhook old-person thing."

They walked a few more steps in silence before Cal spoke again, his voice lower now. "Maybe it's not just the sea that remembers. Maybe some people get pulled back to each other, too."

They stopped, shoulders nearly touching, the water stretched out in an endless blue. A charge had been building between them, familiar and fragile. Something that had always been there, waiting.

"I missed this," Isla said softly.

Cal looked at her, his eyes tender. Their faces hovered just inches apart, close enough to feel the warmth of each other's breath.

"Isla…" he began, his voice nearly lost to the wind.

She tilted her head, searching his gaze. For a heartbeat, hesitation flickered across his expression, then faded into something braver as he leaned in…

A sudden, echoing bark snapped the moment in two. They both startled as a scruffy terrier came barreling up the trail, yapping furiously at something unseen in the bushes.

Suz's voice drifted after him, full of breathless frustration. "Gus! Come back! Stop terrorizing the wildlife!"

The spell was broken.

Cal blinked, dipping his head in defeat before offering a crooked smile. "That's one way to keep things interesting."

"Better luck next time." Isla laughed as she turned away.

"Morning!" Suz called as she passed in the distance, eyes dancing curiously between them. "Enjoy your walk. If you're heading down to the cove, watch your footing. It's slippery today."

With a wave, they continued down toward the beach, the moment left behind.

"So," Cal cleared his throat, "I finally ordered a new bed."

"Oh, big news!"

"Delivered this morning by Murphy's. One of those vacuum-sealed ones in a box. You cut it open and just watch it slowly puff up like a hot marshmallow."

She laughed. "I've seen them in those oddly satisfying time-lapse videos. How is it?"

"Too soon to tell, but I'm hopeful. It'll be great to finally have a bed of my own, and less back pain. They even threw in a free set of sheets." He paused. "Man, I sound old."

"That's great. I look forward to checking it out." She paused, catching herself. "I meant, I'm glad you'll sleep better. Not that I'd…"

Cal raised an eyebrow, clearly enjoying her fluster.

Her eyes widened. "Wait, no, I didn't mean…shit. You know what I meant."

Cal chuckled, hands in his pockets. "Do I?"

"I'll just go throw myself into the ocean now."

Cal gave her shoulder a squeeze and they let the laughter fade with the sound of their footsteps on the trail.

A beat later, Isla tilted her head. "You think Duncan's really okay?"

"I think so. Duncan's tough, but he does seem different now. Distant. I asked him if he remembered falling into the water, and he just said, '*No, but I remember what it felt like to be seen.*'"

"Seen?"

"I don't know what that means, maybe that's about the rescue? Eli said he hasn't been sleeping: he just keeps watching the water and wearing that medallion like it's all that's holding him together."

"Maybe it is. Maybe he's just trying to hold on to whatever version of the story makes sense to him. Whatever is comforting."

"You think it's just trauma?"

She considered it. "Most things are. I don't know. You're bound to come back from things different."

They both fell quiet again. The tide was higher now, but still calm, with small waves curling gently against the sand as broken sunlight cast long ribbons of gold across the water.

“I used to pretend this cove was my secret place.” Isla stepped carefully over a patch of moss-slicked stone onto the sand. “Like it only existed for me.”

“Doesn’t it? You were always so happy in this cove. It’s practically your own back yard.”

“I mean…I loved it here,” she said. “I still do. But as you know, growing up, there was this insinuation like I wasn’t supposed to love the ocean. Not with all Coraline’s rules and warnings.” She paused, letting the words settle. “But down here, it felt different, like none of that mattered. Like if she wasn’t down here, the rules didn’t reach this far. That was the dangerous part, I think. It felt so freeing. I think that’s why I always pushed back so hard.”

At the water’s edge, a band of dark rock jutted out along one side of the cove, breaking the shoreline’s curve. Sand ledges sloped down into tide pools that shimmered like silver mirrors catching the light. Tiny hermit crabs scuttled through crevices, vanishing beneath the swaying fronds of rockweed. Starfish clung to the stone like living jewels, their arms flexing in the sun, while anemones pulsed just beneath the surface, delicate and strange. To the left, a tangle of driftwood lay scattered across the sand, sculpted smooth by months of winter wind and waves.

Isla kicked off her shoes and made her way toward the surf, stepping lightly over the damp sand.

"Whoa, what are you doing?" Cal called behind her with amusement and mild alarm.

Without answering, she stepped into the shallows. The water wrapped around her ankles, and she sucked in a sharp breath. "Oof, it’s cold!"

Still, she took another few steps, shoulders tensing as the chill climbed up her calves. Her body shivered.

Too cold, she thought. *I wish it were warmer*. And then, it was. Not drastically, but enough. The bite dulled, slipping into something more tolerable, and she looked down at her feet, unsure.

"You all right?" Cal asked, eyeing her from the edge of the shore.

"It's warmer than I thought. You just have to get used to it."

"I don't know. That looked like it felt pretty cold to me."

"No, really, it's not bad at all."

He narrowed his eyes at her, and then, as if defending his manhood, kicked off his boots, rolled up his jeans, and stepped in beside her.

"Holy shit!" Cal stumbled back out of the surf. "Isla, it's freezing."

She blinked, genuinely confused. "It's not. I swear."

"Are you secretly immune to hypothermia?"

"Must be." With a chuckle, she shrugged. "Maybe my feet have gone numb."

The water still lapped at her ankles, strangely warm. Something about the soft push and pull made her feel more present. When she finally stepped back onto the sand, her legs were pink and wet, but not cold.

“I have to admit, I've missed being so close to the ocean these past few years.”

“It really never gets old, does it?” Cal said, drawing in a deep breath. Salt, seaweed, and a trace of sun-warmed wood filled his senses. “I do love it here. But we should head back before that cold you're ‘definitely not feeling’ catches up to you and I have to carry you and your ice-block feet.”

“You'd enjoy that too much.”

He didn't deny it.

The air cooled as they walked up the path, and partway Isla finally felt the shift in temperature. Her feet were cold now, the warmth from the water gone almost as quickly as it had come. At the fork in the trail, where one path led toward the lighthouse and to town and the other curved up toward the bluff and the March House atop it, Cal slowed to a stop.

"I'm going to head into town and grab some groceries. Maybe invest in some warmer socks." He gave her a teasing smile.

"I'll see you later?"

"You will."

She turned toward the March House, and he toward Greyhook.

Soft gusts brushed against the back of Isla's neck as she climbed the porch steps. The house had chilled with the afternoon's setting sun as it nestled behind broken clouds. Not bothering to turn on the overheads, she flipped the switch for the small lamp near the couch and tugged out an old blanket from the basket. She settled in, curled up with the blanket on her lap and a journal balanced on one knee. The books had grown familiar in her hands: soft leather, loose bindings, and she flipped to the earmarked section where she'd left off.

The weather's gone strange again. Sun this morning. Fog by noon. The swell is restless tonight, though the wind hasn't changed. There's tension building somewhere out there and it's slipping into my dreams. Always the cove, barefoot. I've been waking up still tired, and last night there was salt on my skin and sand in the sheets.

Isla closed her eyes. This past year, her own dreams weren't far off: barefoot in water, cold rock beneath her feet, something moving just out of sight. The similarities were eerie, but the next entry felt more weighted.

It started again before this last storm. Tightness in my ribs, like waiting for something I can't see. I thought it was anxiety but now I know better. I lose time now, and I keep finding myself at the beach with no memory of leaving the house. Always when the tide is coming in.

Isla's stomach tightened as she read the passage. *Lost time?* Did Coraline go to the water without realizing? Had she walked off thinking she was somewhere else entirely? Unease crept up Isla's spine as this new, unwelcome thought surfaced: what if Coraline hadn't meant to leave at all? What if she hadn't been entirely herself when she did?

Isla turned the page and kept reading. Folded neatly between the next two entries was a photocopied article from the *Berkeley Wellness Letter*, dated in the late 1980s. The page was yellowed, its corners worn, and the headline caught her attention.

Salt-Blood Syndrome: Myth, Misdiagnosis, or Mutation?

Coraline had circled a paragraph in pen that discussed a rare group of individuals experiencing physiological shifts and physical symptoms when spending too much time inland: fatigue, joint pain, mood disruption, sensory sensitivity.

Though largely dismissed by clinical medicine, anecdotal reports of so-called "Salt-Blood Syndrome" have persisted in coastal communities for decades. Subjects described as "sea-adapted" exhibit measurable physiological changes following prolonged periods of time inland. Fatigue, and muscle and joint stiffness, along with disrupted circadian rhythms, are most commonly observed. Preliminary hypotheses suggest these responses may stem from a disruption in electrolyte regulation or a mutation influencing osmotic balance. While no genetic marker has been isolated, several case studies indicate improvement after exposure to saline environments, an IV saline drip, or immersion in natural seawater. This implies an adaptive link between salt concentration and systemic equilibrium.

Coraline's handwriting lined the margins.

It's worse when I travel inland for supplies. Just a few days away from the coast and I feel ill. I feel... wrong.

Isla frowned, remembering those trips. Coraline would drive inland once a month for supplies she couldn't grow or forage herself: pure alcohols, dried valerian root, bulk oils for her tinctures. Isla hated those days as a child. Not only for the long, dull drives into the city, but for what came after. Coraline would return home pale and drained, sleeping for hours, her mood soured and sharp. She'd tell Isla to stay indoors while she rested, leaving the house unnaturally quiet.

Looking back now, Isla realized it wasn't just fatigue from travel. Coraline had been suffering the same symptoms she herself had experienced living away from Greyhook.

The next few pages held more loose entries of folded printouts and cut-out articles from pseudo-scientific wellness papers. The ink was faint, edges soft from handling. Titles included *Aquatic Adaptation and Mutation: Myth or Physiology?* and *Psychosomatic Neurological Disorders Among Coastal Communities.*

An excerpt from one printout read:

Certain individuals exhibit abnormal shifts in serum sodium levels and vestibular sensitivity following prolonged absence from marine environments.

Another warned:

While psychosomatic factors cannot be ruled out, the recorded frequency of these reports among multi-generational coastal families suggests a possible hereditary predisposition.

The margins were crammed with the slanted markings of Coraline's frustration and fear. Joint pain, temperature insensitivity, racing heart. In the corner, Coraline had scrawled in capital letters, *NOT IMAGINED*.

The voice beneath it all made Isla's heart bleed. Though it seemed like Coraline knew more than Isla did now, she had still been searching for sense, for answers.

Isla sat back against the cushions and stared toward the window, where afternoon had deepened into dusk. Her body had felt so different since coming home. The pressure behind her eyes had lifted, the ringing in her ears, gone. Her breathing came deep and clean, without that tight clamp in her chest. The aches and pains, subsided.

She should have told Coraline what was happening to her. So far, these journal entries weren't hysterical; they were logical. Coraline hadn't been spiraling; she'd been tracking. And she had done it all alone.

Isla swallowed. She should have let her in.

Reaching further down the stack, Isla drew out another journal and flipped it open halfway. This entry was dated one year ago.

When the time comes, she will feel it too. Perhaps it has already started, and she hasn't told me. What's written in her blood cannot be unwritten, and I cannot stop it from finding her. I can only try to keep her from meeting her fate too soon.

Isla swallowed hard. Was "*she*" Isla? If so, what *fate* had Coraline been trying to protect her from?

The pieces aligned all at once: the tinctures, the parcels, the deliberate spacing between them. Each of Coraline's deliveries wrapped in brown paper and twine, always smelling faintly of brine. Isla had thought them sporadic, but they weren't. They were timed. Glass vials of tinctures, hand-labeled in Coraline's tidy script, had arrived in her mailbox with measured intervals between. Pickled bladderwrack, dried sea purslane, salt-preserved rock samphire. Strange and bitter remedies pulled from the tide line.

Isla had assumed it was just Coraline being Coraline: half-naturalist, half-grandmother, always convinced she had a remedy for everything. Now, the memories sat under a clearer lens. Those packages were strategic. Coraline had been *trying* to *dose* her with small, salted cures meant to delay the symptoms of this "*salt-blood syndrome*" for as long as possible.

Gently, she closed the journal and held it to her chest for a moment. Tears threatened to fill her eyes as somewhere deeper than thought, deeper than instinct, Isla understood that whatever was happening now hadn't started with her. It had started long before.

It had started with Coraline.

ELEVEN

Cal's dream began in that velvet-blur that comes between asleep and awake. Isla stood at the edge of the cove in blue cotton shorts, the wind churning her hair, the sea stretched out in front of her. She hummed softly, a low, wandering sound without origin, as though it had begun long before he arrived and was destined to carry on long after he was gone.

At first, she didn't seem to notice him, her gaze remained fixed on the horizon, bare feet sinking into the sand, her eyes never blinking. Then, she turned, recognition settling across her face, and she smiled, a cold and knowing grin. Dread filled his every sense as she entered the water, and he started toward her. Then, all went black.

He woke before she disappeared beneath the surface, but the feeling stayed. Just a dream, he told himself. Nothing more. Still, the draw he felt toward her wasn't just desire. It had gravity. Nostalgia was what he used to call it, but not anymore. Seeing her again hadn't been some sudden romantic collision. It was a mechanism finally clicking into place after years of unseen tension. Precise, inevitable.

Isla had changed, there was no denying that. More composed now, more certain in her silence, but she was still Isla. Still funny, still sharp. The girl who ran barefoot down the dock with paint streaked up her arms and across her clothes. The one who smuggled beers to the pier when they were supposed to be studying. The one who kissed him after graduation and left before the night ended, summer still on his tongue and something unfinished between them.

Since he first saw her from the lighthouse on the night she returned, walking the shoreline below, she had lived in the quiet spaces of his day. She lingered in the corners of his thoughts and in the blur between asleep and awake. Cal would often catch himself picturing her without meaning to. There was a natural grace to the way she moved: unhurried, self-contained, never asking for attention, yet drawing it. Her dark hair fell in restless waves that seemed to shift even when she stood still. Her soft lips hovered at the edge of a smile, and her eyes, those strange amber-green eyes that tilted slightly at the corners, caught the light like sea glass turned in the sun.

Yes, she was beautiful. He saw it in the sweep of her cheekbones and the strength in the lines of her frame. But what held him was the way she looked at the world: as if she were always sketching it behind her eyes, translating light and shadow into something only she could see.

When he found himself on her porch that evening, a takeout bag in one hand and an excuse in the other, he convinced himself it was just casual. One friend checking in on the other.

Isla opened the door barefoot, wearing a sweater that hung loose on her shoulders, the sleeves tugged over her hands. Her hair was pulled up in a messy bun on the top of her head, and the scent of something herbal and warm drifted out into the cool evening air.

An unexpected flutter passed through him as his eyes met hers. There was worry behind them, something tired and unspoken, but she smiled anyway. And that smile, the one that curved more on one side of those full, pouty lips disarmed him completely. In that instant, every excuse he'd rehearsed on the walk over slipped away. The reasons he'd told himself to stay home, to keep things simple, to not get pulled back in, evaporated. All he could think was, *This is where I'm meant to be.*

"Hey." He held up a paper bag and a bottle of wine like a peace offering. "I come bearing noodles."

"And no judgment? Because I'm running low on that for myself right now." Isla looked down at her sockless feet and well-loved sweater, dotted with holes and fraying at the edges.

"Never. You look exactly like someone I'd want to share a judgement free meal of mediocre food with."

Moving aside, she waved him in. Coraline's journals sat on the table in the sitting room, and Cal glanced at them as he passed by.

"Any scandalous discoveries in those pages?"

"Not really, no. Just natural remedies. Weather notes. A lot of vague metaphors. Nothing solid yet." *A lie.* A smooth one, but her voice dipped just slightly at the end. He caught it, though he didn't press her.

"Maybe she was cryptic for sport." He followed her back outside with a set of plates and two wineglasses. "She certainly had a dramatic flair at times."

"Did she ever," Isla murmured.

"I wonder what she'd think of this," Cal said as he set the paper bag on the table and pulled out two takeout containers. "The two of us sitting here."

Isla sat down and leaned back in her chair, eyeing the food with a faint smile. "She'd steal half your noodles and grill you about your intentions in showing up unannounced like this."

"Good thing mine are mostly honorable, then."

"Mostly?" Isla raised a brow, smirking beneath her lashes.

Cal flushed as he chuckled. "I mean… I brought dinner."

"True. And wine," she added, popping open a container. "I appreciate it, by the way. I needed a reason to think about something else for a while. How'd you know?"

"I have my ways." He grinned. "Intuition. And maybe a little, albeit rusty, experience knowing how you get when you hyper-focus. You probably haven't eaten since breakfast."

"Guilty. I'll admit, your timing's perfect."

They settled into their meal on the porch, the ocean stretched out below them in soft grays and blues.

"I need to go see Sheriff Wright tomorrow," Isla said after a moment. "Figure out why there hasn't been a proper search. No dive team, no tracking dogs. I just feel like they should have done more."

"It's worth asking," he said. "But if nothing looked off, they probably didn't think it was necessary. She did sign the house over to you, after all. That counted for something with the sheriff."

"Word spreads fast in this town, huh?"

Cal grimaced.

"No, it's okay," Isla sighed. "Nothing's private for long. I just…" She stirred her noodles. "What if she wasn't in her right mind? What if she got confused and wandered off…"

"Have you found something that made you think that?"

"Not exactly. Most of the entries are old, but they're...a little bit bizarre."

Cal watched her carefully and then leaned forward, elbows on the table. "Let me come with you tomorrow. We'll talk to the sheriff together."

"You don't have to do that."

"I want to. I've got time."

"You'll make time, you mean." Her expression softened, appreciative.

"For you? Of course." He shrugged.

Before now, they'd known one another as early drafts of themselves — barefoot kids, reckless teenagers. Life had shaped them since. Whatever moved between them now was earned. They knew each other too well to pretend anything was simple. This wasn't built on memory alone, but on who they were now.

Cal held up a piece of tofu, inspecting it. "I know this isn't big city Thai food, but am I wrong, or does it somehow taste better?"

Isla popped a clump of noodles into her mouth and shrugged. "It's the sea air. It enhances the flavor and numbs your standards."

"Bold of you to assume I have standards." He pointed at her with his chopsticks. "I once ate gas station sushi in Tacoma."

"That *is* a bold, bold gamble. How'd that work out for you?"

"I'll spare you the medical details," he said, waving a hand. "But let's just say it wasn't my closest brush with death."

Without missing a beat, Cal launched into a wildly dramatic retelling of how he'd nearly electrocuted himself fixing a second-hand espresso machine in college.

"I swear to God, Isla, it threw me three inches off the floor. I saw my life flash before my eyes, and it was mostly shitty cafeteria food and mild regret."

"You're lucky it didn't fry your brain."

"I think I may have. It would explain a lot, actually."

"So not just a trauma, but character development?"

"Exactly. It's the origin story of some of my questionable life choices."

A hearty laugh bubbled out, the warmth of the food and his company settling over her like a blanket. Cal had always been a champion at lifting her spirits. It was comforting. Especially now. Easy in a way nothing had been lately. She felt safe with him.

As the meal wrapped up and the candlelight dwindled, they slid their chairs around to the same side of the table. Wine glasses in hand, legs brushing lightly under the table, they took in the view. The last of the sunset painted the water in slow, molten strokes, and they watched.

"What's something you're embarrassingly good at?" She reached over to brush a crumb from his sleeve, her fingers lingering just a second too long.

"That's an interesting question." Cal leaned back in his chair and raised his arm, casually placing it on the back of her chair. "I can fold a fitted sheet, like, really well."

A look of disbelief. "I need proof."

"I held a tutorial freshman year. The whole dorm floor showed up."

Isla nearly choked on her wine. "Okay, that's a very domesticated dad move. I'm impressed."

"I know. It's a very adult skill. I own slippers and everything."

"Slippers? You're really leaning into your old-man era."

"Make fun all you want!" he said, feigning offense. "They're shearling-lined. Very sophisticated, and comfortable."

"Next thing you'll tell me is that you read the paper in a robe and complain about taxes."

"I do read the paper, but only for the crossword section."

"Wow, sexy and literate."

"You don't like crosswords? I've conquered three Mondays and one very forgiving Thursday. Also, you said sexy. Tell me more about that."

Isla laughed, shaking her head. "You used to be cool."

"I was never cool. You just had poor judgment in friends."

"Still do."

"To poor judgment, then." He tilted his glass toward her.

"The one thing we've always been good at. Cheers!" She clinked hers lightly against his.

"All right, your turn. What are you embarrassingly good at?"

Isla took a moment to think. "Packing groceries."

"Define packing. Like, into the house?"

"No. The bagging part. It's an art form. I can fit a full week's worth of groceries into two paper bags like professional-level Tetris. One bag if it's a heavy work week."

"So, you're one of those people who judge the cashier's bagging technique."

"Absolutely. It's painful really. If they put the eggs or bread on the bottom, I have to physically restrain myself."

"That's deeply concerning."

"Hey," she shot back, pointing at him with her glass, "maximizing space efficiency and keeping the soft items uncrushed is very important."

"Optimizing groceries like it's NASA cargo is indeed important."

She shrugged, deadpan. "Someone has to uphold the standard."

They fell into a rhythm of banter, laughter, and trading strange facts and subtle truths. She confessed she was still horrible at parallel parking and never wanted to own a car. He admitted that until well into early adulthood, he thought coral reefs were plants rather than animals.

"I feel like that's not really a brag-worthy thing. Most people don't know coral reef are animals."

"When you grow up ten feet from the ocean and are raised by a librarian, it's definitely brag-worthy-bad. It came up at family dinner on a regular basis for a year."

"Sounds scarring."

"Deeply, but I learned to sit with my shame like a man."

"You always were good at that." She gave him a genuine smile.

"What, man-shame?"

"No, at playing it cool."

"Ah, yes. My greatest talent. How am I doing?"

She arched a brow. "Not bad. Though, it's been a while. You seem mostly normal."

He smirked, considering this. "Eighteen-year-old me had no idea what he was doing. Grown-up me sells it better." Then he added, more to himself then to her, "I think we're all just better at disguising the chaos."

"Speak for yourself. My chaos has a Google calendar now. Color-coded."

Cal nodded with a smile. "Growth."

Just like that, they weren't teenagers anymore, and they were getting to know each other all over again.

"I forgot how loud this place can be at night." Isla eyed the exterior walls of the old house as a breeze whistled through the crevices of the porch. "Some nights it's like it's talking to itself, and it gives me the creeps."

"It probably *is* talking to itself, but I find these old places comforting. I couldn't sleep in the city with the sirens, the people, and the traffic. The ocean makes the world fade away and these old houses…I don't know. They just creak because they're finding your shape again. Think of it as a kind of welcome." Cal looked at her then, and as he spoke, his tone was genuine. "How are you really doing being back here in Greyhook?"

Isla considered for a moment. "It feels strange. And, somehow, completely normal. So, I guess I'm doing okay."

"You were always meant to leave here Isla, even if it was just for a while. We all have to find our path."

Absentmindedly, he reached out and tucked a strand of hair behind her ear. The gesture was intimate, and his fingers brushed her cheek. Then, as he lingered, she leaned into his hand. There was no trace of bitterness in him. No questions or quiet blame about why or how she'd left when she did. There was only a quiet knowing, and a respect for the path she'd had to take. That, more than anything, made her want to stay.

"I'm glad you're back," Cal said, barely a whisper.

Their eyes held each other in that quiet space between them, and they sat, watching the colors change where the sea met the sky in that fragile space between what had been and what might yet be.

~

The view had disappeared into darkness. Inside, the lamps' warm light pooled across the kitchen floor, casting halos on the tile. The dishes were done, the table cleared, but neither of them moved to say goodbye. They hovered close, the distance between them softening in small increments.

Cal leaned back against the counter, at ease, watching her. Isla moved to set her empty wineglass down beside him, allowing her fingers to remain longer than necessary against the stem. When she finally moved her hand away, it drifted toward him, and he reached for it. When she didn't pull away, his fingers threaded through hers.

She hadn't meant for the evening to go like this, but now, with the current of his hand curling around hers and his body just inches away, it was hard to think of a reason to stop it. Eyes down, breath slow and deep, she tried to steady the rush of fire building within her. It wasn't just the wine; it was want. There was no fear in the draw to him this time. No need to run.

When she finally met his eyes, the look he gave her unraveled whatever restraint she had left. It wasn't a decision: it was a current, pulling her under. She reached for him, and he caught her, drawing her in until her body unfolded against his like it had always belonged there.

He kissed her slowly, tentatively at first. Then his hand rose to her face, fingers warm against her skin as a thumb grazed her cheekbone. When her mouth parted beneath his, he welcomed the invitation. Cal wanted this. Not in the way he had when they were young and full of hormones and fire, but in a deeper, more meaningful way. The way that came with knowing what it meant to lose something and to find it again.

The kiss held both the spark of a beginning and the pull of return, and he knew without question that he didn't want it to end. He kissed her again, deeper this time, and she responded without holding back. Slender fingers slid tenderly up the back of his neck and into his hair. There was urgency in her touch: but no hurry, just undeniable want. The heat between them surged. She felt it in the way his hand slid along her ribs and settled at her waist, drawing her closer until her knees slipped between his. In the way his breath stuttered through the slow slide of their tongues.

Their bodies came together with a hunger that had waited for too long. Pausing just shy of the edge, foreheads close, mouths grazing, their breaths caught as the pivotal moment held.

Isla looked into his eyes, then took his hand and led him to the couch. She slipped her fingers beneath the hem of his shirt and pulled it over his head in one fluid motion. Pushing him to sit, her mouth found the hollow of his collarbone as his hands tangled in her hair. She eased him back into the cushions and climbed into his lap. His hands found her waist under her sweater as it slipped off one shoulder, and the touch of his palms on her bare skin sent a shiver through her. A soft sound escaped her as their mouths met again, answered by a low groan as he pulled her closer, as if even an inch between them was too much. He traced his lips along her jaw, then the corner of her mouth, tasting the salt of her skin and the faint sweetness of wine still on her breath. When he finally pulled back, it was only far enough to see her face.

"Are you sure about this?" Cals voice was rough with want.

A single nod, and then she slipped out of her shorts, letting them fall quietly to the floor, and climbed back into his lap. Cal whispered her name, and she kissed the sound from his mouth. With steady hands, he undressed her like the delicate unwrapping of something long imagined and finally within reach. Every detail mattered as he leaned back, tracing each line of her with his eyes, committing her to memory. He listened to the catch in her breath, felt the way her body responded beneath his hands.

When his mouth found the curve of her neck and moved lower, she trembled. They shifted together, breath and body aligned, until she lay beneath him. Soft lips brushed along her stomach, her ribs, the delicate hollow just beneath her breast. She felt undone: not just by the intensity of his touch, but by the reverence in his eyes. He took her in as if he were starving, devouring her with a hunger that was as emotional as it was physical.

"I want you, Cal." It was just a whisper, but it struck deep.

With that, her storm-filled eyes captured his and any patience he'd been clinging to broke apart. He kissed her deeply, and she felt the fault lines opening between them. The ache, the years, the longing neither of them had dared admit. When his body pressed against hers and she guided him in, a broken moan left her mouth before she could stop it. He paused, searching her face, and when she nodded again, he moved with a slow, deliberate care that made her body roar.

Together, they found their rhythm. Her breath brushed his ear in a soft, melodic whisper she didn't fully recognize; a sound rising from a place deep inside, elemental and alive. He drew back, watching as if he was witnessing something divine, something he didn't believe he deserved and yet couldn't stop reaching for. Wonder softened the lines of his face, and he knew that she was the only thing in the world that could undo him. And he would let her.

He listened as she whispered again, her voice soft and lilting as he kissed her neck. Isla groaned when he moved faster, drawing something from him that went beyond pleasure. It was surrender.

His voice broke against her skin. "How are you undoing me like this, Isla?"

She didn't know. She only knew she felt it too, and that whatever had begun between them refused to slow. Isla's voice trembled, threaded with ecstasy and magic; everything inside them tipped. They came apart like a wave collapsing, swallowed in the same breathless fall.

Afterward, they lay tangled together, wrapped in warmth and the sense that something long missing had finally settled into place. With his face buried against her shoulder, calm settled over them, leaving only the soft rise and fall of shared breath.

Outside, the sea kept its steady rhythm. Yet in the hush around them, something stirred. A low, unfinished note hummed through her, and for the first time, she let it rise.

Isla woke alone. The bedroom lay quiet in the pale hush of early morning, sheer curtains lifting gently in the breeze from the open window. She reached across the rumpled sheets, brushing her fingers across the place where Cal had been. Empty, but still warm. She smiled.

After midnight they had made their way upstairs, hands and mouths still hungry. Twice more they'd reached for each other in the dark before exhaustion finally settled over them. Now, lying in the silence that followed, Isla replayed the evening in her head. Skin, breath, heat, the way he'd touched her in the darkness.

She rose from the bed and pulled on the cotton robe hanging from the bedpost. The floorboards were cool beneath her bare feet as she turned on the bedside lamp and crossed to the window. One of Coraline's six journals sat open on the thick sill where she'd left it the day before, a faint ring from her teacup marking the corner edge of the page. It fluttered softly in the ocean air, drawing her eye to an open page.

When the voice awakens, so too do the watchers.

The line unsettled her, no surprise there. *The watchers.* It wasn't a term she recognized, and she didn't like the sound of it.

"Watchers?" she muttered. "What the hell, Coraline. Were you being serenaded by some window lurker? Fantastic. Why are we like this?"

She closed the journal and shook it off.

Something had shifted last night. Subtle, but unmistakable. She couldn't name it, but she could sense it. Had she said something to Cal she couldn't take back? Something she hadn't meant to say. Her body still buzzed with the memory of him, every touch lingering against her skin, but her mind held fragments she couldn't quite assemble. Wine. Heat. Want. The night blurred at the edges, and somewhere in that haze, she was certain, an unintended truth had slipped free. Something unfiltered that she hadn't meant to release.

He lingered in the tingle on her lips, and she lifted her fingers to touch them, trying to hold the imprint of his kiss a moment longer. Into the quiet, she whispered, soft and bewildered, "What did I do to him?"

Then, the answer came from somewhere deeper, through a voice that didn't feel entirely like her own.

You only woke what was already waiting.

~

The bedroom still held the scent of sleep and Cal. Isla sat at the edge of the bed, robe wrapped loosely around her, the cool sheets tucked beneath her legs. Somewhere down the hall, a floorboard creaked, then her door opened.

"Good morning," Cal said, voice still raspy from sleep. He stepped into the room barefoot, hair tousled, a playful grin on his face. In his hands, he held two mugs of hot coffee, and he raised them like an offering.

"Did you wake up with the sun?" Isla asked, biting her lip. "Because that's surprisingly functional behavior for someone who was up to no good half the night."

His eyes were full of mischief as he crossed the room. "I'm not gonna lie, I'm running mostly on adrenaline and muscle memory."

Isla relaxed at his presence. He was still here; he hadn't vanished in the night.

"I wasn't sure how you take it," he said, handing her a mug. "There's no milk in your fridge, so I gambled on black."

"You gambled correctly." She inhaled the scent, letting it curl around her like freshly brewed clarity.

In the soft morning light, Cal looked younger, more open. He sat next to her on the bed, one leg folded under, his other foot brushing the floor as he raked his fingers absently through his sleep mussed hair. *My doing*, she thought, with quiet satisfaction.

"I hope it's okay that I stayed," he said after a beat. "You fell asleep, and I didn't want to wake you just to ask."

"I'm glad you stayed."

Gently, he leaned in, brushing his lips over hers in a soft kiss.

"Hi," she whispered.

"Hi," he murmured back.

For a moment, the rest of the world didn't matter: just them, right here in this sliver of quiet, coffee-scented bliss.

"I don't regret last night." he said quietly, like it needed saying. "I just needed you to know that."

"Good. I don't regret it, either."

"So, was this our second or third date?"

"Why?"

"I never sleep with anyone before the third date."

Isla laughed, tossing him a look. "Are you trying to defend your dignity right now? Because I think it's already too late."

He grinned, hand over his heart. "Wow. Ruthless."

"First of all," she said, pointing at him, "I think you're a liar."

He gasped softly.

"But," she continued, ticking them off on her fingers, "third date, technically. If we combine running into each other on the beach with our coffee encounter in town, that's one. Burgers and your fancy Boudreaux make two. And then last night's surprise Thai food…" She lifted a brow. "That's three. So technically, you're still a gentleman."

"So, it's above board then." He gave an exaggerated sigh of relief, then reached for her free hand, his thumb brushing gently across the back of it.

"I didn't expect any of this." His smile faded just a touch, allowing something real to show through. "But I like it. I've thought about you a lot, Isla March, and I'm glad you're here."

"I'm glad I'm here, too." A moment passed, and then her eyes sparked again. "But, just so we're clear, if you want breakfast, the kitchen is self-serve."

"Oh, I didn't come for the breakfast." His voice was lower now as he moved toward her, closing the space between them with intent.

"No?"

"No."

The Greyhook Police Station didn't look like much. It was a squat brick building with a dull security light and a chipped POLICE sign over the door. Isla hadn't been here in years. Not since she'd gotten caught sneaking onto the old cannery roof the summer she'd turned fifteen. It had seemed larger back then. Now, it just looked tired.

Cal held the door for her. "You ready for this?"

"No," she said, stepping inside. "But I need answers."

The station smelled of musky cologne and burnt coffee. The front desk was empty, but a fan hummed lazily in the corner, stirring the heavy air. A portly woman in uniform emerged from a back hallway, middle-aged, clipboard in hand. "Can I help you?"

"I'm here about Coraline March: she's my grandmother. I need to speak to whoever's handling her missing persons case."

The officer nodded and disappeared again without a word. A moment later, Sheriff Wright stepped out from the back office. His salt-and-pepper hair was combed back; his badge clipped neatly to his chest. He looked tired.

"Isla March," he said, extending a hand. "Didn't expect to see you here today." Then he turned to nod at Cal. "Morning Cal. What can I do for you two?"

"Do you have a minute?" Isla asked.

Sheriff Wright gestured to the open door of his office. Sunlight slipped through dusty blinds and two chairs were positioned across from his desk.

"Come on in. Let's sit."

Cal trailed behind Isla and settled into the adjacent chair, quiet but present.

"I just want to understand what's being done," Isla began. "My grandmother's been missing for God knows how long, and from what I can tell, there's no active search for her. The house was left unlocked; her car is still in the garage and her coat and walking cane were by the door. She couldn't have gone far on her own."

Wright nodded slowly, letting her speak.

"I'd like to know if the water's been checked. Or the woods. Has anyone gone out there?"

"As you know, we did a wellness check the day the disappearance was reported, and then again two weeks later when she didn't turn up," Wright said. "There were no signs of forced entry. No signs of struggle. No blood. No damage. And she moved the deed of the house into your name, which suggests she had no intention of remaining there. I believe she left of her own accord."

"But she hasn't come back," Isla pushed. "She didn't take clothes or any of the things she would have if she'd gone away."

"Miss March, you said yourself that you hadn't been in touch with her in a long time, which tells me, it's entirely possible that you don't know what she may or may not have taken with her if she left."

Isla frowned.

"People are allowed to disappear Miss March," Wright said, not unkindly. "It's not illegal to walk away from your life."

"But she wouldn't," Isla said. "She raised me. She was structured. Obsessed with routine. She wouldn't have left without telling *someone*."

Wright's expression softened. "I understand this may be upsetting, but there's nothing to suggest foul play. There are no mental health flags. No past issues that would raise concerns. Now, that doesn't mean we're doing nothing. We've spoken to neighbors, and we've put out a BOLO with local hospitals, shelters, even the ferry logs in neighboring towns. From what we've learned, Coraline was not an overly social person. If you weren't close, she may not have notified you, or anyone else, of her plans."

"What about the water?" Cal spoke up. "You know how quick the tide can turn. If she slipped…"

"If we had any reason to believe she entered the water, we'd act accordingly," Wright interjected. "But we didn't find any indication of that. No footprints, no drag marks, no discarded shoes or personal effects — nothing to suggest she went into the water."

"Mrs. Danner said she'd seen Coraline swimming on occasion down in the cove. She could have gone in and had some trouble?"

"We didn't find any evidence of that. No towel, no clothing."

"What about the woods," Isla said. "At night, no one would see her if she went foraging after dark."

"We had a team sweep the immediate perimeter, but again, there were no signs that warranted a full-scale search. No evidence of distress, no signs of her having been there. If you have reason to believe otherwise, I'm all ears. Did she tend to forage at night?"

"Well, no…" Isla trailed off.

"Do you have any further information that might warrant a search, Miss March?"

"No. No, I don't."

Wright folded his hands. "Isla, in the eyes of the law, there's no indication of any danger here. No suspicious activity. We can't allocate full search resources for someone who, on paper, appears to have just walked away from her very quiet life. I'm not saying we won't follow up, but our hands are tied unless new information comes to light."

There was a long pause.

"What would count as new information?" Cal asked.

"Witness sightings. A lead. Something physical that contradicts the idea that she left voluntarily."

"She kept journals," Isla said slowly. "Several of them. I've been going through them, and there are some odd entries about the water. Dreams she had, and losing time."

"If you find something that seems urgent, or indicates danger" Wright said, "bring it in. Otherwise, we just have to wait. A woman's journal is not a reason for concern unless something inside it indicates she was in trouble or intended to do harm to herself. Understand?"

Isla nodded as she stood, smoothing the front of her coat. "Thank you for your time, sheriff."

Cal held the door for her, as they stepped outside on to the sidewalk.

"She wouldn't just go," Isla said under her breath. "Not without a reason."

Stroking her back gently, Cal guided her forward. "Then let's find one."

TWELVE

The last traces of daylight faded to gray as night settled over the coastline. Fog crawled intently, inch by inch, across the water, covering the cove like a blanket of cotton. It gathered at the shoreline, wrapping itself around the rocks and moorings. There was no wind, no birds: just the tide slapping against stone. Nature was holding its breath.

Mason Locke stood on the jetty where rustic wood made a narrow path above the tide. Barnacles clung to the concrete beams below, and his lantern swayed in the wind, spilling light into the final moments of twilight.

"The air is heavy tonight."

Mason's brother Jace trailed a few steps behind, hauling their large bait bucket. "Everything's heavy tonight, including this bucket. We should've just stayed in."

"You say that every time. And yet…"

"And yet I follow."

The tide was higher than they'd expected, their path slick with moss and the leftovers of yesterday's swell. They reached the end of the jetty reaching their usual spot: an area wide enough for two chairs, two rods, and a cooler of beer wedged between them. Mason and Jace had only lived in Greyhook a little less than a year, having moved from the next town over, but they'd already considered this quiet stretch on the outskirts of town their own.

Mason set his things down and popped up their lawn chairs.

"It's just so quiet. I didn't expect this fog." Jace set the bait bucket down in front of the lawn chairs and dropped into his seat. He cracked a beer and leaned back, contentedly taking his first swig.

"You can still fish lingcod in fog." Mason didn't sit; he stepped toward the seaward edge of the jetty with his rod, eyes narrowing toward the water.

Somewhere beyond the shadows came a sound, faint and haunting. Delicate as a whisper and barely a melody, weaving through the silence. It lulled him, gentle but insistent. And then, through the haze, he saw her: movement, and a figure in the shadows. Far beyond, half-veiled in mist, was a flicker of light that caught his eye like moonlight glinting on wet stone. She didn't swim; she drifted, a face barely visible above the surface. Long hair fanned out behind her like silk moving in the tide. Her skin shimmered with a glow that didn't belong to the daylight: soft, opalescent, almost lit from beneath. Her eyes, steely, held the endless depth of the deep water. And they were locked onto his. The breath of song was hers. He didn't need to be told: he could feel it.

A yearning inside him awoke, ancient and aching. Not desire, not even fear, but a longing that gripped him low from deep within and pulled. It was as if a piece of him had always belonged to the sea, and now, hearing her, it had remembered. The world around him faded: the cold, the dark, the rationality in his mind. None of it mattered. None of it existed; only her.

What lived behind her eyes wasn't human, but it wasn't cruel, either. It was everything he'd ever wanted, everything he'd ever dreamed of, and it was calling. Not with words, but with promise. A promise of surrender. And so, he moved to the water, toward her.

One pace, then another. No words, no hesitation: he moved like a man with purpose. The fishing rod slipped from his hand, clattering to the ground, and he walked off the jetty and into the water.

"What the…" Jace shot to his feet, the beer sloshing in his hand. "Mason! What the hell!"

Before the last word was out, Jace lunged forward, grabbing a fistful of his brother's coat just as his body slipped under the surface. Cold ocean spray leapt up around them as he leaned over the edge, Mason's weight nearly pulling him in.

What was a calm sea had suddenly turned choppy, the current tugging hard, spinning him sideways and under. Jace locked both hands into the sodden fabric of his jacket and braced against the slick wood.

"Hold on!" he barked, leaning back with all his weight. "I've got you!"

Mason's head broke the surface, sputtering, water streaming from his hair and eyes, but Jace kept him tethered, hauling him inch by inch, upward before the sea could drag him under. He jolted like someone waking up from a nightmare, shaking salt water from his face and mouth.

"What?" he gasped, head above the surface. "What happened?"

With one last heave, his brother dragged him the rest of the way up, both collapsing onto the rough, wet deck.

"You tell me, you idiot!" he snapped. "You walked right off the damn jetty!"

Mason looked stunned, blinking hard in confusion, his breath coming in short bursts. Behind them, the tide was again rolling in a relaxed tempo that murmured against the rocks, as though innocent of any involvement.

Mason, still blinking and dazed, looked down at the water, and then at his brother as he shivered, teeth chattering. "I thought I saw someone."

"So, you jumped in the freezing cold water? What the hell is wrong with you?"

"I…I don't know. I don't really remember."

By morning, the story was already at the diner. By noon, it had made it to the bait shop, the grocer, the general store, and the back table at the pub. By sundown, every old-timer in Greyhook was murmuring the same three words:

"It's happening again."

THIRTEEN

Cal had kissed her softly before leaving; the kind of kiss that lingered even after the door had closed behind him. Though he'd wanted to stay with her, the day couldn't wait. He had a full schedule ahead and couldn't afford to fall behind.

The docket including troubleshooting a temperamental HVAC at the health center, rewiring an aging electrical panel down at the docks, and, if there was time, testing the marina's corroded power outlets to make sure they were running properly before the next spring storm. Salt air chewed through wiring faster than anyone liked to admit, so half his job this time of year was keeping the town's systems running.

Isla had lingered in the doorway after he'd left. A trace of him still lingered in the house: the half-full coffee pot in the kitchen, the button-up cardigan he'd forgotten that hung on the corner of the living room chair, and the scent he'd left on Isla.

After a quick shower, she poured herself another cup of coffee to go, pulled on a sweater, and slipped her feet into worn canvas shoes. With two of Coraline's journals tucked under her arm, she stepped out into the morning. The air held a bite as she walked down the steps and let the door fall shut behind her. Fog clung to the treetops, lifting slowly, the only sound the steady hush of the tide and the stirrings of the cedars.

She followed the path from the March House down to the cove, the one worn smooth by years of bare feet and wandering thoughts. Near the bend where the rocks curled into a crescent over the sand, she spread out a blanket and settled cross-legged. With a deep breath, she took in the view of the wide marine world before her, it's silver reflecting off the sky.

The pages of Coraline's journals were crowded with sketches of coastline, tide charts annotated in her tight script, and fragments of half-formed thoughts. Two paragraphs, scrawled at the bottom of one page under the drawing of the cove, made her pause. Isla skimmed over it once, then again slower. On the third pass, she read it aloud under her breath, as if the sound might help it make more sense.

The sea doesn't choose at random; it calls to what mirrors it. Some it lures gently, others it pulls harder, but it always begins the same way...with the song not heard but felt. Those bound to the land rarely recognize it with their ears. Instead, it rises from somewhere deeper, heard within the marrow of their bones, felt with their whole being. It rises when the sea finds its reflection within them and when its longing meets their own. For some, the song comes like comfort: a tender croon of belonging that grows into ache, then hunger, then need or desire. For others, it arrives heavy with sorrow, steeped in absence and memory. It moves through the bloodstream, patient and precise, listening for their most secret ache, and once it finds it, it begins to whisper its claim.

A burst of chatter floated down the beach, jolting Isla from her focus: two youthful voices, their laughter carrying on the wind. Only pieces of their conversation were audible through the gusts.

"Jetty… water…jumped in…"

No more than that was needed to understand that the whole town must be talking about what had happened: the man on the jetty who'd walked into the sea. Some were frightened, quoting fairytales in hushed tones, while most just rolled their eyes and dismissed it all. Sirens, sea witches, water curses, kelpies…fear gave birth to stories like these, and people clung to them when they didn't know where else to turn.

Isla looked back to the journal and stared down at the lines again, recognition crawling up her spine.

Duncan.

The boy in the cove.

The man on the jetty.

The pull. That strange, quiet longing. Was this what Coraline had meant? The invisible thread drawing people toward the water? These men; lost, found, almost drowned. All drawn too close to the edge, like something just beyond the waves had called their names.

No. It couldn't be. She shut the journal and let it rest in her lap refusing to read on. For a long moment, she didn't move.

"This is ridiculous," she muttered aloud, if only to hear something solid in the silence. She shook her head. *Siren songs. Voices from the deep. Superstition! Poetic nonsense!* And yet, her hands trembled slightly as she picked up another journal and turned the page.

Flipping to a later entry, she skipped over years in a single motion. The handwriting had changed, smaller now and more delicate, as if the pen had become slightly harder to hold.

The date placed Isla at about thirteen.

Isla was always the brave one: fierce, certain, full of fire. Even as a child, she moved through the world like it belonged to her. Nothing shook her. That steady light inside burned bright, and Silas followed it like a compass. She was his anchor, his true north, and he grounded her in return. Two halves of a whole. Around him, she moved more carefully. Her fear was never for herself, only for him. And then the sea took him. Too soon. Too young. It wasn't his time. The pull should never have come for him; not for the twin soul. That choice should've been years away…we should've had more time.

Now, I wait for the pull to awaken in her. Since Silas died, the caution that tethered Isla has unraveled. She walks too close to the edge now, restless and fearless in ways that worry me. Maybe it's grief, or maybe it's something deeper. I do not fear the sea itself, it is a part of us after all, but I fear what will happen if it calls before she understands what it truly means to answer.

I've set boundaries to hold the tide at bay as long as I can. Some she respects, most she tests. I can't explain to her why they matter, not yet. I don't know how to protect her without breaking her, or how to prepare her without revealing truths she isn't ready for…when the song begins, when it rises in her, there will be no silencing it. No rule I've made will stop it. There will be no turning back.

The same melody I've carried my whole life lives in her. The same one Silas heard, somehow knowing it without ever being taught. It runs through our bones, and it waits.

Tonight, I watched her from the window and wondered: have I already lost her? Have all my efforts to shield her only drawn her closer to the thing I fear the most for her? I want her to choose freely, to walk into the truth with her eyes open. Because <u>it is</u> a choice. But until I know what role she's meant to play…I cannot trust the pull. Not yet.

Isla stared. *What the hell.* A new understanding was taking shape now of why the rules had been laid down so firmly, of the warnings that lacked explanation. For the first time, Isla could feel the reason for Coraline's fear but understanding that fear wasn't the same as knowing the truth. The deeper she read, the more her questions gathered like storm clouds on the horizon.

Why her? What role? What had happened to Silas, and what did it mean to be called by the sea? And, if you answered… what then?

Frustration sat heavy on her shoulders. There was no one left to ask, no voice to fill in the missing pieces. Just ink on old paper and the ghost of someone who had loved her enough to protect her but had chosen silence as the shield.

Gradually her attention shifted back to the journal, and she turned to the next page, then the next. Nothing but jumbled thoughts and the times of the changing tides. As she reached for another book, a photograph fluttered loose. Yellowing and torn at the edges, it floated softly into her lap. It was a picture of her mother, Morgan, young and barefoot on a beach that didn't look like coastal Washington. The sun was brighter, the sand pale and dry. California, maybe. Bright and easy, she wore a carefree smile.
From the pages where from the photo had fallen, another entry waited.

Morgan never truly heard the call. As a child she watched the waves but never felt the hum. It wasn't in her. There were no signs; no pull in her veins toward the water, no salt-blood symptoms as she grew and left the shore. I'm certain the legacy skipped her generation. Why, I don't know.

After Silas, she said she couldn't stay. Losing a child is to lose one's soul, so I save my judgement. This place was a reminder of what she had lost and what she was never meant to carry. Perhaps that is why she never felt grounded here: the sea didn't feel like home.

Once, she told me staying felt like an anvil on her chest, that she was drowning on dry land. Morgan wanted distance, normalcy...but the sea has never cared for normal.

Against my wishes, she chose the Severance. The pain was hers to carry, and so the choice was hers alone. It was the most agonising thing I've ever witnessed, and one I will never endure again. I honor it now, even though it left something hollow in its wake. In her. In me. In the family she drifted so easily away from.

The Severance. Isla's heart raced. All she'd ever been told was that her mother had left after Silas drowned and had never fully recovered. That space and time were what she had needed to heal, but this was something else entirely.

Morgan had always carried a kind of untamed beauty. Wind-swept, tan-skinned, with stories that trailed off before they reached their end. A wanderer by nature, she was unpredictable: the kind of woman who vanished without explanation and returned without apology. After weeks away, she'd come home with bruises in the shape of fingerprints, matchbooks from bars no one had heard of, and glitter smudged into the corners of her eyes. She'd moved through the world on instinct, led by feeling over fact, poetry over plans, and the quiet conviction that life was meant to be lived unrooted.

Every few weeks she would kiss her children's heads and whisper words into their hair like, *"I know you'll have a great time with grandma,"* or *"Mommy loves you, but I have to go on a special adventure."* Then, out the door she'd go, with love in her voice and absence in her footsteps.

Isla never doubted that she cared for them, but Morgan wasn't built for mothering. Born into a body that didn't want to stay in one place for too long, she craved freedom like oxygen. She chased festivals, caravans, and any man who made her laugh under moonlight. At eighteen, she'd gotten pregnant by one of those men. A musician, Isla had been told, though Coraline had never said his name. He stayed for a week, maybe two. Long enough to share a few songs and a bottle of mezcal. Long enough to promise the stars and then disappear. Morgan hadn't cried when he left; she'd just moved on to the next adventure with her belly growing beneath her sundress.

After the twins were born, she still couldn't stay put. The longest she'd lasted in Greyhook was a few months at a time. Coraline had done the rest: fed them, raised them, steadied the house and their hearts while their mother floated in and out like the fog. Then, when Silas died, she left and never came back. Not for Isla. Not for anything.

It had been years since Isla had spoken to Morgan. She had been twenty, already at art school, and the conversation had been polite but hollow. Two strangers circling something neither wanted to say out loud. Back then, Isla believed her leaving was part of her grief. A fracture born of loss. But this *Severance* didn't sound like grief. It sounded like ritual. It sounded like a choice.

Closing the journal, she took care not to crease the fragile photo tucked inside. With trembling hands, she placed them gently on the blanket, her eyes fixed on the sea.

Barely above a whisper, she spoke the words aloud. "The Tide Song."

The ocean answered with a long, slow breath, rising, falling, and in that moment, she understood. Whatever this was, it had already begun. An unseen door had opened, and she had already stepped through. There was no going back now.

Isla stood in the kitchen holding a fresh cup of tea. Mist pressed against the windows of the house, blurring the garden beyond into a wash of greens and greys. The house held a tender quiet as she sipped. It felt breakable and weighted with what she'd read in Coraline's journals and the things she'd learned. Truths were unravelling, though never straightforwardly. They came in fragments of small, uneven pieces. Coraline had known so much and said so little, and the pages she'd left behind were proof of that. Entries were scattered and out of order, feeling less like a record and more like a puzzle.

The quiet broke as her phone buzzed with a text.

CAL: Can't stop thinking about you. Dinner at the lighthouse? Say yes.

Torn between the rare, grounding warmth she felt with Cal and the need to keep unraveling her mystery, Isla paused as a familiar flutter stirred in her belly. After a beat of quiet deliberation, she smiled. Maybe a break wasn't such a bad idea.

ISLA: I'll think about it. I'm pretty busy, you know.

CAL: ...Wow. Cold.

ISLA: Just setting some boundaries.

CAL: ...

ISLA: Don't take it personally. I set them with spiders, too.

CAL: Spiders don't text back this fast.

ISLA: They also don't send me cryptic dinner invites.

CAL: What time should I not expect you? I'm going to start cooking at 6.

ISLA: Cooking? What's on the menu?

CAL: Chef's surprise.

ISLA: That sounds suspiciously like "whatever is in the fridge."

CAL: Not totally incorrect. Bring something red?

ISLA: Wine or a warning? 🚩

CAL: Hmmm. Surprise me.

ISLA: I'll bring wine. The warning should come standard in dating.

CAL: So...we are dating! 😍

ISLA: ...there will be wine.

CAL: ...that's not a no.

ISLA: That's a "don't push it." lol

CAL: Copy that. Proceeding with charm and restraint.

ISLA: Proceeding is risky. There is a red flag, after all.

CAL: Consider me warned, but I'm ignoring it in the spirit of romance and poor judgment.

ISLA: Our favourite kind.

CAL: And the most fun.

ISLA: We'll see. Don't burn the food.

CAL: No promises. Fire adds drama.

ISLA: So does food poisoning. Wait, it's not Tacoma gas station sushi, is it?

CAL: Definitely not.

ISLA: Excellent.

CAL: Then it's a date?

ISLA: See you at 6.

The screen dimmed in her hand. In the mirror, she caught a glimpse of the physical aftermath of her morning: mussed hair, a rumpled sweater, the soft disarray of someone lost in books and memories. Clearly, it was time to come up for air. A trip to the wine store first, and then a long, hot shower to rinse off the residue of her past and the dust of Coraline's words.

~

Wine & Beyond sat tucked near the top of Main Street, just half a block from the marina: a newer addition since Isla had left Greyhook. Small but inviting, the shop was lined with tidy rows of bottles, each dressed in elegant, curling script. The mellow hum of old jazz floated through the air as she stepped inside, met by the faint scent of cork and rich, woody fruit.

"Good afternoon!" A man stepped out from behind a stack of crates, voice bright with rehearsed cheer. Looking to be in his early forties, his hair was just a little too well quaffed, and he wore a smile that felt well practiced, likely in front of a mirror. "I'm Gavin. Can I help you find something?"

"I'm looking for a nice red."

Gavin brightened. "Wonderful. Let me show you a few that are popular."

They wandered toward the local reds, where his recommendations came with a little too much enthusiasm. Every bottle he showed her was followed by his gaze lingering on her mouth, then her hands, then back to her eyes.

"Cab Sav?" he asked, holding up a bottle. "Bold. Complex. Good with everything."

"Sounds like a dating profile," she blurted, the words escaping before she could stop them.

He laughed, too loud, too practiced, and ran a hand through his carefully styled hair.

"It's a local Washington vineyard. Very popular."

"You've suggested six lovely wines." She kept her tone light. "Is there one you'd recommend over the rest?"

"Your company makes it worth the effort," he said smoothly. "But personally, if I were sharing dinner with you, I'd go with the Pinot Noir. It's more full-bodied than most Pinots, and the flavor profile is to die for."

Uncertain whether to be flattered or mildly alarmed, Isla smiled uncomfortably. The more polite she was, the more confident he seemed to grow: his voice lower, words slower, with the kind of pauses that felt suggestive.

"Thank you, I'll look around and consider what you've recommended."

"Do you live around here?" he asked, settling in against the wine rack like they had all afternoon.

"Nearby."

"I live across the bridge. I'm not here much, but I could be."

Edging a half step back, she subtly reestablished some space, but he didn't seem to notice.

"Got dinner plans tonight with this bottle?" he pushed. "Anything or anyone special?"

"That's a bold question."

He grinned, unbothered. "I don't know, you just have that look."

"What look is that?"

"Like someone who doesn't eat alone."

She arched a brow. "You've really mastered the art of subtlety."

"You've just got this...energy." He leaned slightly closer. "I noticed it the second you walked in. It's kind of hard to ignore."

Something in his expression shifted; he was still smiling, but it didn't quite reach his eyes. It was glazed at the edges, like he'd wandered into a thought he couldn't shake. Isla felt it then, faint but unmistakable: that low tug in her chest, like a string being pulled tight. His words suddenly felt too close, too specific. She reached past him for a bottle of Merlot, then another, ready to be done. At her movement, his hand twitched like he meant to touch her, then stopped short in midair.

"You know, I rarely say things like this," he began, already far past the point of not saying them, "but you have such a beautiful speaking voice. It's quite captivating. I could listen to you talk all day."

Isla straightened, moving toward the register. "Thank you…?"

"I mean it. The way you speak is so endearing."

"Gavin," she said, calm but firm now. "You've been very helpful, but this… I'm sorry, but I'm not interested."

He blinked, and awareness flickered across his face. "Oh, right. I'm…I'm sorry. I'm not usually that forward. I don't know what came over me."

A bit dazed, he stepped back sheepishly allowing her the space she was attempting to create.

"If you could ring these up for me…"

"Great choice," he murmured. "Superb choice."

The checkout was quiet after that. Gavin worked quickly, eyes averted, and Isla kept her focus on the register. With both bottles clutched tightly to her chest like a makeshift shield, she stepped out into the street. The spell, whatever it was, had been broken.

The day sagged toward evening as the streetlights along Main Street blinked on one by one. Their glow bled softly through the light rain, casting halos over parked cars and puddles. Damp air kissed her cheeks as Isla stepped out of the wine shop, the bottles close against her chest. She drew in a long breath, tasting the sea on the back of it. Gradually, her posture began to loosen, until she spotted Mira Baird approaching on the sidewalk.

"Isla. Settling in?" Mira's smile didn't quite reach her eyes.

Suz followed a step behind, her expression warmer. "Hi, Isla."

"Hi, Mira. Hi, Suz." Isla adjusted the wine bottles in her arms. "How are you?"

Mira carried herself with the confidence of someone who considered every doorway an open invitation. Well-meaning most of the time, her curiosity often wandered straight into other people's business, no matter how firmly she claimed otherwise. She and Coraline had been close once, but by the time Isla reached middle school, their friendship had thinned into something more distant. Now, Mira had taken on the role of Greyhook's unofficial keeper of gossip and speculation, something she seemed to regard as her civic duty.

"I figured you were still in town, given all these strange things going on."

"A pleasure to see you, too."

Mira's smile thinned. "What do you make of it? Think any of it connects to Coraline's disappearance?"

"I really couldn't tell you, Mira." Isla forced a shrug, though the gesture felt brittle. "From what I've heard, it's just a few random mishaps."

"Is that right?" Mira folded her arms in front of her. "Not sure what you think passes as a mishap."

Isla sighed, she didn't have the energy to deal with this. "I don't mean to be rude Mira, but I really need to get going."

"I don't want to be rude either, Isla," Mira replied smoothly, "but since we're being honest, I think all this strangeness has everything to do with you and your family. And truthfully, it might be better for everyone if you went back to where you came from."

"Mira!" Suz's eyes went wide, and she turned quickly to Isla. "I'm so sorry. We were just going to get a bottle of wine for Mrs. Neilsen and her granddaughter: she had a baby. We won't keep you."

Suz tried to usher Mira on, but Mira lingered, her eyes dropping to the bottles in Isla's hands.

"Celebrating something? Or someone?"

Isla's jaw tightened. "Just dinner."

"With Cal?" Mira asked, too casually.

Suz shifted uncomfortably. "Mira…"

"You need to be careful," Mira continued. "Cal's a good boy. He doesn't need to get tangled up in… your complications."

Isla kept her voice even. "I appreciate your concern, but my dinner plans aren't town business."

Mira's smile vanished. "You need to be careful, or you need to leave. Your grandmother isn't here to shield you anymore, and we've had enough trouble."

Suz inhaled sharply. "Mira!"

The words struck, but Isla didn't let them show. She adjusted her grip on the wine bottles, steadying them against her hip before looking back up. When she met Mira's gaze, her expression had cooled.

"I don't need shielding," she said quietly. "And Cal doesn't need permission." With that, she left it, swallowing the fear that, despite everything, Mira's instincts might not be entirely wrong.

As Isla turned to go, Mira stepped into her path, cutting her off with a glare.

"You can brush it off and act like I'm crazy, but I know when something stirs in this town, and I think your family is at the center of it."

Suz, still desperately hanging onto a polite smile, tugged at Mira's arm. "That's enough Mira. Come on."

"I've seen how the sea responds to your family," Mira said, her voice low. "And it makes me question whether your brother's drowning was just bad luck."

Isla stopped short, the air leaving her lungs. "What did you just say?"

"Oh no, Mira!" Suz shook her head, covering her mouth with her hand.

Undeterred, Mira's voice dipped even lower. "The tides are all wrong, Isla. People are seeing things, hearing things, and all since *you* came back. If you care about this town at all, you'll leave before someone gets seriously hurt."

Isla couldn't speak: no words would come. Her fingers curled into fists, knuckles white, as rage simmered just beneath her skin. All she saw was red, and before she could gather a single coherent thought, a deep, guttural gurgle erupted from the storm drain beside them, tearing through the silence like a warning. In a sudden burst, a sharp jet of water hissed upward, spraying into the air. It lasted barely a second, but it was enough.

Mira jolted, instinctively stepping back. Her face had gone pale, but her eyes were locked on Isla.

"That's what I thought." Mira turned and disappeared into the wine shop.

Suz stared at the drain, then at Isla. "Jesus, Mary, and all the saints." She pressed a hand to her chest. "That scared me half to death."

She forced a shaky breath. "It's just pressure in the drains. Happens when we get shifts in the tide. The town never keeps up with maintenance."

Then she reached for Isla's arm, giving it a brief, reassuring squeeze. "You didn't deserve that, Isla. Mira shouldn't have said those things. She's been wound tight lately. The diner's been buzzing with nonsense, and she lets it get to her. But that's no excuse. I'm sorry."

With one last apologetic look, Suz slipped inside.

Isla remained on the sidewalk, stunned and alone. The mist clung to her skin, and she fought the unwanted tears that burned behind her eyes. She glanced once more at the storm drain; it was quiet now. Then she squared her shoulders, pulled herself together and turned toward the road that led to the sea.

FOURTEEN

Mira's words still grated at Isla, but she pushed them down. She refused to let them ruin the evening she'd been looking forward to.

Outside, the sky had deepened to smoky violet. The rain had moved on, leaving the air damp and cool, the distant cry of gulls cutting through the rhythm of the surf.

Isla set the wine on the counter, slipped off her shoes, and headed upstairs with one thought in mind: a long, hot shower.

Steam curled through the bathroom, the hot water washing the day from her skin. Afterward, she took her time, deliberate in the way she dressed, the care with which she styled her hair, and the way she chose to meet the night.

When she set out for the lighthouse, the last light had slipped toward the horizon. From the cliffs, the evening's quiet orchestra rose to meet her: the distant hum of crickets, the low rustle of wind through the dune grass, the birds echoing over the bay. The lighthouse beacon blinked against the darkening edge of the sea, and she followed it until she reached its stone steps.

Cal opened the door before she could knock. "Wow, you look…"

"Like I had a hell of a day and need a drink?"

"No." He stepped forward. "Like someone I wouldn't mind getting stuck in this lighthouse with."

Isla wore a soft, flowing wrap dress the color of deep burgundy. The fabric cinched loosely at her waist, draping just enough to suggest the curve beneath without clinging. The neckline dipped slightly, elegant but unassuming, and a light cotton wrap hung casually over one arm. The sleeves fluttered on her shoulders, and the ocean air had tangled her dark hair into loose, sea-swept waves that framed her face. Her makeup was simple: just a sweep of mascara, a hint of blush that warmed her cheeks and a subtle berry gloss that caught the light when she smiled.

Cal closed the door behind her as she stepped past him, and when he wrapped her in his arms, she sank into them.

"What's wrong?"

"I had a rough day."

Cal pulled back just enough to look at her face, his eyes full of concern.

"I ran into Mira earlier."

"She does have a way of leaving a mark. What happened?"

"Just a casual recommendation that I leave town, and that I'm single-handedly responsible for every strange thing that's happened in Greyhook, at least recently."

"I'm so sorry," he said as he blew out a slow breath. "If it makes you feel any better, last year she accused Walter's dog of being a skin walker." He offered her a crooked smile, trying to coax one from her in return. "She's loud and pushy, but she's wrong."

Isla half smiled and gave him a grateful kiss.

"Listen to me." Cal lifted her chin to look into her eyes. "You're not the reason for any of the things that have happened here. This is a town full of bored people who love to make up stories when accidents, or idiots, happen. Mira just wants an audience. Don't give her one."

Taking the wine from her hands, he led her into the kitchen. "You're here now. I'm going to pour you a giant glass of this lovely wine, and then I'm going to cook for you."

Thankful for his reassurance and the promise of a very large pour, she put Mira's words out of her mind and took in the smells of garlic and citrus that filled the keeper's quarters. "It smells great!"

"I make a damn good pan-fried halibut."

"Is that right? I guess we'll have to see about that."

"Ye of little faith. I even grated lemon zest, which, in bachelor terms means I'm basically a Michelin chef."

Cal uncorked the wine and filled their glasses, the dark red swirling richly in the low light. "This is a great bottle. Did you get it in town?"

"Mm-hmm." Isla said nothing about Gavin or his persistent advances. Instead, she gratefully accepted her glass and lifted it to her nose, drawing in the warm notes of cherry and red currant.

Butter sizzled in the skillet, melting under Cal's unhurried attention. He cooked with a relaxed demeanor that came only from someone at ease in a kitchen. Across the counter, Isla leaned back with her wine, the cool stem resting lightly in her fingers. Eyes drifting over him, she enjoyed the slope of his shoulders, the steady lines of his back, the way his short stubble outlined his angular jaw.

A knowing smile curved his lips when he caught her staring. "You're looking at me like I'm the one on the menu."

"Maybe you are."

"You know, you might have some competition in that department." Speaking over the sizzle, Cal angled the skillet and gave the fish a careful nudge. "I spent part of the afternoon at an 'emergency call' at Mrs. Elwell's, fixing her basement sump pump. I'm convinced she broke it on purpose just to keep me down there."

"I've heard she's quite the silver-haired minx." With a grin, she lifted her glass. "Let me guess: she offered you homemade lemonade, called you 'honey,' and stared shamelessly when you bent over."

Cal shot her a look of mock shock. "Twice! Lemonade *and* shortbread. I thought she was going to offer to adopt me."

"Quite the day! Basement damsels, seductive lemonade, and now dinner. Is there anything you can't do?"

"What can I say? I'm a man of many, many talents." Cal flipped the halibut with exaggerated finesse.

"Clearly. Do you offer a senior discount, or are you only in it for the shortbread?"

He pointed the spatula at her as a playful warning. "I'll have you know I'm very in-demand. Word gets around fast in Greyhook. You're lucky I could even squeeze you in."

"Fair enough. I will leave you a glowing Yelp review. 'Fixed the faulty wiring and made me dinner.' I guess I'll have to see what else the evening brings before I finish writing it." A sly grin, and she took another sip of wine.

"Careful. You keep that up and I'll gonna carry you into the bedroom and burn the fish."

"We wouldn't want to ruin your perfect five-star rating."

"No, we wouldn't." He turned back to the stove, giving the pan a quick shake. "Alright, your turn. Other than your guest appearance on the Mira Baird Show, how was the rest of your day?"

"Well, I spent a good part of the day reading about how I come from a long line of emotionally evasive women who like to write in circles."

"Sounds riveting. Anything the police can use?"

"No, but I did find an entry about my mother, who was more into incense and impulsive decisions than raising us."

"And here I thought you were just mysterious and brooding by nature."

"Don't be fooled. I'm a walking generational trauma sandwich. I warned you about the reg flag, but on the other hand, I make a mean whiskey sour, and I have excellent taste in bad TV. Really, I'm the total package."

Cal was grinning now, full and genuine. Before closing the space between them, he turned off the stove and stepped toward her, heat radiating from his body.

"I think you might be trouble, Isla March. And I am completely okay with it, red flags and all."

Isla set her glass down. "I'm suddenly hungry for something other than halibut."

The kiss began slow and tender at first, as though he were kissing away the wounds of her day. Then, it deepened, stealing the air between them. Arms looped around his neck; she pulled him close. His hands swept down her back and he pulled her in with a certainty that made her knees falter, until there was no space between them left to give.

In one swift motion, he swept her up into his arms. "I hope you weren't counting on an early dinner."

"I like my fish with a side of you."

"Then you've come to the right lighthouse."

Passion simmered beneath every glance, every brush of skin. Dim amber light spilled from the bedside lamp, casting soft shadows across the room as they stumbled in, still tangled in each other's arms, laughter and kisses trailing between them as the bedroom door clicked shut.

Cal traced the soft lines of Isla's shoulder and the faint scar that lived there before he eased her dress over her head and let it fall soundlessly to the floor. His mouth found the hollow of her collarbone, then wandered lower, leaving a trail of heat in its wake until she exhaled a soft, breathless sound. A sound he hadn't known he was starving to hear.

With unhurried calm, Isla unfastened his belt, her fingertips tracing the subtle line of the muscular V below it, savoring the way he shivered at her touch. Their clothes slipped to the floor in quiet succession; an urgency laced with care. When his mouth closed over her breast, she arched into him, fingers weaving through his hair as he moved across her: each kiss, each graze, drawing her deeper into the ache of wanting.

Slowly, he lowered her onto the bed with a tenderness that felt almost sacred. He held her like something precious: something he couldn't bear to let go. Instinct guided her legs, parting in a quiet invitation, and when he hooked his fingers around the edge of her underwear, he drew them down her thighs in one unbroken motion. Bending low, he pressed his lips to the inside of her thigh, each kiss a gentle promise. Moving higher, his mouth found her, and he explored with focused hunger, each motion purposeful and tender, savoring something he wanted only for him. A quiet gasp escaped her mouth as she tilted her hips toward him, urging him closer.

Every sound she made was a chorus, and every meeting of his mouth answered it. Euphoria surged through him. All that existed was the softness of her skin, the salt on her thighs, the way her breath caught just before she whispered his name.

Isla's breaths grew faster as heat coiled in the space they shared, each gasp winding her tighter. It lived in the way she moved beneath him, the urgency of her hands, the rising wave that carried them both higher. It built and surged until she broke against him in a shuddering release. Breathless, weightless, undone.

When he finally moved over her, everything else fell away. There was only heat, breath, and them.

“More,” she sang, her voice airy and tinged with need, hands sliding down to where she found him.

Exhaling sharply, he pressed his forehead to hers, grounding himself for just a moment. Ready in her hand, she held him there, savoring the weight of him. When he finally moved into her, it was slow and gentle. The connection drew a soft gasp from her lips, her body arching instinctively toward him.

As the pace between them built, so did a joyful ache that swirled with longing and desire. From within his mind rose a sound; soft at first, luminous. He didn’t know if it was real or imagined, only that it was beautiful and almost mournful in its sweetness. A resonance he felt only with her that made every nerve stand on the edge of ecstasy, made him want her closer until the world beyond them didn’t exist.

They moved together like they’d done this a hundred times before, finding a rhythm that rose and fell like the tide, pulling them both somewhere they couldn’t turn back from.

Wrapped in blankets with legs tangled, they sat on the kitchen floor eating dinner out of the pan. Cal’s culinary pride was wounded slightly, but they were both content anyway.

“I’m sorry I ruined our dinner,” he said, nudging a crispy bit of fish toward her with his fork.

Isla speared the piece and popped it into her mouth. “You absolutely did. However, I feel I was appropriately filled anyway.”

Cal nearly choked on his bite as pink crept into her cheeks. Eyes bright, she grinned at him. “What? I meant with love.” Her playful use of the L-word suddenly felt too serious, and she paused long enough to see if he noticed, but there was no visible reaction.

"I was right. You are trouble. But I'm hoping you'll be *hungry* again later." With a devilish grin, he reached out to run his fingers along the faint scar on her bare shoulder, then down her arm. He remembered when she got that scar: how she'd shown up at school the following day, scraped and stitched, and grounded for a month, but her spirit completely unshaken. *"Spite stitches,"* she'd called them. He'd admired her even then — stubborn, bold, impossible not to love.

When he kissed her again, he left no space for doubt. It was deep, wanting, and sure. As he pulled her closer, the blanket slipped, exposing skin to the dim light and cool air. A soft whimper caught in her throat the moment his mouth found the line of her neck and the fork slipped from her grip with a soft clatter to the floor.

What followed was slower this time. No rush, no urgency, just a quiet unfolding. Touch gave way to heat, then to something deeper and more intimate.

They stayed wrapped in the warmth they'd made, not speaking, not needing to. Cal kissed her neck, then the curve of her smile. The time he spent with her wasn't just pleasure, it was transcendence: a kind of unraveling. His whole body had opened, and she had drawn something from him. Now, that part of him belonged to her.

~

Isla sat on the top observation deck, curled beneath a blanket. Coffee in hand, she watched the sky shift through layers of light. The night still clung to her skin, the sensation of that glorious hum just beneath the surface.

The air smelled like her childhood: brine and kelp, rust and sand. And beside her, the scent of Cal. Warm skin, cedar soap, a hint of last night's wine, and something natural that belonged only to him.

He leaned against the railing beside Isla's chair, the worn iron cool under his fingers. His feet donned slippers and a navy cardigan hung loose on his shoulders, the collar turned slightly from the breeze that rolled in off the water. His eyes bright, stayed fixed on the line where sea met sky.

"Have you ever been underneath it?"

Isla looked up at him. "Underneath what?"

"The lighthouse," he said, nodding toward the deck beneath their feet. "There's a hidden cavern underneath the foundation. It used to be a dry cache, way back. They'd stash tools and tide goods...probably a fair bit of bootlegged rum during prohibition." He winked at her.

Isla blinked, surprised. "I didn't know that." A pause and a smirk. "Do you think there's any rum left down there?"

"Sadly, no, no rum left to run. And I didn't know it was there either until after Ray passed. I found some old schematics and notes tucked in the back of his maintenance logs. Half of this place isn't on any official records. It's kind of a secret. The tide is low now, so it will be accessible. Would you like to see it?"

A rusted hatch hidden behind the generator shed was the only land entrance to the underground cavern. A narrow metal ladder descended into the darkness below. Cal went first, his boots clanging softly on the metal, and Isla followed.

The air grew dense and cooler the farther down they went. When they stepped off the last rung, the cavern opened around them like a small, ancient cathedral, cold and still but not lifeless. Narrow fissures in the rock overhead let in thin shafts of light, and seawater seeped through in silver threads, spilling quietly down the walls before pooling beyond their feet. Water that would rise and fall with the moon.

There was no other way in, and no other way out but the deep, cavernous pools stretching down below the cave walls. Veins of mineral-rich stone shimmered faintly along the rock, and the drip of unseen water echoed from somewhere deep in the darkness. The scent of raw earth filled the space as ribbons of sunlight filtered through the cracks above, catching on the wet stone and scattering across the cavern in trembling bands of color.

Along the slick edges where water had receded, sea life clung in patient stillness. Anemones curled in like petals in jewel tones, starfish nestled in hollows, mussels clustered in glistening bands. It was a quiet kingdom suspended between tides, brilliant and alive, waiting for the sea to rise and reclaim it.

Isla stood near the center, arms relaxed at her sides, the sound of the ocean clearer here than anywhere above. The rush and retreat of waves and the low hum beneath them was the heartbeat of the sea itself. Closing her eyes, she let the sounds wash through her until the echo of it felt like her own pulse.

When she opened them, Cal had lit a hurricane lamp. Its small flame flickered in his hand, molten gold spilling across the walls as she turned in a circle, the shadows shifting with her. Deep grooves snaked through the stone, carved by years of water tracing the history of the tide's ebbs and flows. An enchanting calm settled over her.

"It's so beautiful."

"I thought you'd like it." Cal stepped back, giving her space to take it all in, their voices echoing off the walls. "I've only come down here a few times. The first time was…not great. It was late, so I creeped myself out a bit, but when the sun's high and the light hits just right through those little cracks, it's magical."

"It really is," she whispered, her voice soft with awe. A rare kind of peace settled over her, the kind that comes when you're exactly where you're meant to be. "This place holds secrets, history."

Cal watched her in silence, the corners of his mouth lifting into a soft, unguarded smile. She was content, light, and entirely herself. "What kind of secrets?"

"Huh?" Isla blinked, confused.

"You said, '*It holds secrets.*'"

"I did?

"You did."

Reaching out, she touched the water-scarred wall, dragging her fingers along the surface like she was discovering a message written only for her. She traced the lines, following the faint grooves as though she were reading braille. The stone was cold and damp, but it quivered with energy.

"Do you ever dream about drowning?"

Cals brows tugged together, considering her question. "I've had a nightmare or two when I was young, especially after…" His voice tapered off. "But not lately, no…do you?"

"They're not really nightmares anymore. Just deep-water dreams, and they don't feel scary, just…inevitable."

Light from the lantern shimmered over her face as Cal watched her.

"I think maybe that's natural after losing your twin brother that way. It's normal to worry about the same thing."

"I think something's happening to me, Cal." The words barely escaped, hushed under the low beat of waves

"Is this about Mira?" The muscles in his jaw worked. "About what she said to you yesterday? Because if it is…"

"No, it's not." The interruption came fast. "I don't know. I think…" Before she could speak again, tears fell down her cheeks. "I think maybe you should be afraid of me Cal."

Taken aback, Cal's mouth opened, but whatever he'd meant to say stalled in his throat. Stillness followed, her words hanging between them.

"What if all of those stories about people walking into the sea have something to do with Coraline, or something to do with me?"

"Hey, stop that." Cal reached for her hand, his fingers steady and sure against her skin. "There is nothing to be afraid of."

"But…"

"Isla," he interrupted, "Listen to me when I say, I am not afraid of you, and I never could be. You've been through a lot. Coraline is missing and you've just come back home after all this time to this town, and then dealing with Mira...it's all just…"

"A lot." She looked up at him with tear-stained cheeks. "Something just feels, I don't know. Different?" The sea seemed to answer through the cavern walls, a crashing wave roaring into the stone before fading into silence

"It *is* different. Things *are* different. *You're* different. We aren't kids anymore, Isla. You're bound to feel like things have changed after being away all this time." He waited, sensing there was more she hadn't said.

"Cal, do you believe Silas drowned?"

He paused, choosing his words with care. "Yes. Of course I do. Why wouldn't I?"

A shaky breath escaped her. "Mira said something about my family, and the ocean and how Silas drowning wasn't just bad luck." A sob escaped her. "What if she was right? What if there is more to it? My grandmother wrote things in her journals: warnings about me, and about the tide taking Silas. I think maybe it was my fault."

Cal's expression darkened with confusion. "The tide *did* take Silas. That's what they say when you drown and they don't find a body."

Isla met his eyes. "There were entries about blood, and water, and something waking up. About Silas being taken by the sea…it's all so cryptic and confusing. I'm scared."

Cal wrapped his arms around her, pulling her into the comfort of his chest, and he held her. Beside them, the lantern flickered: once, then again, its light stuttering. Shadows danced across the stone walls as the flame wavered, dimmed, then flared back to life again, sputtering as if disturbed by something unseen.

"I won't let anything happen to you, Isla. It's going to be okay. Don't let Mira or Coraline's words get inside your head. You've been through enough." He searched her face. "What happened to Silas was a horrible, heartbreaking accident. And it was never your fault."

Head resting against him, she consciously allowed her breath to sync with his, calming the storm that raged in her mind. There was so much she didn't know, and the steadiness in him and this place grounded her. For a few precious seconds, all she could hear was the calming beat of his heart.

"This town can get under your skin," Cal said quietly. "The stories, the legends, the gossip. People hear them long enough; they start to see patterns where there aren't any." He brushed his thumb along her jaw.

"That doesn't make them true." His voice steadied. "Grief doesn't make you cursed Isla. And it doesn't make you dangerous."

She didn't know how to tell him that the fear she felt was not for herself. It wasn't the sea, or the stories, or even the strange current waking in her blood. The fear she felt was for him. Cal didn't know about the pull that had begun to hum beneath her skin, or that he might already be standing in the path of its storm. But she could feel that storm, and it was building.

"We should head back up before the tide rises. This place will start to fill up soon." Cal kissed her forehead and began to pull away, but her arms tightened around him, so he stayed and held her a little longer.

The sea beat steadily against the grotto walls. Its pulse rising, the sound climbing higher as water slipped through the cracks and snaked across the floor, filling the tide pools and spilling around their feet.

Subconsciously, Isla closed her eyes. Not to shut it out, but to listen.

The sharp light of late morning had them blinking as they stepped out of the hatch. A sudden burst of wind teased Isla's hair into her face, and the bite of the air pulled her from the fog of her thoughts, forcing her back to reality. Daylight had stripped away the dreamlike veil of the cavern and the lull of the ocean's spirit, where she'd felt seen and understood.

Now, standing in the crisp morning air, the things she'd said felt too revealing. The trust she felt for Cal was undeniable, but regret needled her. In the dark, her voice had belonged with the salt and shadows. Here, in the cold light of day, it sounded like madness.

Cal pulled the door shut behind them, the rusty latch giving a reluctant creak before clicking home.

"How are you doing?" He placed a gentle hand on the small of her back.

"That was really beautiful. Thank you for showing it to me."

Cal studied her for a moment. "I know this has all been a lot. Is there anything I can do?" His tone was gentle.

"I'm just a little cold." The lie was thin and transparent.

"I'll make you some tea."

Inside, her silence followed them. Their connection still lingered, but her own vulnerability felt exposed now. It was something that belonged in the shadows, in the whispered spaces of the cavern, not up here.

Cal moved through the kitchen, setting the kettle to boil as Isla remained by the window, arms hugged tight across her chest, staring out at a cargo ship crawling across the horizon.

"Chamomile?"

It wasn't really a question, so Isla didn't answer. She didn't trust her voice. The chill had crawled into the room, into her skin, and into her thoughts. Coraline's journals. The cavern. Mira daring to say Silas's name the way she had. One memory brushing against the next, pressing in until goosebumps covered her skin. She shivered.

Turning toward the stove, she caught sight of the kettle that had not yet begun to steam. *Hurry up!* The words weren't spoken; they were felt. *Please, just boil*, she thought. The kettle whined sharply, then whistled. Loud and sudden. Too fast. It startled her.

Cal looked over from the cabinet where he was collecting their mugs. "That was quick."

Steam swirled out and evaporated into the air as Isla stared in disbelief.

Cal poured the scalding water and dropped a bag of dried yellow flowers into each mug, then handed one over. He watched her closely. "Drink this. You'll feel better."

"Thanks."

"Do you want to lie down?"

"No, I'm all right. I think you're right: it's just been an emotionally draining couple of days. Everything's catching up to me." To lighten the air between them, she smiled. "Or are you just trying to get me back into that new bed?"

He crossed his arms and leaned back against the counter. "Naturally. But I meant what I said down there. I'm not going anywhere, Isla."

Without another word, she nodded, the gesture easier than voicing the storm behind her eyes. Better to let him believe it had helped. Better to pretend she wasn't still hearing the whisper of the ocean, deep below.

FIFTEEN

Isla was restless and she itched to move. Her thoughts looped in circles with nowhere to land. Maybe if she walked, breathed, let her body lead where her mind couldn't follow, she could clear the static spinning in her brain.

The afternoon was soft, with faint traces of sunlight slipping through the thick white clouds. There was no breeze. The air held a quiet stillness: the kind that settled just before the weather turned. It was enough to draw Isla out the door.

"Just a short loop. I promise I won't go far. I'll be back before you miss me."

Cal had offered to walk with her, but she waved him off with a tired smile, already slipping on her shoes and wrapping herself in a throw blanket. There was worry on his face, but he didn't push; just kissed her gently, brushing a thumb over her knuckles as he let go of her hand.

Since the cavern, something in her had changed. It was subtle, but it was there. Cal watched her go, concern etched in his eyes. She moved the same, spoke the same, but there was a distance in her now. He couldn't shake the feeling that she'd carried something back he couldn't see or understand. All he could do was let her go and wait.

Step by step, the lighthouse receded behind her, its rotating light still visible in the corner of her eye until a bend in the path and a jut of rock finally obscured it from view. At the rocks' edge, Isla paused beside a salt-scoured post that marked the drop-off into the cove. Below, the land gave way to jagged stone before softening into a bed of wet sand and tangled kelp beds, dark shapes shifting just beneath the water's surface.

There she stood by the ocean, breathing deeply, letting her thoughts drift. This was one of the only places that had truly steadied her these past few days.

Past the foam line, she spotted movement: at first a trick of light, or a school of fish, but then, the surface bulged. Something long and silvered moved with purpose. Gracefully, the shape glided beneath the surface; no splash, no breach. Gone as quietly as it had appeared.

The hair at the back of her neck lifted. It wasn't what she'd seen that had unnerved her; it was the strange awareness that whatever it was, had seen her, too. She stayed frozen a moment longer before taking a single step forward.

"Show me again!" she whispered.

Nothing. A couple of strange coincidences and she was already thinking she could command the tide. The thought made her feel childish.

Light dew clung to the slope, and she followed the narrow trail carved along the cliffside, continuing as it twisted down toward the cove. At the bottom, Isla stepped toward the seashore. Salty mist hung in the air, a hint of spray bouncing off the sand and rock. She let the blanket slip from her shoulders, dropping onto the sand. One bare foot eased forward, her toes curling into the damp earth. She took another step as the tide stretched toward her, lapping just short of her skin.

Instinctively, she extended her arms toward the water like she meant to greet it, and as the sun peeked through the clouds, a faint shimmer moved across her arm: a crystalline dusting of white along her forearms and the backs of her hands. Salt, in perfect patterns of crescent-shaped mirrors, glistening as she moved. She hadn't been in the water yet, not today. Even so, she could taste it on her lips, feel it clinging to her skin.

The kettle. The thought stayed with her. Was it at all possible it boiled because she wanted it to? Because she *needed* it to?

Isla faced the waves. Tendrils of hair danced across her cheeks, and like a spellcaster in a storybook, one arm lifted, trembling slightly. This was not a command, but an invitation. Just a hand, and a hope. Ridiculous, foolish, and desperate, but she couldn't stop herself from reaching, asking. Breath shaking, she closed her eyes. Saltwater kissed her toes, and a resonance stirred within in her chest: a thrum of recognition. The ocean surged forward as if it had been waiting for this moment.

Come closer. The thought wasn't formed in words, but a vibration of will. A summoning whispered from somewhere deeper, in a forgotten language she was bound to relearn.

The ocean responded. A wave larger than the rest gathered from nothing. It rolled toward her, then crashed gently against the rocks beside her. Foam sprayed, and a thick strand of kelp rose in the aftermath and slapped the surface just feet from where she stood. Some secret part of her recognized the movement before it happened, and her eyes flew open.

An invisible thread now stretched between her and the water, thin but real: a pull in both directions so strong she could almost feel it wrapping around her soul. Dropping her hand to her side, she let out a long exhale. The beat of her heart slowed, but she felt like her pulse was racing, strumming in time with the roll of the ocean, matched by the rhythm of the sea, beat for beat.

Show me again. Raising her fingers in an upward motion, the water at her feet rose before her, gathering into a shimmering column that glistened in the speckled sunshine. The surface pulsed, waiting for her next command, and as her fingers lowered, so did the water.

A thrill bolted through her: gratitude. The wave had risen when she'd called; the kelp had shifted in reply. The sea had answered. Thoughts scattered like loose pages in a breeze: Coraline's notebooks, the underlined phrases, the scribbled margins.

The draw will come. Then, the small coincidences. You'll wonder if it's imagined.

Isla stepped forward, deeper now, and step by step the water lapped at her calves, then her thighs. A welcome current moved around her ankles like a silk ribbon, gliding upward in a slow embrace. No pain. No fatigue. No cold. Her spine lifted, her shoulders uncurled: muscles she hadn't known were tight let go. Each step forward felt like surrender. The water rose past her ribs, then her collarbone. It wrapped her like a swaddle, and it felt superb.

Then, gradually, the silence eased. It entered through her bones and her blood; a melody rising within her. Wordless. Endless. Ancient. It pulsed beneath her skin, low at first, then rising into something luminous and harmonic. A song shaped by water. No lyrics: just harmony and sweet, beautiful, ache. It had no name, but she knew it. It had no language, but she spoke it.

Silas had hummed this melody. Not consciously or deliberately, but in fragments when he was small during storms or sleep or play. Coraline, too. On feverish nights, murmuring lullabies with far-off eyes, her voice drifted with this song that Isla now knew had always been a part of her. The harmony rose clear and familiar, and the ocean echoed it back with soothing affection, as if to say, *"You belong here."*

There was no resistance and no fear. Just a wholeness, and the potential of a power that was now awake, liquid and patient, waiting for her to claim it.

Isla felt alive and whole.

At the lighthouse, Cal stood at the window, unease spreading through his gut. He tried telling himself Isla needed some space to breathe, to walk it off, but he knew something was shifting. There was something disconcerting about the way she'd gone, silent and tight-shouldered, with that faraway look in her eyes.

After pacing for nearly an hour, he began to panic. The sky was changing, and the tide was rising. *She should have been back by now.* He checked his watch again: ninety-five minutes. *Too long.*

With his shoes already on, he took off down the path. The trail twisted with loose, dewy gravel between coastal scrubs and jagged rock, each passing bend a blur as he ran.

Now partway down, from this angle, she was easy to spot, like something pale painted into the dark water. Only a shape at first: small, still, and mostly submerged, her hair spread around her in inky swirls, the blanket she'd wrapped around her shoulders abandoned on the shore.

"Isla!" he called. Once, twice, a third time.

No response; not even a flinch. Neck-deep in the tide, she didn't move. She just drifted with the movement of the waves as Cal clambered down the bluff and hit the sand running. He kicked off his boots and plunged into the surf, jeans dragging him down with every soaked stride. The water bit him like a blade, ice-cold, clawing its way into his bones. Not Isla, though.

Even from here, he could tell she wasn't shivering. Appearing almost warm, she looked lit from the inside out, splayed out as if enjoying a soothing swim under a sun-drenched sky.

The water around her was still, unnaturally so. A perfect ring of glass-like calm, like the ocean had formed a sanctuary just for her. Cal waded closer. Something was wrong: she wasn't moving, and his panic surged. Five feet. Three. One. When his hands found her arms, her skin was warm beneath his fingertips. Not flushed or fevered, but radiant.

"Isla! Are you okay?"

Gracefully, she turned toward him. The velvet smile that curved her lips was soft and strange, beautiful and inviting in a way that made his stomach twist. It wasn't romantic or seductive, but seraphic. It was a smile that hinted she knew something he didn't. Or maybe, for a heartbeat, that she was someone else entirely.

"What the hell are you doing?" he gasped, raw with cold and fear. "You're going to freeze to death out here!" His grip tightened slightly, not to restrain but to secure.

As she blinked, it pushed back the fog behind her gaze until the world came into focus again. "It's all right! I just needed to feel it."

"Feel what? The water?"

"Everything." Isla's voice wasn't wild; it was crystal clear. Centered, like she'd been waiting for something and had finally found it.

"Dammit, Isla. You scared the hell out of me."

"I'm sorry." Expression calm, her eyes slid past him toward the horizon. "I was listening to something else."

A chill spread under Cal's skin, colder than the tide lapping around his waist. "What do you mean, something else?" He searched her face for any sign of collapse: cracks, panic, unraveling, but found none. She was present and almost serene. His large hands moved over her arms, instinctively trying to bring warmth to her skin, though he was the one who was trembling.

"You scared me." His teeth chattered from the cold. "You said you were going to be right back."

A slow breath eased from Isla's lips as she looked down at where the water touched her. It still felt warm to her, comforting. "There's something about the sea. When I'm in it… I don't feel sick, or tired, or scared. I feel good."

The words echoed, strange and beautiful, until she noticed the tremble in his jaw. Cal's whole body shivered now, shoulders tight, lips turning slightly blue. His clothes clung cold and heavy.

"Oh my…Cal," she gasped, placing her hands on his arms. "You're freezing!"

"I was w-worried. I thought you…were c-caught in an…undercurrent…or s-s-something." An attempt to speak came out clipped and strangled from the icy temperature overtaking his body. Before he could finish, she moved against him, arms looping around his neck, pulling him in. She pressed her lips to his, and her warmth to his chest. The effect was instantaneous. Heat bled into him like liquid sunlight. More than just surface warmth, it was deep, all-encompassing heat. The surrounding air and water seemed to adjust itself as the cold that had cut through his spine moments before ebbed into something soft and pleasant.

"What's happening?" His voice was barely audible as he began to relax.

Isla stayed in his arms a moment longer, letting the heat pass between them completely. Lazy currents spiraled around their legs, slower now, reluctant to let them go. Then, without a word, she pulled back and took his hand. The swirls trailed behind them, and together they waded from the shallows.

Damp fabric clung to their skin, and as they reached the sand, she grabbed the blanket from where it lay and wrapped it around Cal's shoulders.

The air was cooling quickly, but he still felt warm. Cal blinked down at her, water dripping from his hair, heart pounding louder than the surf. Behind them, the place where they'd stood still gently churned, the sea circling in slow, unnatural spirals. When he looked up, as if it were aware he was staring, it calmed, flattened, and disappeared into the foam.

"Did you see that?" Cal's voice was low, tight with disbelief, trying to make sense of something he couldn't unsee.

Isla followed his gaze, and a faint, haunting smile touched her lips. There was no fear in it, no apology.

"Yes," she said softly. "And I think it saw us, too."

They were greeted by the house's welcome warmth. Isla's wet camisole still clung to her ribs, the chill of the walk home beginning to settle into her bones. Bare feet left traces of sand and grass across the hardwood as she moved past the entryway. At the hearth, she knelt and struck a match. The flame flared, catching the bundle of kindling, and the fire stirred to life, crackling softly in the quiet room. Behind her, Cal stayed in the doorway, uncertain whether to step forward or give her space.

Isla moved into the kitchen, switched on the kettle, and hung the damp blanket over a chair to dry. Her motions were steady, almost careful, with the kind of intentional purpose that came from needing a moment: space to think, to breathe, to shape the explanation that was looming. Then, she paused, braced both hands on the counter, and lowered her head.

"What happened out there?" Cal whispered, running his hands through his damp hair.

"I don't know how to explain it, or even if I should."

"You should." He took a few steps closer. "Whatever it is, I can handle it."

An unreadable expression passed over her as she turned to face him. Gone was the glowing certainty from the water, and in its place was guarded restraint. It was the mask you wear when you're deciding how much truth is safe to share.

"Wait here," she said.

The creak of the staircase quieted as her footsteps vanished upstairs. Cal stayed planted in the kitchen. A minute passed, then two. Long enough for his anxiety to return.

Isla reappeared cradling an old shoebox, the cardboard tattered with age and warped from the damp. Gently setting it on the kitchen table, she peeled back the lid. Inside were stacks of notebooks with curling covers, folded letters tied together with sea-worn twine, newspaper articles, and Coraline's journals.

"I found these hidden away." She pointed to the letters. "Some were hers that she never mailed. Some came from people in other coastal communities."

Cal didn't move; his attention was locked on her. His eyes drifted briefly to the contents, then back to her face.

"She marked pages, underlined passages about bloodlines and gifts passed down. Voices, pulls, and songs." Isla's fingers hovered over the edge of a notebook before tapping it. "I think she knew something was happening to her: some kind of change. I think that's why she left, and I think…" her voice dipped lower, "I think it might be happening to me, too."

A full minute passed before she spoke again.

"I've been hearing things, almost like music inside my head. Sometimes when I'm falling asleep, sometimes when I dream." Isla whispered it like a secret. "At first, I thought I was imagining it, but then I heard it when I was awake, too. It was the strongest when I was in the water today."

Alarm filled Cal's face. Carefully, he asked, "Have you been sleeping?"

"Yes…well, most nights." She hesitated and rubbed her arms. "I think maybe I've been sleepwalking. The other night I woke up with wet hair and damp sheets. I smelled like seaweed. I've been having dreams of swimming and of voices calling to me. And when I wake up, well, sometimes I draw or paint things that I don't remember. But then physically, I feel…better than ever."

A folded piece of paper sat on top of the pile of letters in the shoebox. Isla reached for it and passed it to Cal.

"This is from my blood work a few weeks ago. I'd been sick and exhausted. I wasn't sleeping and I had aches and numbness and ringing in my ears. The doctors said it was all in my head. All my tests were normal except for one thing. My sodium levels were high."

Cal studied the numbers on the sheet but said nothing. His eyes moved back to hers. The concern was clear now. "I don't understand what this means."

Isla pulled out the photocopied article from *The Berkley Wellness Letter. Salt-Blood Syndrome: Myth, Misdiagnosis, or Mutation.* She passed it over. As she spoke, he skimmed the page.

"Salt-Blood Syndrome. It's not widely researched, but there are a few case studies. Isolated incidents of people who have shown strange physiological improvements the closer they live to the ocean. Lowered inflammation, stabilized blood pressure, improved sleep, enhanced memory. For some, the body literally regulates better in the salty sea air, but away from the ocean, their bodies produce higher sodium to create some kind of balance."

"So, what? You need to live near the coast to feel good? I mean, scientifically it's kind of weird, but that seems like a simple solution. A lot of people prefer to live near the coast for the health benefits."

"I don't think that's all of it. Not for me, anyway. It's not just the salt and sea air. It's something inside me reacting to something out there. I don't know what started it, and I don't know why."

Cal stared at her and set the paper down. Then, he sat, hands braced on his knees.

"Let me get this straight. You think Coraline left on purpose?" He rubbed his temples, then added with an edge of disbelief, "And that it has something to do with all of *this*?" He motioned to the box.

Isla nodded. "I think something was happening to her, and I believe she left by choice. I don't know what triggered it, or how long it was happening, but I think she was aware of it, so she began to document it over time. She marked it in her journals and cross-referenced with stories from other places. It wasn't just rambling; she was trying to leave a…a map."

Cal looked down at the table, then back at her face. "And now you think you're on the same path she was."

"Yes. Well, maybe not the same, exactly. But it's a path, and it's heading somewhere I can't ignore. Something is physically happening to me."

The kettle clicked behind her, but neither of them moved to pour it.

"I feel like I should be nervous or afraid of whatever this is, but I don't feel anything bad. I feel good, clear-headed. If Coraline felt it, too, then maybe it wasn't about abandoning us. Maybe she left to search for whatever this is all about. Or maybe she was afraid she'd get someone hurt if she stayed."

"That's what you're worried about? That's why you're afraid."

"Yes. I'm not afraid of what's happening to me, Cal, but I *am* afraid that whatever's unfolding in Greyhook might be because of Coraline, or someone like her. Someone like me. And I'm terrified that something will happen to you." The words landed harder than she meant them to, but the truth rang clear beneath their edge.

Cal sat back, slowly letting the weight of her confession settle in the space between them. "I believe you," he said finally. "I don't get it, but I believe that you're not imagining it."

"I know it sounds crazy."

"I've lived in Greyhook my whole life, and I've seen too much to believe everything can be explained by weather patterns and ghost stories. You're not crazy. I don't like it, but the legends must come from somewhere, right?"

Gratitude shimmered in her eyes, and she let out a slow, shaky breath.

"Whatever this is, it touches people. If this is what pulls them in, I don't know how to protect you from it, and that is what I'm afraid of."

"You don't need to protect me, Isla. I can take care of myself. I choose you, whatever that looks like."

With tears in her eyes, she reached for his hand and held it tight. The reassurance held her, but somewhere beneath it, doubt still stirred: not in him, but in what might come. In what loving her might cost him. Coraline had understood that, and now, finally, Isla did, too.

Cal stayed the night and held Isla until she fell asleep, his arms wrapped tightly around her. The dreams were quieter tonight: no strange tides, no shadows beneath the surface. Just the warm whisper of his breath against her neck, anchoring her.

Sometime after midnight, Isla woke to the sound of the quiet shifting of floorboards groaning under gentle steps. Only listening at first, she tried not to open her eyes, but she knew Cal had slipped out of bed. There were the soft click of locks turning, the low rattle of the back door latch, the faint squeak of a window closing. He moved through the house with purpose, checking every entry, as if securing the house might hold off something he couldn't name.

It touched her: the way he moved so carefully, trying not to wake her. There was something unshakable in him; a man guarding something precious…or dangerous. In the dark, she couldn't decide what unsettled her more: that he felt the need to keep something out, or that, somehow, for her own sake, he might be trying to keep her in.

In the morning, he'd kissed her before heading off to work and promised he'd be back by nightfall.

"Don't go in the water today. Please," he'd asked just before stepping out. The words carried enough weight on their own; he didn't have to tell her why. In fact, he was starting to sound a little like Coraline, but this time, Isla understood the reasons.

After finishing her morning coffee, she climbed the stairs to her grandmother's bedroom. She paused at the threshold; arms folded across her chest. Instinct no longer guided her. It was something deeper now: an insistent, invisible pull. An undercurrent she couldn't ignore. A need to keep moving, to understand.

As she crossed into the room, she wasn't sure what she expected to find. The closet held nothing new. The drawers were filled with the usual remnants of a life long-lived: silk scarves, loose buttons, a few bracelets tarnished by time. Still, she kept searching. Something unseen waited just out of sight, she was certain of it. All she had to do was keep looking long enough to find it.

"Okay," she murmured into the silence, tugging open another drawer. "I'm looking! There must be something you want me to find. Something I *need* to find."

Isla climbed to the attic next, coughing through the dust that hung in the air. Sunlight slanted through the small round window, cutting across rows of brittle cardboard boxes. Remnants of their lives.

One by one, she combed through them. Coraline's old photo albums and Knick knacks. Isla's yearbooks and cassette tapes. Silas's worn-out shoes.

The sight of a red hull and a white sail tugged loose a memory Isla hadn't touched in years. The little wooden boat Silas used to float in the tide pools — he had loved that boat. They couldn't have been more than four or five when their mother disappeared on one of her so-called "adventures." That time, she'd been gone longer than usual. Isla remembered finding Silas sitting in the hallway, clutching that tiny boat to his chest like it was the only thing holding him together; as if, by staying perfectly still, he could will her to walk back through the door and gather him into her arms. Tears had welled in his eyes, his face crumpling quietly, devastatingly broken.

In that shadowed stretch of hallway, Isla had crouched beside him and wrapped him in her arms. She told him stories: outrageous stories of pirate ships and beautiful queens. Of sea creatures who stole lemons from pirates just to make lemonade. Eventually he had laughed; that part she remembered most of all. How his face lit up through tears. How proud she'd felt for making him smile.

A tender ache pressed against her heart. There were so many things they'd never said, so many memories they'd never had the chance to make. She held the little boat in her hands and let herself miss him. Just for a little while.

In a crowded corner nearly swallowed by the shadows, she spotted a blue and green toy chest. White, hand-painted letters curved across the front that said *Silas*. Coraline had given it to him the Christmas before he'd drowned and he'd been so proud of it, eager to fill it with his treasures. She could still see him kneeling by the Christmas tree, small fingers tracing each painted letter like he was learning his own name for the first time.

In front of it now, Isla dropped to her knees and lifted the lid. Memories filled it to the brim: stuffed animals, building blocks, sand molds. All little pieces of happiness that filled his day to day. As she shifted the toys around, a glint in the bottom left corner caught her eye. Half-hidden below a dust-furred dragon sat a small cedar box, its brass hinges tarnished green. She reached for it and dragged it out into the light.

Inside were the books of her childhood: a patchwork library of fairytales and folklore, some with linen spines fraying at the edges, others with hand-stitched bindings and loose pages slipping free. Old cocoa stains and sticky fingerprints marked one cover, while others remained clean and nearly pristine. There were a few she instantly recognized: *The Little Mermaid*, *The Sea Fairies* by L. Frank Baum, and a tattered version of *Grimm's Fair Tales*. Others she'd never seen before.

A wistful smile played at her lips as she lifted each one out, stacking them carefully. The worn edges and faded prints offered the kind of comfort only familiarity could bring. Coraline had once read these stories aloud with animated gestures and a twinkle in her eye, each page a performance, until that day. After Silas was gone, the books quietly disappeared. Had they contained dangerous truths wrapped in bedtime tales? Or were they just too painful to look at?

Isla gathered the books and carried the cedar box downstairs, where she spread a few of the unknown volumes across the kitchen table. Unsure where to begin, she reached for the first, a weathered book with a cracked spine and text half in Latin. The first few pages revealed intricate drawings of shells and star maps. She set it aside and moved on.

The second, *Mermaids: The Legends of the Sea*, contained a few stories she recognized. Romantic tales of women and songs who lured sailors to their greatest loves or to their deaths. Legends of hidden kingdoms, lost realms, and foreboding omens.

The third book felt heavier in her palm. Its cover was slate blue and smooth as stone, unmarked except for a single image carved with silver into the leather. A woman stood knee-deep in surf, mouth open in song. Sea foam coiled around her figure, winding up her legs and hugging her ribs. The expression made Isla pause; her face felt unnervingly familiar. A face not unlike her own, though the figure's hair was longer and wilder than Isla's and writhed like seaweed in a storm. Not quite herself, but close enough for a second look. Below the image, the title was etched in faded black ink: *Of Those Who Sing Beneath the Sea.*

Isla's chair scraped quietly across the wood floor as she sat and opened the book. Chapter titles rose from the page like incantations.

1. *The Voice as a Vessel*
2. *Lures, Laments, and Loss*
3. *The Lunar Cycles*
4. *The Severance*
5. *The Binding of the Tide Soul*

6. The Anchor

The words pulled her forward, her thoughts snapping awake all at once. *The Severance.* Hurriedly, she flipped to chapter four, but there her fingers halted. Several pages had been torn out, the edges ripped clean. Deliberately removed — but why?

A wave of disappointment filled her as her heart sank. The entire chapter was missing. Whatever *The Severance* was, her mother had chosen it and now the truth lay beyond her reach. She didn't know if she would ever have those answers, but with or without the Severance, she couldn't stop now.

After a moment she pulled herself together and turned to the first page.

1. The Voice as a Vessel

They are not sea creatures, but women and men tied to the history and memory of the sea: the echo chambers of the world before land. Their power lies not in the song itself, but in the longing it creates and the connection it ensures. Each song has a shape. Each voice a purpose.

Some anchor themselves to the land, yet their connection to the water does not fade. The power within them endures, but only until the final choice is made. Only then, in the decision to stay or return, does the magic shift. Until that moment, they exist in a state of tension: caught between land and sea, inheritance and identity. It is in that liminal space where both their greatest vulnerability and deepest strength reside.

Further on, in narrower type:

The gift begins gently, and the soul remembers gradually. A soft beckoning in the blood, a memory older than time. When sea touches skin, the shift will awaken. The voice, once ordinary, grows from within and becomes a mirror and a vessel, reflecting what is felt, amplifying what is hidden. It carries more than sound: it carries truth.

Salt links. Moonlight binds. These are the ancient threads, woven through bone and breath, pulling the chosen back toward what they are. The awakening is not always loud, but it is always certain. It arrives like dusk, like dawn, like the tide returning to shore. It is unstoppable. Forever waiting to be remembered.

Isla turned the page.

They speak not only to stone-born men, but to what they have buried.

Memory.

Fear.

Love.

Loss.

Desire.

Need.

Home.

Isla's heart raced as she took in the words on the page. Wind moaned past the windows, and down deep within the plumbing, the house gave a long, breathy sigh. Leaning back in her chair, with the book still open, the words took root.

The next page held diagrams of vocal cords sketched in fine lines, waveforms folding into glyphs, women with open mouths casting rings of sound like ripples from their bodies. Beside one image, off to the side in sharp, hurried script, Coraline had written:

The song waits for no one. This power comes at a cost, but the choice is ours to make.

A thought flitted through Isla's mind as she read Coraline's notes: *power is never free*. What if the cost was Cal? Below the margin, Coraline had scribbled more musings:

I keep thinking about the feeling: the urge to swim, to swim out and to keep going; not because I want to die, but because some days it feels like I'd be going home.

Isla shivered despite the warmth of the kitchen. She closed the book slowly, turning it over in her hands to study the illustration on the cover. She'd seen images like this before in stories and children's books, but this rendering felt older, more evocative, more primeval.

Curiosity drove her, and she flipped to the back of the book. There, more sketches followed of women drawn in careful lines and shadow. Not the wide-eyed, softened figures of her childhood; there were no seashell bras or sparkling tails here. This was something truer, watching her from the pages. These women were sea-forged and strange, beautiful in a way that made her ache. Legs, long and elegant, human-shaped but dappled with subtle scales that shimmered like abalone in the inked shading. The bone at the knee joint curved differently; not wrong but adapted. Hands and feet were delicately webbed with the gossamer threads of a morning spiderweb. Perfectly designed for motion in a world just beneath the surface.

The beauty of their smiles was captivating, each curve of their lips revealing perfect pearlescent teeth, the outermost polished sharp to a point. Hair spilled behind them like dark water, their skin pale as moon-washed stone, and their eyes, vast and deep, were ringed in silver. They looked deep enough to drown in.

Isla pushed the books aside as she took it all in. What she was seeing wasn't just information; it was recognition. She was caught between the shape of who she'd been and the shadow of something ancient that was rising within her.

Far below, past the floorboards and stone, beyond the bluff and into the sea, something had felt the shape of her thoughts. It had always been listening — but now, it knew her name.

SIXTEEN

Cal returned to the house earlier than expected. He'd tried to work, but constant thoughts of Isla unmoored him. By noon, he'd given up pretending and called it a day. When there was no answer to his knock at the door, he opened it and stepped inside quietly, respectfully. A mug sat half-full, cooling on the windowsill, the kitchen empty. From deeper inside the house, a faint, breath-like hum travelled wordlessly toward the entrance, and he followed the ethereal sound into the sitting room.

There Isla sat with her sketchbook balanced on one knee, barefoot in the slanted afternoon light. Charcoal smudged along the heel of her hand, and she faced the ocean through the salt-flecked window. Her eyes were half-lidded, her lips parted. The tune she hummed wasn't conscious, but it moved through her like a sweet and lovely echo.

When she saw him from the corner of her eye, she startled and pressed her hand to her chest before easing into a smile.

"Oh, it's you. You scared me. You're back early."

"You were humming," he murmured, afraid to break whatever spell she was casting on the paper below her.

She flushed. "Oh, I didn't realize."

"I brought something." Cal lifted a thin folder bristling with paper clips and neon post-its. "Can I show you?"

At her quiet cue toward the kitchen, he followed, and they settled side by side at the table, elbows touching, papers fanned across the surface. Scientific journals, deep-sea acoustic studies, fragments gathered from obscure marine biology forums.

"I was up most of the night reading on my phone," Cal said. "I stopped at the library this afternoon on my way here." He slid an article toward her. "Pelagic phenomena. Deep-tide echoes. Low-frequency vibrations that travel through saltwater and are strong enough to affect mood, scramble spatial orientation, sleep cycles, even disrupt motor control. Usually below human hearing, but not beyond human feeling." One finger struck the page. "Some researchers even believe these waves slip into the brain through the nervous system. There've been cases of memory loss, vivid dreams, shifts in behavior. Whales use similar frequencies to speak across oceans. Naval sonar has driven pods to beach themselves. It's not magic; it's biology. It's physics. And I think this could be your answer."

Isla flipped through one of the articles. A diagram showed concentric sound waves mapped in a tidal basin, with annotated notes linking certain frequencies to neurological responses.

"You think this is what's happening to me? That this is what I'm hearing?"

"Maybe. It matches what you've described: the sounds, the dreams, the way it draws you in." Cal's words carried the certainty of someone totally unaware that the same current was already threading through him; faint, but growing.

"But where does it come from?"

"I don't know." Arms crossed, he leaned back. "Some of the research suggests tectonic vents or magnetically active trenches. Places where deep pressure warps sound into something else. What matters is that it's a real thing, and that means there must be a way to stop it from happening."

“Stop it…?” The words felt uneasy on her tongue. The raw energy from the cove still curled wildly through her muscles. The surge that had made every nerve in her body spark awake hadn’t felt dangerous to her: it felt freeing.

“It says here the echoes have been reported everywhere from coastal Iceland to parts of Indonesia.” Cal tapped another line in the document. “Usually in towns near fault lines, or regions with a long history of shipwrecks and disappearances. We’re close to Puget Sound, so it tracks.”

“Do you think it’s possible that whatever it is, it’s listening to me, too? To my vibrations or whatever?”

His brows lifted in curiosity.

“Not like, in a supernatural way,” she added quickly. “It’s just…you saw it. It feels like the water responds to me.”

Isla stood slowly and began pacing next to the window. The shoreline shimmered under a late afternoon haze, the tide beginning its long crawl back toward the horizon.

“When I walked into the cove, I thought it would be freezing, but it wasn’t. It was warm, exactly the way I needed it to be.”

Cal thought of how she’d felt against him, warm and euphoric. He didn’t interrupt her.

“I didn’t even think,” she said. “I just stepped in and something in me… clicked. Like there was this hollow place I hadn’t known existed, and the water filled it.” She glanced at him cautiously. “It moved: not like normal waves do when they hit your body. It moved in anticipation of where I was moving. It felt… alive.”

“That’s not how water should behave.”

“No,” Isla murmured. “It isn’t.”

Cal stepped to stand beside her.

"It feels good." Her voice was small, wrapped in a vulnerability she rarely showed. "Too good. And a small part of me doesn't want it to stop."

An abrupt gust slipped in through an open window, stirring the curtains and rattling the kettle on the stove. Both turned, their gazes meeting, then shifting to the sea beyond the glass.

Isla crossed the kitchen, filled the kettle and returned it to the stove, the running tap now the only sound in the room.

"Boil," she said. As she watched, an airy sound played through her mind in a steady tone that never left her lips: a vibration inside her more than a melody. A sound only in her thoughts.

The kettle began to tick, then hiss, and boil. She stepped back, not surprised but still startled. Then, her attention moved to Cal.

"Okay," he said, eyes wide. "So, you're not imagining it."

"No, I don't think I am."

SEVENTEEN

The bell over the diner door gave its usual brassy clatter as Cal stepped inside, shaking off his jacket. The scents of fried potatoes and coffee filled his nose, and the soft hiss of a frying pan carried through the kitchen. Rory was already there, in the back booth by the window, hunched over a plate of something smothered in gravy. He looked up in greeting as Cal slid into the seat across from him, red vinyl sighing under his weight.

"Damn, you look like hell. Rough night?"

"You could say that. I'm not getting much sleep."

"That much is obvious." Rory snorted before taking a bite. "You've got that 'a woman has emotionally dismantled me' look. New or old?"

"Not your business." Cal smiled at him as he flagged Mira down with a wave.

She approached with a steaming pot of coffee and that same knowing look he remembered all too well.

"So, you're alive." she said with an arched brow.

"Last I checked."

He kept his tone even, but his jaw flexed as she poured. He wasn't thrilled to see her after the way she'd cornered Isla the other night, but he wasn't about to get into it with her. Not here in front of Rory and half the town. So, he swallowed what he wanted to say and let silence fill in the rest.

"Anything else to drink? she asked, already pouring his coffee. "Haven't seen you around the past few days."

"Been busy," Cal said, lifting the mug and breathing in the steam before taking a slow sip. He tipped it slightly toward her in a gesture of thanks.

Mira moved away, but not far, stopping at the counter where two older fishermen hunched over a map.

Rory tilted his head in their direction. "It's been like that all morning. A weird tension in the air. You notice how quiet the harbor's been?"

Cal glanced over. Kenny Bay tapped the map with a thick finger. Kenny was in his mid-sixties, with a thick head of salt and pepper hair and a gait that swayed with the memory of decades spent on boats.

"Crab pots are empty, nets are untouched," he was saying. "Daryl's boat was out for twelve hours yesterday, and he got nothin'. Not even a damn jellyfish."

"It's the tides," Walter leaned in. "They've not been right for weeks now. Low at the wrong time, and too long between swings. It's like the moon's off-course."

"Well, the nets aren't empty for no reason," Kenny muttered. "I guess the sea offers what it wants, when it wants, but it's not great for business."

Mira refilled a water glass. "I've been hearing that stuff all week. Fishing's gone wrong, shoals seem to be nonexistent. Daryl told Walter he saw a family of otters leap out of the bay like they were fleeing a fire."

"Maybe it's just a terrible season," Rory offered.

Mira's eyes narrowed. "It's more than that. Bob Jenkins said his motor cut out in dead calm water just out past the cove. Said he heard something low under the hull, like a voice rolling through the steel. Once he got moving again, he turned right back around and moored his boat. When the tide's unsettled, it'll start taking. We've lost boats before, and people, too. Now it looks like some are going to lose their livelihood."

The bell clinked again as the door swung open to the sound of wet boots and gull cries from outside. Mira turned, already halfway to greet the new arrival.

"You believe that shit?" Rory leaned back.

Cal rubbed at the back of his neck and took a deep breath. The rational part of him wanted to dismiss it as bad luck, poor timing, or tired men, but he'd seen the water swirl behind Isla in the cove. He'd felt the comfort of tepid water where he should've felt ice, and he'd watched her boil a kettle with little more than a thought.

"I just don't know," he said.

EIGHTEEN

Isla walked down the winding path below the bluff and stepped onto the sand, the soft grains sliding between her toes. When she reached the shoreline, she slipped off her robe, exposing the black tank top and shorts she had woken in. Her breath came easier out here, and she expanded her chest greedily, lungs opening wide to the briny air.

It was a picture-perfect morning. The cove was glass-still and the sunlight split the clouds. Though it looked beautiful, it was unseasonably cold, like it was rising up from beneath the surface of the sea.

She slipped off her clothes and dropped them in the sand, then stepped into the frigid spring tide. The bite met her skin in a breathless rush, but quickly, the water shifted, calibrating itself to her body's temperature. It knew her.

Step by step, she walked until the water lapped against her thighs. With a small jump, she dove forward, pushing through the blue and slipping beneath the surface with barely a ripple. The ocean enveloped her as her body moved with effortless grace in long, fluid strokes. Her fingers stretched into the current, water slipping past them, streaming along her palms and wrists. Weightless and wild, her long hair fanned out behind. The sea carried her, cradled her, welcomed her back as though it had been waiting. Every muscle moved as if it were made for this very swim.

Halfway into the cove, she surfaced and let herself float. Suspended, she drifted between the speckled white and gray clouds that hovered low above and the slow-motion water world below. The surface lapped around her ears, and in the muted echoes, there was music: a frequency felt as much by her body as heard by her ears. Eyes half closed, she let the sea hold her for a while, swaying with her tenderly to the sound of her song.

Eventually she lifted her head, turning slowly toward the shore. One hand rose, and the surface around her responded with a faint tremor. Water rippled outward, and she bit her lip to keep from smiling. Next, she swept her hand upward in a gentle, cupped arc, and the sea beneath obeyed. It swelled in an intentional rise, lifting her waist-high, holding her in an unseen palm. The motion rocked her patiently, and then, as softly as it had lifted her, it let her go, lowering her back down.

Laughter burst out of her, sudden and uncontained, with a joy so unexpected that it filled her entire body. It frightened her even as it filled her, because it wasn't just hers. There was an echo: the sea seemed to be laughing along with her.

As she lay in the water, basking in happiness and scattered sunlight, she felt a numbing heat crawling across her shoulder, presence more than pain. Automatically, her hand rose to the crescent-shaped scar she had carried since childhood: a reminder of something delicate that was nearly broken and the rules Coraline had set regarding the sea. She ran her fingertips along the raised seam where her stitches had been and stopped short. The skin was smooth where the mark had once risen, its edges now softened and flat, as though it had melted into her. What remained was only the faintest curve, nearly gone. The ocean was healing her. No — it was rewriting her, remaking her, piece by piece.

The days that followed blurred into salt and water. What began as a single swim became a pull she couldn't ignore. This would become her daily routine, her communion. Entering the water the way others entered prayer: deliberate, respectful, wordless. Each return to shore left her body less fragile, yet feeling more herself. Her limbs tingled and muscles strengthened, every experience revealing something new: how to swirl the current, slow the waves, linger on the surface with little effort. Then back on the shore, wrapped in a towel, Isla would make her way up the bluff and sink into Coraline's old reading chair where she sat surrounded by scattered information in the form of journals, notebooks, and water-warped letters. Now, they were her scriptures: she learned their language page by page. Hours passed that way; sometimes skimming, sometimes examining the same lines repeatedly, willing the ink to reveal the full picture.

Pieces had surfaced. Mentions of the Tide Song, called both gift and burden, able to bend the world around its bearer. Emotion, memory, even weather shaped by thought alone. It could soothe. It could summon. It could destroy.

It seemed Coraline hadn't been the only one discovering these phenomena. There were others scattered across the globe, notes and names in different locations and languages. No explanations or addresses, just fragments and hints of a collective across time, bonded by blood and brine. Who they were, or what became of them, was still a mystery, and Isla was starting to wonder if she would have to live the answers to find them. So, every day, she would read on, and every day, when the words became too heavy and the walls too close, she'd return to the cove: the only place the pages pointed her.

On the fifth afternoon of her ritual swim, a thick fog rolled in and sank low over the cove. The water lay still, a mirror rippling gently, only disturbed as she drifted toward shore. That was when it happened. As she swam, drifting between fog and sea, something moved beneath her: a slippery brush against her calf. When she looked down, all she could see was a blur at first, a shadow wide and sinuous sliding against the grain of the current. Treading water, she straightened and following the motion. Six feet away, a pale shape lingered just beneath the surface, weightless and gliding with an unnatural grace. Not a seal, not a trick of light, but human in its stillness. Then, it slipped away, vanishing into the darker water.

Isla knew that silhouette: not from this place, but from the hollow ache of memory, and from dreams that always ended with water. The same defined chin, now sharpened by time. The same upturned nose, now stronger and bolder. She blinked hard, her pulse now a rapid drumbeat as her eyes scanned the rippling surface where he'd appeared.

"Silas?" The word came out small, breaking the quiet like a dropped pebble. She followed, swimming further out into the bay. "Silas!"

The sea gave no answer until a faint yet clear voice spoke inside her head.

Not yet, Isla. Not yet.

Back at the house, still wrapped in her towel and a healthy dose of adrenaline, she seized her charcoal. Hands moved furiously, guided only by her memory. When the portrait was finished, she stepped back. It was him. Older now, curls wet with sea water, skin luminous, eyes fathomless. Not lost, not gone. Watching…waiting.

NINETEEN

Cal knelt beside an open electrical panel in the marina, squinting against the afternoon light as he toyed with the wiring that powered one of the dock's older utility posts.

"Hey, Sparky." Isla's voice came from behind him. "I hope you're not about to have a repeat of your university espresso machine fiasco."

Cal turned, surprised to see her standing just a few feet away: wavy hair pulled up in a ponytail, sunglasses perched on her head, and a mischievous smirk on her lips. She held a small cooler bag and a six-pack of beer.

"What's this for?"

"The fog has lifted, so let's go have some fun!"

Cal smiled, but hesitated. "That sounds very, very tempting, but I'm kind of behind on this wiring."

"Nonsense. The wind is perfect, so, surprise!"

She gestured grandly behind him as Rory approached and clapped a hand to his shoulder.

"That wiring has survived thirty years. It can survive one more day."

"You're in on this?"

"She needed a favor," Rory shot Isla a cheerful nod.

"So…you're my surprise?"

"In your dreams, buddy! I've seen you brooding the past couple days, so when she called me, I cashed in a favor."

"I haven't been brooding."

"You have." Rory and Isla said in unison.

"Come on," Isla coaxed, grinning. "We're getting out of here."

"Where?"

"There." She pointed toward the far end of the wharf, where a sleek sailboat rocked gently in place. The sun glinted off its white hull, blue striped canvas sails rolled and ready. The name *Sea Whisperer* was painted in silver cursive script along the side.

"You're serious?"

"Very." Isla said. "Now come on, captain. Adventure awaits."

"Have fun, you two!" Rory called, already disappearing back toward the shop.

Before stepping aboard, Cal paused at the edge of the dock, eyes sweeping across the marina and out toward the open sea. He studied the other boats at anchor, watching the slight sway of their masts where the flags atop streamed gently, angled just enough to show a steady breeze coming in from the southwest. Tree branches on the shore leaned into it, too, their ends rustling with movement. Ripples across the water's surface confirmed it: a clean, consistent wind. Good conditions.

He took a deep breath. The scent of brine and sun-warmed fiberglass filled his lungs, laced with the faint tang of diesel from a distant engine and the sharper bite of seaweed baking on the rocks. It was a smell he loved; the promise of a day on the water.

Cal's grin was almost boyish as he climbed aboard the single-hull, the rocking motion underfoot triggering a quiet reflex in his balance. He ran a hand along the polished rail, fingers trailing the edges like he was reacquainting himself with an old friend. This boat was beautiful, sleek, and balanced, every line perfection.

The deck creaked lightly as he moved, hands falling into preparations without thought. He checked the cleats, adjusted the mainline, ran his fingers along the halyard, and coiled the ropes with practiced ease. Every movement was muscle memory. It was in his blood.

"I think I'm in love," he muttered, half to himself.

Isla climbed aboard after him, and he offered his hand, steadying her as the boat swayed beneath her step. He guided her through the directions with light instruction, patient and secretly thrilled by her curiosity. As she moved to adjust one of the sail lines with cautious focus, he nodded toward the tiller.

"She should be a smooth ride. You'll feel it in your bones when the wind's just right and you start to fly."

Cal looked up to examine the mast, eyes scanning the mainsail and then the subtle arc of the hull. An elegant design that promised speed and grace.

"Okay, this is the mainsail. Pull too hard and we'll tilt, let go entirely and we stall. It's all about balance."

As they pushed off from the dock, the bow swung gently into the wind, the boat briefly turning to irons, still and waiting.

"All right, ready?" he said, glancing at Isla. He reached for the tiller and shifted their heading slightly, just enough to catch the breeze. He released the jib first, the canvas unfurling with a satisfying snap as it caught the wind. The mainsail followed a moment later, filling with a deep, clean breath and the boat surged forward.

Isla braced herself as the hull cut through the water, and Cal laughed, the sound carried away on the breeze. Tension melted from his shoulders; tension he hadn't realized he was holding. Whatever weight he'd brought aboard was softened by the sun and wind and scattered with the spray.

As the boat skimmed across the bay, waves lapping at the hull, Isla let out a delighted holler. Cal stole glances between adjustments, watching the way her hair whipped in the wind, how her smile grew along with the speed, and how natural she looked out here. The wind was perfect, steady and playful, and the sloop carved a clean path through the water, white spray arcing off the bow like wings.

After nearly forty-five minutes of flying across the open sea, Isla gestured toward the packed cooler bag. Cal nodded, and they pulled the sails, letting it slow into a gentle sway between the waves.

They stretched out in the cockpit as she pulled out a simple picnic: two sandwiches wrapped in butcher paper, two bottles of beer chilled just enough, and a small container of strawberries dipped in milk chocolate.

"This is the most romantic hostage situation I've ever been in," Cal said, taking a beer bottle from her and popping the top with a smug twist.

“Hostage, huh?”

“Isn’t that what this is? You’ve kidnapped me and brought me out to sea to have your way with me?”

“I only kidnap those who need it.” Isla unwrapped a sandwich and handed it to him. “And you, my friend, were clearly overdue for a joy intervention.”

“A joy intervention? Is that what this is?” Cal took a bite, throwing her a crooked smile.

“Are you having fun?”

“Yes, I am.”

“Then that’s what this is.”

They ate with their legs stretched out in front of them and nothing but the sound of water lapping gently. Cal leaned back on his elbows, looking out at the skyline. The sun was a low blaze now. It glinted off Isla’s high cheekbone as she turned toward him, one perfectly ripe, chocolate strawberry between her fingers.

"Dessert?" she asked.

Cal eyed it with a look of suspicion. "Uhhh, I don't know."

"Seriously?"

"Believe it or not, I've actually never had one of those."

"Wait, never?" Her mouth fell open. "You've never had a chocolate-dipped strawberry? How is that even possible?"

Amused by her reaction, he shrugged. "My mom wasn't a big chocolate person, so we never had them. Since then, I guess I just never sought them out."

"That's tragic. This may be the most important thing I've ever done for you."

"Changing lives, one chocolate strawberry at a time?"

"Exactly." She leaned in, holding the berry just in front of his lips.

In mock reluctance, he opened his mouth and let her pop it in. He chewed slowly, thoughtfully, then gave a dramatic grimace. "Hmm. Not sure about that."

"Oh, come on," she said, already laughing. "You loved it. Everyone loves chocolate-covered strawberries."

"For science," he said, reaching for another, "I should probably confirm and try one more."

"That's what I thought."

He bit into it, then licked a trace of chocolate from the corner of his mouth. "Well, I guess it's not terrible."

"High praise."

"Fine, you're right. I loved it." He smiled, warm and lazy as they floated, both dimples in his cheeks shining through.

"Let it be known I introduced you to happiness."

The sun painted their faces gold as they sat together in no hurry, between sea and sky. Cal caught the quiet curve of a smile on her face; that free, unguarded kind she wore only when she thought no one was watching and something in his chest gave. All of this she'd done for him, simply because she knew he would love it.

"I've always wanted to do this," Isla said softly. "Just...sail away. No plan, no destination."

"I could show you the ropes," Cal offered. "We'll need to teach you port from starboard first and pack a few more snacks."

"I know *port.* It's the one that means left. They both have four letters, so they go together."

He stared at her. "That's actually not the worst way to remember it."

"Tell me a story about sailing." She lay back, closing her eyes.

"All right. I can tell you a story about what *not* to do," he said, chuckling. "First time I skippered solo. I'd bought this crappy old dinghy. Nothing fancy, only big enough for two people, but fast when the wind was right. I was feeling cocky, and the wind picked up out of nowhere. I'd pulled the mainsheet in tight, trying to wring out every bit of speed, but I hadn't adjusted the tiller properly and wasn't trimming for the angle I was on. Rookie mistake."

He paused for effect.

"Suddenly, the hull dipped hard, like the boat was trying to dive under instead of slicing through. The whole thing pitched forward, and I almost flipped. I was staring straight down into the water, holding onto the sheet for dear life."

"Did you capsize?" Isla asked, laughing.

"Almost. Saved it by easing the main just in time and letting the jib luff. Pure luck. After that, I listened to the wind instead of fighting it. Lesson learned. Speed means nothing if you're not sailing smart."

"I don't know what half of those words mean, but I'll take your word for it."

As the sun dipped low on the horizon, casting the world in honeyed light, they moored the boat and stepped back onto the dock. The mood was calm, contented.

"That was perfect," Isla said. "Thank you."

"I should be thanking you," Cal replied. "That was the best day I've had in a long time." Then, he kissed her.

The sun set quickly, its final rays vanishing behind them as they climbed the narrow trail back toward home.

"What a great way to spend the afternoon," Cal said, a little breathless from the climb.

"I'm so glad you liked it. Rory really came through with that boat today. I loved being out there with you. All the swimming I've been doing this week has been wonderful, but I forgot what it was like to be *on* the water, rather than in it."

Cal stopped walking. "Swimming?"

"Yeah, just at the cove. It's been really grounding." She didn't say any more; Cal wasn't ready for the rest.

"Wait, you've been swimming *alone*?"

"Well, yeah." She blinked, confused. "It's not that far, and I'm careful…"

"Isla." His voice tightened. "I knew you were going to the cove, but I didn't realize you were actually spending time in the water by yourself."

"What's the big deal?" Her brow furrowed.

Cal exhaled, running a hand through his hair. "The big deal is that strange things have been happening here. Duncan walking into the sea, that kid in the cove, the guy on the jetty, your grandmother."

"I know, Cal. You don't have to list them."

"You shouldn't swim alone as it is, even without all of this going on!"

"Cal, come on!"

"Why are you pretending it's not a big deal? Why aren't you being more careful? You're the one that said you thought whatever was happening out there was dangerous." His tone had sharpened, more than he meant it to.

"I'm not pretending," she shot back. "I'm just not afraid of it! Not for myself."

"So you are, or you aren't? Because I thought you told me you *were* scared."

"For others. For you!" She crossed her arms, frustration hot on her face.

"If it *is* connected, then shouldn't you stay away from the water until we know more? I just don't understand why you're being so careless."

"What, now I need a chaperone every time I dip my toes in?"

"You know that's not what I'm saying."

"Feels like it."

"Isla, I didn't mean it like that. I just…"

"You sound like Coraline," she snapped. "Like everyone who ever thought they knew what was best for me without actually asking me what *I* felt and what *I* wanted."

Cal's face fell. "I didn't mean to sound controlling."

"Well, you did."

A tension fell between them that hadn't been there before.

"I care about you," he said finally. "I'm worried. I just want you to be safe."

Still flushed from the sun and wind, she looked at him, but her eyes were distant now. "Then trust me to make my own decisions."

Then she turned and walked ahead. Cal watched her go, pained by the wreckage of a day he hadn't meant to unravel.

~

A single lamp illuminated the table, casting a soft cone of light over the chaos of notes, open books, and printed articles. Cal sat hunched forward, elbows braced on the wood while his eyes traced lines of text that had long since blurred with exhaustion. He looked broken in this light, drained and unshaven. He was a man trying to reason with something he couldn't understand.

They hadn't spoken much since the walk home. The silence between them wasn't heavy, just unresolved. He was angry because he cared, but her pride bristled anyway. Maybe it was unfair, but out of principle alone, she refused to shrink into the version of herself this town preferred: the one expected to play it safe. The one expected to stay inside the lines others drew for her.

Standing in the kitchen doorway, she studied him. The weariness in his shoulders, the deepening worry that now seemed to live behind his eyes. He was searching for answers for *her*, and she hated that so much of his time had become this endless vigil. She crossed the room and began to gently squeeze the stiffness out of his shoulders.

"Cal," she said softly. "You need to come to bed. You need to sleep."

With a yawn, he rubbed a hand over his face and attempted a smile. "I'm fine, really. Just a little longer."

"You're not fine. And neither am I."

He looked up at her then, trying to read her eyes. Silent thoughts passed between them: affection, fear, fatigue.

Touching his face with gentle reassurance, she said, "I love what we have, Cal, that hasn't changed. But I think I need a few days to make sense of everything. And maybe you could use a few days, too. Some proper rest, the kind that doesn't come with late nights and research papers."

"You're serious."

"I am."

Cal's jaw tightened, but he didn't argue. In true Cal fashion, he mustered a look meant to pass for understanding, but the hurt in his eyes said more.

"Isla, if this is about me…"

"It's not you, I promise. It's just…I feel like I'm losing my balance. I need to stop and breathe and really take some time to think about what is happening to me and everything I'm learning without any...distractions."

"Do you feel like I'm crowding you?"

"No, Cal, you're not crowding me. You ground me." Taking his face in both her hands, she kissed him. "That's the problem. I enjoy being around you too much and I just need some time to focus. Right now everything feels…louder. The sea, the dreams, the things I'm starting to understand. I just need a few days to process it all and finish reading."

"Tell me the truth. Should I be worried?"

"No, you have no reason to be worried. I just need some space to be figure this out without you trying to fix it."

"I'm not trying to fix it…"

"You are. It's who you are, and I love that about you. I love that you care enough to do whatever you can to help me through this. But you're doing it at your own expense."

Before speaking, he took a moment to gather his thoughts. "Okay. So, what does this look like? A couple days? A week? No contact? What?"

"Cal, I'm not running off. I'll be right here. I just need to find a little quiet that isn't borrowed from you. Give me a few days."

Eyes searching, he studied her. "You know I'll come if you ask."

"I know. And that's exactly why I need you not to."

When he finally nodded, it wasn't agreement: it was restraint. "If that's what you need, I'll give it to you."

"It is."

"Promise me you'll check in. Just so I know that you're okay."

"I promise."

Cal stood, and with a deep breath, he drew her into a lingering embrace, his chin resting against her hair. He wanted to beg her to stay, to ask her not to go to the cove. But he didn't. He kissed her, gentle and reluctant. Part of a promise he wasn't sure he should have made. When he finally pulled away, his hand brushed her cheek one last time before he turned for the door. The latch clicked softly behind him, and the house fell still.

~

Over the next few days, the empty house and silent nights made Isla realize how much she missed Cal. It was apparent in every part of her day. Every so often, a meal would appear on the porch: lunch from The Reef, coffee and a muffin from The Little Bean. No knock, no call; just his gentle way of showing up without asking to be seen.

There'd been a change in her these past few days, terrifying and exhilarating all at once. The faint scar on her shoulder was now gone, erased so completely her fingers couldn't even find its ghost. Every swim had altered her chemistry somehow: her heartbeat steadier, her skin smoother, her body more attuned to the water's shift and temperature, and her senses sharpened. The sea was tuning her to its frequency.

Currents answered her hands when she swam, and salt carried her voice. The cove had become her second home. Twice a day she returned, drawn by need and an ache.

The man whom she believed to be Silas was always there. A ripple before she turned, his face constantly just out of reach. He was a shadow that showed her how to listen and how to command without force, but his voice didn't speak, not really. He simply was, and somehow, she understood his direction. Each night, she woke knowing more than she could explain, the lessons whispered directly into her blood.

Before dawn on the fourth day, beyond the windows, the fog devoured the bluff and threaded through the trees before vanishing over the ledge and into the sea. By mid-morning, a pale light had crept across the sitting room rug, where Isla sat cross-legged on the floor, surrounded by sketchpads and loose, ink-scrawled pages. A cup of tea cooled beside her elbow, its steam faintly scented with lemon and ginger.

Of all the pages she'd read, Isla had never seen them the way she did now. The words seemed to sharpen before her eyes, meaning rising like silt stirred from the seabed. Between the water-stained paper and salt-warped ink, Coraline's warnings took on a new shape. They read now as confessions and discoveries; a record of something ancient and inherited that she had been forced to find her way through alone. Every page carried the persistence of a woman piecing together a secret lineage; one she'd had to learn as she lived.

The page beneath her palm now was thin, and in the margin, a single line had been written darker than the rest, next to a paragraph of what read as directions.

Our Tide Song must rise beneath the full moon, when the equinox tips the world toward spring.

When the song begins to rise within you, you'll know it has begun.

It may be quiet at first, but those closest to your heart will hear it.

The air will shift. The water will stir.

The Tide Song will travel the deepest through bond and through blood.

The stronger the connection, the stronger the echo. Once they hear it...they will never stop listening.

Bond and blood. The words pulsed in her mind. Thoughts of Silas, her twin soul, their shared beginnings, and how his voice now drifted through her mind and her dreams. It wasn't memory or grief pulling him toward her now, but something older. Something written into them both. *Bond and blood.*

A sudden creak shuddered through the ceiling, causing Isla's head to snap up. Stillness, silence, then a vibration. It weaved faintly through the walls: a deep, resonant drone that carried like a whale song through water, moving along the old pipes. She rose slowly, and stepped into the hallway, listening.

"Hello?"

Overhead, the pipes quivered again, the note wavering and unsteady, like the tuning of a cello. Without thought, Isla parted her lips and answered the sound as it waited for her harmony. One clear, note left her body, and the veins of the house replied in kind. When Isla's song stopped, so did the whirr of the water through the walls.

She stood, charged and waiting. The quiet of the house held a presence now: she could feel it around her in an unseen energy that flowed beneath the floorboards and through the walls. The power she'd felt in the cove was here, entwined in the bones of the March House. The realization arrived as both warmth and warning; that water was everywhere. All around her.

She moved back to the sitting room, where the journal she'd been reading lay open. Knees folding beneath her as if in prayer, she turned the page and landed where a red star marked the next entry.

When the Tide Song comes to you in its fullness and the sea claims the voice, guard what you love. Choose with a steady heart, because if you do not, the tide will choose for you.

A small note was tucked into the pages, a delicate fold in its center. It was fragile and thin, the writing barely a whisper. Script curled and swept like it belonged to someone who spoke the language of storms and shipwrecks. No name, no date: just a brief message.

Reading it once was enough. The words hit her like a stone to the gut, and the house finally exhaled. It listened as she read it aloud. The truth she'd finally unearthed shot through its bones, the awareness of her knowing travelling outward through the walls and into the cove.

Isla's fingers tightened around the brittle edges of the message, and with a steady breath, she carefully slipped it back between the pages and pressed the journal closed.

Cal's name flooded her mind.

The truth of her origin lived here now, awake in the walls and the water. Though she couldn't name her place in it, not yet, she knew enough to understand now what she was becoming. And the reality was, it might not be safe for him to love her.

TWENTY

A half-dismantled compass lay open on the bench in Cal's workroom, its copper needle quivering faintly in place. The lantern beside it flickered with the breeze, casting soft, restless shadows across the walls. Cal didn't move; the screwdriver sat idle in his hand, forgotten, as he stared at the compass. Its cover was off and there was no magnetic interference, no reason for it to stir. And yet, it did.

His attention stayed fixed on the trembling point, though his mind was miles away. Instead, he thought of Isla, standing waist-deep in the bay that day, water curling around her like smoke. When he'd reached her, her eyes had been distant and unfocused, as if she'd just come back from some place he couldn't follow.

They'd swum together a hundred times when they were kids, and she used to hold her breath so long he'd panic. Once, she dove straight off a cliffside just to prove she could. This was different, though; it wasn't swimming anymore. This was something else and it scared him.

He ran a hand through his hair and leaned against the window frame, watching the trees beyond the lighthouse bend with the wind as the day's final gleam dipped below the horizon. The weather had taken on an uneasy rhythm these past few days: the sea unnervingly calm beneath the morning fog, then rising restless and wild by the afternoon, with no wind or darkening sky to blame. The barometer in his kitchen rose and fell as if it had a pulse, yet no storms were forecast.

These were the kinds of patterns that had old men whispering on the docks: stories traded over flasks and grizzled years, and talk of omens in the tide, just as was happening in Greyhook now. Cal had always been dismissive of superstition but now, with the image of Isla standing half-lost in the surf, those tales no longer sounded like nonsense.

Worry had been building in him since they'd said their temporary goodbye. There was a pressure that wouldn't ease no matter how he tried to explain it away or distance himself mentally. If Isla was connected to the ocean, and if it knew her, it wasn't finished with her. It wanted her back.

Turning to look out at the cove again, he could just make out the March House perched atop the bluff, pale against the twilight with windows like glowing eyes over the ocean. Growing up, that house had always been in the corner of his world; forever present, but always a little closed off, especially after Silas died, and Coraline had been its gatekeeper. Quiet, stern, and warily kind to him, she didn't trust that he'd take anything seriously, which, to be fair, he hadn't for most of his years.

Coraline was unlike his own parents, who had been easygoing in that small-town-by-the-sea kind of way. His mother, Saisha, was a librarian, and his father, Jason, an insurance broker. As their only child, they'd given him more freedom than most, but it came with an unspoken contract. He was taught and expected to be cautious and capable: raised to know the tides, to move confidently through town and water alike. It had been a good childhood, one of salt air and scraped knees, guided by parents who loved him without hovering. Retired now, they lived in a quiet Oregon community with shops and cafes and a retirement home they had their eye on for the distant future.

Coraline, he used to think, had been too hard on Isla. Too rigid. He'd thought of it as overprotectiveness after losing Silas. Isn't that what people do when the ground breaks underneath them: hold on tighter to what's left?

Thinking back now to that strange day in the cove with Isla and the detached look in her eyes, he'd seen something real; something with weight. Something that he now realized Coraline had been aware of all along.

Cal pressed his palm to the cool glass of the lighthouse window. The sea stretched out in shadows below like the secrets held between them. Isla had asked for space; just a little. Time to read, to think, and to understand the pull she felt, to put together the pieces she wouldn't say out loud. He knew more than she was telling him.

Begrudgingly, he had given her that space and said he'd understood. In the silence now, the pain of her absence weighed on him. It wasn't only desire he felt for her; it was so much deeper than that. His soul felt in tune with hers. When they were together, he didn't just hear her, he *felt* her: in his chest, in his spine, and in the spaces between thoughts. And now that she'd taken a gentle step back, that place inside him felt hollow.

Turning from the window, Cal moved down the hall. As he walked, a cool draft slipped past, carrying the tang of salt and something softly sweet, like rain on sea grass. It was subtle, but he felt it float past him, present enough to raise the hairs along his arms. Overhead, the light flickered twice before settling into a nervous glow. Almost beyond hearing, a delicate sound unfurled around him: a melody without words, thin as smoke, winding through the growing darkness. Sweet, beckoning, and familiar, it rose from somewhere hidden beneath the bluff, moving around and through him. The sound filled his ears and echoed in his chest, reverberating through the center of him. It was beautiful and unearthly in its sweetness, and it was calling to only him.

Cal turned back toward the window, scanning the darkness beyond the cliffs. The voice was distant, yet impossibly near, ghosting through the night. It sounded like Isla, and in his bones, he knew she needed him.

TWENTY-ONE

A storm was coming. Isla could feel it before the first crack of lightning ever touched the horizon. The winds had been rising since dusk, whipping around the house and the surrounding cedar trees, though nothing was in the forecast. It billowed now, howling across the bluff and scattering needles against windowpanes like fingernails on glass. The sea below hadn't yet swelled, but it soon would.

The sitting room glowed with the soft light of a side table lamp and the low flicker of the fire in the hearth. Isla curled up on the couch, legs tucked beneath her, a cotton sweater slipping loose from one shoulder. In her hand, she held a glass of merlot, while a journal lay open across her lap, its pages marked with sticky notes and scribbles. Piece by piece, the puzzle was coming together. Only the final fragments remained.

Somewhere between one page and the next, a soft sound slipped from her lips, unbidden. The melody was delicate and instinctive, something she now knew by heart. So natural, she hadn't even realized she was releasing it.

The phone on the table buzzed, its screen lighting up.

CAL: Storm's rolling in. You alright?

A pause.

CAL: Just want to make sure you're okay. Mind if I stop by?

Another moment.

CAL: Please, Isla. I'm worried about you being alone with this weather.

Closing her eyes, she let the phone rest against her chest. She hadn't noticed the messages. How had she missed them?

Doing exactly as she'd asked, Cal had respectfully given her space, but she could feel his ache through every text and every considerate meal he'd left on the porch. Isla's feelings for him hadn't changed; if anything, the wanting had deepened. It had grown into something more than she was willing to name, but the closer she got to the truth, the more her concern for him grew: concern that whatever thread bound them, might also be the one to drag him under if they got too close.

A sudden gust slammed against the side of the house, strong enough to make her flinch. Quickly, she stood and crossed to the window. The wind had grown even stronger, and it moaned in a long, wild chorus beneath the eaves of the house. Checking the latch, she pressed her palm to the glass and glanced out, inevitably toward the water.

A tall figure stood partway down the far side of the bluff, shoulders hunched, jacket flapping in the gale. Isla squinted as she watched the man disappear down the path that led into the cove.

Cal? Her stomach lurched.

Barefoot, she threw the front door open and stepped into the wind, firelight spilling out behind her onto the dark porch. With no coat and no phone, Isla flew down the steps two at a time, cutting across the grass toward the trail. Louder now, the wind heaved, and thunder rolled above the sea, close enough to shake the air around her.

"Cal!" she called, but the sound was snatched away by the wind.

The path narrowed beneath her and she stumbled as she ran, the ocean swelling louder with every step. The entirety of the beach came into view as she rounded the final bend. Lightning split the sky, white and violent, throwing his silhouette into stark clarity as he reached the edge of the beach and continued to move steadily toward the angry water.

"CAL!" Isla's voice tore free, stretching his name, all lungs and blood and soul poured into the sound.

At last, he turned, his eyes unfocused and dazed as if roused from a dream. The storm snapped around them as Isla skidded to a stop in front of him, grabbing his wrists.

"What are you doing? You can't go in there."

"I heard you," His brows knit as though that explained everything. "I heard your voice. I thought…" He faltered, blinking hard. "I thought you needed me. I thought you were in the water, and with the storm …it's too rough out there for you to swim."

"You *heard* me?" Panic filled her. "I'm not swimming. I was at home."

The melody. Calm and unconscious, she had been humming as she read. Humming without thinking. Had he heard it? Was it her that had drawn him out here, down to the water in an unintentional summons?

"You were…I mean…I swear I heard you." Confusion filled his face, edged with defensiveness. "I was worried. You were calling me from down here…" His eyes cleared. "Weren't you?"

Isla's grip tightened on his arm, her breath coming sharp and uneven as she searched his expression. His shoes still rested on dry sand, not yet touched by the water, but the truth was written in his eyes. He would have gone straight into the sea without hesitation, without fear.

"I'm okay." Her voice broke, and so did something inside her.

"I needed to be sure you were all right." Cal reached for her cheek, cupping it in his hand. "You didn't answer my texts, and this storm is looking to be a big one."

“I didn’t mean to call to you.” A single tear fell down her cheek. “I’m so, so sorry, Cal.”

There they stood, motionless in the wind, the tide churning beside them. Rain had started, with a steady hiss that stung their arms and faces, hiding the rest of her tears. Cal’s hand lingered on her cheek, but she didn’t feel comfort: just fear and dread. Drawn by an unseen force, he had tried to go into the ocean, her voice the only thing he could hear. She should have known; she had been careless. How easily he could have slipped beneath the surface with that vacancy in his eyes, never knowing he was drowning.

A jagged flash lit up the sky, thunder following quickly behind as the storm opened over them. In that instant, she finally understood exactly what the ocean could take — and it was all because of her.

~

They didn’t speak on the walk back. The rain came harder now, needling sideways, wind snapping at their clothes. Isla kept close to him, her fingers tangled in the cuff of his sleeve like she wasn’t sure she could trust him not to turn back.

They dashed up the porch steps, dripping and flushed, and rushed through the still-open front door, gratefully trading the sting of the elements for the shelter of the house. The fireplace had burned low, its orange flicker casting restless shadows across the room. Wind roared through the chimney, but the house held its warmth. Near the door, Cal shrugged off his rain-soaked jacket and ran a hand through his wet hair. Searching for the right words to say, he turned his eyes to Isla’s.

"I didn't mean to scare you." He moved toward her. "I really thought…"

"I know." She cut him off.

Hesitantly this time, he took another step, his palms raised as if calming a startled animal. "I'm okay, I swear. It was just a little walk in the rain." Coaxing, he tried to lighten the mood with his full dimpled smile. "You don't have to worry."

But she *was* worried about him: worried about the way he looked at her and how she knew deep in her soul that the sound he'd heard wasn't just her voice; it was a tether. A lure. It was the Tide Song, and she hadn't meant to cast it.

Isla lowered herself onto the couch, motioning for Cal to sit beside her. He could feel the distance she'd carefully placed between them, though she hadn't moved away. It was in her silence and her stillness, and it terrified him.

"Please don't be upset. Don't use this to pull away." With rainwater still beading along his forehead and lashes, he looked fragile in a way Isla hadn't expected, yet he still stared at her with that same unguarded devotion. The pain of it twisted inside her, love and danger braided too tightly to pull apart. "I just knew I had to get to you. I didn't even think; I just went."

"I know, Cal. It's not your fault, but that's what frightens me."

He reached for her hand and sighed. "I know you're afraid, Isla, but I'm not. I'm not afraid of you or of what this is between us. Today was just a small misunderstanding, and it won't happen again."

Isla examined him; the sharp edges of his face, the familiar fit of his fingers in hers, the sweet devotion. It could destroy him if she let it, and he didn't even see it coming. He was trying to fix what he couldn't, taking blame for a danger he didn't understand. She hated that he was apologizing to her for this, trying to make it right, when she knew it was all her fault. The risk was her burden to carry, not his.

"Let me stay. Let me make you feel safe." He squeezed her hand.

The storm outside screamed against the cliffs as it rolled over the sea, but inside, the fire popped gently with a comforting glow that said they were safe here tonight.

A single nod. The truth was already lodged inside her; the pain of a goodbye she hadn't yet spoken but somehow already knew had to come.

Fingers entwined, Isla guided him slowly upstairs as lightning flashed at the windows, each step a reminder of how fragile this night would be. Her bedroom was dim, lit only by the soft cast of the corner lamp and the storm spilling through the window. As Isla paused in the doorway, Cal stood behind her, patient, waiting, allowing her to take the lead. When she finally turned, his expression was open and unguarded. He stepped forward and cupped her cheek with a kind of adoration that threatened to undo her completely.

Their clothes fell away with the care of a sacred ritual: nothing rushed, nothing wasted. Every touch cut deeper as she savored the details: the feel of his hands, the scent of his shoulder, the curve of his mouth at her throat. She gathered each one, storing them inside herself.

Cal said her name as he touched her, delivering it like it was a vow, and she nearly wept. He didn't know that this might be the last time. Didn't know she had already begun to unravel the threads between them, trying to make peace with what she knew would be the safest thing for him. And so, she let the ache of that knowing flood her body as he kissed her, and she felt all of it.

They moved to the bed, limbs brushing, tongues meeting, breath warming in the space between. The sheets were cool against her back as the storm lit the room in pulses and silver streaks flashed across his chest from the window. Thunder rolled above, echoing the tempest building in her chest as she pulled him to her. In that split second, his mouth on her skin, his hands everywhere, Isla felt the truth of it. She loved him. Fully, fiercely, and just in time to lose him. So, she held him closer, took him slower. Let every taste, every sound, every flicker of light carve itself into her. If this was the end, she wouldn't let it pass unremembered.

When she tried to say his name, to speak as he worshipped her body, her voice wouldn't come, not without breaking. So, she let her hands speak for her, let her mouth press the truth into his skin: that he mattered, that she loved him, that this wasn't goodbye…but it was the beginning of letting him go.

As they finally came together, she held his gaze, the stretch of him familiar and welcome. Her legs curled around his waist, her fingers laced behind his neck, and she rocked with him in time. Skin to skin, breath to breath, heartbeat for heartbeat. It was quiet, it was tender, and it was devastating.

Afterward, they lay entwined until night folded around them. Cal whispered her name once before he surrendered to sleep, but Isla didn't follow. She stayed wrapped in his arms, drinking in the smell of his neck, the weight of his arm across her waist, the steady sound of the beat of his heart. Awake, she could stretch every fleeting minute just a little bit longer and hold on to the illusion that it might never end. For that one small, perfect moment, she let herself believe love was enough: at least for tonight.

The storm had passed by first light, retreating into the sea reluctantly. Rain still tapped along the windows in broken intervals, but the wind had eased, and the sky was transitioning to a washed out, post-storm shade.

Isla lay awake in Cal's arms, her tired eyes tracing the dim ceiling above. Sleep had eluded her most of the night. Each time she drifted, the edges of a nightmare took form, and the same haunting image would pull her back to consciousness: Cal sinking into the black water of the cove, his eyes open and empty, no one there to reach for him.

On the nightstand, her phone buzzed, and she reached for it quietly, careful not to wake a still-dreaming Cal. The screen lit up with a web alert from *The Greyhook Post*.

BODY DISCOVERED AT GREYHOOK MARINA

Isla shifted up on her elbow, her heavy eyes blinking as the headline sank in. Tapping the notification, her browser opened automatically, directing her to the local newspaper's website. As the front page loaded, the headline took shape and the cloud of exhaustion vanished in an instant.

LOCAL MAN FOUND DECEASED

Below, a short article containing very few details was followed by a photo of the scene. It loaded slowly, pixels materializing into shape. Grainy and bathed in morning mist, a man's figure lay on the shoreline at the base of the rocks. One boot was missing from his left foot, a soaked blue parka clinging tightly to a burly frame. A blur box censored the man's face, but his hands remained uncovered. As she took in the details, bile rose in her throat. The parka was distinctive enough, but it was the hands that gave it away. Across the victim's knuckles, large tattooed letters marked the top of his first three fingers; L-E-E, with an anchor etched into the fourth.

Duncan.

A small gasp escaped her and she covered her mouth, gripping the phone tighter. She stared at the screen, willing it to be wrong. Isla wanted it to be a mistake, a cruel coincidence, but her rising nausea said otherwise.

"Cal." She stroked his arm.

"Mm?" He stirred, but didn't open his eyes.

"Cal, you need to wake up."

Groggily, he rubbed at his eyes and sat up. "What's the matter?" Then, he registered the alarm on her face.

Isla turned the screen toward him so he could read the headline. Taking the phone from her, he scrolled down to the photo. "Is that…?"

"Yes…"

Without another word, Cal sprung out of bed and snatched his own phone from the nightstand, fingers flying over the screen as he dialed. The line rang, then clicked in answer.

"What happened?" A pause, then the faint sound of Rory's reply. "I'll be right there." He turned back to Isla. "They found him early this morning. They pulled him from the water…he's dead."

Isla placed her hand gently on his arm.

"They have security cam footage. It looks like he just…walked down the riprap and into the waves. The sheriff is calling it a suicide."

"That doesn't make any sense. Duncan survived *the Lady Marion* incident! I thought he was okay." Dread filled Isla's chest as reality set in. Folding her arms tight against the hollowness she felt, she walked to the window, pressing a panic attack down with everything she had. When words finally came, they were solemn with concern meant for him.

"I can't believe this is happening. I can't tell you how sorry I am, Cal. What can I do?"

Jaw set, Cal stepped closer to her, locking his arms firmly around her waist. "Isla, I know what you're thinking, and this has nothing to do with you."

"Mira was right; it doesn't stop. It keeps calling until it takes what it wants."

"Isla, don't do this. I know something's happening out there. I'd be blind not to. But this isn't you. I was with you all night, and Duncan's been unraveling since…"

"Since he walked into the ocean the first time. The same way you almost did last night!" Her voice quivered but didn't falter. "This isn't a coincidence; this is real."

"No." His reply was fierce, immediate. "Whatever happened last night, you put a stop to. It's not the same."

A raw laugh tore loose. "Yes, it is, Cal. What happens when I *can't* stop it? When I'm not there to pull you back from the edge?" Tears burned her eyes as she buried her face in his chest. "There *will* be a next time Cal! You know there will. Duncan heard it once and then it dragged him back again, and now he's gone. That means if you stay with me, I'll be the reason it happens to you."

Cal shook his head hard, like he could scatter the thought before it rooted. He could see where she was going with this and refused to follow her there.

"I don't know enough about what is happening, what I'm becoming, or what that means for anyone else, Cal. And until I do…" The words collapsed before she could finish, her silence carrying what she couldn't say.

"You're still you," he said firmly, daring her to believe it. "I don't care about the rest. I'm not letting you push me away."

They clung to each other in the silence.

“Duncan heard the Tide Song,” Isla whispered finally. “That’s what pulled him under. And now you’ve heard it, too.”

Neither spoke after that, but the truth remained: the truth that Duncan wouldn’t be the last, that Isla had only just begun to understand what she was a part of, and that they might be powerless against what was rising from the deep.

~

Cal's work truck rolled to a stop near the marina, the flashing lights of the crime scene ahead cutting through the early morning haze. It was blocked off by police cars, and the usual dockside chatter had vanished. There was no thrum of engines, no footsteps on wet planks. Only the groan of boats straining against their moorings and the low murmur of voices trying not to carry across the water.

Coraline’s old raincoat hung loose on Isla’s frame, the sleeves swallowing her hands. Cal glanced at her now and then, concerned about the burden she carried and because his own grief sat close to the surface.

A stretch of yellow police tape cordoned off the scene, holding back a knot of curious locals craning for a glimpse. Ahead, Rory stood rigid beside the coroner, who was already zipping Duncan into a black body bag. Sheriff Wright leaned toward them, speaking low and scribbling notes on his clipboard while Deputy Richardson crouched nearby, carefully bagging Duncan’s boots.

As Cal and Isla drew closer, the sheriff signaled a deputy and the tape lifted to allow them through. He dragged a weary hand across his brow before squaring his shoulders. To Isla, he offered a brief nod, less a greeting than an acknowledgment, then reached out to Cal with a quick, wordless handshake.

"Hey, Cal." Rory's voice was subdued.

"What the hell happened?" Cal said.

"It doesn't make any sense. The coroner found no sign of drowning, no bruising. I found him when I got in this morning, washed up over on those rocks."

"No one should have to find someone like that. I'm sorry it was you." Cal put a hand on his shoulder.

"Me, too, but better than some poor kid, I guess."

"You pulled the dock cams?"

"Yeah, just before the sheriff arrived. The video shows Duncan just standing there. After a while, he walked straight in and out, calm as could be. Then, he was gone until he washed up this morning. They're ruling it a suicide…" He trailed off, shaking his head. "I guess he just snapped."

"Dammit, Duncan." Cal shook his head slowly.

The coroner's van pulled away down the narrow marina road, taking Duncan's body with it. Isla's face had gone pale, arms folded to her chest, eyes locked on the sea as if in question. Gray and silent, it refused to answer.

"I assume someone called Eli?" Cal rubbed at his chin.

"The sheriff tried," Rory answered. "He's been working down in Bridgeport and should be back this afternoon. They reached one of his colleagues."

"Shit. This is gonna hit hard."

Rory nodded. "Eli's been running himself ragged keeping eyes on Duncan these past couple of weeks. Duncan hated it. Told him to stop hovering. Said he wasn't a baby."

Cal swore under his breath.

“I did notice something strange, though. That necklace he made…the medallion with the spiral on it. He wasn’t wearing it. I don’t think I’ve seen him without since the day he found it.”

“You think that means something?”

Rory shrugged. “I don’t know what to think anymore. The other thing is, isn’t it odd that he washed up in the exact spot he went in only hours later? Usually, it takes days or weeks for a body to wash up, and even then, it’s usually up or down the coast depending on the season.”

A mournful silence lingered, thick with questions no one could answer. Rory stared at the water, visibly reliving the morning’s discovery. Grief etched Cal’s expression, tension locked in his jaw. It was all too much, Isla thought. Duncan had mattered to so many people, and now he was gone.

“I’m so sorry, Cal. Rory.” The apology slipped out, though it felt inadequate.

Reaching out, Cal wrapped one arm around her shoulders and pulled her in. His hand found the back of her head and he held her, the only comfort he could offer. “It’s okay. We’re all going to be okay.”

Rory reached out and squeezed Cal’s shoulder, then nodded to Isla. “I’m gonna finish up here, then I’m going to start drinking. You know where to find me if you want to join me.” He stuffed his hands into his pockets and drifted back to Sheriff Wright.

Cal and Isla made their way slowly back down the dock. Ahead, Mira leaned against the railing, waiting. Her eyes were shadowed, her face drawn. Horror had carved itself into the lines of her face.

“Isla.” With a small motion of her hand, she beckoned her over.

Hesitant, Isla stiffened before turning squarely toward her, chin held high. She knew what was coming, and she would face it.

Cal stopped half a step behind her, and when he moved to follow, Mira lifted a hand, palm out. “Just her, Cal.”

"I don't think so, Mira. Not today." Cal hardened his eyes as he reached for Isla's hand. Drawing up beside her, he met Mira's stare. "What is it? Because I don't think any of us have much patience left today."

Mira's mouth twisted into a tired frown, and she looked to their joined hands. "Thick as thieves again, are we?"

"What do you want, Mira?" He asked.

"I knew Duncan better than most, so I think you can spare a minute to hear what I have to say." The usual sharpness in her expression faltered just for a moment, something softer slipping through as she glanced toward the road where the coroner's van had disappeared moments earlier.

"After the incident with the *Lady Marion*, Duncan was different. Sometimes you don't come back the same when the sea calls your name, so I worried this might happen. Poor Eli tried to do all he could." She paused to look down. "You know, he always said he wanted to die at sea." With an empty laugh, she turned her gaze back to Isla. "But I don't think this is what he had in mind."

The hardness had settled back into her.

"There was a boy once…Evan Connelly. You ever heard of him?"

Isla shook her head.

"He was Coraline's first love, in high school. Everyone knew how it was between them. He'd walk her home, bring her wildflowers, that sort of thing."

Cal's hand flexed, irritation rising, but Isla touched his arm lightly, just enough to keep him still. This story was new to her, and she wanted to hear it.

Mira continued. "One summer, we all went swimming out near the point: a big group of us. After a while, most everyone went home, except us three. Evan dove in with Coraline, and I stayed on shore. I wasn't a very good swimmer back then and I was tired, so I hung around to watch them jump. It was all fine…until it wasn't. The water was deep and a bit choppy, but there were no rocks to risk an injury and we had been jumping there for years. On Evan's last jump, he didn't come back up. After about a minute, I noticed Coraline searching the water, diving down and coming back empty-handed, and she was panicking. Evan was lying on the bottom of the seabed, slowly drowning. He sank and stayed there while she dove for him repeatedly. Coraline came up a third time without him, and she pleaded with the water. Literally pleaded. I saw it with my own eyes as she cried and screamed at the sea to let him go. Eventually, the waves calmed, and it did. It let him go."

"You mean she saved him." Cal glared at her.

"No." Mira said. "I mean it *let him go*. It released him. Suddenly, he just floated to the surface, barely breathing."

"And he knew how to swim?"

"He was swimming just fine for the hour before that. Evan said the water was holding him down, keeping him there…but when Coraline begged, it stopped."

There was skepticism in the way Cal looked at her; all the while, Isla stayed silent, listening.

"I remember his face," Mira said. "He was terrified: terrified of the water, and then after, terrified of her. His family moved away after that. No warning, no goodbyes. We never saw him again. Coraline was devastated, and I never went in the water with her after that day."

Isla registered the flash in Cal's eyes. Mira's words had stung, but he didn't want to hear them.

"I think you March women carry something in you, and I think you know it. Or at least Coraline did." Mira's tone dropped to something resembling compassion. "I don't know what it is, but it's dangerous." She tilted her head, studying Isla as though deliberating how much to say. "You ever wonder why Coraline never married your grandfather? Why no man ever stayed with your family?"

"My grandfather was an alcoholic." Isla frowned, defensive. "He ran out on them when my mom was little."

"Alcoholic?" Mira threw her head back and cackled. "You never asked yourself why he drank so much? What he saw? They all leave the March women, Isla. They leave if they want to survive. Not even poor little Silas could survive your family."

"MIRA!" Cal's voice cut through the tension. He tightened his grip on Isla's hand and started to pull her away.

"You feel it, don't you?" Mira called after them. "Like something's building all around us."

Tears had begun to spill down Isla's cheeks as Cal held her hand, guiding her toward home.

"Be careful, Cal!" Mira's words carried on the breeze as she turned to walk the other way. "Love is the very thing the sea will use against you."

The ticking of the wipers swiping back and forth was the only sound as they drove back from town. Though Isla's hand rested loosely in his, Cal felt the distance in it. Neither was ready to talk about what the day had done to them.

Mira's barbed words still plagued Isla, bringing new fire to doubts that had already been simmering. She stared down the road as it unfurled ahead of them, but everything felt distant now, blanketed by exhaustion and guilt.

“I need to check the generator in the lighthouse,” Cal said. “The storm had to have rattled it last night, and if another squall comes in, we’ll need it.”

“I’ll come with you,” Isla offered quickly, not yet ready to go home and sit with her thoughts.

When they reached the lighthouse, Cal swung the truck onto the gravel driveway and killed the engine. The keeper’s quarters were warm, and the air carried the faint scent of burnt dust from a space heater Cal had forgotten to switch off in his rush to the cove. He moved through the motions of making coffee, filling the room with ordinary sounds: the soft thud of mugs on the counter, the kettle beginning to murmur, the measured chime of spoons against ceramic.

“Coffee?”

“Sure.”

Together, they sat by the window with two steaming cups and a plate of blueberry scones that neither ate. Cal reached over and covered her hand with his, his thumb grazing her knuckles.

“What are you thinking about?” he asked, already sure of the answer.

Her expression held both reassurance and grief. Isla could sense his pain in the way his body leaned toward her. She felt the same ache in herself, as if her heart might split in two from wanting to keep him close and knowing she shouldn’t.

“I’m thinking it’s been a really tough morning for you Cal, and I wish I could make it all okay.”

“Yeah,” he said quietly. “It has been. But having you here makes it easier. I don’t know what I’d do if I didn’t have that.”

For a moment, it seemed like he might say more, but he didn’t. Instead, he set his cup down and stood.

“I’ve got to go upstairs and make sure the beacon’s still good; then I’ll check the generator.” He hesitated at the threshold. “Will you stick around for a bit? We’ll talk more after?” A beat. “And Isla… please, don’t be angry with me when I say this, but stay away from the water today. Only for today.”

This time, she understood. “I’ll be right here.”

She sat, playing over the morning’s events, listening to the faint hum of the generator and the steady rumble of the sea. Beneath it, deep in her core, was that other sound: the sweet, round hum that had become a part of her. It stirred now, tugging at her like a summons. She tried to ignore it, tried to stay still, but her body was already shifting forward, legs unfolding from beneath her. At the far end of the lighthouse, just behind the generator shed, sat the hatch for the cavern below. The tide would be low now. The cavern would be open and accessible until it shifted again.

She stood, one hand brushing the edge of the table for balance, the other hovering briefly over her chest where that hum pulsed beneath her ribs, drawing her forward. As the sound tried to rise, she pressed it down as deep as she was able. She would not sing, but she could listen.

Just a quick look, she told herself.

The hatch groaned when she heaved it open, cool salt air exhaling up from the darkness below. The steep metal ladder gleamed faintly in the dark, and the sound of the tide whispered mischievously against the stone, calling to her. By the time she set her bare feet on the first rung, she’d already forgotten about the promise she’d made.

The cavern opened around her. Drops of water fell from the ceiling, ticking like an unseen clock. At the base of the stairs, Isla stooped and picked up the flashlight that waited there. She flicked it on and a narrow beam cut through the dark. Along the edges of the chamber, black pools shone with the thin shimmer of reflected light, each one rippling with the sea's movement.

Isla stepped forward, her footfalls echoing back in a faint, trailing mimicry. A narrow sliver of light spilled through a crack in the ceiling, barely illuminating the cavern floor. She stepped forward, her bare feet sinking into the shallow tide pool that glistened at its edge. Tilting her face toward the light, she closed her eyes and drew a long, steadying breath. The air was still rich with damp stone and the faint mineral tang of crystallized stalactites, just as she remembered. The water lapped gently around her ankles, and her stress eased as she drank in the soundless energy that rose from the sea.

When she opened her eyes, the flashlight beam caught something pale at the far edge of the cavern, half-hidden beneath the surface of a second tide pool. At first, it looked no different from the scattered shell fragments littering the floor, but as she grew closer, she recognized it. Half-buried, worn smooth from years of being turned and shaped by the water, lay an ivory shell with a jagged pink stripe. A clean fracture ran directly down the center, as though it had been split and then carefully laid to rest here.

The sight hit her like a blow, and the flashlight dipped in her grasp as she sank into a crouch. Moving the rocks and sand around to slide it free, she lifted the small conch. The moment it touched her fingers, she knew: it was the same shell Silas had been playing with before he disappeared. The same one that drew him into the water. The same one Coraline had said was never his to begin with. Isla would have known it anywhere, even if a hundred years had passed.

The break was sharp, though the edges had been polished to silk by the movement of the tide. It felt cool in her hands, with a coating of sand, salt and sea…and then, warmth. Not from the shell itself, but from the memory of a small hand in hers.

Suddenly, a little boy's bright laugh rippled through the air before vanishing into the sounds of the sea. It was gone before she could be sure it had been there at all.

Isla's lip quivered as she held it to her chest.

"Where are you?" she whispered.

At first, there was only the slow pulse of water, but then, from somewhere deep in the cavern, a sound began to rise. One note. The same note she'd been carrying in her chest since the sea first began to change her. Only now, it wasn't hers alone. Another voice braided through it, lower, deeper. Isla looked around, turning toward the black tide pool at the cavern's far edge where the water entered from a deep, hidden cave below. It wasn't more than two feet in diameter, but there, she saw him just beneath the surface. Skin pale, dark hair drifting, light eyes bright with recognition. He was smiling, cheerful and familiar, and it said more than words ever could. It spoke of missing her and of knowing her still. It told her he was here; that he had always been here, waiting. Waiting for her to be ready to be guided through what came next.

This was not just his echo carried through water or dreams; this time was different. This was real. This was a meeting, finally face to face, separated only by a thin layer of water.

With the shell still clutched in her palm, Isla moved toward him: slowly at first, then faster, wading into the rising pool.

"Silas!" His name broke loose as joyful tears spilled from her eyes, but just as her hand reached out for him, the vision in the water fractured.

Silas's silver shimmer receded into the deep, slipping downward into the throat of the cave that led out to sea.

Isla fell to her hands and knees, but before she could fall apart, his voice arrived, carried through the water, woven through the currents and into her.

"Soon," he said, quiet and clear. "It is not yet time. But soon."

Then, he was gone.

Her memories carried her back to the story she'd been told a hundred times about the day he'd disappeared. So many questions remained, but she knew one thing now without a doubt: Silas hadn't been lost to the sea; he had been found. Not taken but transformed. Claimed and kept. Saved.

Isla climbed the ladder and pushed open the hatch as she fought to keep her song from rising to the surface. The light stung her eyes after the cavern's dimness, but she barely noticed. The broken shell was warm in her pocket, and she could feel Silas's smile radiating in her mind.

Cal was standing by the outer door at the front of the lighthouse, his jacket zipped to his throat as he scanned the bluff like he was ready to tear it apart. When he saw her emerge from the cavern, his whole body seemed to let go.

"There you are. I was about to go looking for you," he said, meeting her halfway across the room before stopping to take a second look at her. "What happened? You look…" His eyes carried a look more of wonder than worry. "You look beautiful. Like you're glowing." He didn't say holy, though that was the word that tried to rise to his lips.

"Glowing?"

"I mean it. There's something different about you. The light likes you better than the rest of us today." His attempt at humor fell flat under the weight of his awe.

"I'm…" Heat rose beneath her skin. "I wanted to see the cavern again. It's low tide, but I didn't want to bother you while you were working."

"I get it. You wanted to be somewhere beautiful. Today has been hard." Reading every shift in her expression, Cal watched her. When he spoke again, his voice was low and tired.

"The past couple of days have taken it out of us both. I want to be with you today, but I also get it if you need time. I know my little storm-watching stunt last night cut the space you asked for short. Honestly, I might need a little of that, too. I need to go see a few people in town to tell them about Duncan, and I need to talk to Eli when he gets back."

Isla could sense the heaviness in his heart and the grief beneath his words; the weight he carried not just for her, but for Duncan, too.

"I'm sorry you have so much on your plate right now. I just want you to know, Cal, that you don't have to worry about me," she said gently. "I'm safe in the water; you can trust me on that. And even if you see me down at the cove, you can't follow me. Not this time. Promise me."

"I just…" He rubbed the back of his neck. "I can't stand the thought of something happening to you. Especially not after today."

"Nothing is going to happen to me. Look, I know I should've told you before…but there are some things you don't know yet."

His brows pulled together. "What aren't you telling me?" There was no anger, only a look caught between worry and the sting of being shut out.

"I'm close to understanding it. And when I have all the answers, I'll tell you everything, I promise. But right now, I need you to trust me."

The silence held all Cal wanted to say but couldn't. Finally, he nodded and took her hand. "All right. Please call me if anything happens, or if you need anything at all. Text me so I know you're okay."

"I will." Then, she added, "Cal, no matter what you hear, if it sounds like singing or even if it sounds like me calling for you, you can't go to the water. If anything happens, you call me first or you come to the house. Okay?"

"I promise."

Leaning in, she kissed him gently. The sight of him made her want to stay, to let herself rest in something safe. In the doorway, he looked steadier now, but there was still unease. He'd nearly gone into the water once, and she couldn't let that happen again. This time, she'd be more careful.

Just one more day, she told herself. Enough time to uncover the full truth.

With a final glance, she stepped out into the afternoon light, the seashell warm in her pocket and against her palm, buzzing with a current she now recognized as her own.

TWENTY-TWO

The clock in the sitting room ticked slowly, each sound a constant reminder that the time she had left to learn all she needed to know was slipping away.

A chaotic sprawl of Coraline's handwriting and cramped marginalia lay across the table: some neat and thoughtful, others frantic, written in what looked like a storm of mania. Isla had been staring at them for hours, thumbing through entries until the words blurred and her eyes burned.

As she leaned forward, she put her head in her hands and rubbed them both over her face. She needed to put this puzzle together before the springs highest tide, and she only had a matter of days now until the full moon. Time was running out. Whatever was coming, she could feel it building like pressure beneath her skin. Yet she still didn't know what she was meant to do or how she was supposed to do it.

More than once she'd caught herself humming under her breath, the melody slipping out before she realized. Each time, frustrated with herself, she'd push it low and reach out to Cal, making sure he was far from the shoreline and out of harm's reach.

The pull in her was constant now, an everlasting plea in her veins. It lived in her, calling from below in a voice that was almost hers. She wanted it. Needed to be near it, gliding through the waves.

Duncan. Evan. Cal. Isla's great-grandfather, her grandfather, her father. Each name carried its own gravity, holding a space in her mind. Duncan had washed up dead. Evan had nearly drowned. Her father had fled without explanation, as had her grandfather. And her great-grandfather had been lost to the sea decades ago. How many others had there been? How many *more* would there be?

Every answer unlocked another door, each one leading somewhere older, stranger, and more tangled than the last. The sheriff's reports told one story, neat and mortal, but the sea kept its own account. Isla was close now; she could feel it. She had most of the pieces, but until she had them all, every day felt like borrowed time. Every day she waited was another day Cal was at risk.

With Coraline gone and the last journal lying closed in her lap, Isla knew that there was one person left who might hold the rest of the story. A voice she'd avoided for years: one tangled in abandonment, half-truths, and wounds that had never fully healed.

Her mother.

Isla had made a promise to herself long ago: a silent vow never to contact her unless there was no other way. Now, standing alone in the shadows of her past, she knew she'd reached the edge of that promise. Her phone sat on the counter, waiting, and she stared. Heart hammering against her ribs, she wanted to run, to hide, to do anything but make this call.

The pipes within the house sighed softly around her, and the old wood groaned. From beyond the glass, a wave slammed against the bluff with a loud, thunderous roar. The sea was talking, reminding her she wasn't alone.

Slowly, she closed her eyes and reached for her phone, the screen lighting her face as her thumb hovered over the name she'd vowed to leave buried in her past. There were no guarantees, no certainties, but she believed at least some of the answers waited on the other end of that call. All she had to do was break her promise to herself and dial.

~

The phone felt heavy in her hands. Isla paced a few steps, then sat again, feet tapping nervously against the wood floor. Elbows braced on the table, she ran a finger over the journal's leather cover hoping it might drum up her courage.

Finally, she pressed the call button. One ring. Two. Three. Four. Five. By the sixth, she'd decided to hang up when a voice answered on the other end of the line.

"Isla?" Morgan sounded different: older and rougher, like the years had scoured something out of her, leaving only what was necessary to keep moving. Her voice wasn't just tired, it was hollow; not the worn-out thrill of someone chasing too much excitement, but the flat, vacant sound of someone who had stopped chasing anything at all.

"Hi, mom."

There was a pause long enough to make Isla wonder if the call had dropped. She wished she'd greeted her as Morgan instead.

"I'm surprised to hear from you, Isla. How are you?"

"I'm…okay." She wondered if it was too late to hang up, and she traced an anxious circle against the surface of the table before she stood up and began to pace again. "I'm in Greyhook, and I…well, I need to ask you some questions."

"Is it happening to you?"

Isla's pulse pounded against her throat, so loud she thought the phone might carry it to the other end of the line. "Umm…"

"I knew this call would come someday." Morgan's tone was flat, but not unkind. "It's the reason you're calling, right? I thought maybe it would pass you by as well. I'm sure your grandmother had hoped that also, though she never really said as much."

"So, you know, then."

A pause followed long enough that Isla could almost hear Morgan thinking about how to answer her. "Yes, I know. You've felt it?"

Isla nodded, then remembered her mother couldn't see her. "Yes."

"I was younger than you when I first felt it, though it was barely there for me. I didn't know what to call it then: restlessness at first, dreams and whispers."

"Whispers?"

Morgan's voice dropped. "Mostly in my head, I think."

"You mean the song?"

"No. I never heard the Tide Song, just hints of it. Then, it passed me by. I guess it skipped my generation, or maybe just me."

Isla's body loosened and tightened in the same breath, hope and dread fighting inside her.

"But you were a part of it. You must have always known you were part of something…" Isla searched for the word.

"Something different?" Morgan finished for her. "Yes, but that meant very little back then. My mother didn't have the answers, either. There was no one to teach her; no internet, no cells phones, no parents. She had to collect information in pieces over the years.

"How?" Isla's voice felt small.

"She wrote letters to people she thought might be like her, and she'd hunt down old books or listen to legends from half-mad fishermen. There was never a clean definition; just scraps, really. Hints." Her tone was matter-of-fact, but Isla caught the stiffness in it, like each word was being dragged from somewhere she'd rather keep shut. This wasn't a story Morgan wanted to tell, only one she felt she owed.

"Truth is, Isla, I was never really a part of it. Whatever it was for Coraline, it didn't grow slowly in her like a secret. It was just there from the beginning, woven into who she was and whomever she would become. Now and then it would call her, gently, like a reminder, but it never hurried her. She had time: almost a lifetime to learn what she needed to learn. More time than you do if you're calling me with questions."

Isla opened her mouth, then closed it again. She had imagined this conversation so many times: imagined demanding answers, yelling and accusing Morgan of abandoning her, but the reality was quieter. Sadder. Finally, Isla came out with it.

"So, you left me because you didn't have the pull keeping you here?"

Silence filled the other end of the line before Morgan finally spoke. When she did, her voice was not apologetic. "No, Isla. I left because I had to."

Isla's free hand clenched in her lap, nails digging crescents into her thigh.

"When Silas died, the grief was heavier than anything I've ever known. Staying in Greyhook was like standing barefoot on broken glass. Every corner, every shadow, reminded me of him and of the two of you together. A perfect little inseparable pair. And the sea…" She stopped, as if she'd bitten down on the words. "At that point, Coraline thought it had purposefully taken him, and I was just so angry."

"Thought?"

"Silas had an accident, Isla. A terrible one. But he wasn't meant to be taken that day. A rogue wave knocked him over, and the undertow kept him down. It was a horrible, tragic thing, but it was only then that they took him. They saved him from what would have been his end."

The air left Isla's lungs in a rush, and she held the heel of her hand against her sternum as though she could hold herself together.

"They?" To think it was one thing; to hear it spoken aloud was another.

"*Her* kind." Morgan hesitated. "He was pulled under Isla, but he didn't drown. They saved him from that fate, but not in a way that meant he could come back to us; not in a way that belongs to the land."

There it was. The truth of that terrible day.

"I only realized that later," she went on. "After I'd already gone through with the Severance. By then, it didn't matter. I could never have joined him anyway but letting go was easier when I knew the choice had been taken from me."

Isla swallowed hard. *The missing page.*

"Tell me about the Severance. What is it?"

"It's a ritual. An old ritual." There was shame in her voice, and it suggested this wasn't a story she'd ever intended for Isla to hear. "It's a sacrifice that severs your connection to the something, and you must give something up in return. Something that you love. There is a cost to be paid."

Isla's throat was dry, but she felt no empathy for the woman who had left her alone; left her to fend for herself as a child who had just lost her other half, her best friend. A daughter in desperate need of her mother's comfort and care.

"And what was the cost?"

There was no hesitation this time. "The bond. The ability to feel the way a mother feels about her child. That, and any connection I had to the sea."

Isla's vision blurred. She blinked hard, tears welling stubbornly. The line went still except for the faint ringing in Isla's ears and the sound of her own anguish screaming inside her mind.

"That gentle pull I barely felt, stopped. The dreams ended. I could walk past the water without feeling any connection to it. I could breathe without thinking about my grief, and everything stopped hurting." Her voice wavered. "I felt nothing."

Isla held her hand to her mouth to keep herself from shattering, and the warmth inside her tried to answer, low but present, a quiet melody of comfort. Though she wanted to feel it, to let it comfort her, she pushed it back down.

"Tell me about the ritual." She steadied her voice, refusing to give anything away. Morgan deserved none of her tears, and though they slipped hot down her cheeks, she would not let her mother hear the sadness behind them. "The pages from the only book I have that mentioned The Severance were torn out."

"Coraline burned them," Morgan said. "She never wanted to witness it again."

Isla could only imagine the pain that would drive Coraline to destroy the records of an ancient ritual. How it would have felt to watch her only daughter sever herself from the very things Coraline must have loved the most.

"Then tell me about it." Isla's voice hardened, hurt bubbling into anger. "I deserve to know."

"All right. But remember, this ritual doesn't erase the bloodline or your place in it. It only severs your tie. You're the last of Coraline's line. The last alive to carry the Tide Song. If you were to walk away, to sever, whatever's happening there in Greyhook and whatever's got you calling me after all these years will keep moving through the sea. It won't stop without a decision…*your* decision. The tide will wait for the last in line to decide. Whatever it has in store for you must be confronted."

Isla's question rose before she could stop it, angry with years of hurt and desertion. "Why haven't you told me any of this before now?"

"When you were born, your grandmother didn't have all the answers. Honestly, I don't think she even knew there were questions to ask. Coraline was born of both worlds: half sea, half land. There was never a choice for her to make because she already belonged to the ocean. After Silas, after the Severance, she understood. That's when she came to realize that the next in line would have to choose. That's when she started searching for answers; a way to protect you from what she would never have to face herself."

Isla bit down hard on the inside of her cheek. Years of silence. Years of half-truths. Her mother had let her walk blindly into this while questions and answers had sat just out of reach. Frustration surged hot beneath her skin, sharp with fury at every selfish choice that had led them here. The abandonment, the distance, the cowardice. How many nights had she believed she was broken, unlovable, when all along her mother had known the truth?

She swallowed it all, forcing her voice to steady. "Go on."

"You start with a stone. Not just any rock; it has to come from a tide pool. '*A rock the sea has shaped in its own time and in its own dark place*.' Mine was large and oval, speckled with minerals."

Isla pictured it instantly, her mind conjuring a slick and glittering stone in the dark. The song inside her vibrated as though it recognized what Morgan was describing, and she gripped the edge of the table, grounding herself with the wood beneath her palms to keep the song at bay.

"Then you choose what to sever. I used a lock of both your hair; the ones taped into your baby books from your first haircuts, along with one of

Silas's seashells. This one was special to him. The outer edges were pale, but it had the most beautiful shimmering blue vein along its curve, the inside a dark purplish-blue. It reminded me of the clouds after a storm. It held both my children and the sea inside it, all in one fragile thing. I wrapped your hair in dried seaweed and set it on the stone, next to the shell."

Isla knew that shell: a conch with a vein of shimmering blue, the hollow storm-dark violet interior. The same shell she'd found not long ago, wrapped in velvet in Coraline's vanity drawer. The one she'd locked away in her own dresser, unable to explain why it unsettled her so. Now she knew; the shell had been waiting for her to learn of its dark history.

Morgan continued. "Then, I cut my palm. Five cuts for the rope that binds you, one for each of the senses. I let my blood fall onto the shell and stone so the sea would know who was asking to be released. I burned the dried seaweed that contained your hair until there was nothing left but ash." She paused on the other end of the phone as she envisioned it all again. "I never looked away from those flames."

Isla imagined blood dripping over stone, smoke curling into the night, but she stayed silent as she listened to the ritual that had severed her from her mother.

"At dawn, under a waning moon, I carried the stone, the shell, and the ash into the sea. I submerged three times. The first time, the ash and the shell loosened from the stone and from my hands. The second, they were gone, washed away by the water. The third, I held my breath until my chest burned and every part of me was screaming to surface. That was my surrender. That's when I let the stone sink, and I rose without an ounce of breath left in me. Then I walked away, leaving it all in the ocean."

By now, Isla's cheeks were wet and her eyes red, but her mother's voice never trembled. Morgan's detachment told its own story.

"The fire severs, and the water carries it away. The breath you give up is life. The stone you abandon is the weight you've carried. Freedom only comes in exchange for what you return to the water and what you let wash away. That is the Severance."

Isla blinked back her tears and locked her jaw. Every word had landed like a blade, but she refused to let it break her.

"Isla? Are you still there?"

"Yes. I'm here."

"You're quiet," Morgan said at last, with a knowing tone. "I couldn't be a mother anymore, Isla. Not like that. All I could feel was pain, and it was the only path I could see."

No apology: just facts, as though an explanation would be enough. Her mother had purposely severed herself from the ability to love her, her only daughter, after losing her only son. Isla would not allow Morgan's admission to sink its claws into her right now; not when there were still pieces missing.

Isla cleared her throat. "So, it's all true? Where Coraline came from? Found on the shore as a baby, umbilical cord still attached, with a note saying she was John March's child, and that she should be kept near the sea?"

"Yes. I suppose it's a good thing she was born during the warmer months." Morgan chuckled, her tone too light for the gravity of what she was admitting, and it slid under Isla's skin like a splinter.

"Tell me the rest,"

The sea is in her blood.

Isla could see it again: the small, folded note with the truth of their origin, written on a brittle page. Fragile antique paper creased once at its center, the ink so faint it looked breathed onto the surface, the curling script written in an old-world tongue.

This babe is begotten of John March. Let her be kept ever within reach of the tide, for the sea is in her blood and her blood is in the sea.

"Okay." Morgan said simply. "Coraline's father, John March — my grandfather — along with his brother, found her lying on the sand near where John's fishing boat was anchored. She was brand new, not more than a day old. He raised her on his own for a time, and at some point, went out to sea alone and never came back. Some said it was a squall, but Coraline believed he went looking for her mother and that he never returned because he'd found her. Or she'd found him. John's brother and his wife, Coraline's aunt and uncle, raised her as their own in the same house I was raised in. Then, you were raised there too."

The image stuck in Isla's mind: her great-grandfather sailing into a fog that would never allow him to return.

"What was she? What *was* Coraline's mother?" Anticipation filled her, the pieces finally coming together.

"I think you already know. She was of the deep. Not a siren, not a mermaid. Those are human words. The true name wasn't meant for land-bound tongues."

"It must have a name. What is it?"

"I don't know. One of the ocean-blooded. The only name I've heard it called that ever sounded close was Nereid."

"I don't think I understand…" Isla murmured, though the evidence surrounded her. The journals, the photos, the maps, the books, the tides. All of it pointed to the same conclusion.

"They're not so much creatures; they're like a bridge between this world and the water. From what I understand, they don't walk on land, but they do look like us, mostly. Their bodies carry legs and webbed hands and feet, lungs and gills. Hearts that beat for two worlds, but they never stop belonging to the sea."

Isla shivered. "And Coraline?"

"She had half of that blood: half-human, half-Nereid. A direct descendant. Able to spend years on land, decades even…but in the end, the sea calls such people back to where they belong. Those who answer can go on, bound to the water. Those who resist…" She paused. "Well, they age, they wither, and they die."

"So, the ocean-blooded…they never die?"

"I'm sure they do, eventually. Some ocean mammals live for hundreds of years. I get the impression that these are the same." Morgan sighed heavily. "That's it. That's all I know. Have you tried asking Coraline?"

"Morgan, Coraline is missing. I was hoping you would know where she is."

"Huh. Well, if she's gone, then she's gone back to the sea." Her mother didn't sound the least bit surprised, and the words took a moment for Isla to register.

"The sea?"

"Yes. They always go back to the sea."

"And my choice?" Isla's voice was barely a whisper. "What does that mean? What do I do?"

Another sigh ran softly through the line. "I don't know, Isla. She never told me that part."

After Isla hung up, years of pain surged back all at once. An old wound was torn open, each of her mother's words clinging like salt to raw skin. The call dredged up everything she thought she had buried: the abandonment, the Severance, the cold confession of a bond deliberately broken. There was no apology and no regret; only the finality of a woman who had chosen escape over her own daughter.

She sat with the lonely moments that followed, scraped empty and reeling. She hadn't expected softness, but the ruthlessness of the truth left her stripped bare. Any closure she'd hoped for had dissolved, and she was left with wounds that might never mend.

However, the answers *had* come. *Half human, half something else.* Something she now understood. Coraline, her grandmother, had spent her life walking the line between land and water, and now Isla knew why. It wasn't madness, and it wasn't grief. It was blood. It was inheritance.

She closed her eyes, and the images came: Coraline at the shore, her skirt soaked, hair lifted by the wind. Silas in the water with a face that looked so much like her own. The full moon, cold and silver, rising to meet her, to call her home.

Now, only one question remained: how? How was Isla meant to make the choice the journals had warned of? And what were the consequences of that choice?

The table on which her phone sat, vibrated. One new message, from her mother.

MORGAN: If you haven't found all the answers yet, keep looking. Coraline would not have left you without them.

The three dots blinked, stopping and starting. Then, another line appeared:

I'm sorry, Isla.

~

Isla moved like a woman caught between fury and grief, racing up the stairs to her bedroom. The bottom drawer in her dresser stuck at first, but she yanked harder. The velvet fabric inside still held the conch, its presence a quiet confirmation of what had been left behind. Isla lifted it free.

The ritual Morgan had described burned in her mind; blood over stone, the smoke of their baby hair wafting away, and Morgan's absence like a hand squeezing her childhood heart. Laugh lines and lullabies turned to loneliness.

Anger flared hot at her mother for leaving, at the sea for taking, at the whim of fate that had put this instrument in her lap. The choice here was obvious: shatter the relic Morgan had used to sever her love. Reduce it to splinters, the way abandonment had reduced her.

Outside on the porch, she found the hammer. In the shifting light, the conch's blue vein shimmered faintly, catching fragments of sun. Isla lifted her arms, feeling the weight of the wood and metal above her. She pictured the clean crack of shell beneath steel, her rage splintering with it. For one clear, blinding second, that plan was everything. *Destroy it.*

As the hammer suspended high over her head, the thought of seeing this beautiful thing in splinters, destroyed by her hand, made her hesitate. Isla had heard the cost of the ritual in her mother's voice. Destroying the shell here and now would feel small and petulant. It would change her grief into something destructive rather than redemptive. So, she lowered the hammer and set it down, then strode out onto the bluff.

The air at the edge of the overlook carried the chill of impending rain. Below, the surf moved with a measured fury that echoed the restless churn of Isla's thoughts. When she reached the edge where the grass surrendered to stone, she lifted the conch before her like a summons, the wind whipping her hair and tearing at her clothes. The blue vein along its curve pulsed like a heartbeat, a quiet act of defiance against the darkening sky.

Everything the shell meant and the choice it had been a part of: the woman who had walked away, the ritual that had unmoored Morgan from motherhood, stood there with her now. Isla thought of Silas, of Cal, of all the names that had become stones in her chest. The urge to smash it returned, fierce and animalistic, but another current ran beneath that. It was the knowledge that what she needed was not to destroy the past, but to let it go.

With a deep and grounding breath, she raised her arms and released a primal scream, raw and full, carved from grief, rage, and sorrow. Then, she hurled the shell over the cliff. It spun through the air like a defiant comet before descending toward the sea. The sound it made when it hit the water wasn't the brittle crack she'd imagined, but a muted, sorrowful splash. The surface rippled once, then stilled, drawing the shell quietly beneath.

Release. There was no salvation in it, no absolution; only an unburdening. A knot inside her finally loosening as the grief that had been held there for so long washed away.

TWENTY-THREE

Isla sank deeper into the claw-foot tub, hot water enveloping her shoulders. Steam slithered lazily along the walls, blurring the mirror and muting the small room's edges. The heat moved intently through her muscles, unwinding what tightness was left. For once, there was no heaviness in her heart, no ache for Morgan. Only quiet. Only breath.

Letting her head rest against the porcelain, eyes half-closed, Isla let her fingers drift just above the surface, tracing slow circles in the air. Beneath them, the water followed in small, perfect spirals, blooming and vanishing. The motion soothed her as she felt the ripples fade. The past had finally loosened its hold, and now there was only one thing left to face: the choice.

What she knew so far:

Coraline: Found as part of some kind of beachside baby dumping on the shores of Greyhook, with a note about her life being bound to the sea.

Coraline's fate: Most likely ghosted everyone and returned to the sea in a dramatic homecoming.

Coraline's Lineage: Half-human, half ocean-blooded. Nereid? Semi-siren? And so, in part, were Isla and Silas, which for all she knew came with more baggage than benefits.

John March (her great-grandfather): Vanished in what was probably a Tide Song-induced stroll off his boat and into the ocean, most likely while chasing after Coraline's mother, a literal sea-seductress with whom he'd had some kind of offshore entanglement that resulted in knocking her up.

The Pull: Not psychological, but biological. Blood calling to the sea and the sea calling back. Legacy singing through her veins.

The Echo: The stronger the connection, the stronger the resonance between the person and the Tide Song, unfortunately making Cal a walking bullseye.

Silas: Alive, or something like it. Rescued by Coraline's mer-mafia as he was drowning. Unable to return him to shore, they'd claimed him.

Morgan: Took the express lane out of grief-ville thanks to a handy blood ritual that essentially hit the unsubscribe button on parenting. Checked out and moved on with no further tie to the ocean or to Isla.

The Tide Song: Not music; more like a presence. A too-pretty voice in your head that jailbreaks your nervous system, amplifies every emotion, and turns love or longing into compulsion. Side effects include visions, euphoria, madness, and the occasional walking-smiling-into-the-sea.

Tide Song bonus tip: Sometimes when you think you're only breathing, you're broadcasting.

The full moon: Nearly here, along with some kind of mystical life-or-death decision. No instruction manual included.

Everything else: Congratulations, Isla. You're flying blind.

The burden of it was present, but after today's catharsis, she breathed deeply, letting herself shed what she could. Bit by bit, her mind opened, surrendering as she drifted somewhere between sleep and waking.

Without intent, her soul did what it had always been meant to do: it sang. It slipped out unnoticed, smooth as water over stone, curling into the hazy, humid air. It moved through her and back again, a self-made sedative she didn't realize she was dosing. The notes lulled her from the inside out as tranquility spread, and a subtle signal broke free.

TWENTY-FOUR

Finally climbing out of her relaxing water coma, Isla slipped into bed, where sleep came deep and heavy, pulling her down. She drifted through the darkness and opened her eyes in a place between worlds.

The water was warm and laced with golden light. A subtle tilt of her palm turned her, and a soft kick sent her gliding, her hair drifting behind like dark wings. She soared and moved the way you do in dreams.

As she turned, the world widened. Ribbons of kelp hung like banners. Anemones opened and closed in bruised purples and sugared pinks. Tiny fish flashed like coins of blue and tangerine through streams of sunlight, then stitched themselves back into shadows. Urchins stippled the rocks in constellations while starfish waved with the motion of the water. The current combed past, and the light poured down in soft columns just for her.

The purr of the song inside her answered a larger note that found the same key. The taste of salt touched the tip of her tongue, and she turned once more with a flick of fingers, waters parting like a curtain.

There he was: sea-grown, and a man. His hair drifted, his skin flawless but for the faint shimmer of iridescent scales dusting his brow, shoulders, and hands. Smiling eyes gleamed in shifting hues of blue and green.

When he reached for her, his voice harmonized with hers, though his lips did not move.

"I was never meant to leave you, Isla. I was meant to guard you and guide you through your awakening. The current of life swept me away before I was ready, so the sea found and kept me. I remain your guide: not to pull you under, but to help you rise. You have a special purpose. You are a tether between worlds, one born to rise where others would fall. The sea will always call, but you are not meant to follow blindly. You are meant to choose. To chart the way.

"It is your time. The sea is changing, and if you don't hold it, it will continue to take without asking."

No sound came when she opened her mouth to ask how. She wanted to speak, to tell him she didn't know what to do, but he only shook his head gently, as if time was too short.

Then, he opened his hand, spilling fragments of light between his delicately webbed fingers. It scattered into the shapes of pages, a locked drawer, the faint outline of a cedar box, journals, letters, a corner…and then, a vision of the moonlight streaming through the windows of March Manor onto a floorboard just below the stairs.

"Search where only *we* would once have known to look."

Before she could ask anything further, the water around them began to shimmer, small pockets of light and bubbles rising, swirling upward from below. Then, the world folded in on itself, and the vision collapsed into darkness.

Isla woke with a gasp. The bedroom was perfectly still: no wind, no sound. As her breathing slowed, she rubbed her eyes and felt a sudden heat flowering in her palm. It felt like the throb of a recent burn, subtle but persistent. She turned her hand over and stared.

Etched into her tender skin was a fine spiral marking, just broader than the whorl of a thumbprint. The lines appeared to glow in a muted bluish tone that glittered beneath her skin. It wasn't raised, nor cut, but pressed into her flesh like a brand that had always been there just beneath the surface. With her other hand, she traced the spiral. It was cool, slick, almost glasslike beneath her touch.

She stared at the etched coil, in awe of its beauty but also shocked by its presence. She recognized it. This mark wasn't new to her eyes: it was the same one on the medallion Duncan had worn around his neck, the one he'd been clutching when they'd pulled him alive from the sea. And the one that had vanished with him when he'd died.

This wasn't a coincidence. Whatever the symbol meant, it belonged to the same deep thread that ran through her blood; the same birthright that was reshaping her from the inside out. It was tied to where she came from, what she was becoming — and now, it had marked her.

The edges of her dream still lingered, and when she sat up, a single droplet of water ran down her forehead. Hands drifted to her hair; it felt damp against her cheek. Her cotton t-shirt clung to her skin, and had soaked through to her bedsheets, leaving a wet stain where she'd been laying. Something weighted hung just above her left ear. When she reached up, she found a slick thread of green seaweed, long and glistening. On a glance down, she saw that wet markings streaked the floor, and when she stood, her bare feet met a trail of wet footprints that stretched from the door to the edge of the bed.

"Shit."

A fresh flood of panic rose. *Cal.* If she had gone to the water unknowingly, there was little doubt in her mind that she would have cast her song. Had he tried to go to her? Was he already lost beneath the waves?

The thought brought her to her knees. Her need for him and her need for the sea blurred together until she couldn't tell which her body might have chosen while she slept.

Seizing her phone, her fingers flew over the screen, searching for Cal's number. She dialed once with no answer. Again; nothing. Dread flashed through her as she left a voicemail and then switched to text, tapping out a message with unsteady hands.

ISLA: Are you okay?

Seconds crawled to minutes. She rushed to the bathroom and met her own reflection in the mirror above the sink. Wet hair clung to her cheeks, but as she leaned closer, expecting the usual sleep-tangled look, she found a faint sparkle glimmering beneath her skin, gliding along her cheekbone. There, then gone, then back again as she moved into the light. Tilting her head, she caught it once more; a glow woven into her skin like moonlight playing on water. When she touched it, her fingers met cool, smooth flesh. Nothing more.

"What the hell?"

A sudden buzzing against the porcelain pulled her from the mirror with a start.

CAL: Sorry, I took a sleeping pill last night and slept with headphones on. Trying to keep my promise to you. I'm fine. Is everything okay?

Isla nearly wept with relief, and she had to brace herself against the wall. Speedily, she returned his message.

ISLA: Good. Just checking in. I miss you.

Trying to play it cool, her heartbeat settled, reassured that Cal was safe and sound. However, her mind refused to follow. It spun, snagged on what she could no longer deny. What she'd thought was as a dream hadn't been a dream at all: she had gone to the sea unknowingly in her sleep. How many times had she done that? If she couldn't trust herself to stay on land, if her body could answer the ocean's call without her consent, what did that mean? How much longer would she be able to control it at all?

Descending the stairs, she rounded the corner toward the kitchen and the night's visions surged back. The memory of what Silas had shown her sharpened. She could see it now: the narrow space beneath the stairwell, the loose floorboard they'd pried up with a butter knife. Little knees pressed to the wood, fingers dusty with the effort. Their secret place. She had forgotten it entirely until now.

As children, they had hidden their treasures there: bottle caps, bits of sea glass, small mysteries meant for no one else. Coraline had pretended not to notice, allowing them their secrecy, though Isla suspected she'd always known.

The memory lit up inside her, fast and vivid, and she turned around to kneel at the base of the stairs, fingers searching the scuffed wood until she found the loose board. It was stubborn, but she worked it free with her nails until it gave with a groan. Not far in, past splinters, dust, and cobwebs, her fingertips brushed a stiff, folded object. She closed her hand around it and pulled it free.

Half afraid to open it, half desperate to tear it apart, she turned it over in her hands and then rose quickly, her steps urgent until she reached the front door. The handle turned under her newly marked palm and she was outside, gulping down the sharp coastal air that steadied her.

Coraline's wicker chair faced the horizon, and she sat. In her hand was an envelope, her name written in Coraline's unmistakable hand. With it was a small pocketbook bound with cloth. This was something that carried more importance than just ink and paper; she could feel it. Whatever was inside would change the shape of everything.

Isla broke the seal and began to read.

My Dearest Isla,

If you are reading this, I am already gone, the moon is waxing with the next full night close, and the sea is unsettled. It nears the time for you to make your choice.

By now, you've uncovered the truth of our bloodline. What lives in you is not myth and not some pretty tale of mermaids or sirens. We are older than that. We are the sea's memory, its firstborn. It moves through us, and we through it. Our bodies hold its tides. Our voices carry its call. The Tide Song is not taught: it rises unbidden, like the breath from your lungs. Our voices were never meant for land, and when we forget, the sea reminds us. Not to punish, but to reclaim.

And yet, there is danger in what we carry. When it harms, it is not out of cruelty, but out of yearning. It reaches for connection, for what was lost. It finds the hearts left open, softened by grief or love, and sings through them until they no longer know where they end and the sea begins. Though we do not lure with intent, when the sea is restless, the sound of our song will draw others before they realize they are drifting. This is the burden in your blood now. Yours to understand, and to carry.

In this season of making your choice, you may hear the Watchers. They are kin to us and our most ancient ones. On nights of high tide and bright moon, you may hear them echo your song: not only in longing, but in answer. A chorus to remind you that you are not alone, that your kind are near, and that you still have a place among us.

As the pull within you grows stronger, you will have to choose, and there are only two paths: anchor, or return.

To anchor is to bind yourself to the land. The anchor must be offered freely by one who loves you without condition. Anchoring is not a rejection of the sea, but an embrace of the love that steadies its pull. It is a tether to that love, and it quiets the song and holds the gift in balance. Then, in time, it passes on to the next.

To return is to surrender completely. To give yourself back to the water, to take your place among those who came before. It is to guard what is sacred and to add your voice to the deep. You will be welcomed as kin of the current, keeper of its truth. But you must understand this clearly: there is no coming back to the shore. Returning to the sea is to be remade, and thus you must choose the sea forever. To go back after would come at great cost.

I do not know the weight of the choice you face. My blood runs differently. For me, the decision was simple. I had always been more sea than shore, for it is half of my whole. I could not resist what I already was, and land had begun to hollow me out. To stay would have been to fade away.

For you, a choice <u>must</u> be made, one way or another! If you do not choose, the sea will choose for you. Its unrest will not quiet on its own, and it will continue to reach, to take, to search for resolution in the only way it knows how. It will not linger in uncertainty; it will demand an answer.

Leaving without a goodbye was the hardest thing I've ever done, but I knew that when the time came, you would come home. I am sorry for the years you felt alone. I know I was hard on you, and harder still as you grew. I feared the sea would come for you before you were ready. I set rules to protect you, not to cage you. I thought distance would keep you safe. I see now it only left you unprepared. For that, I am truly sorry.

Whatever you choose...choose it with your whole heart. Let neither fear nor grief decide for you. You are not alone, Isla. I will be watching with the tide.

Always,

Coraline

Isla stared at the words until her body trembled from the sudden and unbearable weight of what Coraline was asking her to do. On the back of the page, she scanned over a neatly-written set of instructions. Chest rising and falling too fast, she knew inevitability was finally at her doorstep.

The full moon. Anchoring. Returning. Changing. Silas. Coraline. Cal.

One choice.

TWENTY-FIVE

Heavy clouds rolled toward Greyhook, bruising the sky with a swollen gray that transformed the sea into a monochrome landscape. As dusk gave way to night, rain came in sharp bursts, slanting against the windows of the March House. Below, the ocean thrashed, its swells white-capped and restless, lunging and retreating in a mounting rhythm. Overhead, the waxing moon climbed higher, nearly full now, glowing like a countdown etched into the sky.

Isla tried calling Cal and then followed up with a text.

ISLA: Can I see you? It's time for me to tell you everything.

She stared at the screen, willing it to light up again. She needed to see him, to tell him what she had learned. So many things were spinning through her mind, a tangle of all she now knew. The choice she had to make. And everything that was at stake.

The cedar box sat open on the kitchen table, a mess spilling out in front of her. The letter from Coraline was set safely inside, and Isla now held the small clothbound volume she had pulled out with it. It was small and looked to be antique, containing no title on the front. The only wording was on the tiny, faded spine that read: *Nērēis.*

Exhaling a half-breath, Isla lowered herself into the chair and opened the small book with care. Its pages crackled softly, aged and delicate. The handwriting inside was unfamiliar but elegant, winding script inked in a style no one used anymore. The penmanship belonged to another era entirely, but the voice lingered here, laced through each line as a whisper pulled forward in time.

Between the strokes of ink, a silent power stirred as her eyes moved across the page.

Nērēis, Nērēidos: The Latin word for Nereid. Nereids: daughters of the sea god Nereus, or Νηρεύς (Nēreus), son of Pontus (the sea) and Gaia (the Earth).

Isla read the unfamiliar words aloud, testing their shape on her tongue. Denser paragraphs followed with ink browned and water-stained.

Not bound to water in the way of the herring-kind or beasts of brine, they can move between the shallows and the deep. A few walked the land in elder times, carrying the sea inside them: its murmur in their marrow, its song in their blood.

Isla read on.

Wardens of the strand and their sea-born kin, their song could summon as swiftly as it could forewarn. The yearning they stirred in mortal hearts was no work of ill intent nor gentle grace, but the awakening of a deeper truth: the echo of their own longing. The song was not oft given voice, though the gift was theirs to wield aloud. It dwelt beneath the skin, loosed by thought or by stirrings of the heart. When feeling surged, so too did the sea.

Through this yearning were the first unions wrought between the Nērēides and those of the land. Some were born of love, others of chance or of burning obsession. Each union bound sea to soil in ways neither realm had foreseen. From such unions came issue. The offspring bore the strength of the sea and the ache of the shore, their voices able to still or stir the waters. When wrath held the tongue, the sea rose fierce; when love or true seeing guided the song, the tide yielded. Yet this interweaving bred unrest: tempests that knew no respite, tides that rose unbidden, whole coasts reshaped by desire unruled, and men who were called and lost unto the sea.

To restore the balance, the eldest among the sea-kin wrought the Ritual of Anchoring: a choice laid upon the bloodlines born of both realms. To dwell upon the land, they must bind themselves to a mortal tether strong enough to hold them fast; yet in so doing, they forfeit their sway over the sea. Should the binding come too early, or prove frail, the deep may cast off the anchoring and madness may follow. Some do not survive and are lost to the pull, to never return.

To go back into the sea is to be unmade and made anew, to take up the water-flesh and rejoin their kind. It is to forsake the land entirely. Without the choosing, the blood grows wild, the pull quickens, and the sea takes what it desires.

Isla leaned in, drawn deeper with every line. The words blurred together as she turned page after page, skimming more than reading now, chasing understanding as it unfolded. There were descriptions of the body: how it shifts, reshapes, remembers the water. Mentions of the Watchers; the elders of their line, bound by rites she didn't yet recognize. Isla barely paused to absorb them. She only knew the answers were here, layered beneath names she didn't know and histories half-told.

Suddenly, a bottomless rumble rolled through the house, strong enough to rattle her teacup in its saucer. A rapid flash of lightning bleached the room in stark white, like the flash of a photograph. The building storm had arrived over the bluff, over Greyhook, and it had found its voice.

Her phone vibrated sharply on the armrest, startling her. Waiting for Cal to call back had her nerves wound tight, and she grabbed it.

"Cal?"

"Isla."

"Cal, I've been trying to call you. I need to see you. Can you come over?"

His voice came fast, scattered. "Isla…" A pause, as if he were trying to find his footing. "I...I can't…"

She froze. Behind his voice, she heard the churn of water, the roar of the thunder.

"Cal." Fear filled her voice. "Where are you?"

Another pause, his breathing ragged.

"Isla…I can hear you."

"What?"

"The song. I didn't notice it at first, but now…it's all around me." He broke off again. "I was at the marina, helping Rory with the storm lines. I was leaving to go home…" His voice cracked, the next words almost swallowed by wind. "I don't remember turning off the road."

Her hand tensed around the phone. "Cal? I need you to turn around and go to the lighthouse or come here. Can you do you that?"

"I'm coming to you…wait, it's okay. I know where you are now." His breath came out in a long, relieved sigh, his voice no longer fighting, but oddly calm. "I'm almost there." Waves. Closer now. Crashing.

Lightning flared outside, and the signal crackled.

"Where are you?" She closed her eyes as she whispered, but she already knew. Because now, in the quiet between thunder, she could feel it…that soft, beautiful melody surging around her ribs, ancient and alive.

The line went dead. Isla was already on her feet, the book slamming shut behind her.

~

Rain slashed down in icy sheets, needling her skin as she scrambled along the bluff path. Waves pounded the shore below in a steady roar and the air cracked, thick with electricity, every sharp inhale filled with the storm. She rounded the final bend, boots slipping on the slick stone, and stumbled onto the open stretch of rock above the sand. There, in the surf, was Cal: chin-deep in the water, black hair plastered to his face, pressing onward into the seething dark.

"Cal!" The flurry around her tore at her words and she knew he'd never hear her. She barely slowed, thrusting out her hand toward the sea.

"Stop! Let him go!" she shouted, pouring power into the command, but the water didn't listen. It heaved and crashed, indifferent.

By the time she reached the edge, Cal was gone. Only a scatter of bubbles broke the surface where he'd slipped below.

"No…" She heaved forward into the surf. "MOVE!" she shouted again, raw, urgent and filled with authority.

This time, her touch found the water, and the sea obeyed. Before her, the surging tide calmed and the waves eased, folding back into a glassy channel shallower than the rest. She stumbled forward, heart pounding, feet slapping through the pools. Salt spray lashed her face, but she didn't falter. The ribbon of still water stretched ahead, a narrow vein carved into the chaos. When she reached where the water deepened, she plunged headfirst without hesitation, feeling her temperature adapt to her surroundings. Isla kicked hard, eyes straining in the dark until they adjusted and her eyesight cleared into perfect, goggle-like vision.

There. A shadow standing calmly on the bed of the ocean deep below. The murk cleared, and she could now make him out perfectly even in the moving water. He wasn't struggling and did not appear to be afraid.

With speed, she swam toward him. Both hands shot out and her fingers closed around him. She pulled hard, and they glided upward, breaking the surface together. Cal gasped, chest heaving and dragging in sharp, ragged breaths of air. His eyes darted, wild and glassy. Rain and sea streamed down his face as he blinked against it. Then, he saw her, and he smiled.

"You're here. I knew you'd be here." He didn't move right away; just stared. A rawness lived in his expression, like her presence both calmed and unsettled him at once. Underwater, his hand found hers, and he squeezed tightly, fingers laced as if finding the reason he'd come this far.

She knew then that she should have dragged him back to shore, but when their eyes connected, something in her broke open. Relief, fierce and hot, followed by a feeling more consuming. It was her love for him, interwoven with her deep, unshakable bond to the sea. The string connecting them pulled tight, as Cal and Isla fell into each other's arms.

As her song pulsed within her, sweet and sure, it flowed through the water until the whitecaps around them stilled, swells softening until the area was calm. It was as if this tiny corner of the cove had drawn a curtain between them and the storm.

Lightning flashed beyond, over the open water, catching on droplets that clung to her skin. In the darkness, Isla looked lit from within, and Cal gasped in awe at the sight of her.

"You're glowing," he whispered, coming out of the haze that held him.

Carefully, he reached for her as if touching something divine, something dangerous. Cal's cold, trembling hand found her cheek, and she leaned into it, light blooming beneath his touch in a flowering bioluminescence. With wonder, he watched her hands as she seemed to command the water, keeping the furious storm at bay. When his lips parted, no sound came; what was there to say? He wasn't just looking at Isla; he was watching as she became one with the sea.

Words felt too fragile for what was happening, so neither spoke as the waves rocked them together. There, in that strange pocket of calm, cradled by the sea, they came together urgently.

Tide gathered at their thighs, soft foam wrapping around them like a living thing. The water shimmered with tiny sparks drifting from the places their bodies touched in pearlescent trails of blue and green that swirled like constellations, a dormant magic awakening.

Cal slipped off her clothing, watching each curve of her bare body shimmer before him. She tilted her head back and let the tide cradle her, hair fanning out in a dark halo. Salt clung to her skin as his fingers traced the slope of her neck, the arc of her collarbone, and the gentle curve of her breast. Then, he took her into his mouth, his tongue brushing the peeked tip as she gasped, body arching into his touch.

Hands tangled in his hair, Isla moaned. "I love you, Cal."

The glow deepened, curling around them in shimmering streams that responded to every movement, every press of skin against skin. Isla reached for his clothes, and he helped her ease them away. As the last layer slipped from him, a shiver ran through his body, gooseflesh rising along his arms. Her hand skimmed the surface of the water, sending a soft ripple through the light.

"Warm," she commanded.

A rush of heat unfurled, flowing along his legs and spreading upward, wrapping him in the same velvet grip that held her. It coaxed the cold from his bones until the shivers eased beneath her touch. Along with that heat rose something else: her song. It was bound to the very water that now cradled them, engulfing him in slow, sinuous waves that curled along his spine and settled deep in his chest until he could hardly breathe for the beauty of it. His need for her, already fierce, grew intense and unstoppable. In his eyes lived not just desire, but surrender, and part of him knew there would be no turning back.

Cal stood before her where she leaned back, buoyed by the water, held by the tide. Her legs floated open around his waist and his fingers slid inside, thumb circling the place that made her gasp. Isla pulled him closer, and their mouths met in a kiss that was made of hunger and need. Her lips parted as their tongues tangled, salt and heat mingling: the taste of him, of the sea, of an unspoken bond rushing between them.

Cal slid his hands to her hips, guiding himself into place. Hard and ready, she felt him pressing against her, teasing, testing. A groan sang from her lips, her body aching for him to fill it, and her inner song swelled, deepening into something more intoxicating. With a rush of need, he entered her in a single, fluid thrust. Isla gasped, her stomach arching as he began to move, each thrust claiming her with unrelenting rhythm. The water swirled around them, swaying with their motion. The pleasure was different here; denser, fuller, flowing from her into him and from him back into her. The song thrummed through every movement, every quiver: a pulse beneath the pulse. Each nerve lit up with a bright, weightless euphoria.

When she opened her eyes, the glow between them was brighter still, each spark binding them closer in a silent vow that whispered the language of the sea.

"I want to feel you shatter around me." Cal's voice was low and husky in her ear.

Trembling, her moan spilled into the air as release built, wave after wave, until it crested and she came undone. Cal followed seconds later, his own climax pulled from him in perfect, breathless tandem. Together they collapsed into one another, bodies trembling with the aftershocks of pleasure. He brushed her lips with a soft and tender kiss, holding her close as they floated together, suspended in waist-high water, the storm still raging just beyond their reach.

In that perfect moment, Isla understood: this was the origin of the longing. This is what her ancestors had carried inside them for centuries. It was not hunger and not harm: it was the impossible ache of wanting and being wanted. The pull and the tether all at once.

"I love you, Isla." Cal's lips brushed against her ear.

"I love you, too."

The storm beyond their unseen shelter was growing impatient, its howl rising as wind sliced through cracks in the rock face. Isla felt the tide shift, the waves pressing harder, rolling faster, and she knew the cove wouldn't hold for long.

"We have to go." Reluctant to leave this place where the world had felt only theirs, Isla planted her feet.

Cal's eyes were clear and present now, but still bright from her song's lingering echo. If she kept him here another moment, the sea might pull him in again.

“Come with me.” She took his hand and turned toward the shore. “We can ride out the storm back at the house and I’ll tell you everything.”

Something in her tone cut through the euphoria, and he nodded. They waded to shore together, gathering their scattered clothes from the shallows and pulling them on as best they could before hurrying hand in hand up the path toward the house.

The higher toward the bluff they climbed, the wilder the storm’s voice became, until the sea below was a boiling black mass smashing against the cliffs with resounding roars.

By the time they reached the house, rain slicked the steps, and the front windows rattled in their frames from the thunderclaps. Isla pulled Cal inside, shutting out the storm with the heavy slam of the door. Wind and rain still pushed against the walls as Cal stood dripping in the entryway.

She drew a steadying breath before meeting his eyes. “I need to tell you some things, Cal. If you’re going to stay here with me tonight, you deserve to know everything.”

TWENTY-SIX

Cal stood still, water pooling around his feet, his soaked blue shirt clinging to his chest and dark hair mussed and dripping. Outside, silver rivulets streaked the windowpanes, blurring the world into shadow.

His gaze held steady on Isla. In his eyes were a tangle of things she couldn't unravel: gratitude, wonder, and a shred of uncertainty just beneath the surface.

Pulling a thick wool blanket from the couch, Isla crossed the room. Cal still stood near the door, his wet jacket and heavy jeans sagging in his hands. She took them without a word, then reached for the T-shirt and peeled it away gently.

"Boxers, too," she said, glancing up. "I'll dry them."

Once he was wrapped in the blanket, she guided him to the couch and bent over to coax the fire to life.

"Let me do that."

"It's okay, I've got it. You need to warm up."

Striking a match against the stone mantle, she lit the kindling and newspaper already stacked in the hearth. Then, she pulled off her own wet clothes, tugged a loose sweater from the back of a kitchen chair, and slipped it over her head. Without looking back, she walked toward the laundry room.

"I'll throw these in the dryer. Sit, and stay warm."

Isla's heart was still alive with the energy of the cove, her steps too light for someone who'd just dragged Cal from below the deep. The way the sea had listened to her, the way it had wrapped around them both, had been sublime. The Tide Song wasn't just a gift: it was a bond, ancient and binding.

When the dryer rumbled to life, she returned to the sitting room wearing a t-shirt and sweatpants, crossed to the couch, and lowered herself down beside him.

"There are a lot of things I haven't told you, Cal." Cross-legged, she turned to face him. "Things I didn't want to involve you in. Things I thought might be too much for you or put you at risk."

"You thought I wouldn't believe you after everything we've been through?"

"No. I know you would have. I just wasn't ready to believe it myself."

The fire Isla had built was burning low and steady, but Cal stood and added another log, creating a comforting glow and crackle. When he sat back down, he took her by the hand.

"So, tell me."

"When I'm in the water…" She glanced down at their hands. "I feel powerful. You've seen what it's allowed me to do. It's who I am and, apparently, where I come from." Her eyes caught the firelight as she looked up at him. "It's changing me."

"I know." Cal's jaw flexed. "I can see it; in your skin, in the way you move in the water, and in the strength of the song I heard tonight."

Isla held out her hand, revealing the small blue swirl marking her palm.

Shock filled his eyes. "Is that..." He reached out and ran a finger over the symbol. "How?"

"I don't know."

"Do you know what it means?"

"No. I woke up and it was there. I think I had been in the water during the night, and when I woke up…" He leaned forward, face concerned and about to speak, but she held up a hand. "I'm fine. What I'm saying is, it just appeared. I don't know how I got it, and I don't know what it means. Do you recognize it?"

"Yes."

"Then you know it's connected to whatever happened to Duncan."

"What happened today in the cove…"

"It's getting stronger. That feeling you feel? That draw is not something you can stop, Cal."

"I called you, and you answered. When I realized I was walking toward the cove, I managed to call. That's something!" His eyes searched hers.

"Cal, this is so dangerous."

"Dangerous? You protected us out there. You created our own perfect little ocean. It was amazing."

"It's not just hearing something captivating and following it to the sea, Cal. I pulled you from the bottom of the seabed. If I hadn't been there…" She stopped herself. "Look, the pull rewrites your sense of what's safe and what belongs to you. It makes the ocean feel more appealing than the shore, and that's what makes it dangerous. It isn't the waves, it's the wanting and the need. You don't understand, I can't seem to control how or when I'm sending that call out to you."

"I do understand, because I know exactly what it feels like." Cal's voice was rough, but his words came like a confession. When he spoke, it wasn't with reason or defense: it was with ruin.

He squeezed her hand as he tried to explain. "I don't just want you, Isla: I am made of wanting you. It lives in my bones, in my breaths, and in every part of me that keeps me alive. It's an ache without a language, and a hollow only *you* can fill. I *do* know."

The words made her heart ache so wildly it hurt.

"But your song isn't what burns inside me. I'm in love with you, Isla. Completely, hopelessly in love with you. And I didn't *just* fall in love with you; I remembered how much I already was. When you're away from me, it's like I'm walking around with only half of my soul. Loving you has unraveled who I was before, and what's grown in its place is better, fuller. Whole. Your song draws me in, but it's not why I love you. I would follow it, though, to the ends of the earth, because it leads to you. I would follow you anywhere, with or without it."

A single tear ran down her cheek. It was beautiful: more beautiful than she had ever imagined anyone could feel for her. Yet beneath that beauty was the truth she could never escape. If the Tide Song blurred love and longing so intrinsically, then his devotion could become a death sentence.

"I love you too, Cal." Her strength wavered, and her voice broke. "More than I can ever tell you. But I'm terrified: for you, and for us. The Tide Song was meant to guide and protect, but over generations it's grown stronger." Revealing the symbol on her palm again, she said, "Duncan didn't fight it because he *couldn't*. It twisted his sense of safety and I'm afraid it's going to continue twisting yours. You are in danger *because* I love you."

"So, you really do love me, then." Relief brightened Cal's face, a playful grin spreading, though its warmth betrayed how much her words really meant.

"Of course I do. But that isn't shaping up to be a great thing for you, Cal."

"That doesn't scare me."

"It sure as hell should." Isla's arms folded tight across her chest.

"Maybe it should, but it doesn't. I'm not walking away, and if the sea takes me because I love you, then let it take me." His hand cut briefly through the air, as if offering himself to it. "I'd rather drown than live without you."

"Case in point, Cal."

"I know what I'm doing. I'm a big boy. I'm not wandering into this blindfolded, and since I can't hear your siren-playlist in my head right now, I'm safe right here beside you."

"I'm not a siren."

Cal leaned in and kissed her gently. "I think this just means I have to stay with you all the time, to make sure we're both safe." He winked before turning serious again. "There must be something we can do."

Coraline's words from the letter: *anchor or be swept away.*

"There is something…but first, we need to keep you away from the water, at least for the next twenty-four hours."

"Okay, no problem. What else?"

"The full moon is tomorrow night, which means I have a choice to make."

"Choice?"

"Let's open a bottle of wine." Thunder clapped above the house. "I have a lot more to tell you."

Isla told Cal everything: what she believed had happened to Coraline, the truth about Silas, the story of her own bloodline, what it meant to be born of the sea, and what it demanded of her. She spoke of the cost, and of her mother's choice to sever herself and turn her back on it all.

Cal listened intently, wide-eyed, elbows braced on his knees. The words settled like stones, but his gaze never wavered. Beside them, the fire had burned to a low glow, and the rain had softened to a gentle patter against the windows. Their half-empty wine bottle sat abandoned on the table beside their forgotten glasses, lost amid the letters, notebooks, and scattered stories.

When she was finished, Cal exhaled with puffed cheeks and leaned back in the armchair. After a brief silence, his mouth quirked.

"Holy shit. Mira is going to be one smug old lady."

"Ha!" Isla laughed, short and surprised. "I'm glad you're taking this so well, but you're probably right. I can practically hear the 'I told you so.'"

"Do you think Coraline saw what we did in the cove?"

"I like to tell myself there's a boundary there. Rules about peeping water-people."

He grinned faintly as Isla chuckled, but the humor faded. "You talked to your mom. Wow. What did she say?"

Isla picked up her glass and stared into the dregs of her wine. "She told me the truth, or her version of it. That she chose a ritual of separation after Silas died, or whatever. Something to…" She searched for the words. "To remove her from her own grief. And remove her bond with us. Claimed it was the only way she could keep going. It's called the Severance."

"She chose that? To just cut it out of herself?"

"Apparently. She seemed to feel it was a kind of mercy." Isla rolled her eyes. "More like emotional amputation."

"That's horrible, Isla. I'm so sorry."

"Thank you, but I'm not. Not anymore."

"That doesn't make it less cruel to leave you with all of it: even now, but back then you were just a child."

"I've spent a long time being angry at her. Now, I'm just…done."

"You didn't deserve that." He took her hand in his. "You deserve to be loved by everyone who should love you, and by anyone who is lucky enough to. You *are* worthy of it."

Isla raised her hand to his cheek, his words filling the hollow parts of her heart. "Thank you. No one deserves what she did, but maybe if she hadn't done it, I wouldn't be here."

He studied her. "I bet Mrs. Ellwell would love to adopt you."

That drew another laugh. "I don't think I want to compete with you for that roll. Though I would enjoy her shortbread on the daily."

They smiled at each other.

"So…this choice; anchor or return to the sea. Does it *have* to happen on this full moon? It can't wait until next month?"

"It has to be tomorrow," she said, the reality of the deadline upon them. "High tide on the full moon of the spring equinox."

"And this Severance thing is not an option in this case."

Isla shook her head, a pang of nausea rising at the thought of severing herself from all she now knew.

"All right, then. I guess we'd better make sure you have everything you need before tomorrow night."

As the words left his mouth, Cal realized Isla had never said what her choice would be. A future was being planned in his mind that she might not intend to share with him. Trepidation at the possibility she may not decide to stay.

"Isla, tell me you're going to stay. If you need me to say it, I will. I want you to anchor!"

Of course she wanted this. She wanted him. She wanted a life with slow mornings wrapped in warmth, sunlight filtering through linen curtains, and Cal's presence steady, always beside her. Afternoons spent with hands intertwined, salt on their skin, and laughter in their mouths. Dinners beneath an open sky, the scent of rosemary and wood smoke curling in the air. A home where land met water, where they could build something rooted; something no tide could carry away. She wanted children with him. Children who would know both the land and the sea. A slow life that began and ended with Cal.

Beneath those wants also lay a quiet insecurity. What if Cal didn't really love her by choice alone, but because the Tide Song had wound itself into him and he just didn't realize it? What if his feelings weren't truly his, but something borrowed and summoned from the deep? If it was the song holding him, not purely his own heart, then none of it was truly real, and she would never know unless she tried to anchor. If she failed, it would break her, and the anchor would be unsuccessful.

On the other side of that choice was Coraline, with a legacy knotted in secrets, and Silas, the brother she barely knew. Older now: a bridge into a world she had only glimpsed in dreams. What would it mean to turn her back on them, on all that lost time? There was still a chance to know the woman behind the silence, to see her grandmother as she truly was. And Silas not as a mystery, but as a man, a brother, a friend.

For a while, they sat with her silence, her unsaid words gathering tension. She had known Cal for what felt like lifetimes: childhood friends and teenage confidants, together through grief and growing pains. And now, friends folding into lovers. But she didn't just love him: she belonged to him the way the moon belongs to the tide.

Finally, Isla smiled a smile that came from the certainty of knowing that she would choose fully and without fear. *With your whole heart,* Coraline had said. Isla stood at the edge of two worlds and wanted to turn only toward him.

"I want that, too," she said at last. "It's always been you Cal. I want to anchor. This…" She reached for his hand, lacing her fingers through his and then placing them over her heart. "This is the life I want. *You* are what I want."

Cal let out a breath he hadn't realized he'd been holding: a soft, trembling exhale that broke into a quiet laugh of relief. Then, he kissed her: tenderly, and he understood exactly what she'd given him.

"I'm going to need your help," she said.

"You have it. Let's figure this out, together. Tell me what we need to do."

"Well, first we'll need some supplies. A stone from the cavern to start. Coraline called them 'memory stones' in her instructions. '*A tide-worn rock touched by the moonlight. The ones that shimmer will hold resonance.*' That stone will bind the choice." Isla pictured her mother, the story of the Severance with her glimmering rock.

"Okay. Sounds easy enough. What else?"

"We need to figure out where all of this will happen." Isla read from the back of Coraline's letter. "'The choice must be made in a place touched jointly by moonlight and tide.' The cavern beneath the lighthouse could fit, but only when moonlight is strong enough to leak in through the cracks in the stone. If it's at all stormy at high tide, it won't work."

"What about the cove?" Cal asked.

Isla considered. "It just feels too simple, doesn't it?"

"It fits the criteria. And it's where you've been learning about all of this, so why not?"

Ruminating on Coraline's words, she considered the paragraph about song and bond and how the anchoring only worked if offered up freely and with free will.

"There's one more thing." Isla swallowed. "The anchoring needs to be tied to something, or someone. A person whose bond can hold me here."

"And if you don't have that?"

The storm flashed over the cliffs, a crackle of lightning illuminating the room.

"Then I have no choice but to choose the sea. And if I anchor and fail, then all hell will break loose. The ocean will not settle, and it will continue taking."

Without pause, Cal's voice came clear and sure. "Let me be your anchor."

Relief flooded her, though it twisted almost instantly into guilt. To be her anchor was to tether her, not with chains, but with love. The song would coil around him, binding them together and to the land through his presence, his heartbeat, his love. If his love was pure, it was the solution they needed to remain together and to calm the hungry seas. If not — if it was at all clouded by the pull — then the ritual would fail.

"Are you certain? You don't know what you're offering." Her voice was softer than she meant it to be. "It won't be a walk in the park."

"Maybe not," Cal admitted, "but I'm offering it just the same." He smiled his disarming smile. "If we need those rocks from the cavern, we should go tomorrow morning."

"Low tide is at six a.m." Isla pointed to the tide chart.

"Guess I'll set my alarm."

"Second low tide is at six twenty-five p.m., which means the following high tide hits at twelve thirty-seven a.m."

"Right at the height of the full moon," Cal noted.

“What if we can’t find the rock we need?” A feeling of impending doom began to settle on her. “What if we don’t find the right one, or if there are none?”

“We will,” he said simply as he took her hand in his. “We’ll find it.”

Cal gathered her into his arms, pressing her head to his chest until the rhythm of his heart slowed her own. With each rise and fall, the panic ebbed.

“As promised, I will make great sacrifices and stay here with you tonight.” The warmth of Cal’s breath carried his playful words, ever bent on brightening her mood and lifting her up. “That way, I can’t sneak off without you to try to hurl myself into the ocean.”

The wind whistled at the windows, and the sea answered with a restless growl. The air seemed charged as the ocean anticipated her choice. Already knowing, already waiting, ready to reclaim her if she faltered.

By tomorrow morning, she’d be standing in the place where her future would begin to take shape.

Couch and chair cushions, layered with blankets and bed pillows, made a low nest on the sitting-room floor in front of the glow of the hearth. Cal stretched out, looping an arm around Isla’s shoulders and drawing her against his chest as the slow crackles of the burning wood filled the silences between their sentences.

The conversation drifted from nothing to everything: the first time they’d climbed the lighthouse as kids, the night the entire town lost power in junior year and they drank cheap wine under the pier. The private replay of what he really thought the moment she waltzed back into town, and how he knew then that he was going to fall for her all over again

They played an old record on Coraline's battered player and dug into a microwave-warped bowl of popcorn, laughing at lyrics and trading stories between buttery handfuls.

"You still eat all the half-popped ones," Cal said, nudging her foot with his.

"They're the best ones," Isla grinned. "It's like eating tiny, angry rocks that pop open and taste like butter. The crunch is amazing. You're just mad I beat you to them."

"You always did," he said. "You always did dig for them like a gold miner."

"You would wait until the steam cleared like a gentleman and then wonder why there were no good ones left at the bottom."

"I *was* a gentleman; I gave you the last slice of pizza the night of Amanda Nielsen's birthday."

"Yeah, after you dropped it face-down on the grass."

"It still counts," Cal said. "It had the shape of a piece of pizza, and the soul of a piece of pizza, so it was still a piece of edible pizza. Plus, you brushed it off and you ate it."

"I was hungry."

"We were tipsy on Coraline's homemade strawberry wine. I think you would've eaten anything at that point."

"You're impossible."

"And you're a half-pop hoarder."

For hours, the world outside the windows didn't exist.

"You know…" Cal shifted a little, elbow propped on a pillow. "I was nervous as hell when I heard you were back."

Isla glanced over, surprised. "Really? Why?"

"Because I knew I'd still be stupid about you, that I'd see you and dive straight back in. And I didn't know if you'd even want to see me again."

"You thought I wouldn't talk to you?"

"I was just afraid of old feelings. But then I saw you standing on the beach that night and…" He trailed off.

"You didn't look nervous."

"I wasn't. All that fear faded away, because it was you, just as you'd always been."

"Older, though." She cocked her head playfully.

"Wow. You're really never going to let me forget that."

They laughed, enjoying small ordinary things that made the night feel normal again. Cal asked what the future might look like if she could truly choose: not land or sea, but the life she would want if none of this were real and there was time enough to build it. She'd hesitated at first, and then began to paint a picture for him, her voice light with imagined tomorrows. This house, warm and full of sunshine, restored to its original glory. Slow mornings, the cove between the March House and the lighthouse as their private shore. Long, lazy summer days on the sand and candlelit takeout dinners like the ones they loved to share.

"You'd finally be fixing up that old sailboat," she said. "You'd make her seaworthy again and you'd take me out every Sunday."

"You'd be my first mate, but you'd try to name her something ridiculous." Cal chuckled.

"Absolutely. Like...the *Salty Queen*."

"Maybe I won't let you be my first mate, then."

Amused, she settled deeper into him.

"We'd sail to Hawaii," she murmured. "Or Mexico. Or just…disappear for a while. Be nobodies, everywhere."

The dream widened. Children, if they wanted them; names and numbers tossed back and forth.

"How many would we want? Don't say eight."

"I was going to say nine," he smirked. "We could field a baseball team."

"Try again."

"Two? Maybe three, but only if we had two boys or two girls already."

"You'd end up with three girls for sure."

"I think I'd be okay with that. They'd all be as beautiful as you are."

"Cheesy!" Isla laughed. "I like 'Charlotte' for a girl. Sophisticated, but a little bit wild."

"It sounds like a queen's name," Cal laid back, smiling at the scene they were painting. "She'd definitely rule us."

A conversation that might once have felt too soon flowed easily now, stitching small, ordinary hopes together into something they could foresee. There was no speaking of the full moon or the choice hanging in the balance. They curled up together, her head on his shoulder, his fingertips tracing gentle circles on her arm.

If she closed her eyes, she could see this as forever. She could pretend that tomorrow wouldn't come.

TWENTY-SEVEN

At dawn, a fragile calm had settled. Above the cove and the clustered rooftops, the sky was mottled in soft pre-sunrise hues, streaks of lavender and orange stretching across the horizon. Though it remained still, the wind had shifted, bringing an icy northern push that carried the brackish tang of deep water and the indication of another storm brewing far out at sea.

The water should have been calm on a morning like this, but the waves struck the shoreline with thunderous pulses, each one heavier and drawn from some deeper, mounting rhythm. With every swell, the spray leapt high, curling into mist that reached for the cliffs. Its echo hurled upward, shattering against the face of the rock.

Dressed for the chill, Cal threw on the same jacket and jeans that had hung overnight after the dryer hadn't quite finished the job. The fabric was stiff, the cuffs damp where his hands had brushed against the morning dew. Isla wrapped herself in an old fisherman sweater, thick with soft brown wool that smelled faintly of cedar. The sleeves swallowed her hands, and the weight of it felt like a kind of armor; a borrowed comfort against the day ahead.

As the sun rose, they climbed the weathered steps into the lighthouse, stones slippery with lingering spray that glistened underfoot. Isla's heel slipped, but Cal caught her arm without a word, steadying her and guiding her forward. They passed through the main area and on to the generator shed, through the groaning hatch and down the metal ladder. At low tide, the cavern's mouth yawned wide: a black, waiting hollow. Stalactites hung like jagged teeth overhead, their tips weeping drops of runoff into the small pools below.

"Do you see anything that might work?" Cal picked up rocks, examining them before dropping them back into the shallow waters.

Isla stepped forward. The air was alive with the same energy she'd felt the last time she was here. She glanced around, and then, for a moment, closed her eyes and listened.

"Yes," she said finally, eyes opening again. "I can feel it. There's a current here; something I feel connected to."

They moved deeper into the grotto's winding crevices, where the ceiling dropped so low Cal had to hunch, his head brushing against the rock above him. Isla crouched just ahead, her fingers grazing the edges of a narrow tide pool nestled in a hollow beneath the overhanging rock. It was a shallow pocket, half-hidden in shadow and close to the ground. At her touch, the water glowed with pale bioluminescence, each ripple awakening soft pulses of light beneath the surface as her fingers coaxed it from the dark.

Cal stared at the shimmering glow in the water. "That's…not common down here. Are you doing that?"

"In part, yes. I can call, but it's the sea that's answering this way. I'm just asking it to show me."

The ghostly shimmer continued to spread in a small, tight path leading toward a narrow cut in the rock wall where the water pooled the deepest. Isla slipped off her boots and waded in to where the glowing road ended. Arm outstretched, her hand sank below the surface, where she found a hard, smooth object. It was oval, with an uneven texture that caught the light when she pulled it free, water streaming off its surface as she raised it up. It was about the length of her forearm and surprisingly light in her hands. It had veins of deep green and flecks of silver. No ordinary rock: Isla recognized it. This was a memory stone.

"Is that it?" Cal leaned in for a closer look.

A single nod. It looked just like the stone her mother had described: same size, same shape, flecked with silver like captured starlight. A stone of resonance. A stone meant to bind a choice.

"Yes, this is it. This is the one." The calm it brought with finding it, was also edged with unease. Holding it made everything real: the stories, the legacy, the choice she could no longer pretend was distant.

The cavern, once dense with mystery, now seemed protective. Peace clung to the walls and in the salt-damp air, it wrapped her in a sense of belonging. She felt at home here in this space, and now, the thought of leaving, of stepping back into the storm of what came next, was a burden she didn't feel ready to shoulder.

Cal stepped forward and carefully took the stone from her, slipping it into his pack and drawing the zipper closed. The straps rasped as he tightened them and settled the weight against his back. When he turned to Isla again, a reassuring look softened his face. He extended his hand, waiting until her fingers slid into his. With that one small act, came the reminder that she wasn't alone.

"Come on; take a deep breath, and then let's finish what we need to do." With that, he led her toward the mouth of the cavern and up the ladder.

Back in the lighthouse, he set his pack down and tipped his head toward the bedroom. "I'll grab a few things to bring over. Just give me a second." Then, he disappeared through the doorway.

Isla paused, taking in the familiar space before climbing the narrow spiral staircase to the upper viewing deck. From here, the lighthouse's beam swept slowly across the edges of Greyhook and back out over the ocean, its glow steady in the overcast morning.

The town huddled close to the shoreline, rooftops covered in dew, window lights flickering to life as the day began to stir. Beyond, the harbor rocked in quiet motion with a scatter of tethered boats, their masts swaying like restless reeds in the push of wind and tide.

It struck her then. What if things went terribly wrong? What if this was the last time she ever saw Greyhook from above? The March House's roofline in the distance, the narrow streets she'd wandered as a girl, the lighthouse always bracing against whatever swelled in from afar. It all felt painfully finite, like her memory might have to hold it forever.

The rotating light swept again, catching the sea in a pale stripe before the rising morning swallowed it back. As she followed it beyond the cove, just past the rocky lip where the waves curled inward, something silver moved in the glint of the beam: not one shape, but several slender, glimmering bodies refracting the first hints of daylight. They slid through the water with an elegance that felt both alien and familiar, reflections catching and scattering along the arcs of their movements.

The Watchers.

A living record passed down in memory and song. While the younger, less experienced sea-kin sang to express, to soothe, and to mourn, the elders sang to remember. Their voices held their history; the cadence of every choice made at the water's edge. They sang to tally bargains, to mark thresholds, to note when a human life had become an entry. Their song was the ink, their voices the parchment. They did not sing for love; they sang for keeping.

Isla felt the gravity of their gazes from within the water, waiting. Their presence was not a casual curiosity; they were here to bear witness. She felt the pull within her and heard their melodies, velvet and beautiful, threading into hers. The time was almost here.

When Cal emerged with a small duffel on his shoulder, Isla had fixed her face from a look of awe into something more stable.

"You ready?" he asked.

With a nod, she took his hand, and together they made their way down the stairs, out of the lighthouse, and toward whatever waited on the other side of the choice.

TWENTY-EIGHT

When they arrived back at the manor, Cal pulled the stone from his pack and carried it to the kitchen, passing it to Isla, who set the shimmering oval in the center of the table. Light struck its surface and splintered, scattering like an explosion of trapped stars. Flecks of mineral inside the stone shimmered into a hundred pinpoints of gold that danced across the walls. Around it lay the journals, tide charts, notebooks, and an old sea-stained map of the coastline. Together, they formed a kind of archive: a record of patterns, discoveries, and everything the sea had taken from her family. And everything it would ask for next.

"At high tide, when the moon is at its peak, the light should cut down right through the middle. If it falls across the water here," Cal pointed to a spot on the map, "it'll connect the land to the sea on this side of the cove."

He was studying the topography, tracing the lines of the coast and the projected path of the moon, but Isla's attention had already shifted back toward the window, where the cove shone below streaming fingers of cloud broken sunshine. She could feel him now. Silas was nearby.

As Cal murmured something to himself, she stepped away, moving toward the glass. She looked to the familiar sweep of the bluff and on to the restless motion of the sea, where, once again, she saw movement. A lone figure cut swiftly and elegantly along the surface, moving with purpose. When it reached the cove, it rose until its shoulders broke the water not far from shore. Isla narrowed her eyes, straining to see into the distance, when suddenly, her sight seemed to clear, sharpening until she saw him as though he stood only feet away.

There Silas was, standing in the shallows where sea met rock and sand. His shoulder-length hair stirred in the wind, calm eyes smiling, presence marked by the same gentle patience he'd carried as a boy. Isla exhaled, and a faint bloom of condensation touched the glass in front of her, ghosting the space between them. She could hear him now, inside her mind, slipping into her thoughts.

"Here." Just one word, and then he was gone, slipping back beneath the waves.

Behind her, Cal was still speaking; something about the tide charts and the moon, but his voice had faded, like it belonged to another room entirely.

"It's the cove," she whispered. "You were right; that's where it's meant to happen."

"Okay, we should head down there now, then." Cal didn't question her certainty. "Let's check it out while it's still light out and before the rain hits."

He rolled up the map and put the stone and journals into his pack, tucking it safely out of sight. They left the house together, boots crunching over the damp gravel, hands intertwined.

The switchback trail down to the beach was slippery from the rising mist of crashing waves, and a fine electric charge tingled over Isla's skin like static. At the final bend, they broke from the trail and stepped through the sea grass, wet blades brushing against their legs, until they reached the rocky stretch where stone gave way to sand. The place in front of where Silas had appeared.

"This is it," Isla said quietly. "This is where it has to happen. Right here."

Cal stood beside her, eyes scanning the cliffs. "Okay," he said, simply. He could feel the tension flowing through her, the heaviness of standing in the very place where everything would change. "We'll be ready."

When the moon rose, this ground would remember, and it would bear the weight of her choice.

Lacework patterns made from a film of foam and water pulled back and forth across the sand as Isla traced the line where the high tide would reach tonight. Mentally, she marked it while Cal watched, admiring her.

"You know, this where I first saw you. Right here in this cove."

Isla looked up, surprised.

"Not the first time we met, but the first time I saw you. We'd just moved back to Greyhook. I was five or six; young, so it's a bit of a scattered memory. My mom brought me down here to explore, and I remember walking along the shoreline kicking at the sand when I saw you. You and Silas were over there." He smiled at the memory as he gestured toward the shallow water along the beach in the distance. "Silas was throwing rocks, and you were trying to catch them before they sank. Your mom was sitting there," he pointed just beyond, "with a book."

"I don't remember that day."

"You would have only been four or five. I was too shy to come say hi, but Silas spotted me when you were putting your shoes on and came running up the beach like he knew me." Cal's face carried a look of fondness and loss in equal measure. "He said hello, and then he ran back to where you were. That was it; that was the first time."

Isla couldn't see the memory in her mind, but it sounded like Silas; approaching someone he didn't know with kindness. Maybe he had been the bridge between her and Cal even back then.

"Guess I've been finding my way back to you ever since." Cal spoke with tenderness.

The words turned her heart liquid, marking her soul in a way she'd never forget. She turned away, blinking against the sting rising in her eyes. Somehow, Cal made this choice feel so simple.

The rest of the morning unfolded quietly. Time ticked away as hours slipped by, with Cal and Isla orbiting one another like magnets, never far apart. He brewed coffee while she stood at the sink, rinsing the dishes from the night before. Each time her cup neared empty, Cal filled it again, as though caffeine might pin them to the present a little longer.

She wiped down surfaces and tidied clutter, holding true to Coraline's old mantra to always tidy before a storm. *Chaos outside calls for order inside.* And a storm was coming, in more ways than one.

By early afternoon, the heavens had grown restless, a sure sign the weather would shift again by nightfall. They worked side by side as the day stretched on, storm-prepping in small tasks to keep their minds and hands busy. Cal split the last of the wood and carried it inside while Isla stacked it by the hearth, commenting how Coraline always kept a dry pile inside, even during the summer. Then she built a small cone out of kindling that surrounded pieces of scrunched-up paper and dryer lint, creating the perfect fire starter.

"You make it look so easy, like you've done it a million times." Cal brushed the wood dust from his palms and leaned against the doorframe.

"I probably have. Coraline made us always prepare for a storm, no matter if they were forecast." She tied back her hair with an elastic band. "Do you think this one's going to hit hard?"

"Maybe not in the kind of way that shows up on weather maps."

"That's not ominous at all."

"Sorry." He laughed, tilting his head toward the darkening sky. "You have to admit, when things get serious around here, the weather throws a fit."

They gathered the flowerpots from the porch, pulled down laundry still fluttering on the line, and latched the upstairs shutters one by one. Between each task, Isla found herself sharing things she had never thought to voice: the way Coraline marked the turn of seasons by tides instead of calendars, what it had felt like to spend so many years away from Greyhook, and how much she had enjoyed being back here these past few weeks. Cal listened intently, asking questions as though learning the language of her life piece by piece.

They cooked a late lunch; chopping vegetables, stirring the pot, moving around each other in that easy way. Then, they carried their plates to the porch to eat while Isla watched the horizon. Between bites, Cal told her about a fishing trip he'd taken with his uncle when he was just a boy and how they'd caught nothing but still stayed out all day.

"That's when I knew I always had to live near the water." He let the memory unspool.

"When was that trip?"

"Uncle Ray's old boat, the summer I turned ten. That boat barely floated and it smelled like diesel and mildew, but I thought that thing was the most beautiful ship in the world."

"Ray was such a good guy. With an affinity for sun-faded ball caps, if I remember correctly."

"That was him, but only blue ball caps! He had to have had over a dozen." Cal laughed. "He used to say the secret to a good day on the water wasn't catching anything; it was staying out long enough that you stopped caring if you did. And we rarely did. We'd sit out there for hours, just the two of us. I learned all the sailing knots from him, and he taught me about reading the stars."

Isla rested her chin on her hand, listening. "Sounds like you caught something after all."

"I guess I did. I really do need to get back to fixing that old boat. She's a mess, but she's got good bones."

"You still think I'd make a hell of a first mate?"

"Of course!"

"Even after all of this weird sea business?"

Cal reached for another slice of bread, shrugging. "I'd say you proved yourself when we were out on the water this week. You've got good instincts and strong arms. We know you can hoist a sail. And all this ocean drama will be behind us by then, anyway."

Isla raised an eyebrow. "Strong arms? Is that your new move? Flattery by way of manual labor?"

"Maybe. Is it working?"

"You haven't seen me try to tie a knot in ten years. The last one I made for you unraveled itself."

"We'll work on that," he said, topping off their wine glasses. "You handle the snacks, I'll handle the rigging."

"Perfect division of labor," she said, lifting her glass. "To surviving the storms, both literally and figuratively."

"And to boat dates. Imagine us, sunburnt, half-lost off the coast of British Columbia, sailing through the gulf islands."

"Honestly, that sounds pretty great."

Cal leaned back on his elbows, watching her.

"I think about it more than I should," he said. "That kind of life: slow days, water all around. You. Me. No curses. No moon rituals. Just…us."

He swirled his wine. "Sometimes I wonder…" His voice softened. "If things had been different; if you'd never come back. I'd still be waiting here without even knowing I was."

"But I did come back." Isla reached across the table.

"Yeah. You did."

After a moment, Isla broke their comfortable silence with a teasing glint in her eye. "So, how sunburned am I going to get on this future boat of ours?"

"You? Lobster red. Absolutely no awareness of the sun."

"I'll have you know I am meticulously SPF-aware. And if I must, I'll wear a hat. But then I'll have to take dramatic selfies from the bow while yelling nautical phrases I don't understand."

As the mostly cloud-covered sun traced its slow arc toward the sky, they continued to trade tales and dreams, laughing the kind of laughter that made everything feel possible. By late afternoon, the air had sharpened, carrying the first threads of night.

Isla felt time slipping away too quickly. When the dishes were washed and set away, she drifted to the fire, gazing into its hypnotizing blaze.

Cal's arms encircled her from behind, and he bent close to murmur against her ear. "It feels like the end of something."

"It's the edge of something," she whispered. "The beginning."

A gentle hand brushed down her arm until their fingers found each other, and he turned her around to face him.

"I need to say this just once more, before everything happens tonight." He squeezed her hand. "I've loved you longer than I can remember, Isla, and I want you to stay. If this really comes down to a choice…choose me. Choose us. I'll be your anchor, and I'll spend my whole life showing you that you don't have to be anywhere else to feel whole. That you don't have to *be* anyone else." His voice caught, but he smiled. "I'll spend the rest of my life loving you. I hope you already know that, but I needed you to hear it again."

The fire popped softly behind her and she rested her forehead against his. She had foolishly believed that once the decision was made in her head, the stress of the night would loosen its grip; that the fear would dull and something would relent. Instead, as sunset crept closer, everything seemed more tense. It wasn't doubt, but fear; already moving, already here, breathing down her neck as the light began to fade.

"I can hold you here if you'll let me. Just keep saying you'll stay."

Cal had been there in almost every chapter of her life. The one who came to her rescue time and time again. Once again, she let herself imagine it fully: this house as their home, the cove their playground, his boat rocking steady, anchored there in the water. A life built together, simple and vast all at once. She had never loved anyone like this; had never even believed herself capable of it until him.

As her eyes met his, she felt her decision re-settle like the tide returning home, and she smiled. "You're my anchor, Cal. You always have been. I'm not going anywhere."

They let the next hours of fading light unfold wrapped in each other's orbit: nothing elaborate, just time stretching on, the evening belonging only to them. Isla curled into him on the old sofa, her bare feet tucked beneath his leg. Cal rested his chin on the top of her head while his fingers traced the pattern of the blue swirl on her palm.

"I wonder what it is…what it means."

"I don't know. Maybe it has something to do with whatever happens tonight. Or maybe it's some kind of genetic marking or fingerprint, like a way of saying I belong."

Cal bent and pressed a kiss to the mark, letting his lips linger there. "It's wrong. You belong here, with me." He leaned in, brushing his mouth against hers with a kiss that offered her his heart.

As they moved into each other, it was with the kind of deep intimacy that lives in shared breaths and long silences. In making love without urgency and for the sake of knowing one another completely.

Isa stood, stepping between Cal's legs where he sat on the couch. She lifted one knee and settled into his lap, her baggy sweater pooling over her thighs like ink spilling across water. The scent of her: clean cotton, warm skin, and something wholly her own, rose to meet him. When he looked at her face, he softened completely, his quiet breath leaving him. She smiled, the softest curve of lips, brushing her thumbs over the stubble along his jaw. Their eyes stayed locked, pupils wide, neither of them looking away. His fingertips found her hips, then slid to the small of her back, drawing her closer until no space remained between them.

Letting her forehead tip to his, she whispered, "I need to feel all of you tonight."

His hands stilled at her waist, his thumb tracing once along her spine in answer, understanding passing between them without words. No rush, just skin meeting skin for the sake of knowing and being known. He found the hem of her sweater, and she raised her arms without being asked, allowing him to lift it over her head. A simple cotton bra remained, and he traced one strap from shoulder to back, lingering, then unhooked the clasp. It loosened and she shrugged it off, letting it fall somewhere behind her, unnoticed.

Cal leaned forward and pressed his lips to the soft curve of her breast, his breath warm before the kiss itself landed. Goosebumps rose, and she sighed, weaving her fingers through his dark hair. She tugged gently at his T-shirt, and he helped her guide it off, their movements unhurried, almost absent-minded in their focus on each other. The rest of their clothes slipped away, forgotten in the folds of the couch beneath them.

Cal reached for her hand, and Isla climbed back onto his lap, knees bracketing his hips, the fabric of the cushions below rough against her shins. Skin met skin, warm and unhurried, every movement an exploration, not a race. Eyes still locked with his, she reached between them, fingers curling around silk and steel. She angled him upright, letting her softness meet him with a tentative, searching press. As they met, he inhaled sharply, hands steady on her hips, guiding but never pushing. Slowly, she lowered. The first inch drew a hum from her throat as her body opened to him, and stilled, letting her lead. When half of him was sheathed inside her, she paused, adjusting, breathing, settling onto him as if learning the shape of him all over again.

She draped her arms around his shoulders, her brow against his, and he cradled the nape of her neck with one hand, the other resting on the curve of her backside. They stayed there for a breath, wrapped in the moment of utter closeness, their hearts pulsing in sync.

At last, Isla rolled her hips in a gentle wave, and Cal met her with a soft press upward, matching her rhythm. Then again. Retreat, return. The pace steady and tender. Each motion became a meeting point: the velvet drag of him, the soft clutch of her, the hush of breath between mouths that brushed more often than kissed as their eyes remained locked and heavy lidded.

Cal's lips returned to the slope of her breast and collarbone, scattering damp kisses that lingered instead of traveled, while Isla's thighs pressed tighter around him, heels now tucked behind his back to keep them connected.

The room narrowed until there was only breath, heat, and the quiet rhythm they built together. When Isla felt the slow bloom begin, she whispered his name. He heard the change in her: the quickening he had come to recognize, and followed it instinctively, moving with her as though he'd been waiting for that moment. His hand slipped from her neck to her jaw, guiding her lips to his so he could share the breath she suddenly so desperately needed.

Their kisses grew messy, real, and when her body finally unfurled around him, he waited half a second, savoring the grasp of her, before letting go himself.

When they stilled, Isla let her forehead rest against his, neither of them moving as they caught their breath. He pressed a kiss to her temple, then her neck and shoulder, his lips tracing her outline, while they lingered, connected, a moment longer.

Tangled in each other's safe embrace, they lay together until the clock on the mantle whispered eleven. The fire burned low, its gentle embers flickering like hot jewels in the hearth, painting slow light across their skin. Neither of them moved to pull away. There was no point in stoking it; they wouldn't need it much longer. Midnight was coming. The tide would be high, the moon full, and the path of light across the water would soon be waiting for her.

"We should get ready to go." Cal whispered.

Isla nodded but didn't move. "Just a few more minutes."

TWENTY-NINE

At eleven-thirty, Cal and Isla walked out the front door. The air was already alive with the storm's arrival: the wind pushed hard in ragged bursts, tangling Isla's hair across her face and yanking at Cal's jacket. Salt spray hurled by wind stung their cheeks even from where they stood high above the surf.

The sky was a blanket of deep grey clouds piled on top of one another, churning low and impatiently. Now and then, the moon's full face broke through in shards, painting the wet pathway in quick flashes of silver before the darkness swallowed it up again. Farther out, above the open water, lightning crackled along the skyline, a jagged streak that made the incoming swells glimmer before returning to black.

In one hand, Cal carried a flashlight that illuminated their path ahead; in the other, he held the oval stone wrapped in a strip of burlap. Isla walked barefoot beside him, her boots tied by the laces and slung over her shoulder. The contact with the earth steadied her, each grounding step a quiet calm in her veins.

When they reached the tight trail that wound down into the cove, the sea's rumble grew louder in anticipation of her arrival. A half-moon of dark water stretched out before them, the king tide almost at its peak. Lightning flashed again, closer this time. In its brief illumination, she caught the movement of the clouds, thinning, shifting, revealing glimpses of the clear sky beyond. It wouldn't be long before the full moon broke through, spilling its light wholly onto the water.

They descended into the heart of the cove, where sea, sand, and stone met. The seam between land and water. This was the place: the ground where the ritual would bind itself to her choice.

Cal set the bundle down on a dry ledge of rock next to the sand, unwrapped the stone, and looked over at her. "Tell me again what happens."

"Pass me your knife."

Though he obeyed, apprehension manifested in the set of his jaw as he placed it beside the oval stone. Isla pulled off her jacket and then tugged her sweater over her head, folding both and setting them beside the stone. Now she wore only a thin tank top and cotton shorts. The chill bit instantly at her skin, and she stepped, shivering, into the shallows, cold lapping against her ankles. This time she asked for no softening, no warmth from the water. There was to be nothing comfortable about tonight.

"I'll stand here." She positioned herself where the moonlight would touch both sea and shore. "When it comes, I'll hold the stone out in front of me."

"And me?"

"You stay here." She pointed to the small strip of sand just beyond the reach of the waves. "As my anchor, I need you to hold my hand. Do not let go. You're the tether between me and the land, and it must hold until the ritual is complete. If you let go…"

"I won't," he said firmly.

Wet wind plastered his hair to his forehead, his black jacket dark with spray, but his eyes were firm and unblinking. Fierce support lived there, something that felt like home. The quiet strength he had given her these past weeks had carried her, and love filled her so completely it was too vast for words.

"Whatever happens, Cal, promise me; no matter what you hear, no matter what you see, you will not come into the water. No matter what."

"I promise. I'll stay here."

"It's almost time."

Cal stood just above where the sand surrendered to the sea, his boots kicked off to the side, bare feet planted firmly on land with Isla's hand joined in his, her fingers warm in his grasp as his thumb drifted over hers in an unconscious, nervous motion. The quiet around them held magic: something unseen, but palpable nearby. The moon's pull had done its job, and the water lapped at its furthest reach; the tide would go no higher.

"It's time." She drew a long breath, held it, then exhaled slowly. "Here we go."

Letting go of his hand temporarily, she knelt and picked up Cal's knife. Then, she stood just inside the tideline, where foaming waves lapped over her feet and ankles. The azure spiral shimmered faintly in her palm under the knife's blade as she turned and pressed the tip to her skin.

"I've got you." Cal crouched beside her, close but not touching. "I'm here, and when it's time, I won't let go."

"I know you won't." She smiled. It wasn't brave or forced; it was real. He was her anchor, the man she loved, and a glimpse of the life that waited on the other side of this moment.

"Five small cuts for the rope that binds."

A single cut for every sense: taste, touch, sight, sound, and scent, etched into her hand as the offering began. When it was done, she set her bleeding hand against the shimmering rock that lay on the shore, marking it with her blood. Then, placing her other hand in Cal's, she waded out until the waves reached her calves, stretching as far as she could while still holding his hand in a firm grip.

The pull was overwhelming tonight, like thousands of unseen hands winding through her hair, curling around her waist, and coaxing her deeper into the water. Her bleeding hand hung loosely at her side, fingers reaching to skim the surface as salt licked at the fresh cuts. As her blood mingled with the surf, it was more than just a wound: it was an invocation.

Cal picked up the oval stone, ready to pass it to Isla at her signal, and as he stood, the water ahead of Isla shifted: first, a faint shimmer of light bending over the surface just past where she stood; then, one by one, *they* appeared.

The Watchers rose from the depths both near and far, half in the shadows of the clouds and half shimmering in the speckled light of the moon. Their bodies, the perfect marriage of human grace and oceanic otherness, held limbs long and sleek, shoulders and elbows dusted with scales so fine they shimmered like powdered silver. Long hair black as kelp drifted with the water's movement, framing faces both fierce and flawless. Webbing stretched between their fingers, delicate as the gossamer wings of a dragonfly. Along their forearms, translucent fin ridges flexed with each subtle movement. Eyes pale as sunlit tidal pools, with deep-sea depth behind every stare, were all fixed on her. They were here to watch; here to witness.

Cal's breath faltered, his grip tightening around her hand. A gasp of fear or wonder…maybe both. She felt him flinch as the first figure stepped forward into the slow-gathering light of the emerging moon.

"Isla." Cal's voice was barely a whisper. "Are they…really here?"

A nod was all she managed, throat too tight for words. Behind her, the surface broke, and Silas rose waist-deep from the tide. The current bowed around him, framing broad shoulders and a jaw carved clean and sharp, but the spark of boyhood lingered still in the curve of his mouth and the softness behind his eyes.

They found Isla's, then Cal's, and understanding settled over his face, heavy with the weight of the burden he carried in part for her.

"Silas?" Disbelief and joy tangled together in Cal's recognition of his childhood friend, his eyes welling with emotion.

Before Isla could speak, the sea stirred again, and another figure surfaced several feet back.

Coraline.

Hair once streaked with silver now spilled over her shoulders in strands of midnight. Face smoothed of time's wear, she was younger, yet still utterly herself. Serenity shone through her.

"Coraline…" Cal's eyes widened.

With a smile as her only salutation, Coraline stepped to take her place beside Silas. One glance toward Isla carried all the words she needed to say. *You are not alone.*

Above, the wind clawed at the cliffs, howling as the storm dragged its nails across the sky; yet within the cove, the sea held its calm around them.

Isla looked at the faces gathered before her and felt Cal's hand wrapped tightly in hers. The choice was no longer distant; it wasn't on the horizon. It was here. Now. And they were all waiting. Waiting to see if she would anchor…or return.

THIRTY

Silas spoke once, his voice carrying clear across the water despite the roar in the clouds overhead.

"It is time, Isla: time to choose the home that will keep you."

Isla turned to Cal. "Remember, whatever you do, do not enter the water." The gravity in her eyes said more than her words ever could.

His knuckles tightened around her hand in a gesture of understanding. In his other, slick with rain, the stone rested, waiting to be passed into her free palm. The instant it touched her skin, it pulsed faintly, mirroring the spark in the mark in her flesh. Like a circuit closing, energy crackled to life between her and the stone.

The clouds above tore open in a single moment, revealing the moon in full. Its silver light poured in a perfect column from the sky, spilling its glow directly upon her. Where the moonlight touched, her skin shimmered. Shoulders, cheekbones, and forearms glinted with the pearlescent sheen of scales just under the surface. The moonlight had awoken what the sea had hidden in her all along.

Cal had to catch his breath. Beauty like this had no place on land, and yet it was hers: terrifying and magnificent all at the same time. In that shimmer he saw not only the truth of where she came from, but the sea's intent to claim her.

Silas's gaze lifted to the sky, then back to her, giving a single nod of instruction for her to raise the stone toward the moonlight. Then, his voice echoed directly into Isla's mind.

"You must hold the stone in the light until it touches the sky. When they connect, you will make your choice. Hold that choice within you and choose what will bind you."

Isla tightened her fingers around the stone's wet surface as the Watchers, standing in perfect stillness, began their chorus. It started as a single vibration before spreading outward into harmonies that seemed to come from every direction. It was music, the ocean's memory in sound, and it was unbearably beautiful. Its notes curled around her ribs and down her spine, meeting her own song, filling her. It was warmth after years of cold: a memory she'd forgotten was hers, restored. Every voice carried belonging, and it spilled over her until her own song intertwined completely with that of her ancestors, swelling into a vast chorus.

The storm answered in kind with wind that screamed against the cliffs, rain that needled her face, and thunder that shook the ground. Her outstretched arm trembled from holding the stone aloft, her shoulders aching as the song around her grew.

Beneath it, another sound held steady: Cal's heartbeat echoing through their joined hands, anchoring her with its own steady rhythm. His feet were driven deep into the sand, one arm braced behind him against the growing pull. She felt him through the storm, through the song. He was the tether that kept her from being swept away, his lips shaping her name in a quiet plea.

For an instant, the storm and the Watchers and the pull all quieted, and there was only him. The sight of him there, rooted for her, ready to hold no matter how hard the elements tried to take her, showed her then and there that he was here because he truly loved her: pure, authentic, and real.

Isla saw their future in a flash: together years from now, drinking coffee in the sunlit kitchen. Dark-haired children with light eyes, full of happiness as they played in the cove. She saw them growing, changing, falling deeper into one another. Grandchildren. Years of life and love flashed before her eyes. A life she had never dared to want and only ever dreamed of.

Then, like a shadow sweeping across clear, calm water, she saw the cost: those children, grown, standing where she stood now under the same full moon, with the same pull clawing in their chests. She saw the Watchers waiting for them in the dark water, the anticipation of choice in their eyes. Love on one side, the call of the sea on the other. Every child who carried her blood would have to make the same difficult choice. The cycle would not end, and Greyhook would go on keeping its quiet tally of the taken.

Tasting her hesitation, the storm surged harder, slashing sideways as lightning splintered across the heavens. The Watchers' song rose further, swelling with the tempest as it filled her; unrelenting, demanding an answer.

Cal's desperation rippled through their bond, deepening the torment in her soul. They could build the most beautiful life together: the life her heart wanted, the only one that mattered to her now. But that life would come with a price for someone, someday, to pay. Isla saw it as clear as the path of moonlight on the waves: the cycle stretching on for generations, the unrest beginning all over again in a never-ending sequence. This ritual was not about power, but surrender…and whichever path she chose, it would cost her.

Blood, sea, and storm blurred together, and in that moment, she felt the full weight of both choices: the pull of the sea below, the draw of the land behind.

Suddenly, lightning exploded, stitching the clouds above her with fire, and a jagged vein struck down to meet the shimmering stone in Isla's hand.

The surge raced into the blue spiral etched in her palm, coiling through her like a living current, flooding every vein until she was nothing but light and sea. Her marked hand blazed as the sky poured into her, searing the weight of her choice into blood and bone. Pain flared through her palm, and the stone tore free from her grasp, hissing as it flew into the sea. The ocean roared in recognition. The answer had finally come.

Instinctively, Isla plunged her burning hand into the water, desperate to cool the fire lacing through her veins. The shock had driven her to her knees and ripped the air from her chest — yet Cal's grip held firm, his hand still locking her to the shore, anchoring her.

In her head and inside her song, she heard Silas's voice again echoing through her mind with urgency.

"*MAKE YOUR CHOICE!*"

The price of her happiness was too high: too high for Cal, too high for their children, too high for Greyhook. Tonight, she could end this; end the cycle for all of them. She could protect him, even if it meant losing him and shattering her own heart.

Isla looked into Cal's eyes with tears in her own and said a thousand words with one aching look. Then, she reached her burning hand toward him, rested it on his, and mouthed the words.

"I love you. I'm sorry."

Then, she released the grip on his fingers and let go.

~

Release came at once. The scattered lightning faded overhead, and water folded around Isla like a velvet cloak of calm, easing every physical ounce of discomfort she had felt.

The tide surged between her and Cal in a single violent push, knocking him backward into the sand. He scrambled up, shouting Isla's name, but as he lunged toward the water, her will poured through the sea. A wave struck, spinning him hard against the sand and pinning him there on the shore.

Light erupted in the shallows. Bioluminescent ribbons unspooled from the water's depths, coiling up her legs, winding around her torso, tangling in her hair until she glowed like a star. The Watchers retreated into the depths, pulling their voices back with the tide as the ocean eased.

Silas rose before her, the mist and rain dissolving between them like a veil lifting. His smile was just as she remembered; only now, it held the beauty of the ocean's oldest secrets. His eyes shone, wise and knowing, and he extended his hand to her. Palm warm despite the cold, he bore the same mark that lived on her skin. The tidemark. The claim of the ocean. Their shared birthright, binding them to the sea.

When Isla's fingers touched his, the world above seemed to fall away. Sound from ashore became thin and distant until only the low, echoing harmony of the Tide Song remained.

Silas drew her into his arms, something long-lost finally returned. Beyond, Coraline waited in the moving waves, and in an instant the water rose around them, lifting before lowering their bodies into the depths of the cove and drawing them out to sea.

Isla's heartrate slowed, settling into a new cadence, syncing with the ancient world around her. Each beat sent warmth flooding through her, unraveling the last threads of her human weight. The clarity of her vision sharpened to show her every stone on the seafloor, every darting fish viewed in perfect detail. Sounds honed; the roll of distant currents and the click of shells carried to her as if whispered in her ear. Between her toes and along her fingers, delicate webbing shimmered into place, gossamer-thin yet impossibly strong. Behind her ears, soft gills unfurled like petals, catching and releasing the sea's breath. Isla moved through the water with ease, her body no longer foreign here but radiant, made whole in the ocean's embrace.

Rising fast and clean, she breached the surface in an arc of silvered spray, the rush of it flooding her with something wild and electric. It felt like flying. It was powerful, unbound, and utterly hers.

The last thing she saw before the water closed above her was Cal's figure on the shore, struggling to his knees, his face soaked with rain and tears. She wanted to tell him she loved him — not softly, but with the whole of her. With every moment they would never get to live. She wanted to beg his forgiveness; to say she was sorry for breaking the life they might have built and for leaving him to carry its ghost alone.

Isla's heart broke for the hollow her absence would carve in him, for the one already opening inside her. She needed him to know she had chosen the water out of love. Not to abandon their future, but to protect it and to protect him. Because the only way he could ever really be free, truly safe, was if she let go.

She longed to spill every word. To explain and to soothe and to promise that his grief wasn't his alone, but the water had already taken her voice, sealing the truth inside her.

Soaring deeper, she did not rise again. Beneath the waves, her transformation had begun, and the girl she had been slipped silently away.

Cal collapsed to his knees on the sand. The cold cut through his jeans, and his breaths came in ragged pulls as every muscle in his body trembled from the strain of holding her and the violence of losing her.

He stared out at the ocean, desperate and wild-eyed, searching for any sign of her. A hand, a shadow, a ripple…but the tide had already smoothed itself. The storm's edges had dissolved into moonlight and a million scattered stars. It felt obscene. Wrong that the world could turn so gentle while his soul was splitting open, every beat of his heart cracking against the void she had left behind.

"Isla. Isla, please." His ragged voice went from whisper to scream. "ISLA! Come back! I was supposed to keep you safe."

He folded until his forehead touched the sand, his body racked with tremors as a sob broke loose, raw and involuntary. Salt spray kissed his cheeks, cooling the fevered path of his tears as they fell to the beach beneath him. All he could hear around him was her: with every wave came the faintest echo of her laugh, a shadow of her voice, fraying at the edges and slipping further from reach.

"WHY?"

Again and again, the word struck through him. Why had she let go? Why had she chosen to vanish when he would have spent his whole life keeping her tethered to this world? Hadn't he been enough? He knew he could have been. They could have had years, decades: a house full of her wild laughter and a future that tasted of her lips. Isla had known what she meant to him; he knew she had. Even so, she'd left him on this shore alone, emptied out and scorched.

A faint sound lifted then, almost lost to the wind, and drifted across the water to him: her song. It ebbed and flowed with the roll of the surf, thinning, fading but echoing his deep ache. Both hands clutched his chest, holding that sound like it was the last piece of her he would ever have, as if holding it could keep his heart from breaking apart.

By the time he was able to gather the scattered pieces of himself and force his body to move, the horizon was already paling with the first light of dawn. A beautiful day was breaking in scattered pinks and golds, the world blissfully unaware of what the night had taken from him.

Cal's feet felt like anvils with every step up the bluff, his grief holding the weight of a thousand stones. The gale had calmed, the storm swept clean from the air, and the stillness made her absence louder. When he reached the March House, Isla's wool sweater was still draped over the armrest of the couch where she'd left it. Pulling it into his arms, he collapsed, pressing his face into the soft weave and breathed in desperately, as if he could feel her with his lungs. It still smelled faintly of gardenia, woodsmoke, and her.

Her small traces still lingered in the room around him. An open notebook where she had paused taking notes mid-thought. The leftover remnants of their dinner packed neatly away on the counter. The shorts she'd slipped off before making love to him laying loose on the sitting room floor. The bottle of wine corked beside the sink that they had planned to finish when this was over. None of her belongings had been cleared away, everything had been left exactly as people leave things when they believe they'll be back.

In that moment, Cal knew she had loved him, and she had intended to stay.

Minutes passed, or maybe hours. Time had no meaning anymore. He stayed where he was, curled in on himself, barely breathing and bone tired in a way that sleep couldn't possibly touch. Broken in a way that didn't bleed but that ached everywhere.

At some point, he pushed himself upright, still clutching her sweater, and he crossed into the kitchen for a glass of water. Each step was impossible, but his hands moved by memory as he filled the glass from the tap and lifted it to his parched lips. He drank greedily, draining it in heavy gulps that cooled his raw throat.

As he set the glass down, something in the distance caught his eye. Propped against the back door, just off-centre, was an envelope, Cal's name written across it in Isla's beautiful handwriting. Transfixed, he stared as if it might vanish like a mirage. With shaking fingers, he walked over and picked it up, breaking the seal.

Cal,

If you're reading this, then something didn't go the way I believed it would. It means I made the impossible choice. The one I never intended to make, the one I never thought I would have the courage to.

My love for you is the purest thing I have ever carried. It has shaped every part of me throughout my life – the softest and the strongest, the pieces that endured and the pieces that healed. Loving you has been the truest, most beautiful thing I have ever known.

This legacy began long before us. My purpose was to complete the bloodline, one way or another. If I am not here, it means this curse will never risk haunting our children, or theirs. Its shadow will not hover over the life we might have made. You will not spend your years wondering if it would come for us one day, if it would hollow out our children or their children with this choice, the way it has hollowed me.

Know this above all… If I'm not here, it's not because I loved you less, but because I loved you more than I loved my own life. I did not walk away from you. I walked toward something I believed would free you.

Right now, you may hate me, and I will carry that if I must. But please understand that none of this was because you were not enough. You are everything. I will never be whole without you. Not in this life. My choice always has been, and always will be, you.

The house is yours. The paperwork is in my bedroom, signed and only needing to be filed. I signed it only in case I failed. I never believed you would need it. If I do not make it back, promise me you won't let the rooms sit in silence. Fix it up. Make it shine again. Fill it with laughter and life. Have a family and raise them on the water. Love them and let this be their home. Live the life we dreamed of, Cal. If I cannot stand beside you, then live it fully: not as a monument to me, but as the future we wanted.

And when you stand at the cove and the wind shifts just right, you'll hear me in the waves. Not as a ghost, not as a memory, but as love. A love still yours, still reaching for you, loving you with a depth even the sea can never touch. To love someone enough to let them go... I understand now, that is the deepest kind of anchor.

Forever yours,

Isla

The words began to blur before his eyes reached the end. Isla's letter quivered in his hands, the paper shivering with the emotion in her words. Isla's sweater lay in his lap, catching the salt of his tears as they fell soundlessly. Cal let his head fall back against the door, heart clenching with the pain of knowing not just that she was gone, but that she *had* truly loved him and chosen him, even as the tides claimed her.

As he wiped his eyes and drew a slow breath, he saw a flash of color tucked away to his left, hidden beside the coat closet: a canvas, barely visible behind the doorframe. Carefully, he reached for it, pulling it forward. What emerged stole what was left of his composure, and he fell apart.

A painting, Isla's touch visible in every brushstroke, her presence felt in every detail. A piece of her left behind in an underwater seascape unlike anything he'd ever seen. A visual witness to what had claimed her, a window into another world. The world she now belonged to.

Brushstrokes of light spilled through water in soft, radiant shafts, gold and opaline, sky melting into the sea. Colorful coral formations rose like ancient temples from a floor of pale sand, their edges veiled in drifting gardens and deep green kelp. Iridescent fish moved in sweeping, celestial spirals, trails of silver and blue weaving in and out of the current. Every surface shimmered, as if dusted in starlight, the water aglow with silent tranquility.

Deep within the painting's heart, nearly hidden in the folds of color and light, was a silhouette: a woman, her form rendered in soft strokes, rising gently through the current, her face tilted upward toward the surface. She wasn't swimming or rising: she was simply *looking*. A stillness, a knowing, and a message meant only for him.

Cal traced the strokes of her brush with his eyes and for the first time, he understood that she was finally home.

Beyond the windows, the tide whispered along the rocks, carrying her love back to him again and again for all the days he had left.

EPILOGUE

One Year Later

Cal leaned against the new porch railing of the March House, coffee cooling in his hands as he watched the first thin light of daybreak touch the bluff. The house stood taller now, brighter: a fresh coat of white paint catching the dawn, sage-green shutters neat against the clapboard, a new roof snug beneath a sky blushing with the tender pinks and blues of morning. Renovations were slow, but steady.

Inside, sunlight reached into every room, finding corners with new bead-board and fresh flooring. Isla's joyful ocean paintings hung along the hallway walls: vast, moody blues and silver-tipped waves, windows into her world, each one capturing the wild beauty only she had been able to see.

But the one most luminous, the most alive, the last one she'd painted, hung in the master bedroom: a world beneath the waves rendered in her hand, soft light threading through the endless blue of a quiet kingdom she now claimed. Cal had hung it there himself, where he would see it each day. It reminded him not only of where she'd gone, but of the peace she must have found in the life that claimed her.

Outside, beside the porch steps, a small bronze plaque gleamed against the fresh white siding:

March House — Established 1862, Registered Heritage Home

Cal had filed the papers himself, combing through old township records and sea-worn deeds, assembling the fragments of a family line that had shaped this coast for generations. The designation meant the house would be preserved, its bones protected, and its stories safeguarded. It was his quiet offering to the legacy Isla had carried.

In the attic, a cedar box lay tucked beneath the rafters, sealed and locked, filled with Coraline's journals, notebooks, and letters: the long thread of their story bound and waiting. Safely kept out of reach of curious hands, but not out of reach of time, so that one day those stories might be carried down carefully by the generations to come. The answers would be waiting if ever the sea came calling again.

Greyhook had quieted in Isla's absence. The fishing boats returned heavy with their catch. Tourists and locals alike returned to the water, lingering along the sun-warmed docks and wading through the shallows, the gulls above them wheeling in loose, lazy spirals. The town's sea glass light had returned, painting the harbor green and gold on its soft spring evenings.

On nights when the moon was full, Cal would walk the bluff, always to the cove and back: to the place where he had last seen her. Tonight was no different. Stopping where the sand was damp and cool, he admired the surf folding over itself in silver froth. From his pocket, he took a smooth shard of azure-blue sea glass, the kind they had once filled jars with as children. The shard warmed in his palm before he touched it to his lips. Then, he raised his arm and let it fly into the waves.

No words: only the hope that wherever she was, Isla was happy. A softness came over him, his lips breaking into a gentle, crooked smile. A smile meant only for her. The sound of her laugh still lived in him, as did the memory of her song.

And sometimes, in the still hours of dawn, he swore he could hear both in the calming hymn of the sea.

One Mile Out

Isla drifted with the tranquil rhythm of the waves. Dark hair streamed around her like glistening silk, her eyes open and fixed on the distant outline of the March House above.

With effortless grace, she swayed with the water, heartbeat steady, keeping time with the swell. Now and then, she surfaced only long enough to breathe his name into the wind.

Around her, the voices of her kin wove tighter, binding her to the sea – her first and final home. And when she slipped once more into the deep blue that had claimed her, she carried with her the quiet certainty that her story — *their* story — was safe, imprinted into the bones of the house on the bluff and kept alive in the heart of the man who would always remember her.

Isla March. Salt-blooded. Tide-bound.

ABOUT THE AUTHOR

Heather Cavill lives in a quiet beach community in Vancouver, BC, where the sea, fog, and coastal folklore inspire her writing. *The Echo Below* is her debut novel.

www.ingramcontent.com/pod-product-compliance
Lightning Source LLC
LaVergne TN
LVHW030916080826
845145LV00013B/2925